THE
HOUSE
AT
THE END
OF THE
WORLD

ALSO BY DEAN KOONTZ

The Big Dark Sky · Quicksilver · The Other Emily · Elsewhere · Devoted · Ashley Bell · The City · Innocence · 77 Shadow Street · What the Night Knows · Breathless · Relentless · Your Heart Belongs to Me · The Darkest Evening of the Year · The Good Guy · The Husband · Velocity · Life Expectancy · The Taking · The Face · By the Light of the Moon · One Door Away from Heaven · From the Corner of His Eye · False Memory · Seize the Night · Fear Nothing · Mr. Murder · Dragon Tears · Hideaway · Cold Fire · The Bad Place · Midnight · Lightning · Watchers · Strangers · Twilight Eyes · Darkfall · Phantoms · Whispers · The Mask · The Vision · The Face of Fear · Night Chills · Shattered · The Voice of the Night · The Servants of Twilight · The House of Thunder · The Key to Midnight · The Eyes of Darkness · Shadowfires · Winter Moon · The Door to December · Dark Rivers of the Heart · Icebound · Strange Highways · Intensity · Sole Survivor · Ticktock · The Funhouse · Demon Seed

JANE HAWK SERIES

The Silent Corner · The Whispering Room · The Crooked Staircase · The Forbidden Door · The Night Window

ODD THOMAS SERIES

Odd Thomas · Forever Odd · Brother Odd · Odd Hours · Odd Interlude · Odd Apocalypse · Deeply Odd · Saint Odd

FRANKENSTEIN SERIES

Prodigal Son · City of Night · Dead and Alive · Lost Souls · The Dead Town

MEMOIR

A Big Little Life: A Memoir of a Joyful Dog Named Trixie

DEAN KOONTZ

THE HOUSE AT THE END OF THE WORLD

THOMAS & MERCER

Published by Thomas & Mercer, Seattle

www.apub.com

Amazon, the Amazon logo, and Thomas & Mercer are trademarks of Amazon.com, Inc., or its affiliates.

ISBN-13: 9781662500442 (hardcover)
ISBN-10: 1662500440 (hardcover)

ISBN-13: 9781662508073 (paperback)
ISBN-10: 1662508077 (paperback)

Cover design by Damon Freeman

Interior illustrations by Edward Bettison

Printed in the United States of America

First edition

To Gerda. To mark fifty-six years of marriage—the halfway point!

ONE
ALONE

———

THE LAST LIGHT OF THE DAY

Katie lives alone on the island. She lives less for herself than for the dead.

This is just another day in April, a Tuesday defined by isolation and hard-won serenity—until it isn't.

Built in the 1940s, her small house is a sturdy structure of stone. In addition to a bath, the residence has a kitchen, bedroom, living room, armory, and cellar.

The house is on a knoll, surrounded on four sides by a yard, on three sides by woods beyond the yard. The front door faces a slope to a shingle shore, a dock, a boathouse, and open water.

Her domain is a quiet refuge. She has not heard any human voice but her own in a few months, and she rarely speaks aloud.

Lacking television, radio, or internet, she hoards seven CD players with six-disc magazines, which are no longer manufactured. For a few hours a day, she has music, always classical—Mozart, Beethoven, Brahms, Chopin, Haydn, Liszt.

She has no interest in pop tunes or American standards. Regardless of how beautiful the voice, the lyrics too poignantly remind her of all that she has lost and all that she has forsaken.

Having found peace in isolation, she won't put it at risk.

Set into the hillside, a flight of concrete stairs with a painted-iron railing leads to the shore. As she descends, a pied rock dove waits for her at the bottom, perched on the newel post.

The bird seems always to know when she will walk the shoreline or come down from the house for another purpose. It is not afraid of her, never takes wing at her approach, but seems merely curious.

Katie wonders if the scent of civilization has so faded from her that the creatures of the island now consider her one of them rather than either an interloper or a predator.

Soon more than a thousand blue heron will migrate to a rookery on another island far to the north of Katie's retreat. When breeding is done, one will now and then stalk the shallows of this shore for sustenance, like a beautiful descendant of the Jurassic era.

Tied up in the boathouse, a twenty-foot cabin cruiser with an inboard-outboard engine controlled from the wheelhouse offers range and speed. She uses it two or three times a month, taking a cruise to nowhere and back.

As necessary—*only* as necessary—she goes to the mainland to have the boat serviced at the nearest marina. She has not gone into town in five months, since visiting her dentist.

She parks a Range Rover in a rented garage there. She pays a local to drive it twice a month and keep it ready for her use. There is nowhere in the world she wishes to go, but experience has taught her to be prepared for all contingencies.

Even the islands at this remote end of the archipelago now enjoy cell-phone service. She rarely makes a call. She sends text messages to no one but Hockenberry Marine Services.

Hockenberry delivers groceries, tanks of propane, and other goods twice a month. They are pleased to carry any items up the stairs to the house, but she always declines, as she does today.

She is only thirty-six and in superb physical condition. She needs no assistance. Besides, she has given Hockenberry a boat-house key and prefers not to interact with anyone.

The boathouse is of the same stone as the residence. At the inland end, a separate and well-soundproofed chamber houses the propane-fired generator that provides the electricity for the residence and for the pump that brings water from the well.

The cabin cruiser is belayed in the lower, forward chamber, tied to cleats in the floating slip and snugged against rubber fenders. It wallows almost imperceptibly as mild currents wash beneath the big roll-up door.

A gangway leads up from the slip to a storage area at the same level as the dock. Here, among other things, is a refrigerator in which the deliverymen leave perishable goods. Sturdy cardboard boxes contain the other items and stand beside the fridge.

When propane is needed, they leave the tanks in the generator room, where they also leave three-gallon cans of fuel for the boat.

Now Katie straps the grocery cartons on a dolly with large wheels designed to climb steps easily, and she pulls it up to the house. Two trips are required to transfer the entire order.

After she returns the dolly to the upper level of the boathouse and closes the door, she stands at the end of the dock, surveying this world of hers in the last ninety minutes of daylight.

The sky is for the most part blue, though a filigree of white clouds decorates it randomly, like a long ribbon of lace unraveling. When the sun westers a little farther, those scrolls and arabesques will be transformed to gold in the oblique light.

Decades earlier, the water was murky. The introduction of zebra mussels, which feed on algae, improved the clarity. The rocky floor and some shipwrecks are visible to a depth of eighty feet or more.

Here at the tail of the archipelago, facing south-southwest, she can see only two other islands. When she purchased this property—which is more than half a mile long and somewhat less than half a mile wide—its remoteness suited both her mood and bank account.

In 1946, when the first resident moved here, a young World War II veteran, the island had no name, and he didn't give it one. The second owner, Tanner Walsh—a poet, novelist, and mystic—called it Jacob's Ladder, a reference to the Old Testament prophet who claimed to have seen a treadway to Heaven.

In the first week of her occupation, gripped by bitterness and anger, Katie thought of her new home as Bottom Rung Island. Back then, the climb to Heaven seemed impossibly long and arduous, the attainment of grace forever beyond reach.

The smaller of the two nearest islands, Oak Haven, lies half a mile to the east, nearer the mainland. It's a third the size of her sanctuary, with a large, shingled Cape Cod house that has a charming, white veranda.

She doesn't know the names of those who live there, and she has no desire to know.

The other interruption in the wideness of water looms two miles south-southwest of Katie's position. It is four times the length of her property and perhaps twice as wide.

Watercraft and helicopters—some big twin-engine models—traffic between the mainland and that last, most isolate island, some days more frequently than others. The stone quay is long and formidable, with a deepwater port; on a few of Katie's outings, she's seen the dock bustling with workers off-loading vessels.

A facility of some kind lies at the heart of the place, but those structures can't be seen. A dense pine forest encircles the island, needled palisades that screen out prying eyes.

The island is Ringrock, named for the immense pillar, a natural formation, on which it stands. Even the Hockenberry deliverymen know nothing more about Ringrock, and never go there.

If the helicopters bore the insignia of one service or another, that would be proof that Ringrock is a military installation. Except for the registration numbers on the aft section of the fuselage and shorter numbers on the engine cowling, however, none of the aircraft is ever identified. Likewise, the boats that visit there.

The week during which Katie first toured Jacob's Ladder and made an offer for it, distant Ringrock had been in a period of relative quiet. She hadn't been concerned about it.

The Realtor, Gunner Lindblom, implied that Ringrock was a research station operated by the Environmental Protection Agency.

That seemed benign.

It also proved to be a mere rumor.

Perhaps some residents on the hundreds of islands northeast of hers or those in the shore communities know what facility occupies that last island in the chain. However, Katie never associates with the other islanders, rarely with mainlanders, and when she does interact with the latter, she never gossips.

If she asks questions of others, they will surely ask questions of her. By sharing her past, she cuts herself with sharp memories; having stopped bleeding at last, she is determined not to reopen the wounds.

Her hope is that the mysterious island is nothing but a retreat for corporate honchos or serves some other purpose for a private enterprise. People who are driven by the profit motive do not scare her. With rare exception, their ultimate intention is to get rich by serving customers, not by crushing them.

If the installation is under the auspices of the EPA, the CDC, the NSA, the CIA, or some federal black-op outfit with no name, that is more problematic.

Katie is suspicious of authority. She distrusts those who prefer power to money or who seek money not by working but by exercising their power.

She isn't a survivalist, but she intends to survive. She's not a prepper, though she makes preparations.

She does not believe that she's living in the End Times, even if on occasion she wonders.

Isolation is a wall against fear and despair. Only nature, quiet, and time for reflection can heal her. If she can be healed.

After twenty-six months on Jacob's Ladder, her fear has largely faded, and her despair has gradually eased into a settled sorrow. She is not happy, nor is she unhappy; she takes pleasure in her endurance.

Now, as she turns away from the water, intending to go to the house to have a glass of wine while making dinner, an eruption of activity at Ringrock startles her. She pivots toward the noise and squints into the slant of late-afternoon sunlight.

As though they are elements of an elaborate Swiss clock as it strikes the hour, two helicopters abruptly rise out of the center of the island—the first a pilot-and-passenger model, the other perhaps with four seats—just as a flotilla of fiberglass racing boats departs the quay. The latter are sleek, low in the water; she thinks there are six. The shriek of turbine engines, the hard clatter of air-chopping rotors, and the growl of outboard motors slap across the water like skipping stones.

One chopper heads south, the other north. They appear to be searching for something on Ringrock, traversing the ground from right to left, then left to right. Sunlight slides like molten gold across the advanced-glass cockpit of the aircraft heading in this direction. Two racing boats follow the shoreline to the northeast while two speed southwest, and the remaining pair sweep back and forth along the quay—a perimeter patrol.

Ringrock is not a prison. The presence of a penitentiary would be known to Gunner Lindblom and other locals, both as an important employer and as an object of concern.

Most likely, she's witnessing not an escape, but a penetration. If the facility is a high-security operation, those guarding it will react like this when an electronic fence is breached.

Whatever is happening, it is none of Katie's concern. She is in retreat from the company of strangers and is acutely aware of the danger of calling attention to herself by being concerned about the activities of others.

She has no family in the outside world. They are all dead.

Life insurance proceeds and the sale of two houses were a significant contributing factor to her ability to buy this remote and little-valued island. Enough funds remain to support her longer than she expects to live.

As the searchers at Ringrock rattle the day with their frenzied actions, Katie leaves the dock.

The rock dove has abandoned the post at the foot of the stairs.

As Katie ascends, she sees a raven on the chimney cap. The bird faces east, as if it is a sentinel charged with welcoming the night that, just beyond the horizon, crawls up the turning world.

A LITTLE FORTRESS

Joe Smith, the war veteran and first owner who oversaw the building of the house in 1946, was a superb carpenter; he lovingly crafted the interior himself. The ceiling beams, the shiplap between them, the paneling—a golden, encompassing warmth of knotty pine finished to a gloss—comprise a masterwork of design and joinery that storms and time haven't warped or worn in any way.

He also built most of the furniture, some of pine and some of oak, which remains as well. The second owner, Tanner Walsh, merely reupholstered to his taste; Katie has done the same.

The stone fireplaces—one in the kitchen, one in the living room—are capable of heating the entire house. Walsh preferred to avoid the mess of burning wood and installed electric space heaters in all four chambers; Katie has updated them.

She has replaced the faux Persian area carpets with Navajo rugs by a weaver with a special talent for producing traditional designs in softer and quite beautiful variations.

The front—and only—door is of ironbound oak. Three inches thick.

The casement windows are smaller than she prefers, and they open inward. Screens keep out flies and mosquitoes, but each window also features one vertical and one horizontal bar of steel solidly seated in concrete casings.

In the 1940s, the nation enjoyed a low crime rate. Even these days, while foolish water-traveling thieves might rarely target houses on the hundreds of closely grouped islands at the head of the archipelago, felonies in this remote region are all but unknown.

Tanner Walsh had researched the life of Joe Smith and recorded his own thoughts about the house and the island during the year before his death. Being a mystic as well as a writer, Walsh was of the opinion that Joe intended the two bars to be cruciform, and this conviction led him to see symbolism in nearly every aspect of the building.

Katie believes the reason for the bars is less otherworldly. For one thing, the two crossed lengths of steel require the minimum expense and labor to ensure that no one can gain entry through a window.

For another thing, in 1945, Joe Smith was in the contingent that liberated the prisoners in Dachau. What this farm boy from upstate New York saw there haunted him for the rest of his life and drove him to live apart from most of his fellow human beings. Thirty boxcars filled with decomposing corpses. A "skinning room" where freshly murdered prisoners were carefully peeled to provide "quality lampshades." A decompression chamber in which experiments regarding the effects of high altitude caused subjects to go insane and made their lungs explode. All had been done in the name of the people, in what the authorities insisted was a pursuit of a more just society. There can never be too much justice in Utopia.

She has thought of this place as the house at the end of the world, her world.

A WORK OF ART

Initially, the thick stone walls prevent the continuing ruckus at Ringrock from disturbing the tranquility of the house.

After pouring a glass of good cabernet sauvignon, Katie does not at once begin preparations for dinner. Instead, she takes her wine into the armory.

She mocks herself by using the word *armory*. Unloaded and propped in one corner are a pistol-grip pump-action 12-gauge shotgun and an AR-15 that is often called an assault rifle by people who don't know anything about guns. She also keeps a substantial supply of ammunition for each weapon.

Most of the room, however, is furnished with a large drawing table and adjustable stool, an artist's easel, cabinets containing art supplies, and an armchair into which she sometimes sinks to contemplate a work in progress.

In addition to the three mortal fears—of terrible pain and disability and death—everyone needs at least one additional reason to live, a task that inspires. Since her adolescence, Katie's art has been one of her reasons for being. In her life on the island, art has become her *only* inspiration.

During her twenties, she enjoyed a flourishing career. She achieved major gallery representation at twenty-two. Her paintings sold at steadily increasing prices.

Currently, she creates solely for herself, because not to create is to die inside. She has no intention of returning to the art market. She destroys more finished works than she keeps. None hang on the walls of this house.

She paints in rebellion against abstract impressionism and all the soulless schools of modernism and postmodernism. Her signature style is hyperrealism, an attempt to capture everything a photograph might and then much more: what the mind knows about a scene that the scene itself does not reveal; what the heart feels about the subject before it; how the past lives in the present and how the future looms real but unrevealed; what any moment on the Earth might mean, if it means anything at all.

Now, wineglass in hand, she stands before the canvas that is mounted on the easel, a work in progress. It's four feet wide, three high. The mundane subject is a trio of storefronts in a seven-store strip mall—a nail shop, an ice cream shop, and a neighborhood pizza parlor.

To any eye but Katie's, the painting is finished, a work of photorealism with the depth of trompe l'oeil. For her, the scene remains incomplete; tomorrow the hard work on it will begin.

Most artists would deem this room an inadequate studio. They would insist on larger windows, good northern light.

Katie wants nothing more than what she has. In this diminished life, she is content to paint by artificial light. Sometimes lately, she does her best work surrounded by shadows, with no light but what she focuses on the canvas.

Wine almost slops out of the glass when she is startled by a distant explosion that, though muffled, rattles the windowpanes and creaks the ceiling beams.

DEPTH CHARGES

Common curiosity, perhaps underlaid by lingering paranoia from her mainland life, ensures that Katie has an interest in any unusual maritime traffic. She keeps a pair of powerful binoculars on a small table in the living room. Now she snatches them up before stepping outside. As she opens the door, a second muffled explosion throbs through the afternoon.

She hurries across the yard, pauses at the brink of the bluff above the shore, and brings the binoculars to her eyes. The racing boats with outboard motors have retreated from the scene.

Katie doesn't know—doesn't remember—as much about US Marine helicopters as she should. The aircraft patrolling the water a few hundred yards off Ringrock is larger than the pair that quartered the island a short time ago. It appears to be akin to a Sea Horse or Sea Stallion. Like the first two, it bears no insignia, which would be required of any military ordnance. Not many private companies have a use for rotary aircraft with this power and load capacity.

Unlike the smaller helos, this one is engaged in violent action that makes no sense in this place and time. While the craft hovers, crew members dispense a barrel half the size of an oil drum from the loading ramp at the rear. As the object plummets a hundred feet to the water and sinks below the surface, the big chopper moves on. The detonation is a muffled whump, though of sufficient power to suggest it occurred within a fathom or two. The lake surface swells as though a leviathan is breaching. White water boils. A momentary geyser spouts high before collapsing. Another depth charge drops.

Stunned, Katie lowers the binoculars just as gentle waves from the initial explosion wash against the pilings of her dock and lap the shingle shore.

She can imagine no explanation for the event she's witnessing. What are they attacking? No submarine could make its way into this system of freshwater lakes. Besides, no war has been declared; this isn't ever likely to be a naval battleground. Nor is it a suitable place for such training exercises.

The fourth detonation appears to satisfy whatever mandate inspired this foolishness. The Sea Horse—or whatever it is—arcs back toward Ringrock, ejecting nothing more.

From around the northeast end of the island, the larger of the previous two helos reappears, a type of Bell executive chopper common in the business community. She pulls it close with the binoculars to confirm the pilot, copilot, and two passengers in the rear seats. They are figures at this distance, silhouettes, and she isn't able to discern if they're wearing uniforms.

Following the course of the craft that dropped the explosives, the pilot commences quartering that stretch of water in much the way he earlier searched a portion of Ringrock island.

An instrument of some kind, not visible until now, has extruded from the belly of the fuselage. Katie can assume only that it is an array of sensors of various kinds, seeking evidence that the four depth charges have achieved their purpose.

Because there can be no submarine—neither Russian nor Chinese, nor a vessel commanded by Captain Nemo that has manifested here out of the imagination of Jules Verne—perhaps they are looking for the body or bodies of one or more scuba divers.

Who were guilty of what? Penetrating the island's security? Escaping with top-secret material or evidence of grave crimes?

That might be a sequence in a James Bond film. She isn't able to convince herself that this sleepy archipelago is a likely venue for such glamorous melodrama.

Furthermore, if such divers existed, meeting their incursion with mortal force, especially employing massive quantities of high explosives against them, was not a proportional response, was in fact absurdly violent. The law required arrest, indictment, a trial in a court of law. Whether the facility on Ringrock is an operation of government or private enterprise, in neither case are those in command of it inclined to risk their freedom by exposing themselves to charges of excessive force resulting in manslaughter or murder.

The outrage of environmentalists, who might have witnessed the explosions from watercraft or the mainland, is enough to dissuade Ringrock authorities from doing what they appear to have done.

In spite of what Katie has seen, it must not be what it seems to have been. She lacks crucial information that would allow her to imagine a logical and reasonable explanation.

The sole remaining helicopter moves right to left, left to right, across water that is three hundred feet deep in that area.

As the late-afternoon sky slowly dims, the enormous lake has less blue to reflect. Below Katie, gray tongues of water lick the shore stones that centuries of wet caresses have worn as smooth as the granite of grave markers.

Gone to gold, the filigree of clouds graces the sky like ornamentation spun with jeweler's wire.

For whatever reason, atmospheric or otherwise, the clap of the helo's rotary wing comes and goes, so that sometimes, in an eerie silence, the craft seems to remain aloft without a functioning engine, floating as if it were only a figment of her imagination.

The strangeness of the moment encourages a feeling of being exposed and vulnerable, even watched.

Those who work—or live and work—on Ringrock no doubt also have binoculars. However, considering how bold and noisy they've been, they shouldn't be concerned that she is curious about them.

Nevertheless, she returns to the house and locks the door and finds her unfinished glass of wine.

She doesn't need to know what they were doing. They are of that world she shuns and to which she will never return. She has a world of her own. Only here can she live to fulfill the Promise she made.

TURNING DOWN THE BED

After selecting a book that will be her dinner entertainment and putting it on the kitchen table, Katie repairs to the bedroom, where she folds back the quilted bedspread and drapes it over the footboard.

Every morning, she plumps the pillows and draws the bedclothes taut and smooths everything just so, as though she wishes to avoid being mortified if someone should see the sheets and blankets disarranged.

She has never admitted a visitor since she moved here. That doesn't matter. Standards must be maintained. Routines have to be followed. Untidiness can lead to slovenliness and worse.

Her mental health, such as it is, depends on maintaining this house as she had done the one before it—as though it still matters. As though someone she thought lost will miraculously appear on her doorstep. She must be prepared even for the impossible. Failure to be prepared is a failure to hope.

As she turns back the top sheet and the blanket, a disturbing thought occurs to her regarding Ringrock. Whatever had happened over there, they had expected that it might one day occur. They had been *prepared* for it, even to the extent of having depth charges at hand.

Her preparedness is a defense of sanity, but *theirs* seems to suggest that they are engaged in some enterprise so dangerous that it is madness.

AN ARTIST IS A MATHEMATICIAN WHO KNOWS THE FORMULAS OF THE SOUL

Katie is three weeks short of her thirteenth birthday, home early after the last two classes of the day were canceled following a failure of the school's heating system. She is alone in the house.

As usual, she is done with her homework in half an hour. She sits at the kitchen table, her big drawing tablet on a slant board, striving to perfect her skill at rendering in pencil.

Calm water is not easy to represent because it acts as a mirror that reflects sky, trees, buildings, people. Such inverted images present perplexing problems of perspective.

Still water can be portrayed with smooth horizontal strokes that benefit the artist by justifying a slight distortion of the reflected images.

Another fine technique requires that the reflections be drawn entirely in vertical lines, which are then strategically interrupted with a few horizontal blurs created by an eraser to suggest the stillness of a pond.

Katie is struggling with the second approach to the problem when she becomes exasperated with the drip-drip-drip of the kitchen faucet. Each drop is marked by a reverberant *plonk* when it strikes the stainless-steel sink.

Standing at the sink, she studies the problem. She puts one hand under the spout. The drop that strikes her palm is warm.

"Gonna teach you a lesson," she tells the faucet, which is what a mean girl at school told her a couple of weeks earlier.

That fight was a draw, but only because Mr. Conklin, a teacher, broke it up. He said, "Katie, I'm surprised at you." She had never been in a fight before, but that wasn't what he meant. The other girl was two years older, bigger, the toughest bitch in middle school—and Katie was winning, which surprised Conklin.

Now she goes into the garage, where her father has a workbench and cabinets of tools. She gathers what she thinks she needs.

Her dad is handy around the house. She has watched him make repairs a few times, but not often.

She is operating on . . . well, intuition.

Under the sink, she shuts off the water supply. Then she turns a faucet to be sure that what she's done has worked. The spout dribbles and then runs dry.

She removes the faucet handle. Using an adjustable wrench, she loosens the locknut from the stem assembly. She unscrews it by hand the rest of the way and sets it aside.

The stem assembly fits snugly in the faucet. To remove it, she jiggles it slightly as she pulls up firmly.

If she were eleven years old, she might at this point lose the confidence to continue. But she'll soon be thirteen.

With a screwdriver, she extracts the retaining screw holding the deteriorated washer in place. She pries the washer out.

Next she inserts the new washer into the stem cup, making sure the beveled side is facing the faucet seat. She doesn't know the terms *stem cup* and *faucet seat*, but she doesn't need to know them. She can see how this has to work.

She fastens the new washer in place with the retaining screw, tightening the screw until it compresses the washer slightly. The stem assembly slides back into the faucet. She uses the adjustable wrench to tighten the locknut. Replaces the handle. Gets under the sink to turn on the water. It works.

After putting the tools back where she found them, she sits again at the kitchen table and returns to the task of representing still water with graphite pencils. She is no longer distracted by the dripping faucet because it doesn't drip.

That night at dinner, Katie's mother smiles at Father and says, "Oh, by the way, thank you for finally fixing that faucet." When he says he hasn't had the chance yet, Katie admits to the deed. Mother is suitably amazed.

Father, however, is not surprised. "She's an artist."

"Yes," says Mother, "and not a plumber."

This response encourages Father to wax philosophical, which he is wont to do, though fortunately not so often that he becomes an embarrassment. "You know, of course, that music and mathematics are closely aligned. Indeed, music is a form of mathematics, and many musicians have a natural aptitude for trigonometry and the like."

Mother reaches out to pat Katie's hand, to show that she does not mean to criticize or demean when she says, "I believe all those torturous piano lessons prove our girl is no musician."

"Nor does she need to be," Father says, "considering what an extraordinary talent she possesses as a visual artist. My point is, it's clear to me that any great artist—musician, painter, sculptor, a fine prose stylist—is on a subconscious level a mathematician and a carpenter and a mason and an engineer. A great artist intuitively understands how the world is built and how it works and how people best fit into it. That's how they're able to create beauty—because they know the truth of things. An artist is a mathematician who knows the formulas of the soul. 'Beauty is truth, truth beauty.'"

Mother sighs. "Next time the air conditioner goes kaput, I'll call Andrew Wyeth."

"Undeniably great. But I'm afraid he's dead."

Katie says, "What's that thing called you stick the washer in?"

"The stem cup," Father says.

"So maybe just knowing the names of all that junk, I'll get better at drawing water."

As the years pass, she takes pleasure in learning to fix things that are broken. Some things, however, *can't* be fixed. By the time she is so handy that she's self-sufficient, she will wonder if being alone on Jacob's Ladder has been her inevitable destiny from birth.

SHADES

That morning, Katie had baked six chicken breasts. She slipped five into plastic bags, vacuum-sealed them with her FoodSaver, and put them in the freezer.

Now she cubes the sixth breast, chops asparagus, and slices several raw mushrooms. Frozen snow peas have been thawing on a paper towel. She puts everything in a bowl, to which she adds olive oil and seasoning. A bag of buttered rice with raisins is heating in a pot of boiling water.

Burnt-orange light burns beyond the cross-barred windows.

She pours a second serving of wine, corks the bottle, carries the glass into the hallway, opens the front door, and steps outside.

To the east, the sky is deep sapphire going to black. In the time it's taken her to pay a visit to the twilight, the western sky has darkened to blood-orange.

Although a stillness has settled with the dusk here at ground level, the lacy clouds have been blurred by a high-altitude wind. No longer a filigree, they are like a dark smear of some unpleasant organic substance.

No helicopters are aloft. If boats ply the lake, they do so without running lights.

Ringrock is a flamboyance, radiant splendor, kingdom of beams and beacons. She's not seen it a tenth this bright on any previous night. Until now she has never imagined that the far island is so lavishly electrified.

She stands just outside her door, puzzled, vaguely disquieted. It's as if they have turned on all their lamps, the better to see into every corner and under every bed.

Wondering gains her nothing. And though she has little left to lose, what remains is precious. She won't risk it by indulging in curiosity. This is a time in America when those who make the rules view inquiry as inquisitiveness. The curious are called meddlesome; they are accorded no respect and little mercy.

She returns to her house and locks the thick oak door.

Moving room to room, she lowers the pleated shades at all the windows. She isn't driven to do this by the spectacle at Ringrock. Every evening at dusk, she routinely bans the night with the shades.

During the more than two years that she's lived here, no one has ventured onto this island uninvited, at least not to Katie's knowledge. She's never seen a face at a window. In her countless long walks over these one hundred and thirty acres, she has never come across a footprint other than one of her own.

She suspects that the ritual of the shades is more symbolic than practical. Subconsciously, she is shutting out something other than the attention of potential trespassers. She has yet to deduce what that might be.

DINNER WITH DAPHNE

The kitchen includes a dining corner with a table and four chairs. The furniture is handsome and sturdy, the work of Joe Smith when he came back from war.

Katie takes her meals here, always in the same chair, the one with its back to the wall, which provides a view of the entire cozy room.

Joe never married, and he lived alone all his life. He had no need of four chairs, and yet he built the extra three, perhaps as an expression of hope.

Sometimes Katie wonders if he might have foreseen that, three-quarters of a century later, she would take residence here and need the full complement of four dining chairs.

Although she often has music with dinner, she resorts to none of her CDs on this occasion. Whether Mozart or Beethoven, she would be straining to hear through it to whatever sounds the night might bring.

She always reads with dinner. She uses a small blue-gray stone, found on the shore, to weigh down the left-hand page when it wants to fall to the right.

Although she has read all of Dickens and all of Dostoevsky more than once, she will read it all again. Jane Austen, Balzac, Joseph Conrad. She despises the smugness and mad intensity of James Joyce's prejudices. Her dislike for the work of all nihilists further limits her reading list.

Tonight she has chosen lighter fare, one of Daphne du Maurier's novellas, "The Split Second." The author is a storyteller first and foremost, but her work has more depth than has been recognized by those who claim the right to define art.

Du Maurier has sympathy for the suffering of others but avoids sentimentality. Her stories are often dark but never spiral into nihilism. She knows that true compassion is noble and demanding, but that tenderness is a vain form of pity indulged in by those who want to feel good about themselves without being put to the inconvenience of doing something.

In recent years, that distinction has become important to Katie.

She is finished eating dinner, halfway through the fiftysome pages of the novella, considering a rare third glass of wine, when the quiet is broken by a high-pitched buzzing like an immense swarm of angry wasps. The source is not in the kitchen.

Glancing toward one shade-covered window and then the other, she gets up from her chair, as the buzzing grows louder. Stepping into the center of the room, she realizes that the sound beyond the windows is also coming down the chimney.

She stands listening, analyzing without success, and then steps quickly to the cutlery drawer beside the cooktop. In addition to a few knives that serve culinary purposes, the drawer contains a 9 mm Glock pistol. She stashes the gun here, in addition to another in a bedroom nightstand, in case of a crisis that unfolds too rapidly for her to get to the weapons in her studio. This is the first time she has taken it in hand other than for target practice and to clean it.

The drawer also contains an eighteen-inch-long Tac Light. She retrieves that as well as the pistol.

By the time she reaches the front door, the sound has grown still louder. It is a buzzing, yes, but combined with a shriek as thin as a paper cut but as piercing as an ice pick.

She disengages the top deadbolt, then the bottom one, and hesitates only a moment before opening the door.

SCANNERS

Katie prefers to have a two-handed grip on the pistol. However, the moon is not yet risen, and the crazy light show on Ringrock is two miles away. Her island lies in a nearly blinding darkness, and she needs the Tac Light.

She is confident that she can use the Glock effectively with one hand. She trains with weights to have sufficient bone and muscle strength to cope with recoil, and she exercises her hands with a hard rubber ball to maintain a strong grip.

Nothing leaps at her. A sweep of light reveals that no one stalks her. The action is overhead.

The powerful Tac Light exposes a moving swarm, mechanical and strange. Wheels. Struts. Quadripartite configurations of rotary wings. Stabilizers. Antennae. What might be cameras seeking infrared heat signatures. What surely are the receiving barrels of sensors probing for things other than visual bogeys.

"Drones," she says, though these are a kind she has never seen before. They're twenty to thirty feet above the house, moving slowly northeast. Even with the Tac Light playing over them, it's difficult to gauge their size, but they appear to be large, no less than five feet in diameter and perhaps as much as six.

They are traveling in a phalanx, parallel to one another. Even when she constricts the beam to make it more powerful, the Tac Light lacks the reach to confirm what she suspects: that the machines are ranked at intervals the width of the island, at least thirty or forty of them, which accounts for the volume of noise.

As they move across the yard, they gain altitude in anticipation of the trees.

Katie finds herself running to keep up with the drones, for she is overcome by a compulsion to shoot down one of them. The size and complexity of the machines and the sheer number of them seem to be proof that the people on Ringrock are engaged in an extraordinary project. And evidently an individual on their team or an intruder has stolen something of enormous importance, something that could not be gotten by hacking their computers. They need desperately to find the thief, and they believe he or she might have gotten as far as Jacob's Ladder, her island, her *home*. She feels violated. They appear to have put her at risk. And if they're like so many other reckless and deceitful sonsofbitches these days, they'll deny what they've done, hide the truth at any cost. If she can capture a drone, that will be evidence.

She wishes she had the pistol-grip 12-gauge. A quick double blast of buckshot would be sure to bring a drone crashing to the ground.

Having gotten ahead of the phalanx, Katie drops the Tac Light and takes the Glock in both hands. One foot forward, one foot back, in a modified isosceles stance, she locks her arms. Like all the other drones, the nearest oncoming one lacks running lights, but it's a discernible gray geometry against the black sky. She waits until the thing is passing overhead, squeezes off a shot, then a second—but thinks better of firing a third.

The chance that the facility on Ringrock is operated by the government, either through the military or in partnership with a private enterprise or a university, is at least fifty-fifty, more likely eighty-twenty. The justice system as currently constituted has given Katie no justice. If she shoots down a megadollar drone that's government property and finds herself in court, she'll have little hope of triumphing, considering that the *federales* have the deepest pockets on the planet. She might lose everything, including her island and, for a time, her freedom.

If that were to happen, she couldn't keep her Promise. And the only reason she gets up every morning and struggles through the day is to keep it. The Promise is everything.

Frustrated, she lowers the pistol. She watches the precisely arrayed drones slowly fading to the northeast. Less gray with every yard of distance, the machines deliquesce into the blackness. Their motors and rotors continue to cry down the night, the source of the sound now invisible, as though the woods are haunted by despairing spirits that can't find their way out of this world in which the bodies they once inhabited have long ago moldered away.

A chill rises off the dark water. The faint breeze smells of shore mud and dock creosote and something that she can't name.

She plucks the Tac Light from the ground and heads back to the house. Halfway there, she stops and turns, playing the beam across the yard. Although the drones apparently cleared this territory to their satisfaction, Katie feels . . . a presence. In spite of what she feels, no one is there.

South-southwest, Ringrock remains as bright as a fairground midway at the height of carnival.

THE MYSTIC

Katie washes her dinner plate and utensils, puts them away.

The insectile chorus of drones is faint now, and yet unnerving, like a distant sound that a dreamer might think is mere tinnitus, when it's a warning that the dream is phasing into nightmare.

The pantry is open. Her attention is drawn to a calendar fixed to the inner face of the door. Easter has passed. Passover ended. The squares with dates in them foretell restful weeks, with no occurrence more momentous than a full moon two days hence.

She no longer trusts that benign forecast. She lived on the island two months before she came to believe she might be beyond the reach of evil. For two years, she has felt safe. The events of today have shaken her sense of security, and she closes the pantry door.

These occurrences have stirred up her long-settled sediment of fear. Worse, they rankle. She tries always to avoid anger, which leads individuals to self-destruction and entire nations into ruin.

She considers using her cell phone for something other than texting orders to Hockenberry Marine Services. She could place a call to the county sheriff or to the lake patrol. Not to lodge a complaint. She doesn't want to draw too much attention to herself. She could inquire in a concerned-citizen sort of way, expressing the hope that all the commotion at Ringrock—the explosions and the sky full of drones—doesn't mean people have been injured over there. She might learn something that will set her mind at rest and allow her to sleep through the night.

No. A third glass of wine, which she seldom permits herself, will be less risky and more effective than a phone call.

As she is pouring the cabernet, she recalls Tanner Walsh's recordings. Something she heard on one of them a long time ago suddenly seems pertinent.

Alienated from most of his relatives, Walsh left his entire estate to a questionable charity providing legal defense to needy persons believed to be wrongly accused of elder abuse. His hatred for his own parents, expressed in his recordings, was such that he might have wished they had lived long enough to be dependent on him, so he could have had the opportunity to abuse them. His sympathies in such cases might have extended even to those accused of following the Lizzie Borden model for the settlement of family disputes.

Directors of the charitable foundation were interested in their benefactor's bank accounts and the proceeds from the sale of the island and Walsh's boat. They weren't keen on sending someone to dispose of his clothing and other personal effects. Among those items were a hundred and six one-hour audiocassette tapes on which he recorded everything from his observations regarding the ecology of the island to ruminations on such matters as reincarnation, poltergeists, astral projection, and spontaneous human combustion.

In the early weeks here, Katie listened to a few recordings, but her interest waned. Walsh was as credulous as a child, though without the charm of innocence. Opinionated. Conceited. He is not good company even if he can be shut up with a flick of the switch.

She hasn't disposed of the recordings because, even as foolish as Walsh seems, she is moved by a vulnerability that underlies his pomposity. He was no less human than she is. To toss out more than one hundred hours of his ruminations on his beliefs and the meaning of his life . . . well, that seems too much like throwing away his life itself. She is acutely sensitive to how little some people value the lives of others these days.

The microcassettes are stored in four shoeboxes on the top shelf of the hall closet. She brings them to the kitchen table.

Walsh had labeled every cassette as to subject. He separated them into four categories, each with its own box: My Life Before Jacob's Ladder, Island Life, Literature, and Paranormal.

Among other things, Tanner Walsh had been a novelist—a most fortunate one. His first work, *Orchids in Winter*, was the initial selection of a TV talk-show host's hyped book club. Three million hardcovers flew off shelves. Film rights sold in a frantic auction. The book was translated into forty languages. It was said that *Orchids* earned him in excess of twenty million dollars.

For two years, he mingled with the literati and Hollywood's elite, mounted stages to opine on everything from postmodern poetry to politics, and swanned through glittering parties here and in Europe. Then he purchased his island with the announced intention of committing himself exclusively to his art for a year.

The first tape in the box marked Literature features Walsh, alone in this very kitchen, speaking to posterity about the Great American Novel that is soon to pour forth from him. It's the only recording in this category that Katie has had the fortitude to play—which she did in a state of morbid fascination—from end to end.

His second novel spent one week on the bestseller list, sold forty thousand copies, and was poorly reviewed. His third never made the list, sold fifteen thousand copies, and was savaged by critics. His fourth novel could not find a publisher.

The island, purchased as the artist's retreat, in time became his sanctuary from ridicule and humiliation. He rarely left it after the woeful reception of his third book.

The tape that Katie remembers is in the box marked ISLAND LIFE. She sorts through the cassettes, reading labels, and settles on one titled OBSERVATIONS OF THE LAKE.

The micro recorder is in the same box, sans batteries. She fetches a pair of AAs from a kitchen drawer, and the refreshed device proves to be reliable.

She listens to Walsh describe a boat that he observed passing Oak Haven Island; he is scathing about the pilot's nautical skills. She fast-forwards the tape, listens, reverses it, hears a faux poetic passage about the play of morning light on the waters of the lake, zips ahead, ahead again, listens, then winds backward, seeking until she finds what she remembers.

Walsh's voice is inflated with less pomposity than it sometimes can be. Indeed, there is the haunted note of a man who is beginning to recognize the inadequacy of his long-held view of the world. *"I wonder if Jacob's Ladder has made a mystic of me. Reincarnation, bilocation, possession—I see some merit and relevance in it all. The isolation must be the reason. Though preferable to the corrupt culture of the New York literary swamp, it's isolation nonetheless, and the mind seeks to fill the emptiness by considering what once seemed outré. And how strange it is to live surrounded by water, as if by the flood of injustice that drowned my hopes and ambitions. I had a dream last night that was like no other in my life. So vivid. Compelling. Deeply disturbing. I dreamed that I was sleepwalking. I passed through that stout oak door as if I were a ghost, and found myself on the dock, gazing at Ringrock. The usual soft lights that glow there during the night had been extinguished. The far island appeared deserted. No, it was worse than that. In the dream, I thought I must be in the underworld, that the water before me was the River Styx and that Charon, the boatman, would arrive soon to ferry me into that land of everlasting darkness. Yet I was not afraid. Something called to me, called reassuringly, but not with words. How do I describe this? I felt wanted, not wanted as Death wants us with his bloody scythe and bony grin. Instead, I felt needed. More than needed—cherished. In the dreaming, I stepped off the dock and found myself standing on the water. I began walking toward Ringrock, as if I were Jesus Christ himself. I could feel the cool water under my bare feet, the way it gently undulated and yet supported me. A tremulous kind of joy grew in me, step-by-step, but there came a quiet fear as well, and I said aloud, 'That is the land of the dead over there. I'm not ready to die.' Then I knew, again without words being spoken, that someone was on Ringrock who was thought to be dead but was not, and that if I walked two miles of water, all the way to that island, there would be something I could do to help him, something that would give my life more meaning than it had ever had before. I began to walk faster across the water, so excited, my joy growing—until I remembered when I was a boy, only five years old, how my father tried to teach me to swim by throwing me off the bank and into the pond, a very deep pond. I remembered how he came into the water, pulled me out when I almost drowned, then threw me in again, and again. My dream of Ringrock became a nightmare of the pond and my father. I woke in terror, thrashing in the sheets as if the bedclothes were my father's arms, that hateful fucking bastard."*

Walsh had grown agitated, almost breathless. Now he took a moment to gather himself before continuing.

"*This morning, I couldn't find my slippers. How strange not to be able to find one's slippers beside the bed where they are every morning. I couldn't remember where I'd left them. After dressing, I brewed a pot of strong Jamaican blend and filled my favorite large stein, which holds the heat just as well as it keeps beer cold. I meant to go down to the water and sit in the dock chair, let the blissful tranquility of the lake encourage my production of alpha waves before setting to work on the book that will prove how wrong the critics were about me, how lacking in insight. At the door, I discovered the deadbolt hadn't been engaged. Even after all these uneventful years on Jacob's Ladder, I still lock the door every night. I'm not getting forgetful. I'm not that old. Yet first my slippers, now the door lock. Not worried exactly, but puzzled, I went down to the dock—and, my God,* there were my slippers, *side by side, as if I'd stepped out of them. As if I'd actually contemplated setting foot on the water. I sat in the chair, drinking my coffee, staring at the slippers, the water, and Ringrock, wondering if I'd acted out part of my dream even while dreaming it. Had I really gone sleepwalking? I became increasingly disturbed. I'm a man of singular self-control, as steady as a gyroscope. I am not one to go rambling about in a fugue state. At last, quite agitated, I removed my shoes and socks to inspect my feet. I always shower before bed, in order to get a quick start in the morning, the artistic impulse being such a demanding master. The soles of my feet ought to have been clean, but they were quite dirty—as though I had indeed visited the dock while sound asleep, left my slippers there, and returned to the house barefoot. That discovery chilled me. I have been unable to work on the novel all day. The more I think about it, this strange experience seems to be something more profound than a dream, more than somnambulism. It almost seems that some entity from a higher realm has spoken to me, that I am in some way chosen for a special role. Which would not surprise me. But a role in what?"*

The tape runs out. The recorder clicks off automatically.

Katie switches it on again and reverses a little beyond the beginning of the passage she just heard. Walsh usually starts by citing the date on which he is laying down his wisdom on the tape. He has done so in this case. The recording was made four months before Katie bought the island.

If memory serves her, that was the month that Tanner Walsh died.

A MESSAGE FROM THE DEAD

More than two years earlier, the first time Katie listened to Tanner Walsh's account of sleepwalking, the story had meant little more to her than that the man's fall from celebrity to nonentity, exacerbated by his years of isolation, had left him bitter, perhaps somewhat deranged, and given to self-dramatization. Now, after the events at Ringrock and the fleet of drones that must have come from there, his words resonate with her as they had not done before.

She assumes there must be a subsequent recording. Surely Walsh had ruminated further on this event that encouraged him to feel "chosen for a special role." She sorts through the cassettes until she finds one labeled DREAMS.

The entry on his new tape had been made two mornings after the final recording on the previous cassette. Following an uneventful night, Walsh endured another during which he dreamed again of being called to Ringrock by someone who was "thought dead over there, but who was not dead." He had gone sleepwalking as before, this time barefoot from his first step.

"In the dream, I suddenly found myself in the night, floating above the house, then gliding over the woods, banking and turning with the aid of my arms, in a state of rapture, as in those dreams of flying that most adolescent boys experience. Needless to say, I had not enjoyed such an exhilarating dream in decades. In time I found myself standing in midair, forty feet or more above the house, facing toward Ringrock. As before, I felt needed and understood by someone on that island, my value known by him as no one else in my life had ever

recognized it. Without words, he called to me. I knew without being told that if I came to his assistance, then the gift of flight would be mine forever, and I would regain the status and acclaim that always should have been mine. I drifted to the ground in front of the house. The power had been granted to me only as a demonstration. To earn it, I was required to reach Ringrock by my own initiative. I can't express how emotional this dream was, how much I felt wanted, cherished, loved. Yet . . . yet under my ecstasy, perhaps at the level of instinct, I felt threatened. Nevertheless, I stood there, yearning intensely for Ringrock—and woke to discover that I wasn't in the yard but on the shore, standing barefoot on the stony beach, water lapping at my toes. As I realized that my flying had been fantasy, my sense of ecstasy evaporated. Fear overwhelmed me. If I were not as sound-minded a man as any who has ever lived, then I might worry about my mental health. If something is awry, however, it isn't me. It's Ringrock. I've been told by locals that it's a facility of the Environmental Protection Agency, which they finished building a year before I purchased Jacob's Ladder. Maybe. But when I go online to research the public records, it seems that Ringrock does not exist. Something is amiss. I believe it behooves me to learn what I can of the place. When I finish this recording, I'm going to the mainland, to the county seat, to discover what the records have to say about that mysterious island. I have a sense that, through the agency of some extraordinary power, I have been chosen as the writer whose talent is great enough to make of this material a book of singular importance."

When Walsh's recording ends, Katie switches off the little machine. She stares at it for a long moment. She looks at one of the shade-covered kitchen windows, then at the other. She sips her wine.

Outside, the buzz-shriek of the large drones gradually grows louder as they return from the far end of Jacob's Ladder. Evidently, they haven't found what they're seeking, but they continue to search for it.

Whoever monitors the cameras on the drones knows that Katie is in residence and hostile to this imposition. The muzzle flash of her pistol, perhaps now in video archives, is proof that she took two shots at the unmanned aircraft. Although she failed to hit one of them, authorities could decide to pay her a visit tomorrow.

Katie wonders who might come and what they will want from her. If she says that she acted emotionally, in defense of her property and in fear for her safety, that claim isn't likely to earn their sympathy. This is an age when freedoms are fragile. Those in power speak loudly, ceaselessly about compassion but rarely exhibit any.

She switches on the recorder, turns up the volume, and listens to Tanner Walsh's next entry, which he'd made seven hours after the previous one, upon his return from the county seat.

"What to make of this? According to county records and back-issue files of the surviving newspaper here, the Department of the Interior seized Ringrock by eminent domain forty years ago. A real estate investment trust that owned it didn't protest. The property transfer was done under a nondisclosure agreement, so I assume the trust was well compensated. The Army Corps of Engineers, working with a private contractor that specializes in sensitive military and government projects, built a facility on Ringrock. Some say the EPA operates a lake-monitoring station. Bullshit. It was likely once a biological warfare lab; that's my guess. Whatever it is these days, the people who work on Ringrock live there. As if it's an Antarctic

research facility a thousand miles from anywhere. What's that about? If a journalist or state official gets curious, they always back off fast, almost in a panic, as though someone maybe took one of their children for a day just to show them what could happen. More than ever, I think there's a big story here, a career changer. There are rumors that the military conducts successful research into psychic powers. Is Ringrock where it's done? The person calling me to Ringrock—is that evidence of telepathy? Is some gifted individual imprisoned there? I must be careful. Think this through. I'm not a reckless man. I'm also not one to fuck with. Some power has chosen me, called out to me. How often does that happen—to be called to greatness? But consider the cost. Prudence is required. I am not the kind of man to shrink from danger, but I must be prudent. If a telepath is seeking my help, he is surely a victim, an abused innocent. But he—or she—might quite innocently compel me to put myself in grave peril. I will do the right thing, as I've always done. But I must think this through from every angle. Until I decide what action is wisest, I'll take precautions against sleepwalking. While ashore today, I purchased a simple battery-powered security device that I will insert between the front door and the jamb each night. When the door opens, a siren sounds. It is very shrill and will wake me. I fear nothing and never shrink from danger. But something exceedingly strange is happening here, and I need to understand it before taking bold action."

The recording ends. The cassette still contains more than forty minutes of unused tape.

Outside, the night seems to be an infinite webwork of crossed wires stressed with frustrated currents, but the sound is only that of the drones droning as they return to this southern end of the island, passing over the backyard, over the house.

Katie stares at the ceiling. The hive's worth of agitation peaks and gradually fades as the flight formation cruises south, over the dock and boathouse, over the water from which the noise reflects with a flatter pitch. They are returning to Ringrock.

Sorting through the cassettes in the box, she's unable to find another one labeled DREAMS or bearing any word that suggests that it picks up with an account dated subsequent to the day when Walsh returned from the county seat.

Tomorrow she can peruse the tapes further. She's had enough of Tanner Walsh for one day.

Her wineglass is still half-full. She stares at the cabernet as the sound of the drones fades to silence. She takes the glass to the sink and pours the wine down the drain.

JUST IN CASE

She must assume that someone will be coming, if not tonight, then in the morning. To explain the drones. To tell her lies and set her mind at rest. Perhaps to conduct a boots-on-the-ground search of Jacob's Ladder and confirm that whoever the drones failed to find is in fact not here. To inquire about her pistol.

Instead of replacing the two depleted rounds in the 9 mm Glock, she returns it to the kitchen drawer from which she retrieved it earlier, where it can be easily found in a search.

In her studio, one wall provides cabinets, two pairs of tall doors that serve two sets of shelves. She rebuilt these herself, soon after moving to the island, matching the aged pine that Joe Smith used back in the day.

A hidden release unlocks the shelves behind the doors on the right. They roll out on wheels, bringing the concealing base molding with them. Hidden behind is a foot-deep space with shelves laden with airtight cases of ammunition and spare magazines for her various weapons.

She loads two magazines for the 9 mm pistol that she keeps in a nightstand drawer in her bedroom. She pockets them.

The shelves behind the left-hand cabinet doors also roll out. This second secret space is deep enough to accommodate the 12-gauge and the AR-15. She clamps them to the wall and rolls the shelves into place once more.

On the easel, her current painting draws her attention. The nail shop, the ice cream store, and the pizza parlor.

If someone were to buy the canvas and hang it on a wall of a building across the street from the strip mall that is portrayed here, anyone might think it wasn't a painting, but instead a window, so passionately executed is the hyperrealism, so cunning the trompe l'oeil. However, it does not yet convey the truth of the scene, the meaning, the horror.

She retreats to the bedroom. Closes the door. Locks it.

She retrieves the second Glock from the bedside drawer and puts the gun on top of the nightstand with the two spare magazines.

Minutes later, in bed, she switches off the lamp. She is not afraid of the dark. She has lived in darkness for two years, ten months, and eighteen days.

3:26 A.M.

Something wakes her, and she turns her head on the pillow to look at the digital clock.

Although her eyes are dark-adapted, the room is so black that she can see nothing except the green numbers on the readout and a pale square that is the pleated window shade.

The moon is high and soon to be full. If that lunar lamp were absent, starlight alone might not have allowed her to differentiate window from wall.

She lies faceup, listening to the deep quiet. She cannot hear her heart or even the rhythm of her slow, shallow breathing.

Perhaps a dream took an unpleasant turn, causing her to shake off sleep. If so, she has no memory of it.

The quiet persists.

As recently as three years ago, when Katie was thirty-three, enduring silence would have lured her back to sleep. Now continual quiet can seem as suspicious to her as any sound that breaks it.

To avoid insomnia, she closes her eyes and tries to focus her mind on remembered images of tranquility, paintings that always calm her. Childe Hassam's snow-blurred *A City Fairyland*. Pieter Claesz's *Still Life with a Lighted Candle*. She settles on that remarkable, magical work by John Singer Sargent—*Carnation, Lily, Lily, Rose*.

Something knocks against the wall of the house, a soft thud.

Katie opens her eyes, sits on the edge of the bed. In the emerald glow of the clock numerals, she takes the pistol in hand.

A softer sound follows the first. It seems to come from the wall with the window.

Although barefoot, she's gone to bed in jeans and T-shirt, lest the drama that disturbed the evening proves to have another act. She stands, her toes clenched in the short nap of the Navajo rug.

Quiet returns, sustains for a minute, two, but she doesn't believe it.

This island is not home to large animals—no deer, no bobcats, certainly no bear—that might rub or knock against the house. The largest predators on Jacob's Ladder are red foxes. The few owls are night hunters that are silent on the wing; when roosting, they tend to announce themselves with their signature word or not at all.

Moving cautiously around the bed, Katie makes her way through the dark to the window.

When she moves off the rug, the oak underfoot is cool, sending a brief chill from soles to spine to scalp. As she steps in front of the window, a floorboard creaks.

The moonlight is strong enough on this west side of the house to project faint shadows of the security crossbars through the glass and onto the translucent fabric of the shade.

The casement window is a thirty-inch square, large enough to admit an intruder if not for the bars that divide the opening into four squares. Each quadrant is only fifteen inches on a side.

She stands staring at the large, vaguely imprinted plus sign, listening. A soft breeze had sprung up earlier, when she'd been outside. If it has strengthened into a wind, she can't hear it.

Her breath catches in her throat and her heartbeat quickens when the glow abruptly dims and the crossbar shadows fade until they are hardly discernible—as if someone has stepped close to the far side of the window, blocking the moonlight.

Katie chastises herself for being too easily spooked. Nothing more has happened than that a scarf of cloud has wrapped a portion of the bright, cratered face.

Beyond the shade, something clicks against the windowpane.

Startled, she sucks in a breath, but her finger doesn't move from the trigger guard to the trigger. Most likely, there is a light wind that just blew a brittle scrap of something against the glass.

Click, click. Click, click, click.

Either it's a busy wind or someone is testing the glass. But why test it when the crossbars prevent entrance even if the pane were to be shattered?

Click, click.

If someone is out there, he can't be taunting her, aware that she's standing at this side of the window, for there's no light in here to reveal even the merest shape of her.

Click, click, click.

In early summer, June bugs will spend themselves against the windows for a week or two, though it's too early for those beetles.

She waits. She listens. The outer light grows brighter, and the shadows of the bars darken again on the shade.

So relax. It's only a cloud that has now unraveled from the moon. And the breeze is just a breeze bearing this or that.

Katie feels for the shade cord and finds it.

In the thick stone walls of this house, the windows sit behind deep ledges onto which the bits of windblown debris might have fallen. Moonlight is now perhaps bright enough for her to see what was blown against the glass.

She's about to pull the cord, raising the shade—but hesitates. She doesn't know why she fails to yank it. Rather, she knows why, but doesn't want to admit to trepidation because, damn it, she isn't that kind of woman.

A noise elsewhere in the house turns her from the window, and the cord slips out of her hand.

AN INQUIRING MIND

Katie knows this compact house as well as a champion gymnast knows her own body. The place is no less familiar to her in deep darkness than in full light. She moves through the rooms with the sureness of someone who has been blind from birth and has lived nowhere but here.

She keeps a small flashlight in her nightstand, but she leaves it there. If someone is testing the defenses of the residence, she doesn't want to risk betraying her position to him. The best she can hope for is that he decides the house is at the moment unoccupied. If he reaches that conclusion, he will be bolder, even reckless, in his attempt to gain entrance. If worse comes to worst, the element of surprise will then be hers.

She moves quickly from her bedroom into the adjacent kitchen. The digital displays on the appliances provide meager illumination, the quality of which gives her a feeling of being underwater.

A rattling noise draws her into the hallway, past the living room on the left and her studio on the right, to the front door. Someone seems to be aggressively—stupidly—twisting the doorknob back and forth, as if under the drunken conviction that it will disintegrate if agitated enough.

Beneath that hard clatter, she thinks she hears the subtle sound of oak under pressure, as though someone of formidable size and strength is straining against the door. But that might be a product of her imagination.

The would-be invader relents. The night falls into silence.

Pistol now in a two-handed grip, she waits.

"Avi," she whispers, which is a summons that can't be answered, but also a reminder to herself of the Promise she must keep. Her lives will not end here, not this night.

A new commotion compels her through the archway on her left, into the living room. A scrabbling noise. As if something is clawing at the stones that form the front wall of the house. Clawing for purchase, *climbing*.

She follows the sound with her eyes, and knows the moment when the trespasser transitions onto the roof.

A year before his death, Tanner Walsh paid a roofing company to come in from the mainland to replace the deteriorated substrate and install new slate. The roof sheathing is solid, the slated slopes easy to negotiate.

The modest living room is furnished primarily with armchairs, four of them with footstools, though she always sits in the same one and reserves the other three. With no guidance from the ghostly glow of the window shades backlit by the moon, she navigates among the chairs and stools, arriving at the hearth just as a tinny twang and then a thin screech echo down the chimney.

The intruder seems to be examining—or attempting to wrench loose—the spark arrester that is fixed to the chimney cap. This effort is soon abandoned.

As the visitor crosses the ridgepole to the slope at the back of the house, Katie follows. Living room to hallway, to kitchen. She arrives at the second fireplace just as the other spark arrester is tested with a twang and screech.

Neither chimney has a flue wide enough to admit a man. Because she employs space heaters rather than wood fires, the dampers are always tightly closed against the possibility of mice, which can squeeze through a gap as narrow as a quarter of an inch. Nothing can enter the house through either of those vertical passageways.

Silence returns. She stands listening for the intruder as he—or it—seems to be listening for some sound from her. After perhaps a minute, a ruckus overhead leads quickly to the eave. A rain gutter produces a vibratory note as the roof is abandoned.

She stands in anticipation for a while. Then she sits at the kitchen table to await developments, of which there are none.

"Raccoon," she says into the renewed quiet.

The behavior of the trespasser is consistent with that of a curious raccoon.

Except for one inconvenient fact, she is inclined to dismiss this incident as the work of just such an animal. However, in the twenty-six months that she has lived on Jacob's Ladder, she has never seen a raccoon.

Squirrels, rats, mice, shrews, chipmunks, rabbits, martins, foxes, muskrats, birds of numerous species—the island supports a diverse population. Katie walks her domain for a couple of hours nearly every day. She often draws and paints from nature. She is familiar with most of the animals with which she shares her water-encircled home.

If raccoons are on the island, she would have seen them often. Although they hunt by night, they are curious and always exploring. They are frequently bold, occasionally even dangerous because of their razor-edged claws, but never shy.

Furthermore, the largest raccoons might weigh twenty-five or thirty pounds. Judging by the sound of it, she believes the creature on the roof, if perhaps not a man, weighed at least fifty or sixty pounds.

Unable to return to sleep, she makes coffee in the near dark. Sits at the table, drinking cup after cup. Thinking about Ringrock, depth charges, swarming drones. Her waking life has become stranger than any dream.

The blinded windows brighten. Dawn comes, and with it nothing good.

TWO
VISITORS

———

GUNNER LINDBLOM

Katie has not spoken to the Realtor since about a month after closing escrow on the island. With business concluded, he asked her to dinner. She'd realized earlier that he was attracted to her, but she'd been careful to give him no reason to believe the attraction was mutual. He was a nice man—smart, kind, amusing. Therefore, she had declined the invitation as gently and graciously as she could.

He'd been so cultured and courteous when she turned him down that Katie wished she could have told him why romance was the last thing she could accommodate in her new life as an islander, so that he would know her rejection truly had nothing to do with him. If she had been using her married name, Lindblom might have understood; however, to avoid being defined by tragedy, she had reverted to her maiden name, although in her heart she remained who she had been ever since her wedding day.

To share the truth with him—with anyone—will invite pity she can't tolerate. Furthermore, she's sure that sharing her feelings will inevitably trivialize them. There is something sacred about great suffering, and it is the sacredness that makes the pain endurable. To speak of the past, to describe her ordeal, she has nothing but words, and words are insufficient to the task; mere words will reduce the sacred to tabloid-newspaper sensationalism. And then she'll have nothing.

Now, Gunner takes her call, as though they had spoken only yesterday. "Katie, how lovely to hear your voice."

"You sound well," she says, and the words seem wrong to her, as if her social skills are withering in this isolation. "I mean, I do hope you're well."

"I'm very well," he declares. "Always busy. What about you? Have you found the tranquility you were seeking on Jacob's Ladder?"

"Oh, yes. It's beautiful. Beautiful and peaceful. Life moves so slow here that time seems almost to have stopped. None of the hectic rush I came here to get away from."

He sounds surprised, perhaps slightly disappointed. "Frankly, I thought you might have had enough of it by now, might be calling to put Jacob's Ladder up for sale. You know, Katie, farther north in the archipelago, there are islands clustered closer together. You can have privacy and tranquility up there, too, but also a sort of neighborhood. Some islands are even connected by footbridges."

"No, what I've got here is good for me. In fact, I've been writing about Jacob's Ladder, waxing philosophical about nature, pretending to be Thoreau with a bigger pond."

"I'd love to read what you've done."

"I may always be too embarrassed by my prose to try to have it published. But recently I've included some history in my journal, in addition to observations about flora and fauna and weather and life in general. I don't mean to be macabre, but I realized I don't know how Tanner Walsh died. I thought it was of a heart attack, but then I realized no one ever said as much."

After the slightest hesitation, Lindblom says, "As I'm sure you know, he was something of a sad case—famous, acclaimed, and then a long, hard fall. Nevertheless, he wasn't depressed, always plotting a comeback. According to the autopsy, his blood-alcohol level was high, quite high, but there were no drugs in his system. The cause of death was drowning. A boater spotted Walsh's body floating in the lake, wearing his pajamas. Later, one of his slippers was found on his dock. The second one must have gone in the water with him. As likely as not, he fell in rather than jumped. The shore shelves off abruptly there. It's deep enough to have given him serious trouble if he couldn't swim, or if he was too intoxicated to swim well."

Or maybe, Katie thinks, *he tried to drink himself into a sleep from which he couldn't be roused to sleepwalk, but something calling to him nevertheless persuaded him that he could take a two-mile hike on water.*

"How terrible," she says.

"I didn't withhold the information for any nefarious purpose when you bought Jacob's Ladder," Lindblom assures her. "It just seemed the guy suffered enough humiliation in his life. There wasn't any point in making his sad and rather foolish death part of local lore. I hope knowing this doesn't diminish your love of the island."

"Not at all," she assures him. She doesn't ask him if he can recall the date of Walsh's death. She has no doubt that it happened the night of the day that the writer went to the county seat to research Ringrock. She says, "There's nowhere on Earth where people haven't died in sorry ways. I asked, you told me, and that's that. One other thing. Have you heard about all the explosions at Ringrock yesterday afternoon? Do you know what happened there?"

"Yes, we heard it on the mainland, but we didn't have a front-row seat like you. Rest easy. No real explosives were involved."

"They sounded like depth charges."

"According to the EPA, all the booming was—I quote—'only mechanical sonic devices that simulate the sound waves produced by explosives.' They were conducting an experiment to learn to what extent sound has an effect, positive or negative, on algae."

She says, "The zebra mussels that were introduced decades ago have cleared up the water."

"They sure have. But EPA wants to find a way to deal with algae that doesn't require injecting a nonnative species into the water."

Katie doesn't say that the EPA is spouting bullshit. Lindblom is obviously among those naive souls who believe what authorities tell them in the name of science. These days, "science" is often nothing more than a cover story. She doesn't ask him about drones. If they were aware of drones on the mainland, he would volunteer whatever lies the people on Ringrock concocted to explain them.

EVIDENCE

Before raising the window shades, Katie stands in front of the canvas that is clamped to the easel in her studio. Nail shop, ice cream store, pizza parlor.

The problems of infusing this mundane scene with the truth and meaning of it are manifold. She can't use color as a tool. She must remain faithful to the colors of the real-world strip mall that is her subject. Because she won't—dares not—attempt to portray the meaning graphically, she must approach the truth of the place by symbolism, subtext, and suggestion. The instruments with which she might achieve this are limited to light, shadow, and reflection.

When working with pencils, drawing water hyperrealistically in all its myriad conditions is difficult. Window glass is no easier. As demanding as such pencil work can be, rendering water and clear glass in her style and with acrylics is even much harder.

The windows of the stores provide a lot of glass. The sky is clearing, blue breaking through gray clouds; rain is puddled on the pavement, providing mirrored surfaces in addition to the windows. Light and shadow she can manage. The reflections might undo her.

She moves through the house, putting up the shades. No one is waiting at any window.

In the bedroom, she threads a holster onto her belt and slips the 9 mm Glock into it.

The day is cool. She shrugs into a beige sport coat and drops the two spare magazines in its pockets. She does not always carry a concealed weapon when outside. Henceforth, she will.

She steps out of the house and locks the door.

A fog has grown out of the lake during the night. In the east, above the sea of atmosphere, the sun is not its fierce self, but more like a bright moon. Lazy currents of mist eddy across Jacob's Ladder, like a vision of some future flood that will submerge it.

When she circles the building, she finds no footprints where the soil is soft enough to take impressions.

The mist has quieted the morning, suppressed most sounds, kept the birds silent in their nests and on their roosts.

At the back of the house, she spots a section of rain gutter that, though still attached to the eave, is bent, which it hadn't been before. She recalls the vibratory note the gutter made when, the previous night, the trespasser completed exploration of the roof and went away.

Under a kitchen window, the earth is gouged; torn clumps of grass are scattered about. Sometimes crows will tear up turf in this manner when foraging for grubs.

What gives her pause is the ammoniacal stink. She has never encountered anything like it.

A patch of grass and divots of exposed soil, approximately six feet in diameter, has a powdery, frosted appearance unrelated to the fog. When she stoops to study it, the stuff resembles downy mildew. However, mildew should have a musty odor, not an astringent alkaline smell, and it shouldn't be thriving in the open air.

The affected area is directly below the torqued gutter, but that doesn't mean there's any connection between them. Following the weird events of the previous afternoon and night, she is inclined to be suspicious of things that, on any other day, would seem mundane.

Life on a small island in these climes requires her to keep a supply of mildewcide on hand. Later, after the fog has lifted, she will return here and treat the affected area if necessary. Most likely, when the fog dissipates, this fungus—if that's what it is—will quickly perish in direct sunlight.

At the end of the front yard, the concrete steps vanish into the fog, which thickens further near the water. She can't see the boathouse below, although she hears the lake gently lapping at the deep bed of tide-polished pebbles and stones that form the shore.

As she descends, a new malodor rises to meet her, different from that behind the house, less intense and more familiar.

At the bottom, visibility is ten or twelve feet. She turns away from the dock, venturing onto the beach, where the pebbles are so tightly integrated that they shift only slightly underfoot.

Within half a dozen steps, she discovers the source of the smell, which is what she expected. Dead fish have washed up during the night, twenty or thirty of them just in the arc of visibility. Their white bellies are bloated and glistening with a viscous film.

"'Mechanical sonic devices that simulate the sound waves produced by explosives,'" she says. "'No real explosives were involved.' Try to sell that bullshit to the fish."

To her trained eye, the stones and fish become a tableau, a white-and-gray composition that makes a disturbing statement. The stones represent life, which is a hard slope. The decomposing fish allow no evasion from the cold truth of where the shingle beach of life inevitably leads.

The fog assumes a new character, morphs into the toxic miasma of a nightmare, in which monsters wait to be revealed.

A dire sense of suffocation overcomes Katie, as though the air has grown too dense to inhale. She hasn't been stricken by this disabling dread in more than two years, and she isn't of a mind to surrender to it now.

"Hell, no," she says. She turns away from the fish, refuses to scan the fog for threats that are mere figments of her imagination, and proceeds to the dock.

From the water comes the low, distant growl of a passing craft. An outboard engine. The boat probably isn't big enough to have the requisite radar and electronic navigation for this weather, so the fog that is pushing ashore must be winnowing away out on the lake.

By the time she climbs the dock steps and makes her way along the railing to the boathouse, the panic that threatened to seize her has passed. In spite of recent events, Jacob's Ladder remains a refuge where, after a time of weakness and doubt, she has regained much of the strength and confidence that she once possessed in abundance, the courage that she needs to keep the Promise.

The boathouse door is locked, as she left it. Inside, the cabin cruiser remains belayed, snugged against the rubber fenders. Water softly chortles. The floating slip creaks where its flat decking meets the gangway. She steps outside, locks up.

At the back of the structure, she opens the generator-room door. All is as it ought to be. She can see no indication that anyone attempted to force entrance. She engages the lock.

As she climbs the steps from the shore, the fog is thinning.

She can return to the house, to the painting that resists a satisfactory completion, and write off the events at Ringrock as being none of her business and beyond her control.

It is likewise easy to argue that the post-midnight trespasser had nothing to do with Ringrock, that it must have been a raccoon, and that she had been in an agitated state that encouraged her to make more of it than it was. Just because no raccoons have troubled her in the past doesn't mean that one hasn't recently found its way to Jacob's Ladder. If the animals live on Oak Haven, one might have crossed the channel. Raccoons could swim, couldn't they? They waded into streams in search of fish and crawdads to feed on.

But Oak Haven lies half a mile away. The channel isn't a mere stream.

At the top of the stairs, she looks beyond the house, toward the woods that are manifesting out of the mist, dark and smoldering in the early light. She's aware that the motor noise of the outboard boat that passed in the fog did not fade gradually out of hearing. In this still morning, sound travels a great distance. The craft had fallen silent abruptly, as if it put to shore near the north end of her island.

BEFORE JACOB'S LADDER:
THE THERAPIST

The office is Scandinavian contemporary, with furniture that looks more uncomfortable than it is. Instead of a couch, the patient is provided an armchair identical to the one the doctor occupies. The three large paintings are abstract expressionist works blazing with colors, shapes, and illusions of movement that allow for an infinite number of interpretations but mean nothing.

Dr. Allyson Wynn-Sperry, thirty-five, is a modern therapist in every way. She is physically sleek, dedicated to a diet of organic foods low in carbs and rich with antioxidants. She swims for half an hour every morning and attends a Pilates class three times a week. She dresses not in the staid manner of previous generations of women in her profession, but with style and panache, though without ever being flamboyant, as if she is perpetually on her way to an upscale restaurant to have lunch with a trio of friends whose Ivy League bona fides might as well be stamped on their foreheads. She drives a Tesla and carries an attaché case rather than a purse; however, she isn't embarrassed by retro impulses, so she sports a Cartier watch and often wears Hermès scarves. Dr. Wynn-Sperry encourages patients to develop high self-esteem, to regard feelings of guilt and regret as relics of an oppressive culture that is dying, and to lean in to life with an aggressive expectation of fulfillment.

At Katie's election, this will be her last day of therapy, and Dr. Allyson Wynn-Sperry is deeply concerned that her patient is making a terrible mistake. "You've got a successful career, one that so many women would envy. With the inheritances and insurance money and your savings, you can remain here, in a new home of course, but in a desirable neighborhood, where you'll have the inspiration that only the city can provide an artist."

"Andrew Wyeth lived in rural Pennsylvania part of the year, in rural Maine the other part," Katie says.

Dr. Wynn-Sperry presses her lips together for a moment as if frustrated in her composition of a reply. Then she says, "Katie, I understand you well enough to know that you aspire to recognition."

"Not at all. Not anymore."

"Well-earned and deserved recognition," the doctor persists. "You want to paint something that endures. Frankly, I don't know anyone who would collect Wyeth. As young as you are, just coming into your most creative decades, you can't just give up and walk away from your career."

"I'll continue to paint. I'm just not interested in selling, the gallery shows, the interviews, the art scene. For a few years, maybe forever, I want to paint just for me."

Wynn-Sperry looks toward a window, at the cityscape beyond, at the life into which she leans with such intensity that any painting taking her as a subject might, with symbolic intent, depict her as she soldiers down an avenue where the skyscrapers bend noticeably away from her, cowed by her determination. "You've been through hell," the doctor says. "Many people would be broken forever by what happened, but you're not most people. Yes, right now, you're bitter, you're lost—"

"I'm bitter, but I'm not lost. I'm in pain. The grief. The void. The stupid, evil, damn irrationality of it all. The fear."

"All of which you should feel, need to feel. But as difficult as it might be to believe, even grief will not always remain as sharp as it is now. Grief becomes sorrow, and sorrow becomes—"

"Enduring," Katie says. "I suspect sorrow can inspire art better than any city can."

After a silence, Wynn-Sperry says, "What about the Promise that's so important to you? How can you keep it alone in a castle, surrounded by a moat?"

"It's a lake, not a moat. Wide water well beyond the mouth of the river. Tranquil. I'll live to paint for myself and for them."

Wyatt-Sperry regards Katie with pity. "For them—who can never see what you paint."

"They'll see," Katie says. "Anyway, it's not a gloomy castle, just a bungalow. I think Joe Smith built the place as his defense against Dachau, his refuge from the possibility of it."

Wynn-Sperry puts aside her pen and notepad, having written nothing. "Dachau, Auschwitz—the past is past. You're a young woman with a future if you want it."

Katie slides forward on her chair. "Do you really believe the past is past? I think the past might be our future, that we're busy laying the groundwork for new Dachaus, new Auschwitzes, all in the name of compassion, progress, justice, prosperity. Of the hard lessons that humanity learns, how many are retained? How very few? The passion of angry ideologues, the ignorance of the arrogant, the ferocity of utopians—how can such people lead the world to anything but its end?"

The doctor reaches out to Katie. "I'm worried for you."

Katie squeezes the offered hand. "And I for you."

FOXES

The fog rises to the heat of the sun, not in one curtain, but like long, cottony, decorative garlands of faux snow lifted from the pines as though they are Christmas trees being undressed after the holiday.

As the haze ascends and withers, the woodland clarifies even if it grows only slightly brighter. Shadows sharpen as though they have been stropped on the scarves of mist. The light filtered through the interlaced boughs of the hardy evergreens, through the newly leafing branches of sycamores and maples, blurs its way to the forest floor, painting everything with more mystery than revelation.

The main trail that Katie follows is not a straight line, but winds from south to north, adding a little less than a quarter of a mile to what would otherwise be a half-mile walk. Dwarf periwinkle, honeysuckle, ribbon grass, snowy woodrush, potentilla making an early recovery from winter—the island offers a rich variety of plants, far more than she can name, and the undergrowth is dense.

Rock formations intrude here and there, sometimes draped with myrtle or purple-leafed Japanese creeper. Farther north in the shallower waters of the archipelago, many islands are sedimentary, formed from centuries of accumulated silt, but her refuge is born from a spine of bedrock that here and there reveals a few of its vertebrae.

On her way to the north end of Jacob's Ladder, when she rounds a thrust of smooth gray rock, she is confronted by three adult red foxes that appear to be fleeing some threat. At the sight of her, two creatures depart the trail and disappear into the undergrowth.

The third fox, by the grace of its sharp curved claws, climbs straight up a tall sycamore with an alacrity almost equal to that of a squirrel, its thick bushy tail trailing like a wool scarf.

Katie has never previously seen more than one fox at a time. They live together only when mating and during the early months of their pups' lives. Otherwise each keeps to its own den and hunts alone. She has no idea if the island supports as few as four or five, or twice that number.

Because its tail is redder and speckled with much less black than the tails of the others, she recognizes the one in the tree as the boldest of their population. This guy, and he alone, hunts close to the house for field mice and birds. He has a keen curiosity. He never vanishes at the first glimpse of her, but stands and watches intently. On a few occasions, he has even approached her, coming to within ten feet. She has given him the name Michael J. Fox, because he possesses a charm not unlike that of the actor, whom she adored when she was a young girl, but also because this Michael appears to have a large measure of courage, as does his human namesake.

Now Michael J. watches her from high on the sycamore. He looks back along the trail, in the direction from which he and the other foxes came. When he turns his attention once more to Katie, he makes a noise that in part is an expression of distress but that is also a low hiss and growl of disgust and perhaps a warning.

Having lived so long with little human contact, the animals on Jacob's Ladder are likely to be sensitive to the sudden arrival of two-legged visitors.

Convinced that the watercraft she heard earlier has put to shore at the north end of her property instead of passing by, Katie hurries toward whatever confrontation awaits.

At the northeast corner of the island, in a small cove, a boat has been drawn out of the water, onto the sand. An outboard racer. The drive shaft pulled up and secured. It appears to be one of the flotilla of such vessels that searched the water near Ringrock the previous evening.

THE GROTTO

In the damp sand, the footprints of two men arc from the beached boat to the stairway that leads to the grotto. No doubt about it this time—trespassers have violated her property.

During the decades that Joe Smith lived here, he engaged in a construction project more ambitious than the bungalow in which Katie now lives. He didn't know what he was creating until he'd labored on it for almost forty years. Even when he felt that it was complete, he didn't know if building it had any value beyond filling his life with a purpose that distracted him from dwelling too much on his darker memories.

Smith had written extensively about the construction process in his diaries, which Tanner Walsh preserved and which were markedly more interesting than the failed author's own audiotapes.

The veteran's ruminations reveal to Katie a kindred soul. In his swift transition from farm boy to warrior, Smith's recognition of the human capacity for evil vaporized his innocence, which he longed to regain, though he knew it was a thing that, once lost, was gone forever. When the world proved chaotic and its meaning obscure beyond discovery, he tried to build his own meaning stone by stone, brick by brick.

This end of the island is a rampart of shelving limestone. With his skills as a stone carver and mason, Smith fashioned a six-foot width of the steep bluff into twenty-four steps that ascend to the headland.

Warmed by a simmering indignation, Katie climbs the stairs. At the top, a narrow brick pathway of Smith's creation, deteriorated by time and weather, leads thirty feet through a swath of scrabbly grass. Thereafter, it descends to the mouth of the natural grotto that the troubled veteran toiled for decades to shape into a wonder.

The opening to the grotto is at the center of a curved, twelve-foot-high cliff forming the back wall of a crescent-shaped declivity in the land. The original access to the cavern had been through an irregular maw overhung by vines.

Joe Smith had regularized it with a sixteen-foot-wide, ten-foot-high surround and a deep vestibule featuring a barrel-vaulted ceiling, all of matte-textured burgundy brick over concrete block. This might have appeared to be the entrance to a train tunnel if the obsessed mason had merely laid the bricks in simple bonds. Instead, he achieved patterns Katie had never seen before, waves and whorls that seemed not to be structurally sound, but obviously were.

Consequently, the striking grotto entrance suggests that past this portal might lie the hallowed hall of a mystical order of monks or knights. Something magical and strange.

In producing this and the amazing work in the grotto itself, Smith was periodically assisted by a deaf, mute craftsman named Jude Macabee. At especially challenging points in the project, the silent mainlander visited the island for weeks at a time. Evidence suggests that Jude was the only friend Joe Smith had. He never spoke a word to Jude, nor Jude to him, yet they shared a profound friendship.

For Joe, silence was a defense against the ever-louder madness of the world. For Jude, it was what fate provided for him.

Katie ventures under the arch, into the vestibule. She listens. The voices are soft, and the echoes are softer, and the words convey no more meaning than do the subterranean drafts that whisper out of the throats of ancient stone below, their source unknowable.

The grotto appears as dark as a closed coffin, but that doesn't mean the intruders aren't using flashlights. If the main cavern is likened to a theater, there are loges and a backstage out of which little or no light escapes; if it is likened to a cathedral, there are vestries and apsidal chapels and baptisteries that the intruders might be exploring.

Lacking a flashlight, having failed to foresee the need to go spelunking, preferring a confrontation in sunlight, Katie shouts into the void, her voice echoing in a chorus of demands. "You are trespassing. Come out of there and identify yourselves."

She retreats from the vestibule, backs off fifteen feet from the entry arch, and tucks the right panel of her sport coat behind the grip of her holstered pistol, to make sure they see that she is armed and realize the need for a respectful response.

After a few minutes, two men appear. They are tall and fit and the very definition of potential energy, the kind who are capable of going kinetic in an instant and acting with lethal decisiveness. Their black boots, black pants, and black crew-neck jerseys are uniforms without identifying insignia.

They wear gun belts with sidearms. They also carry AR-15s on which are mounted flashlights aligned with the muzzles. The rifles are slung over their shoulders.

One of them is fortysomething, with salt-and-pepper hair and eyes the steel-gray of flensing knives. The other is younger, his face too sweet and his stare too tender for his profession.

The older man smiles a smile that Katie finds disturbing.

A SLIGHT INCONVENIENCE

The sky is mostly clear, the morning sun revealed. The last serpentine shapes of fog writhe slowly across the ground.

The two men produce laminated, holographic-photo ID immediately upon Katie's request. The older man is Robert Zenon. The younger is Hampton Rice. Both are with the Internal Security Agency.

"The ISA?" Katie says. "I've never heard of it."

"Nonetheless," Zenon assures her, "it exists."

They don't ask for her name. Obviously, they know who she is.

"What're you doing here?"

"Looking for someone," Zenon says.

"Who?"

"Classified."

"You're from Ringrock."

Zenon shrugs.

"What's going on over there?"

He says nothing, merely meets her stare.

"If someone came from there to here, am I in danger?"

Glancing at her holstered Glock, Zenon says, "Depends on how quick and accurate you are with that."

She frowns. It seems a stupid thing for him to have said—or something worse than stupid. "Is that a threat?"

"No need to get hysterical," he says. "It's just an observation. We're here to ensure your safety."

That smile again. The arrogance and contempt irritate Katie.

"This is my island. By what authority—"

"By the authority of this search warrant." He produces the folded document from a pocket, shakes it open, and hands it to her.

At a glance, it looks real. She doesn't want to read it because that would mean looking away from these men.

"Why didn't you come to the house to present this?"

"We didn't want to alarm you unnecessarily. We just need to search the cave, and then we'll go."

Puzzled, she says, "Just the grotto? Why couldn't this person you want be anywhere?"

"The rest of your island has been searched already."

She considers and then says, "The drones. But that was last night. Since then he could have come out of the grotto and—"

"This morning, we have other, more powerful ordnance at a loftier altitude. A second search was concluded minutes ago."

Katie glances at the sky. "This is crazy."

"What we want is either in the cave or not. Just return to your home and leave this to us. That's all that's required of you. A slight inconvenience. But it *is* required. And it's required now."

She looks at the younger man. "Do you ever talk?"

"Oh, yes. Though not as much as you."

If anything, his smile is more of a sneer than Zenon's. With this impudence, his boyish face turns as soft as spoiled fruit.

Their effrontery doesn't surprise her. She has dealt with their kind before, almost three years earlier. Back then, however, this new wave of fascists made at least a small effort to pretend to be something other than what they were. Now, in this matter, they seem to feel their time has come to act as they wish, without concern about blowback.

Jacob's Ladder is her last redoubt. She can't risk having it taken from her. If she lets them search the grotto, maybe they will leave, as Zenon has said. All she wants is for them to be gone.

In spite of the events of yesterday and this morning, the peace of the island can be restored. She can live as she wishes, as she wants. She can fulfill the Promise. She has to believe that is true, for it's all she has.

THE GULLS AND THE FOX

Returning from the grotto, north to south on Jacob's Ladder, Katie indulges in a slow burn that never escalates from mere vexation. Life has taught her that it's mentally exhausting and spiritually depressing to waste energy and time fanning the flames of anger when the reason for her outrage is someone who can't be affected by anything she does or some malignant force in society that, when challenged, will engulf her and dissolve her in a metastatic frenzy. Patience, steadiness, and hope are healthier than anger; therefore, in spite of evidence to the contrary, she still trusts that the world has been shapen to a purpose and that the purpose is not the triumph of evil.

Repeatedly during her trek from grotto to bungalow, she halts, gripped by the intuitive perception that her island has changed. Rock formations that have been the same for hundreds of years seem to have been resculpted in an indefinable way. The undergrowth, the trees, the way sunlight channels through the limbs and boughs—none of it is quite what it was this time the previous day. And although the changes are not drastic, they are profound and terrible.

She imagines that this is how she might feel if she went on vacation for a month and, on returning home, discovered subtle indications but no hard proof that, in her absence, some uninvited guest had lived there.

Of course, this is just a reaction to her treasured solitude having been violated by the ISA agents and whomever they might be seeking. The rocks and trees have not changed, nor the trail she follows, nor the house of native stone that now appears beyond the last of the evergreens.

And yet . . . A sense of wrongness prickles as if a burr has somehow gotten under her skull.

As the trail departs the woods and Katie steps into the meadow behind her house, she hears the gulls. The high, thin *keeel* of their flight calls. The squeals and short, excited phrases of those who are on the ground and in a feeding frenzy.

At the head of the concrete stairs, she looks down on the beach and shallows, where perhaps a score of ring-billed gulls are gorging on the dead fish that washed ashore during the night. Others swoop overhead, white kites, the black tips of their wings seemingly as sharp as flinders of flint.

Soon the birds will leave only fish shapes of fragile bones that gentle lake tides will carry away and disassemble and dissolve.

Katie's attention is drawn beyond the beach, to the boathouse, to the dock that runs along the side of it and another fifteen feet into the water. At the end of that pier, something small and furry sits with its back to her. When it turns its head toward her as though aware of being watched, she realizes that it is a fox.

Never before has she seen a fox near the boathouse, though that doesn't mean they haven't prowled out there on nights when they are hungry and hunting.

Foxes will eat dead animals, and they will spring on birds to take them by surprise. For whatever reason, this specimen appears to have no interest in either delicacy.

When the fox turns its head to stare at the lake once more, the contrast between the raucous birds and the contemplative creature at the end of the pier increases Katie's sense that this small world of hers, by water wrapped, is yawing ever so slightly, like a boat wallowing in the merest presentiment of an oncoming storm.

She descends the stairs to the shore and then climbs stairs to the dock. Staying close to the railing, to give the fox space to run past her if it chooses to flee, she approaches him slowly.

When she is twenty feet away, she knows for sure that he is Michael J.

She is ten feet from him when again he turns his head to look at her. She ventures no closer lest she frighten him. His coat is reddish, flecked with black and gray, except for a white ruff at his throat and white fur lining his perpetually pricked ears.

"What are you doing out here?" she asks.

After favoring her with a long stare, he lies down with his front legs extended, his head raised, gazing under the lowest horizontal bar of the railing, toward the lake. Toward Ringrock.

Katie has seen foxes gamboling in play and stalking prey. She has seen them sniffing forest trails and meadows to read the news of the day. But she has never seen one of them meditating, which almost seems to be what Michael J. is doing.

As the satiated gulls finish their meal and leave the picked-clean bones and eyeless skulls to lie like omens of the eventual death of the lake, Katie realizes that the fox is shivering. Tremors course along his flanks.

The perception of wrongness, with her since the grotto, now intensifies. Closer consideration of the fox leads her to wonder if he has come to the end of the pier because he wants to put as much distance as possible between himself and the land behind them. He looks as if he would flee the island if he could.

She regards the sky. She remembers the drones. She wonders about the "more powerful ordnance at a loftier altitude." From miles above, a surveillance satellite can scan Jacob's Ladder; an analytic computer program can differentiate the heat signature of a rabbit from that of a fox—or that of a human being.

Anyone sheltering in the grotto is safe from being scanned by drone or satellite. But then anyone in the house or the boathouse is likewise beyond discovery. And yet Zenon and Rice did not insist on searching those structures.

Why not? After all, as far as they know, she might have given sanctuary to a prisoner or spy or some other enemy of the state who escaped Ringrock. They should want to have a look in the buildings, even if they have been locked since before the commotion at Ringrock the previous day. Furthermore, if some outsider has stolen secrets or some insider has betrayed the project at Ringrock, Zenon and Rice ought to insist on questioning Katie to learn where her loyalties lie.

The wrongness she perceives involves not just an undefinable change in the nature of Jacob's Ladder, but also the inexplicable failure of the two men at the grotto to follow the long-established and logical procedures of a search for a fugitive.

Their behavior suggests that they have no reason to suspect her, which can only mean there is no fugitive to whom she might have given shelter. They aren't seeking an escaped prisoner, a spy, or a traitor. They are seeking something other than a person.

The fox rises, changes position, sits on his hindquarters, his glorious tail blooming behind him. He makes eye contact with Katie for a moment, and then rests his chin on the lowest horizontal of the railing. He has refocused his attention from Ringrock to Oak Haven. Irregular tremors flutter along his flanks. His mood appears to be one of both longing for the island beyond his reach—and dread.

Katie says, "What do you know that I don't?"

The fox does not reply.

BEFORE JACOB'S LADDER:
THE ATTORNEY

Their offices occupy the four top floors of the high-rise, a realm of gleaming marble and polished mahogany and stunning city views that confirm the power of those who work here.

Lindman's reputation is that of a fighter. He—and the firm that bears his name before the other three—is equally revered and envied not only by those who work for and with him but also by this nation's legions of attorneys who make of the law what it is and, more than any other profession, shape the future of America. He has stood fearlessly against the wealthiest corporations and cracked through their seemingly impervious defenses. On behalf of a sexually abused woman, he sued a man worth forty billion dollars, an oligarch thought untouchable, and won a settlement of four hundred million. He has brought down a senator and a governor, and through his pro bono work perhaps contributed significantly to the abrupt fall of a president.

Sixty-eight years old, Lindman is a beefy man, though by all appearances fit. When his secretary ushers Katie into the attorney's ultramodern office with its high-contrast display of ancient fired-clay horse sculptures from the Sung and T'ang dynasties, the attorney springs up from his chair as might a twenty-year-old. He rounds his desk, strides to her, takes her offered hand in both of his, and expresses his sympathy with a grace and chivalry that has been all but lost by later generations than his.

In this vast aerie, two seating areas can accommodate clients. The first provides two sofas and two armchairs. The second is much smaller, with four armchairs near the wall of windows, which offers a floor-to-ceiling panoramic presentation of the lesser buildings of the metropolis all the way to the distant sea.

Confronted with this vista, a severely acrophobic person might find himself facedown on the floor, gripped by a paralytic panic. The attorney escorts Katie to the chairs nearest the wall of glass, where they sit facing each other.

Lindman's countenance is broad, unconventionally handsome, and seamed in such a way that suggests experience rather than advanced age. His blue eyes are uncommonly clear. The directness of his stare suggests her every word matters to him, and she feels that she has his sincere sympathy rather than unwanted pity.

He has thoroughly familiarized himself with her ordeal, but he wants to hear it from her in detail. She unburdens herself with more emotion than she intends, but without tears.

When she's done, he apologizes for the blunt questions he must ask. What does she want? Does she want money as compensation? If it's money, how much?

"I want justice," she says, "but they won't give me that. I want the guilty put on trial, but they're above the law. So, yes, the only way I can hurt them is to take the one thing that matters to them, as much of their money as I can make them pay."

He nods in understanding. He turns his head toward the view. After a thoughtful silence, he says, "Two fine men died during the construction of this building. Ironworkers who walk the naked frame of a skyscraper, bolting and welding and bracing—they're a brave breed. It's a long fall from thirty or forty stories, a short span of seconds that must seem like an eternity." His stare returns to Katie. "Do you understand the risks?"

"Litigation is expensive. I could lose. I'm aware of that. But they'll have to endure a lot of bad publicity, public scorn."

"These are very powerful people."

"After all I've lost, what's left to lose?"

He bows his head. "Do you know Aesop? The fable titled 'The Great and the Little Fishes'?"

"If I've ever heard it, I don't recall."

His gaze fixes on his hands, which are folded in his lap. "'The fisherman drew up a net that he had cast into the sea. It was filled with all kinds of fish. The many Little Fish began to slip through the meshes of the net and back into the deep. The Great Fish cried out at the injustice of this, but the fisherman was unmoved. All the Great Fish were caught and hauled into the ship, but all the Little Fish escaped.'"

When he meets her eyes again, Katie says, "So you think we can catch these people, haul them in?"

He shakes his head. "I'm afraid that's not the meaning of the fable. Aesop intends to say that the insignificance of the little fish is what assures their safety." He pauses to allow her to think about that. "If you should try to bring a civil action against these people, you will have made a Great Fish of yourself."

Katie sits up straighter in her chair. "So be it. I'm not afraid of them."

"My best advice is to be as tiny a fish as you can be. Take your savings, your inheritance, the proceeds of the two insurance policies—and make an offer for that island you're considering."

She hasn't said a word to him about her finances or the island that she has considered buying as a refuge. And yet he knows.

When he places his arms on the arms of the chair, he taps the fingers of his right hand to express his impatience. "If you find a law firm naive enough to represent you, I expect you'll have a fatal accident before you ever get into a courtroom, perhaps even before you can file the action. In fact, I guarantee it."

What Katie has taken to be sympathy and kindness has instead been smug calculation. "You represent them?"

"No. Let's just say they and I are in the same club. They're my kind. You can never be." He rises from his chair, and she from hers. "You think you've hit bottom. Believe me, you still have a long way to fall, a very long way. You can't even imagine what all could happen to you in a fall as long as that."

A well-barbered, polished, thirtysomething man wearing a four-thousand-dollar suit, showing exactly half an inch of shirt cuffs at the end of his coat sleeves, sporting a gold Rolex with a gold face and gold checks instead of numbers, as self-possessed as a prince of the realm, escorts her to the elevator and enters the cab with her.

As they descend, he says, "Do you know the fable titled 'The Vain Wolf and the Lion'?"

Any curse with which she might reply will not affect him and will only diminish her.

He smiles. "Roaming by the mountainside as the sun was setting, the Wolf saw his own shadow magnified, greatly extended. He said, 'Why should I—so immense, nearly an acre in length— be the least bit afraid of the Lion? Why, *I* should be acclaimed the king of all the beasts.' While he was expressing these proud thoughts, the Lion attacked and killed him." Her escort pauses long enough for two floors to go by, and then he says, "Do you grasp the meaning?"

She says nothing.

"By thinking too highly of himself, by gravely overestimating his strength and his place in the world, the Wolf brought about his own destruction. Do not think too highly of yourself."

He accompanies her all the way down to the second subterranean level of parking. He remains in the cab as she steps out of it.

He says, "Have a nice day."

KEEPING WATCH

Katie fetches two protein bars, a bottle of Diet Pepsi, and her binoculars from the house. She quickly returns to the stairs that lead to the shore, where she sits on the top step.

She intends to wait until she sees the outboard racer make its way back to Ringrock with Zenon and Rice aboard. She wants to know when her island is once more hers and hers alone.

The last of the gulls have gone.

Michael J. remains on the pier.

This Wednesday well before summer vacations have begun for most people, there are only a few pleasure craft passing on the lake. A greater number of commercial shippers ply those waters, some bound for busy ports to the south, others for a farther lake. Each type of craft has its particular voice: Some growl while others moan; some sound like a saw meeting wood, while others purr. A few larger vessels, passing miles wide of Jacob's Ladder, seem as silent as ghost ships.

Katie eats the protein bars and washes them down with Pepsi and watches and listens. She will recognize the outboard engine of the racer even from a distance.

All appears to be quiet over on Ringrock. No boats patrol its shores, and no helicopters arrive or depart.

She has been sitting on the step for half an hour when she hears semiautomatic rifle fire in the distance. The clatter comes from the north, perhaps as far away as the area around the grotto. One sustained burst and then a shorter one are followed by a pause, and then by a series of shots spaced slightly farther apart than those preceding them. In this nearly windless morning, even at a distance of half a mile, the sound of an AR-15 can't be mistaken for anything else.

If it's not a man that Zenon and Rice have come after, then what have they shot? Or attempted to shoot?

An animal of some kind, contaminated or infected.

If Ringrock is not an EPA facility, perhaps it operates under the authority of the Centers for Disease Control or another agency. Maybe scientists there are engaged in gain-of-function research on exotic viruses. The CDC had often indirectly funded such legally prohibited work at foreign laboratories, eventually resulting in an accidental leak and a global pandemic. Maybe they decided it is safer to conduct such potentially catastrophic research, whether legal or not, on an isolated island in the United States, where the laboratory protocols and security are much better controlled—until they aren't.

Katie gets to her feet, facing the woods, anticipating further gunfire or the sudden appearance of a fugitive animal that has been shot at but not hit. Dogs are often used in experiments. More often, monkeys. Sometimes, even chimpanzees.

An angry chimpanzee can be as dangerous as any animal on the planet. A seventy-pound chimp is as quick as a cat, stronger than a man twice its size, and capable of a blood frenzy that not even the most deranged human being can match. Katie recalls a news story from her childhood, when a pet chimpanzee attacked a woman, in less than a minute biting off her fingers, gouging out her eyes, and ripping her face away from the bone. In yet another case, a furious chimp blinded and tore off the genitals of the man who had kept him as a pet.

The previous night, it might have been a chimpanzee that climbed the wall of her house, explored the roof, and tested the chimney caps.

Drawing the Glock from her holster, holding it at her side, she considers retrieving her own AR-15. But she doesn't want to miss Zenon and Rice if they pass in the racing boat while she's in the house. The pistol should provide adequate protection.

She stays on her feet. In that posture she will be quicker to react to any threat. Although she paces, she never turns her back on the meadow and the woods beyond. Compared to the land, the lake seems less a source of menace.

That judgment reminds her of an Aesop fable titled "The One-Eyed Doe." A doe with one eye grazed near the sea, where she felt safer. She kept her one eye toward the land, on the lookout for hunters and lions, and her blind eye toward the sea from which nothing could approach her. Sailors rowing past in a boat saw her, notched arrows in their bows, and shot her. Our troubles often come from where we least expect them.

Flocking southward, Canadian geese pass over in silence and are gone as if they were more dreamed than real.

The Wedgwood-blue sky is clear and still, although in the heights, beyond the envelope of atmosphere, an eye in orbit might even now have its unblinking gaze focused on Jacob's Ladder and Katie.

She has been pacing almost half an hour when she hears the distinctive outboard engine. She holsters the gun.

THREE MEN

Eyes to the eyecups, Katie searches the sun-spangled water with the binoculars, seeking the low profile of the boat.

She expects it to cruise along the east flank of the island, following a direct line to Ringrock in the south. However, after a minute or so during which the outboard engine grows steadily louder, the pitch of its growl subtly changes, as might be the case if the racer is no longer coming directly south toward her.

As the signature sound slowly fades, she finds the boat heading due east, on a course that will take it north of Oak Haven Island and eventually to the mainland. It's already at such a distance from Jacob's Ladder that it's little more than a shape moving through the bright and ceaseless capering of the sun fairies that dance across the riffling wavelets.

Katie adjusts the focusing drive, clarifying the craft. She pulls its image closer, until there can be no doubt that it is the type of boat that Zenon and Rice had beached at the north end of her island.

Three dark shapes seem to be three men. So the ISA agents came here in pursuit of a man, after all, not an animal. One occupies the stern seat, near the outboard—either Zenon or Rice—operating the steering-and-throttle arm. Two sit side by side on the forward thwart seat.

She is unable to determine if one of the two on the thwart seat is wounded and in captivity, or perhaps dead.

In fact, they are at such a distance that she can't identify Zenon or Rice. They are nothing more than three tiny figures veiled by the sun's infinite reflections that flare off the rippling lake.

Nevertheless, she is all but certain that the receding boat carries the agents and their quarry. If they are taking the captive to the mainland instead of to Ringrock, it is probably because he requires urgent medical attention or because they intend to bring him before a court to charge him with whatever crime they claim he has committed.

The boat passes Oak Haven and maintains a course due east. It vanishes into the shimmer and sheen. She lowers the binoculars and listens to the engine noise as it repeatedly fades and returns, until it fades and doesn't return.

The fox remains on the pier.

Katie makes her way to the house with the binoculars, the empty bottle of Pepsi, and the protein-bar wrappers. She disposes of the trash and puts the binoculars away.

She could spend the rest of the day reading. Maybe Dickens. Maybe Balzac. Maybe Austen.

She could begin to deal with the reflective surfaces in the unfinished painting. The shop windows. The rain-puddled pavement.

Outside once more, she stares at Ringrock. She turns north and regards the woods, beyond which lies the cove below the grotto.

All is quiet on her island. Peace and order have returned. Or the illusion of peace and order.

Katie is not a one-eyed doe. The truth of things can never be assumed. It must be confirmed by action and inquiry.

She fetches her Tac Light, locks the door, and sets off to confirm that the beached boat is gone and the ISA agents with it.

THEIR NAMES

The strangeness cultured by recent events continues to make mysterious these woods that were previously as familiar as the rooms of her small house. Some of the shadows appear to move independently of anything that casts them; in places, daylight bends through the branches in ways that deny the spectrum physics of the real world and make a moment dreamlike. Or so it seems.

The one thing that reassures Katie is the birdsong, which is everywhere as it should be. The sweet, high, clear notes of yellow warblers. The unmusical buzz and *zid-zid-zid* of northern parulas. Redstarts, waterthrushes, scarlet tanagers, rose-breasted grosbeaks, dark-eyed juncos—she knows their names, studies them all, and recognizes their distinct voices.

Perhaps because there were three men in the boat and because boats frequently appear in classic paintings as symbols of fate, three other names come into her mind unbidden. Lupo. Hamal. Parker. They were the three men, three instruments of a demonic fate, who stole from her the life she had and can never hope to regain.

As she follows the trail through the trees, those faces pass repeatedly through her mind. In the aftermath of the horror, she'd obsessively studied photographs of Lupo, Hamal, and Parker. Every smallest detail of their faces is etched irrevocably in her memory, as if she has painted their portraits in her signature style.

For a time, she fantasized about surveilling them one by one, waiting for a moment of opportunity, and shooting them dead. That was the one time in her life when anger consumed her. During those dark weeks, she learned definitively that anger can never conjure justice where justice does not already exist. The tragedy that she wished to avenge was capped by another tragedy, after which she wanted not revenge but only sanctuary.

The trail descends now, comes to the shore, and curves around the northeast corner of Jacob's Ladder, to the cove where the boat was beached when last she came here.

It's gone. The sand is deeply scored where they dragged the craft back into the water.

This discovery eases her mind, but her relief is not complete. Shots were fired. Blood was probably spilled. She might not be able to learn much from whatever evidence remains of that confrontation. But this is *her* island, and whatever facts she is able to glean from an inspection of the grotto, where perhaps the violence began, might be essential to a restoration of her peace of mind.

She climbs the twenty-four steps to the brick walkway that leads across a sward of scraggly grass and down to the elaborated entrance to the grotto. She halts two steps onto the path.

On this occasion as on no other, this place reminds Katie of a mausoleum. The eccentric patterns in the brickwork of the wall seem like whorls of runes or hieroglyphics that anyone desiring to enter would be wise to interpret first. The darkness in the open vestibule and beyond looks so dense as to have substance that even the Tac Light won't penetrate. The arched entrance is like a passageway to some medieval castle, where a portcullis might at any moment crash down to deny access—or exit.

She knows that no portcullis exists, that the Tac Light will carve away the darkness, that good Joe Smith's masonry is nothing more than an expression of his creativity. The sinister impression the grotto makes on her is just a consequence of the encounter she had with Zenon and Rice.

Or it's a portent, a foreboding. She's not one for auguries, omens, supernatural signs. She *does* believe in intuition. Maybe intuition is what she's feeling, more intensely than ever before.

She is not a timid soul. She is certainly not a coward. She has already lost everything, lost more than her life. If Death comes for her, it will be like dying a second time, therefore the less to be feared. But she won't die easily, not when she has the Promise to keep.

Perplexed by her apprehension, she retreats to the head of the twenty-four steps and hesitates there.

Below her waits the beach. Once the land meets the water, the topography becomes dramatic. The shore doesn't slope gradually out into the lake. Ten feet beyond the waterline, the floor abruptly drops off to a depth of forty or fifty feet and becomes much deeper a little farther out.

If she were standing here an hour later, when the morning sun reaches its noon apex, the lake would be a mirror, preventing her from seeing what she sees now. If zebra mussels had not been introduced decades earlier, the water would be clouded with algae. From this elevated perspective, the crystal-clear fathoms reveal what she couldn't have seen from the beach. A sunken boat. The outboard racer in which the ISA agents arrived. She sees the vessel clearly from bow to stern—the thwart seat, the engine.

They must have either chopped a hole in the bottom before launching it or weighed it down with stones.

The three men she'd watched motoring past Oak Haven toward the mainland hadn't been who she'd thought they were. They hadn't come from Jacob's Ladder but from farther north in the archipelago.

Robert Zenon and Hampton Rice are still on her island. And for the time being, they don't want her to know it.

THREE
LOCKDOWN

——

THE LONG WAY HOME

Sunlight slants through the lens of water, as fish and their shadows pass over the boat that lies seven fathoms down.

Katie is wary about returning to the southern end of Jacob's Ladder by either the direct or the winding trail, which both pass through the woods. Too much undergrowth. Too many shadows. Numerous places where someone could lie in wait for her.

Even though Zenon and Rice know she's armed, they're not the kind to lurk in the bushes on the off chance of taking her by surprise. They're professionals, heavily armed, sure of themselves to the point of arrogance. If they come for her, they will most likely make a bold and forceful approach.

If they're still able to come for her. If they still exist.

The ISA agents could be dead, in which case she might soon be stalked by someone else.

On seeing the submerged boat, she had initially assumed that Zenon and Rice sunk it. Now she realizes it makes as much sense—or more—to suppose that whoever they were searching for has killed them and scuttled their vessel. Unlike the ISA agents, this unknown person might have no desire to leave Jacob's Ladder; he may intend to hide out here at least for a while.

If Zenon and Rice are dead in the grotto, their killer could be a foreign agent or a whistle-blower intent on eventually telling the truth about Ringrock, or another individual whose purpose she can't yet imagine.

Possibly, he is her natural ally. Whatever project is underway on Ringrock, it seems to be dangerous if not reckless, perhaps even wicked. A whistle-blower, on a crusade to reveal the truth, would have no reason to harm her.

However, experience has taught her that allies in a righteous cause are rare in a world of self-interest. Expect deceit. Distrust is essential to survival.

Behind her, the grotto probably holds the answers to the fate of Zenon and Rice, answers that will only raise new questions. She is not fool enough to enter that place without knowing if it is a rabbit's warren or a lion's den.

She draws her pistol and descends the limestone steps to the cove. Approximately a third of the eastern flank of the island is a sheer rock wall that ranges between ten and sixteen feet high; for that stretch, no shore exists to allow passage on foot. She must follow the longer route around the north end of Jacob's Ladder and along the western shore, which presents some treacherous footing of its own.

Because she must be cautious to elude an ambush and to avoid sustaining an injury in a fall, the trek is likely to take forty-five minutes. As she follows the arc of the small cove and rounds the northwest point, Katie wonders what awaits her at the southern end of the island.

A YOUNG MAN'S ACCOMPLISHMENTS

Back in the days before Jacob's Ladder, when grief and anger are all-consuming, when the district attorney and the judge and the mayor fail her, when the impotent sympathy of the police is of no consolation, when fantasies of revenge seem like realistic schemes that she can carry out successfully, Katie is obsessed not just with photographs of Lupo, Hamal, and Parker, but as well with the three files in which have been gathered hard-gotten information on their histories.

When Lupo is eleven, he finds the gang. During the next five years, he is charged three times with trafficking drugs, which means he isn't selling them but serves as a runner between the cartels that import the merchandise and those who peddle it on the streets. Twice he is remanded to rehabilitative therapy, and on the third occasion, he serves four months in juvenile detention. He leaves school when he's sixteen. That same year, he is one of nine boys under the age of eighteen who are indicted as adults for the gang rape of a twelve-year-old girl. Charges are dropped when the victim commits suicide and key evidence in the case is declared tainted, thus making a conviction unlikely. At nineteen, when he is a suspect in the beating of a priest who suffered severe brain damage, his life path crosses Katie's. She is thirty-three at the time.

FEVERISH CALCULATION

Katie is on the move, her thoughts faster than her feet as she negotiates a rocky shore that is cleft and perpetually spalling. For centuries, in the worst of winters, currents have carried ice floes into this western flank of the island, where they crash one atop the other, their tonnage and sharp edges leaving evidence of their work after they have melted away. The resulting obstacle course provides countless places where anyone in too great a hurry is sure to twist an ankle and tear a tendon, maybe even break a bone.

She wants to get to her house as quickly as this route allows, but she doesn't want to arrive there without a plan that she can swiftly execute. The right plan. The smartest plan.

Her first inclination is to hunker down and dig in. This is *her* property. The Internal Security Agency and the fools who seem to be striving toward some apocalypse on Ringrock have no right to be on Jacob's Ladder. Not if the Constitution still means anything.

Of course, maybe it doesn't mean a damn thing anymore. She has made a point of avoiding the news for more than two years. A lot can happen in that length of time when a country is on a fatal slide.

Constitution or no Constitution, if her life is threatened on her own land, she is within her rights to defend herself with mortal force. But against agents of the government who have a legitimate mission to fulfill? She knows how that will turn out. Pretty much the same way it will turn out if their mission *isn't* legitimate.

To take a stand that might require violence to be used against violence, she needs to know *precisely* what the situation is, who all the players are—how to tell the good guys from the bad guys—and what the stakes are. She doesn't have a clue.

The thought of fleeing in the face of provocation galls her. She cherishes her self-reliance. It's who she is.

If she splits for the mainland, she'll have to go to the county sheriff and report trespassers, gunfire, possible murder.

Then what? Federal authority trumps local. Property rights are bendable when a matter of national security is involved.

She will be kept off her land until the authorities have done whatever they came here to do and have cleaned up every trace of what it was they did. When she returns, Jacob's Ladder might never again be what it has been to her—a place of peaceful solitude, where she feels safe, where she can fulfill the Promise.

When she's little more than halfway to the bungalow, a short burst of gunfire rattles the day.

She halts, pivots toward the rampart of pines, listens, waits. The clatter was so brief that she can't guess where on the island it originated.

A minute passes, two. When no further shots are fired, she is on the move once more.

Although she is loath to admit it, she can't stay here, can't be sure of doing the smart thing, the right thing, when she doesn't know the who, what, and why of the situation.

She needs to go to the house, get her checkbook, retrieve the small backpack stuffed with hundred-dollar bills that is hidden in the pantry, and retreat to the mainland.

When the right thing to do feels seven ways wrong, it's still the right thing, and doing it is what separates the quick from the dead.

Remembering the doe with one eye, she proceeds with caution, scanning the shadows between the trees that crowd along the low bluff above the shore, but remaining alert as well to the passing marine traffic, which is sparse and at a distance.

She reaches the southwest corner of the island and continues east. Shore grass sprouts out of the sandy soil, and the footing is less treacherous. She moves faster, taking the Glock in both hands.

The bungalow comes into view above and on her left, set back from the bluff. When she rounds the southeast corner, the soft beach transitions into shingle.

Ahead lie the boathouse and pier. She takes only a few steps before she realizes that the door of the boathouse is standing open.

ONE LESS OPTION

If he wants her dead, she's dead. Whoever's out there—Zenon or Rice, Zenon *and* Rice, or someone she's never met, some guy who has perhaps already killed Zenon and Rice—he's armed with an AR-15, and he probably has sniper training. Katie can dart from one pathetic patch of cover to another, run in a crouch, crawl on her belly—and none of it will matter. From higher ground, from the roof of the house, from wherever he is, he can scope her, track her, and with one round take her head apart as if it were a soft melon. Using a .300 Win Mag, a sniper can squeeze off a kill shot from a thousand yards, even fifteen hundred; in this case, although he probably doesn't have a sniper rifle, just an AR-15, the distance from muzzle to target might as well be point-blank.

She hurries across the bed of water-smoothed pebbles and the fish skeletons that splinter underfoot as if they were spun glass, climbs the pier steps, and follows the planking to the boathouse door.

An analysis by Sherlock Holmes isn't required to determine that the lock has been shot out with a burst of rifle fire, which was no doubt the brief clatter she heard when she'd been halfway along the western flank of the island.

After a hesitation, she steps through the door and flicks the light switch. The twenty-foot wooden cabin cruiser is where she left it, belayed with the bow toward her, still afloat.

She is alone here on the upper level. No intruder is either on the slip below or, apparently, aboard the boat. Everything seems to be in order.

Except. Except that the gunman hadn't blown the lock out just to step inside, have a look around, and satisfy his curiosity.

Descending the gangway, Katie sees the problem even before she reaches the vessel. Her rib cage constricts or her heart swells—a tightness in her chest that signifies mental rather than physical distress—and for a moment, but only a moment, her knees grow weak. She might as well turn back. There's no reason to go farther, no reason other than a refusal to believe her eyes. She keeps moving.

Always keep moving, Avi used to say. *The Fates are master sharp- shooters, and the easy target is the one who's standing still.*

Katie steps between the belaying lines, sits on the gunwale, swings aboard, and stands on the deck aft of the cabin. From skeg and propeller to swivel bracket, the driveshaft remains firmly clamped to the transom. The engine has been removed.

The cabin of the small cruiser has no back wall. She doesn't need to step inside to see that the engine hasn't been left there. It will be neither elsewhere in the boathouse nor anywhere she is likely to find it.

Someone intends to leave the island in her boat at such time as he chooses. He or they. Meanwhile, she is not being allowed to flee.

She swings out of the cruiser and stands on the slip, her mind racing.

Cone lights hanging on chains brighten the upper level and cast undulant reflections, like luminous fish, on the dark water, though shadows live between the pilings and under the decking. The place smells of the lake, wet concrete, creosote, and damp teak planks. Water softly burbles and purls, as though dogs unseen are lapping from their bowls in every corner, and the gangway creaks with the subtle movement of the slip, and among the rafters a bird—at this hour, surely an owl—flutters its wings as it adjusts its position on a beam.

All this is familiar in every detail—and was once comforting—but she is increasingly aware of a new eeriness in the scene. ISA agents and national security and spy-movie skullduggery do not explain what is happening on Jacob's Ladder. Both intuition and common sense tell her that the hidden truth is deeply strange and that the trouble she thinks she's in is much less terrifying than the trouble she's *really* in.

A USELESS APPLE

She still feels like a target as she climbs the stairs from the shore, as she crosses the yard and stands at the door of the house.

Here, the lock has not been shot to pieces. She uses her key, enters the front hall, and closes the door behind her. She listens.

Just because the lock was engaged doesn't mean the premises haven't been violated.

She knows how to sweep a house and ensure that it's safe. Move with her back to the wall. Both hands on the Glock. Never peek into a room. Peekers get shot in the face. Lead with the gun, low across a threshold. Quickly clear the doorframe, back against the wall again. Closets are a bitch, but they have to be checked.

She clears the four rooms and bath. Only the cellar remains. The house has no accessible attic.

From the exterior, there is no indication that the bungalow has a cellar. Any intruder who searches the house will find no evidence of a door to that lower realm.

Joe Smith had placed an obvious cellar door in the bedroom. Working alone, Katie had built a wall forward of the existing one, creating three closets, each with its own door. Those to the left and right are smaller than the third closet and contain hanging clothes. The center door opens to a ten-foot-wide space; in the center are floor-to-ceiling three-foot-wide shelves holding shoes and other items. The cellar entrance is behind this set of shelves that, unlatched by a hidden lever, can be rolled aside to reveal steps leading down.

The island is her retreat, the house her refuge, the cellar her last redoubt.

She releases the catch on the shelves and pushes them aside, and steps onto the landing. She flips up the light switch.

The rising silence has a sinister quality, but she descends. Leaving a search incomplete is as bad as conducting no search.

She doesn't know for what purpose Joe Smith used the cellar, but Tanner Walsh filled it with what he referred to as his "literary archives"—every scrap of paper he produced, including many drafts of his manuscripts, letters, journals, canceled checks, shopping lists, and reams of cringe-worthy poetry—as well as a supply of the finest Scotch whisky that should have lasted him twenty years if the nation ever reinstituted prohibition.

This last redoubt now contains two long rows of eight-foot-high shelves that she assembled herself from kits that were delivered from the mainland by Hockenberry Marine Services. They are stocked with scores of three-gallon hermetically sealed cans of freeze-dried food, twelve hundred bottles of water in forty-unit shrink packs, a thousand candles, and other basic supplies needed to ride out a two-year pandemic worse than Covid-19, a collapse of the electric grid, or another crisis that might prevent her from acquiring anything from the mainland for an extended period.

As she winds through the three aisles between the rows of shelves, her preparations seem alternately excessive and inadequate. Excessive because she has lived here more than two years, and the world beyond the water hasn't fallen apart. Inadequate because, with the current invasion, Jacob's Ladder has proven to be a less secure retreat than she imagined.

Paranoia can be a serious mental illness.

It can also be the proper state of mind for prey in a universe of predators.

After returning to the main floor, she extinguishes the cellar lights and rolls the concealing shelves into place.

She no longer feels as strongly as before that a target is painted on her. If they wanted to take her out with a bullet, they could have done so outside—or been waiting for her in the house.

Yet from deep in flesh and blood and bone, where thousands of years of human experience are condensed in her genes, the intuition arises that what awaits her is something worse than death.

In her studio, Katie plucks her iPhone off the drawing table, where she'd left it after speaking with Gunner Lindblom, the real estate agent, earlier in the day. She's loath to seek help from the county sheriff's office, from *any* authority, leery that those who are sworn to protect the innocent will fail to do so again, but at this point, she sees no alternative.

She enters her pass code in Apple's finest. Cell service has been available in the archipelago since long before she purchased this island. It is not available now. A moment later, though her phone shows a 72 percent charge, the screen goes dark. She clicks the phone off, waits, and then clicks it on—to no avail.

SHOW NO FEAR

Katie no longer thinks that anyone with a badge will use a trumped-up charge to confiscate her weapons. They won't make even that pretense of operating according to the Constitution. Having put her into lockdown by disabling her boat and somehow rendering her iPhone useless, her enemy—or enemies—have made it clear that they assume laws are made to be broken, that no rules apply to whatever game is being played here.

After retrieving the pistol-grip semiauto shotgun from the hidden trove of weapons in her studio, she stashes it in the kitchen broom closet with a box of shells. She loads her AR-15 and three spare magazines.

In the kitchen, she puts the rifle on the table while she has a quick, late lunch—a ham sandwich with Havarti cheese, mustard, and sliced tomato. She accompanies it with an icy beer. In the current circumstances, a touch of alcohol seems better for the nerves than yet another jolt of caffeine.

She could remain in the locked house, guns at her side, ready to repel anyone who attempts to force entry. One interpretation of events to date suggests that all the authorities want of her is to stay out of their way and not alert anyone on the mainland that something has gone wrong on Ringrock and the consequences of the event have spilled over to Jacob's Ladder; when they've found their fugitive or mopped up whatever mess they've made, they will leave her alone, bewildered but safe. It seems easiest to hunker down and wait for whatever is happening to conclude, for life to return to what, by her wrenched definition, is normalcy.

That plan does not account for the sunken boat. Nor does it allow that the ISA agents might not be who they claim to be or that they might be dead, which leaves her alone on Jacob's Ladder with one or more strangers of even lower character and worse intentions.

Locking herself away is acquiescence to those who have violated her privacy and property. A half step from cowardice. Appeasement never works. Weakness invites further abuse.

She shouldn't challenge them so aggressively that she backs them into a corner. Yet she must show no fear, let them *know* she's ready for the worst if they insist on infringing on her rights any further.

When she has finished the sandwich and the beer, she leaves the house with the 9 mm Glock on her right hip, the AR-15 slung over her shoulder, and the binoculars in hand. She locks the door.

She's making a show of being armed and on patrol, but she's alert to more than threats. The possibility exists that she'll see something, however seemingly insignificant, that will help her make sense of what is happening.

At the head of the stairs to the shore, she studies the beach and boathouse before raising the binoculars and focusing on Oak Haven Island, half a mile away. The large Cape Cod residence with columned white veranda circling three sides looks like a citadel of sanity and peace.

A woman sits on the front steps of the veranda. A young girl stands on the lawn, using a pair of binoculars of her own to study distant Ringrock.

Katie's glasses are the most powerful on the market. They pull in the scene so clearly that she's sure the girl is the one she has seen three or four times, when she's passed Oak Haven in her cabin cruiser. The kid is blond, thirteen or fourteen, and athletic. On two occasions, she had been practicing handsprings and cartwheels on the lawn.

Although the girl's interest in Ringrock might indicate concern—or at least curiosity—about recent events there, the adult on the steps seems entirely at ease, judging by her posture and by the fact that she isn't obviously gunned up. The distance is too great for Katie to read the woman's facial expression, but the family on Oak Haven doesn't appear to be under duress of any kind.

Katie lowers her binoculars and moves along the bluff, past the southeast corner of Jacob's Ladder. Fifty yards farther, she pauses. After turning to confirm that no one has entered the yard behind her or the meadow beyond the yard, and after studying the dark line of trees in the distance, she faces south and raises the glasses.

Nothing moves at Ringrock. Whatever crisis occurred there the previous day must have been resolved. No boats or aircraft are en route to or from the island. No one is visible on the long stone quay or anywhere along the shore.

She remembers Tanner Walsh's diary entries about the psychic "call" from someone who needed him, a summons that compelled him to walk in his sleep and that perhaps eventually led to his death by drowning.

During twenty-six months here, she has not received such an entreaty while either asleep or awake. If what Tanner Walsh claimed he experienced was the truth, why has she not been likewise called by whatever extraordinary individual might be restrained somehow on Ringrock? Maybe to hear and feel that mysterious attractor, you have to be massively inebriated. Some nights, she has her way with too much wine, but the volume of Scotch that Walsh imbibed makes her occasional indulgence in cabernet seem no more intoxicating than taking communion on a Sunday.

As she glasses Ringrock, her impression of it changes. Instead of connoting the restoration of order after a calamity, the current inactivity might mean that no one has survived whatever befell the place. A presentiment of catastrophe slithers out of the darkest cellar of her subconscious, where the scaliest of superstitions resist banishment even in the most modern of minds. An icy chill of intuition prickles through her, and she knows that whatever happened on Ringrock is not finished, that it has only just begun.

The mysterious island shrinks away from her as she lowers the binoculars. Without the magnification, it seems even more to be an isle of the dead.

Far past Ringrock and low along the horizon, across the south and west, dark-gray clouds are slowly rising, as though the entire continent is on fire beyond the curve of the Earth.

Since coming to Jacob's Ladder, she's never consulted a weather forecast. Neither sunshine nor downpour nor blizzard has the power to make her day better or worse. The weather will be what it is, and she will pass through it as indifferent to its effects as is the Earth in its timeless turning.

Based on past experience, she expects the storm to be here by nightfall. Perhaps the rataplan of rain on the roof will help her to sleep.

THE CRY

After walking most of the length of the low bluff above the southern shore, making her statement by refusing to hide, showing the flag, resisting intimidation, Katie finishes her first patrol of the afternoon by returning to the house and circling it, making sure everything is as it should be.

Thus she rounds a corner and finds Michael J. crouched in an intense investigation of a smell that intrigues him, his woolly tail straight out behind him. He lifts his head to stare at her, but only for a moment, and then returns to his sniffing.

The fox's hackles are raised the length of his back, and this detail wakes Katie to the realization that this is the area—under the torqued section of rain gutter, below one of the two kitchen windows—where, that morning, she'd found the ground torn up as if crows had been plucking out chunks of turf in search of grubs. The site had reeked of something like ammonia. The divots of exposed earth, the torn turf, and the undisturbed grass had all appeared frosted with a powdery substance that resembled downy mildew. She had meant to return here with mildewcide, but it had for damn sure turned out not to be a day for lawn care.

The ammoniacal stink is gone, as is the pale powdery substance. The lawn has . . . repaired itself. Impossibly. Fully. Vigorously. In an irregular circle approximately eight feet in diameter, where the spring grass had been short and sparse and recently plucked apart, there is now rich, green grass four to six inches tall, as thick as the fur on the fox's tail, growing right up against the wall of the house. The chunks of plundered turf are still there but nearly lost in the new, deep forest of blades. No fertilizer she could purchase would grow grass this lush—*and in a matter of mere hours.* Nor has the ground been watered to facilitate such growth.

The red fox moves as foxes do, warily and with grace, sniffing along the perimeter of this circle of inexplicably wild growth. His hackles remain raised, and he avoids stepping on the new grass, as if it might suddenly grow around his legs and pull him down like an insect in a Venus flytrap.

Katie is wondering, stooping with the intention of sweeping a hand through the grass, when the first cry rips the fabric of the day. It's a roar and a shriek unlike anything that she's ever heard before, at once human and unhuman, a wail of despair that seems also to be sharp with glee, as if two voices—that of prey and predator—are so harmonized that they sound like one.

The fox and Katie startle. Michael J. springs erect, onto his hind feet, for an instant poised as if for a wildlife ballet. Then he launches away on all fours, racing past the house, toward the eastern shore, perhaps to the end of the pier where earlier he had taken refuge.

The cry comes again, from beyond the meadow and out of the far woods. It is as if a creature with fierce teeth and razor-sharp claws is tearing itself apart, simultaneously screaming in agony and ecstasy, triumphant in self-destruction.

When the loud, shrill plaint dies down the day, Katie stands as alert as she has ever been. Although great music and great writing move her, she is most deeply affected by images freighted with meaning and emotion, which makes sense for one whose talent lies in the visual arts. Until this, she would never have imagined that a sound could chill her as profoundly as Goya's *Saturn Devouring His Children* or the same artist's untitled painting of the head of a panicked dog about to disappear in quicksand. The cry is the voice of nihilism personified, an insane and ferociously empty scream of rage at the very fact that the world exists.

In the pregnant silence that follows, Katie is paralyzed by vigilance, because instinct warns that such a horrific cry will be accompanied by a sudden attack that might come from anywhere, out of the sky or out of the earth itself, though the scream seems to have issued from the woods.

Hundreds of birds of all kinds abruptly explode from the trees, as if they, like Katie, were briefly frozen by the weirdness and the implied extreme violence of the scream. Their different flight calls clash in a chorus of alarm and distress. They soar, swoop, and dart without their usual grace, like a squall of leaves tossed in a thrashing wind, and for a moment it appears they might settle back into the trees. Then, as though crows and warblers and tanagers and juncos and grosbeaks are of the same species, in unison they wing away to the east, past the shore and over the lake, apparently departing Jacob's Ladder for the mainland.

Katie looks at the impossible grass greening at her feet.

She stares at that part of sky into which the birds vanished.

She looks to the south, where Ringrock is dark against the low black wall of clouds ascending.

When she turns her attention to the woods, into her mind's eye comes a work by Henry Fuseli, *The Nightmare*, which he painted in 1781. A woman, sprawled on a disarranged bed, is either dead or dreaming of death, while a gross mad-eyed demon sits on her chest and from the shadows, a crazed, blind horse attends to the scene, its eyes white with cataracts.

Katie shudders. The spell is broken. She finishes circling the house. When she unlocks the door, the key is slippery in her sweat-damp hand.

LUPO AND HAMAL TOGETHER

Back in the day, when Katie is obsessed with revenge that she will never take, when she studies the photographs of Hamal, she can see in his sweet face no evidence of the cruelty in his heart. He is a good-looking teenager, and then even better looking by the time he is a young man of twenty-two. His stare is always open and direct. His smile is winning. In a portrait, the honest artist seeks by subtle techniques to convey something of the truth of the subject, but Nature is a deceiver modeling monsters after lambs.

When Hamal is fourteen, he is six feet tall, a hundred and eighty pounds of muscle. He and two other gang members are charged with the murder of a Jewish restaurateur who was hacked to death with machetes. Because of the extraordinary violence and its status as a hate crime, Hamal is tried as an adult. His codefendants *are* adults. They are convicted of murder. Because of the jury's sympathy for a misguided youth of such angelic appearance, Hamal is found not guilty. By the time he is seventeen, he is known to be a brutal gang enforcer who also enjoys beating women whom he dates. He's suspected of murdering three girls ranging in age from thirteen to fifteen. Police are frustrated when those who first wish to testify against Hamal always subsequently rethink that decision.

Hamal is sixteen and Lupo is thirteen when the former becomes the mentor of the latter. They are soon fast friends because they share many interests and attitudes—such as a love of all superhero movies, a determination to advance to more profitable positions in the gang, a belief in Bigfoot, a taste for preteen girls, contempt for those who work for what they want instead of just taking it, cool designer socks, venomous antisemitism, inspiring mobs on Twitter to bring hellfire down on any public figure whom they consider to be an asshole, and the desire to build a lucrative protection racket in a suburban area that the gang has granted to them in return for 50 percent of their take.

Hamal is twenty-two and Lupo is nineteen, going about some important business in a stolen Dodge Charger, on the day that they bring Katie's life and hope crashing down around her.

HAMPTON RICE

If at some point they decide not to allow her the comfort of light and heat and running water, they will sabotage the generator.

She retrieves four Coleman lanterns, a one-gallon can of fuel, a box of candles, and a chemical toilet from the supplies in the cellar. She places a lantern in each of the four rooms, ready if needed. She reserves the candles for the kitchen table and sets up the chemical toilet in a corner of the bedroom.

Built of stone, with a slate roof, the house is pretty much fireproof. However, she has half a dozen fire extinguishers in the hall closet; she distributes those throughout the rooms.

Whatever will happen will happen. Katie isn't going to pace the bungalow, chewing her fingernails to the quick, trying to anticipate the next turn of events.

Fear is useful when it's on a leash, Avi once said, *but it's always a bad dog when you let it run free in your mind.*

Since coming to Jacob's Ladder, she has prepared as well as she can for another eruption of terror and chaos into her life. Although she hasn't imagined a Twilight Zone scenario like the one in which she finds herself, she needs to trust in the fortification this house provides, her skill with firearms, and the quickness of her mind.

Even in war, life goes on, and one of the few things that still gives her pleasure in life is food. More than three hours remain until dinner. She intends to use the time to prepare a special meal.

She takes an eight-ounce vacuum-packed filet mignon from the freezer, unwraps it, and places it in a pan to thaw.

One of her favorite dishes is sliced potatoes and onions and green peppers fried in butter, with a little salt, a little pepper, more than a little cilantro, and chopped black olives added at the finish. She starts by peeling two potatoes and slicing them into a bowl of cold water.

The window above the kitchen sink faces south-southwest. From time to time, as Katie proceeds from potatoes to onions to green peppers, she gazes toward Ringrock and the thunderheads many miles beyond the island. The black clouds are moving slowly. They do not yet register as a stormy overcast, but instead present the illusion of a great wall dividing the continent. At the rate they're moving, the rain won't be here until after dinner.

When next she looks out the window, a man dressed all in black is standing near the edge of the bluff, his back to her. Judging by his height and dark hair, she's all but certain that he's Hampton Rice. He's not carrying the AR-15 he had before, and his partner, Robert Zenon, is nowhere to be seen.

He turns his head to the right, then to the left, surveying the lake, and even at a distance of a hundred feet, his profile confirms that he's Rice. When he faces Ringrock again, he stands very erect, his shoulders back, his head raised. His attentive pose, which he holds and holds, suggests that he's listening to something.

Inevitably, Katie thinks of Tanner Walsh's description of the summons to Ringrock that was not a sound but a feeling, a sense of being wanted and needed by someone on that island, a drawing power like a magnet asserts on a scrap of iron.

Rice holds out his arms full length, his palms toward that far island, as though to say, *I am here. See me. I am here.*

No. That's not the right interpretation. He isn't signaling any-one. As the man continues to hold out his arms, Katie suspects that he's expressing a longing for something, even adoration. This is similar to the posture of a believer in a sect that conducts clam-orous services, and she will not be surprised if he shouts hallelujah over and over again.

Keep fear on a leash and keep moving. Never retreat from a confrontation that might have something valuable to teach you about your situation.

She picks up the AR-15 from the table. The magazine capac-ity and the recoil control offered by the weapon make it preferable to the pistol in these circumstances.

At the front door, the only exterior door, she hesitates. Zenon could be lying in wait for her—crouched below a window, around the corner, back pressed to the wall.

No. Rice's behavior is too strange to be that of a decoy. If he intends to lure her into Zenon's line of fire, he will pretend to be disabled by an injury or even fake death.

She unlocks the door and quickens through as it opens, lead-ing with the rifle, left hand on the handguard, right hand on the pistol grip, finger lightly on the trigger. She sweeps the day from left to right, from right to left.

Zenon isn't there.

As she locks the door, she realizes that she should attach the key to her belt with a length of cord or chain, so she won't have to dig it out of her pocket and then tuck it away again. Less time with only one hand on the rifle. Less chance of dropping the key, having to stoop to retrieve it.

Sidling toward the back of the house, she is acutely alert for movement at the periphery of her vision.

Hampton Rice is still standing on the bluff, facing Ringrock, reaching out with both hands as if he might be able to grab the far island and pull it closer.

Light slants from the west at forty-five degrees, the sun still above the slowly rising ramparts of black clouds, the lake as blue-gray as slate.

She would prefer to stand with her back pressed to the wall of the house and call out to Rice from there. But she has the nearby patch of inexplicably lush grass to consider. Michael J. was wary of it. Katie is of a mind to respect the instinct of the fox.

Besides, she isn't likely to learn much of anything from Rice at a distance of a hundred feet. Like a muscle, courage requires constant testing to ensure it will be strong when terror weighs heavily on it. She moves toward the ISA agent.

As she draws closer to him, she realizes that he's disheveled. His black shirt is untucked and rumpled. The legs of his uniform pants are spattered with mud to which have adhered bits of dry grass, fragments of dead leaves, brown pine needles.

When Katie hears the sound he's making, she halts about thirty feet from him. He's crooning softly, like a father lulling a baby in the cradle.

"Rice," she says. "Hampton Rice."

He continues to croon, and his raised hands work the air as if the day is hung with curtains that he yearns to grasp and pull aside to reveal something beyond.

"Damn you, Rice, talk to me. What's happening? What's wrong with you?"

He falls silent. He lowers his arms. Slowly he turns.

His hair splays over his brow, tangled and greasy. His face is slick with sweat, though the day is not hot.

Regarding her with puzzlement, as if he can't remember who she is, he stands with his arms slack at his sides, his mouth agape. His teeth are stained, shreds of something caught between them.

On his right side, his shirt is rucked up over his holster, which lacks a pistol.

"What's wrong with you?" she asks again.

He covers his face with his hands and peers at her between his fingers, as though he's a child who's been caught doing something naughty.

WITHOUT TEA AND TABLE

"What's wrong with you?" Hampton Rice asks, returning the question to Katie, watching her through the interstices of his overlapping fingers. He gives those words a different emphasis. "What's *wrong* with you?" And then again, "What's wrong with *you*?"

Katie's residual hackles, less impressive than those of a fox, raise on the back of her neck, and the skin of her scalp shrinks on the skull.

Covering him with the rifle, she glances behind her, to the left, the right. She scans the bluff top beyond Rice, expecting someone to scramble over it.

No one. Nothing. No squirrel or fox. No birds or birdsong.

"Where is Zenon?" she asks.

From behind his mask of digits, he says, "What is where is?"

"Zenon. Robert Zenon. Your partner."

"Partner, particle, corpuscle. Combine, integrate, aggregate."

He begins to croon against his cupped palms.

The sound he makes is not merely what she first thought it was. It is a crooning, yes, but then it flows from a croon into a groan and back again, as if his thoughts keep shifting from something that delights him to a subject that is distressing.

Either his behavior is an act, with a purpose she can't fathom, or he is in the grip of delirium caused by a drug or toxin or fever. Delirium is always temporary. Rice can't have been rock-solid sane this morning, at the grotto, and already hopelessly, permanently insane.

In his confusion, a man suffering delirium is still capable of knowing truth and occasionally speaking it.

"What have you done with the boat's engine?" she asks. "Where have you hidden it?"

His hands slide off his face, down his flanks, to his hips, and hang at his sides in white-knuckled fists. He sneers, and his sneer becomes a grin, a drunken leer. He nods and winks. "Hidden, cloaked, interred. The marrow. The marrow in the bone."

When he takes a step toward her, she fires a round over his head. Even if he doesn't mean her harm, she must now consider the possibility of disease, which might be the cause of his fever. Maintaining distance is crucial.

In the receding roar of the shot, she shouts, "Stay away from me. One more step, and I'll fucking kill you. I mean it. I swear, I'll kill you."

His grin falters and something like grief contorts his face. His eyes flood and tears spill down his sweaty cheeks. "Combine, integrate, aggregate. Who was isn't. Who will be won't be. So hard. So hard to make one and one be one other."

Katie feels as if she's gone down the rabbit hole, where she and the Mad Hatter are conversing without the amenities of tea and table.

She perseveres. "Damn it, where have you hidden the boat's engine?"

He shakes his head. "Five thousand times five thousand years and then five thousand more. Who knows where, why, how long? Learn what it is, and you'll wish you hadn't. Pride and ignorance, all the ignorant geniuses who were and aren't, know-nothings who know everything. And now what? Now what?"

He seems to be spewing blather and babble, but Katie senses a revelation in the weave of those words, a thread that she might be able to unravel from the nonsense.

Before she is able to bore into him with other questions, Rice rolls his eyes like a terrified horse. Shudders violently. Hocks up a wad of phlegm and spits it on the ground. He tosses his head as if trying to throw off a hood that's been forced onto him. He presses his hands to his skull and grimaces like a man whose brain has been cleaved by a sudden migraine. "No. No, no. *NO!*"

She backs away from him.

When his eyes meet hers, they are pellucid for the first time since she confronted him, his delirium having for the moment abated. *"Run!"* he urges. "For God's sake go, get away, save your-self. This is the epicenter. Everyone living here will be dead soon. Everyone within a radius of miles. Miles and miles. Until they stop it, if they can stop it, and they won't, the ignorant fools."

With that, he turns away from her and starts along the bluff, in the general direction of the stairs to the shore.

After a hesitation, Katie follows him for a few steps, but she stops when she hears him arguing with himself. She can't make out what he's saying, but he's conducting the dispute in two dis-tinct voices, the one with which he spoke to her and a varia-tion that is pitched lower and has a rough edge to it. He sounds increasingly distressed. And perhaps, after all, he is less delirious than insane.

Without a boat, she can't heed his advice to flee. She has the stamina to swim the half mile to Oak Haven Island, although not all the way to the mainland. In either case, she'll have to strip down to make the crossing, and she can't take a firearm. She would arrive exhausted and defenseless.

The sun is in decline, the black clouds ascending.

Ringrock is growing a formidable shadow. The lake darkles.

The oblique sunlight fills the windows of the bungalow with an illusion of fire.

She returns to her house and locks herself inside.

ALONG FOR THE RIDE

In his photographs, Parker tries to look street, but he is preppie to the core and never appears other than a child of privilege costumed for crime. According to the file Katie kept on him, back in the day when she dreamed of justice, Parker's greatest satisfaction comes from rebellion against all norms. By the time he receives a high school degree, he's been booted from three expensive private schools. The fourth institution, grateful for his father's generosity, endures the kid, but in time everyone from the milksoppy headmaster to the most homicidally inclined Marxist teacher feels so put-upon by Parker that they are driven to Prozac. To show him the door a year early, the administration concocts an academic record full of classes he has never taken, grades he never earned, and community service he never performed; as a junior, he graduates with the senior class that, tongue-in-cheek, awards him the title of "most likely to exceed."

Beneficiary of a seven-figure trust fund, destined to inherit a greater fortune, Parker possesses the resources to acquire whatever he wants in the way of recreational drugs, off-market firearms, and gangster gear as defined by *GQ* and various pop-culture magazines. Furthermore, his family's connections and highly successful history of bribing public officials have taught him more than he has learned in school, and he is a wizard at persuading police not to arrest him even when, at twenty, he's caught naked with a fifteen-year-old girl as he's teaching her how to self-inject DMT. On those rare occasions when he *is* arrested, charges are quietly dropped within forty-eight hours; the single exception involves a stubborn cop and a young assistant district attorney who believe that no one is above the law, and they soon find themselves excoriated mercilessly by the judge who dismisses the charges as "utterly without merit, based on manufactured evidence," even though the evidence was indeed evidence and was "manufactured" by Parker during his commission of the crime.

Parker's relationship with Lupo and Hamal is initially one of buyer to sellers. He is a customer for their drugs. Soon they learn that Parker can acquire certain exotic military-quality weapons for them that even they can't source. His wealth and connections open a door that allows him to be accepted as a sort of honorary member of the gang, although some who are higher up the chain than Lupo and Hamal often refer to Parker as the "ladies' auxiliary." A bonding occurs among Parker and Lupo and Hamal, the kind of alliance that men incapable of genuine friendship nevertheless believe is true friendship. They share the same interests from Bigfoot to "baby dolls," which is their term for young girls. All three are nihilists, though none is likely to be able to define the word or spell it, and all enjoy that ultra-high level of self-esteem common to psychopaths. Parker frequently rides along with Lupo and Hamal when they are doing business or just looking for an outrage to commit to reassure themselves that they are powerful and superior. Parker is twenty-three years old, celebrating his birthday, on the morning that Lupo and Hamal pull back the curtain to reveal to Katie that California can be Hell on Earth.

MOTHER, ARE YOU THERE YET?

After the disturbing encounter with Agent Hampton Rice, Katie continues dinner preparations. This is how she's managed to function through personal catastrophes that should have destroyed her: Focus intently on quotidian needs and trust that maintaining routines will eventually restore meaning to life and quiet fear. Cook, clean, make the bed, do the laundry, scrub the floor. Idle hours are sharp; they open new wounds in the heart and prick the mind with anxiety.

The ingredients for the potato-and-onion dish are in the refrigerator and need only to be assembled in a pan to be cooked nearer mealtime. Later, she will slice the filet mignon against the grain and sauté it in butter and brown Madeira sauce.

Now she whips up the filling for walnut-and-kumquat crepes. She puts six ounces of soft, unsalted butter in a metal bowl. One cup of sugar, three large eggs, three tablespoons of cognac. She opens a can of kumquats in syrup, finely dices six fruits, and adds them to the bowl. She pulverizes six ounces of walnut meat and beats all the ingredients together. She covers the bowl with plastic wrap and puts it in the freezer so that, when congealed, it won't immediately liquefy and spread when the crepes are baked.

During these two and a half hard years, the most encouraging thing Katie has learned about herself is that she's more resilient than she ever imagined. Perhaps she can be broken, but it has not happened yet. She can be bent so severely that it doesn't seem as though she can ever straighten herself out again, but she always does. She gets on with getting on.

Conversely, if she has learned one thing about herself that is the most discouraging, it is that she is immune to the illusions in which so many people take comfort. Even though comfort based on an illusion is itself illusory, it is for a while a deliverance from the anxiety and existential dread that the world today can generate in abundance. She does not believe that any political ideology can shape society into a utopia. She knows that, instead, even the most earnest utopians always and everywhere create horrific dystopias. She does not believe that scientists are always honest, that rapidly advancing technology will inevitably save us, that everything that is called "progress" is in fact progress. She knows that "experts" are often frauds, that "intellectuals" can be as ignorant as anyone, and that those who most strenuously signal their virtue and are celebrated for it will always prove to be among the most corrupt. Such innate clearheadedness ensures that comforting illusions will elude her, though there are times, as now, when she might welcome the comfort of them.

When a majority of people in any society share the same array of illusions and cling passionately to them, they will encourage one another until illusion becomes delusion, until delusion becomes mass insanity. Whole societies do go mad. History is filled with chilling examples. Joe Smith knew it when he built this house.

Katie refuses to dwell on what life might be like for her in a world gone mad, when by her nature she will be one of those denied the comfort of illusion, the armor of delusion, and the fellowship of mass insanity.

For later, when the crepes are ready, she now prepares the sauce in which she'll flame them. Sugar, butter, kumquat syrup, cognac, and four kumquats cut into julienne.

She's putting the sauce in the refrigerator when Hampton Rice raps on the window above the kitchen sink and calls out, "Mother?"

Although Katie has been expecting something unexpected, she startles, pivots.

He doesn't appear markedly different from how he looked less than an hour earlier, and yet he's a ghastly vision. He's a fright not because he's glaring at her aggressively, which he isn't, but because his features are slack, his face moonish, as if his flesh is soft and swollen. His eyes are not fierce, not bright with hatred, but instead they seem like windows to a vast and empty room.

He raps on the pane again and says, "Mother, are you there yet? Are you there?"

"Go away," Katie says.

Rice flattens one hand against the glass. His voice trembles with anxiety. "Mother, please. I'm not combining well. It's been six hours. Nothing is happening like it should. I'm in a condition of rejection. I want to be us. I need to be us."

A couple of hours of daylight remain, but the malignant clouds have now arced up from the horizon and swallowed the westering sun. The afternoon is gray and seems bleak, as though the clock of the seasons has been rewound from early spring to late winter.

Rice presses both hands to the glass, like a small boy—a very strange boy—peering through a shop window at something he yearns for but cannot have.

"Go away," Katie says again, and she lowers the pleated shade.

Before she can move to the other kitchen window, Hampton Rice is there, rapping on the glass. "Mother, please help me."

The glass slightly muffles his voice and gives it a tinny quality. "Nothing is happening. Don't forsake me."

Although she is not likely to learn anything useful from this man whose mind is so obviously deteriorating, Katie engages him. "Who is this mother of yours? She isn't me. She doesn't live here."

Rice opens his mouth to speak but says nothing, as a look of puzzlement returns a modicum of character to his pale-pudding face.

"You're not combining well? 'Combining'? What does that mean?"

As he tries to look past her and into the kitchen, his eyes slide to the left in his sockets, to the right, like those of a mechanical doll in which counterweights act to simulate the eye movements of a living creature. "Mother's in there somewhere."

"What happened six hours ago?"

His puzzled expression melts into a soft frown. "Six hours? What happens in six hours?"

"You said it's been six hours and you feel in 'a condition of rejection.'"

He shakes his head. "Did I? Did I say? I don't know."

"It's what you said. What happened six hours ago?"

"Oh. Well, maybe . . ."

"Maybe what?"

"I guess . . . in the grotto. Was it in the grotto?"

"What about the grotto?"

His features have settled once more into the expressionless face of a mannequin. "I don't feel well."

Katie presses him. "What happened in the grotto?"

"I feel wrong. I should feel many, but I feel less than one."

"What happened in the grotto?"

"Happened?"

"You and Robert Zenon went to the grotto."

"Robert *who*?"

"Zenon. Your partner. You went into the grotto to search for someone. Who were you searching for?"

"Am I Robert Zenon?"

He isn't looking at her, but through her, or maybe no farther than the surface of the glass between them. He doesn't seem to be faking confusion. His mind is failing him.

"Your name is Hampton Rice."

He considers what she's told him, blinks, blinks, blinks, and then denies that he's who he is. "No. Not Rice. But I think . . . I think I knew him once."

He turns away from the window and walks out of sight.

As Katie lowers the shade, she hears Rice at a window in the bedroom. "Mother? Mother, are you there yet? Are you in there?"

She goes into her bedroom and lowers the shade as Hampton Rice, like a moth knocking itself insistently against a lighted pane, taps the glass.

Tap, tap, tap, tap, tap.

By the time she reaches the living room, he is at one of the windows, calling for mother.

Lowering those shades, Katie wishes that she had added interior shutters. The crossbars will prevent him from gaining entrance. But he might break the glass and throw something inside. Something that he's set afire. She has the extinguishers; she can deal with fire. Shutters, however, would be a comfort.

From the living room, she crosses the hall into her studio and puts down the shades before he gets there. She hears him rattling the front doorknob.

In the hallway once more, she stands watching the door. He rattles the knob and calls for mother. He can't get through that thick slab of ironbound oak with its two deadbolts.

She returns to the kitchen.

She puts a place mat on the table. A napkin. Knife, fork, spoon.

Four candles in red-glass cups.

Her hands stop shaking with the third candle.

Whatever the coming night might bring, there will first be the pleasure of dinner. Filet mignon sautéed in butter and served with brown Madeira sauce. The elaborate potato dish. Two or three well-stuffed crepes for dessert, possibly with a scoop of ice cream on the side.

It's good enough to be a prisoner's last meal on death row.

"Fuck that," she says. "It's just another dinner."

She has half a bottle of cabernet sauvignon from the previous night. Putting out a wineglass, she considers filling it now.

Better to wait. She'll need it as a sleep aid.

FOUR
STORM

IN MEMORY OF THE DOG

With time to pass before the final preparation of dinner, Katie sits at the kitchen table, reading T. S. Eliot. She finds solace in the elegance of his lines, in his profound trust that mercy and meaning are woven through the fabric of this world. His belief, like hers, isn't just of the heart but is also of the intellect; perhaps she shouldn't need the latter, should rely solely on the grace of hope, but she is who she is. As an artist, she can create only when using two brushes, one of emotion and the other of meaning: *Here is what I feel and here is what I know, and on this canvas is a small slice of the world not merely how I see it, but how it truly is.*

On the table before her are four bronze urns, all simple in design, one smaller than the other three, each standing behind a candle in a red-glass cup. She has brought them from the bedroom closet, where they have stood on a shelf, out of sight, for a year.

She is not a sentimentalist, indulging excessively in tender emotions that, with gaudy flourishes, paint over the stark truth of loss and pain. Loss is the basic fact of life; all flesh is grass, and withers away. Pain is not her nemesis but her ally. She doesn't want to dull the scalpel of pain until it's merely melancholy, because its sharpness keeps her focused on what matters in life and in her art. And it reminds her of the Promise she must keep.

The four urns stand on the table not so she can use them as an excuse to drink too much wine and wallow in sorrow as a distraction from fear. She wants them nearby in the event that a contingent of sheriff's deputies or national guardsmen or other authorities arrive to evacuate her from her island. Slung from the back of one of the chairs is a satchel into which she can tuck the urns. Whatever has happened on Ringrock is no small matter, and the consequences have not been contained; they are spreading. If the authorities aren't aware of that, they soon will be, and they will act to cordon off the threat, even if ineffectively.

She reads aloud from Eliot—"'I said to my soul, be still, and wait without hope, for hope would be hope for the wrong thing'"—and then she closes the book and sets it aside.

The smallest and simplest of the four urns holds the ashes of a golden retriever, Cassie, who lived twelve years in the splendid joy and innocence that is the lot of beloved dogs. Katie was twenty when Cassie came into her life, thirty-two when Cassie was taken from her by cancer. The pain that racked Katie on that day of parting would in a short time prove to have been a gift; it was a preparation for a loss that, without a past experience of terrible grief, might have destroyed her.

She sets about preparing dinner. As the ingredients of the potato dish are crisping in a deep-walled skillet, she begins to slice the filet.

When something thumps against the window above the sink, she looks over her shoulder at the pleated shade. "Go away," she says, assuming that, in his delirium, Hampton Rice has returned.

After a silence, a mewling noise like that of an animal in distress causes her to put down the knife and cross the room to the sink. The cry is thin and pitiable, too childlike to be the work of a grown man like Rice.

When the whimpering doesn't relent, she raises the shade and discovers Michael J. has sprung onto the deep window ledge. The fox stares at her, as he has often done before, but this time his gaze seems not curious, but instead beseeching. He begins to punctuate his whimpers with urgent panting.

Earlier, on the pier, Katie had thought that he was yearning to escape Jacob's Ladder for Oak Haven or the mainland. She's even more convinced that she understands his current anguish. If he isn't able to leave this island, he wants desperately to be granted the shelter of the house in these last two hours of daylight.

Her island is free of rabies. No reason to fear a twenty-some-pound fox. His kind feeds on birds, eggs, lizards, mice, berries, nuts, grasses, roots.

Nonetheless, she hesitates as his panting grows more frantic. She looks toward the candlelit table, at the smallest of the four bronze urns. Michael J.'s whimpering reminds her of the sounds that Cassie made as the veterinarian prepared the catheter through which the dog would be relieved from cancer and receive a merciful death.

In memory of Cassie and with a sense that all the creatures of nature are perhaps at as much risk as she is, Katie decides to go outside and, depending on the behavior of Michael J., encourage him to join her in the house.

As she turns away from the window, the fox panics. He thrusts onto his hind feet, hooking his forepaws through the horizontal bar, and scratches at the glass with his claws, which make a sound like chalk skreeghing down a blackboard. His whimpers grow louder and longer, shrill expressions of terror.

She turns off the flame under the skillet. Hoping to calm the creature so that he'll wait for her to come outside and lead him to the door, she unlatches the casement. The halves open inward.

Michael J. at once drops to all fours on the window ledge and thrusts his head through the lower right quadrant formed by the steel bars. As Katie warily backs away, the fox—lean, lithe, and driven by panic—squirms through the opening, drops into the sink, scrabbles against the stainless steel, panting frantically, his eyes so very wide. He erupts onto the counter, leaps to the floor, and scurries to the far end of the kitchen.

Katie watches as her visitor paces and sniffs the floor, no longer whimpering, as he smells the narrow vertical space where a pair of lower cabinet doors meet, as he assesses the gap at the bottom of the door to her bedroom. Whether he is reassured or not, he's panting less rapidly. He stands watching her as she watches him, his tail held straight out behind him, like it is when he is running or preparing to run.

Katie talks to him as once she had talked to Cassie, with the conviction that either by the action of instinct or by a psychic ability to read emotion and intent, he has a general sense of what she's saying to him, although of course he does not follow her word by word.

"I'm beginning to think you're a bellwether of what's coming. If I'd paid attention to you when we met in the woods this morning, thought hard about the fear that drove you up the tree, then after I met Zenon and Rice at the grotto, I might have taken my boat to the mainland while it still had an engine. What's next, Mr. Fox?"

He lifts his head high and sniffs the air and stares past her. When she turns to see what has his attention, she discovers the open casement.

She returns to the window. A cool breeze stirs her hair as she closes the hinged halves and latches them.

Although the sun is drowned in the unspent sea of the storm, though the light of day is now indirect, half the sky remains blue. The spreading woolpack appears clotted with soot, but lightning does not yet craze the sky, and thunder remains trapped in the storm's dark throat.

Ringrock lies under the shadow of the clouds. On any other late afternoon, with such bad weather gathering, lights would already be visible over there. Not today.

She lowers the shade and looks again at the fox.

He regards her solemnly for a moment, then sniffs the floor, circling as if following a spiraling scent, until he curls up to the right of her bedroom door. He rests his chin on his crossed paws and watches her, his perpetually pricked ears suggesting that he is alert and that his current safety is not to be taken for granted.

With a rough sponge, soap, and hot water, Katie scrubs out the sink. She fills a bowl with water and places it in a corner, where Michael J. can drink whenever he wishes.

She returns to the filet mignon, which she was slicing when the sound came at the window. She keeps about four ounces of the eight-ounce steak for her dinner, slices the other four into a bowl, and places the raw meat two feet from the fox.

He raises his head and sniffs the air. But then he props his chin on his paws once more.

At the cooktop, switching on the flame under the skillet, she says, "If you're concerned about the environmental effects of the flatulence of cattle, don't be. It's a myth. What'll kill us all is the flatulence of politicians."

She turns the potatoes, onions, and peppers, which are browning nicely. When she is slicing the remaining steak, she hears Michael J. at the bowl.

Having quickly finished what he was offered, he stands licking his chops, watching her. Either by instinct or a psychic ability of her own, she can read the fox as well as he reads her.

She finishes slicing the second half of the steak and brings it to his empty bowl. He backs away as she approaches.

"It's okay. I have meatballs in the freezer. I'll microwave a couple for me. Just don't think it'll be filet mignon every day."

As she's putting the meatballs in the microwave, Michael J. visits his bowl once more.

She is as alone as ever in defense of her freedom and her life, but the mere presence of the fox has to a surprising extent relieved her loneliness.

Watching him eat, she wonders why she has not brought a dog with her to Jacob's Ladder, a companion as sweet as Cassie.

Not much thought is required to answer the question now that she has posed it. She's surprised that she has lived here more than two years without previously asking it of herself.

She has chosen to live alone rather than give her heart again to anything that will die. She has done this unconsciously, without considered intention.

By the time that she sits down at the table with her dinner and a glass of wine, she has arrived at the disquieting thought that she has kept the Promise in only the most minimal sense, not in the true fullness of its meaning. She's done what Avi asked of her as he lay dying, but she's been miserly in her interpretation of the key word of the Promise.

He had *not* asked her to paint a portrait of him, that he might be immortalized by her talent. But if he'd made that request, she would never have imagined that a canvas as small as a postage stamp would fulfill his request.

Instead, fearing that grief would destroy her, he had made her promise that she would live. *"Live, Katie. Live for me. Live for the girls. Live for us. As long as you live, we'll still live in you."*

She has not been living in the sense that he meant.

She has been *surviving*. A postage-stamp existence.

She looks across the table to the fox that lies curled on the floor, to the right of her bedroom door. He is sleeping.

The last daylight has waned beyond the window shades.

Four overlapping pools of candlelight and shadow glimmer and pulse on the ceiling. Filtered through the votive glass, mists of red radiance glow in the golden pine cabinets and paneling.

An almost subliminal sound incites the fear that strains at the leash she has on it. Perhaps it's the first roll of distant thunder, the storm breaking far to the south and west.

AN ERROR OF TIMING

For Lupo, Hamal, and Parker, Saturday is party night, a night for doing shots and drugs, and doing a girl together. Their theory of parties is that a good one has to be hard on them, has to leave them wasted and sweaty, bloated from their indulgences and yet as drained as overworked stud horses. If the girl is the kind who expects to be paid, then by the end of the night, they want her to be in such a condition that she almost needs to crawl out of the venue on her hands and knees. They want her to feel there isn't enough money in the world to induce her to party with them again. If the girl is the unpaid kind who believes one of them might learn to love her, they aren't as physically demanding; instead, they want her to finish the night emotionally knocked out, wondering if she is as worthless as she feels; they want her to be unable to forget the thinly veiled contempt with which they complimented her on her looks and skills. If they crush her spirit in precisely the right way, the poor confused thing will want to be with them again to prove to them and to herself that she has value.

On those occasions when the party starts late because Lupo, Hamal, and Parker have slept the afternoon into the evening, fortifying themselves for what lies ahead, they are sometimes still together at the break of dawn, although finished with the girl. In that case, they often have the energy to cruise in search of some adventure that will confirm for them that they are princes of this world, above all laws, impervious to consequences, with cojones that are the envy of ordinary men. If they can find an old Jew walking alone and daring to wear a skullcap to announce his religion, or a kid whom they know to have dodged an invitation to join the gang, they are able to work off what energy they still have and gain the affirmation they seek.

This Sunday, they are in a Dodge Charger that Hamal jacked the previous day when a mother outside the office of a pediatric dentist chose to surrender her vehicle rather than have her eleven-year-old daughter's face slashed. No one is looking for this car now, because Hamal swapped the plates for those on a Lincoln Continental that is parked in a long-term lot while the owner is on vacation.

They don't need to find an old Jew or a stupid kid who thinks the gang doesn't own him. They already have a preferred target. In the territory that Lupo and Hamal operate a protection racket, under the aegis of the gang, a seven-store strip mall includes six shops whose owners are realistic enough to pay their monthly insurance and get on with their business. The seventh store, a busy ice cream shop that offers forty flavors and is a popular source for specialty ice cream cakes for parties, is owned by a Vietnamese family who think they are tough enough to defend their American dream. They are a bad example to the other entrepreneurs who have gotten with the program, and something needs to be done about them.

Wearing blue cloth masks and the darkest sunglasses on the market, as if they live in perpetual fear of another deadly virus out of China and retinal melanoma, Lupo and Hamal and Parker arrive at the strip mall at 10:10 a.m. Sunday morning. The nail shop opens at eleven o'clock on Sundays, the pizza parlor at noon, three other stores not at all. Lupo and Hamal are under the mistaken impression that the ice cream shop doesn't open until eleven o'clock, and they assume that if anyone is inside, it will be a member of the family that owns the place. In fact, it opened at ten o'clock.

Clouds hang low, but the heavy rain ended a quarter of an hour ago. Large puddles glaze the blacktop. A Ford Explorer and a Honda sedan are parked in front of the pizza parlor, and the assumption is made that they belong to employees preparing the place for the noon opening. Hamal is driving. Lupo has the AK-47 with a thirty-round magazine, and Parker is packing a Heckler & Koch VP70 machine pistol with an eighteen-round magazine. Later, it will occur to them that it is never a good idea to engage in protection-racket enforcement after a long night of partying. But the various substances that they ingested have compromised their judgment on this occasion.

Hamal parks parallel to the curb in front of the ice cream shop. Lupo throws open the front passenger door, gets out, and trains the assault rifle on the storefront. The morning light has made a mirror of the big windows, and the interior of the business is further obscured by a banner advertising five new flavors. As far as Lupo can see—or cares to see—the place is deserted. He spends thirty full-metal-jacket rounds on the shop, shattering the windows and blowing the shit out of whatever equipment and freezers might be in the way. Parker, who has emerged from the back seat of the Dodge, has set the selector switch on the VP70 for three-shot bursts. He depletes the magazine with six quick pulls of the trigger. He has no expectation that he will add much damage to what Lupo creates; he just wants to be part of the fun.

A minute after stepping out of the Dodge Charger with all the swagger of characters in a Tarantino movie, they're aboard again, and Hamal is accelerating the hell out of there. Five blocks from the strip mall, they leave the car, as prearranged, in a warehouse where chop-shop specialists will dismantle it and sell the parts in Mexico. Hamal's Cadillac Escalade is waiting there; he and Lupo and Parker conclude their night of debauchery and their morning of client persuasion with breakfast at IHOP.

They do not expect to have gunned down anyone in a deserted ice cream shop, although if members of the family that owns it happened to be there and took a few bullets . . . well, it was pride that did them in, a refusal to bend to the will of their betters.

In fact, one member of the family was behind the ice cream display coolers. Two others were in the kitchen. But none was injured.

The fatalities occurred in the area where customers wait to have their to-go orders filled or sit at small tables to eat. The victims include Harry and Emma, Katie's mother and father, who were buying a quart of cherry delight and another of blueberry swirl to serve at lunch. Harry and Emma came to the shop directly from church in the company of Penny and Regina, their eight- and ten-year-old granddaughters, whom they were entertaining for the day. The girls sustained multiple horrific wounds to their bodies and heads. When identifying Penny and Regina for the medical examiner, their father, Avi, a former Marine who had seen combat in the Middle East, began the descent into despair that would lead him to take the law into his own hands and result in his destruction.

MEANWHILE, ON OAK HAVEN

After failing to come home the previous day, at last Francesca pilots their boat back from Ringrock, arriving just when Sarah and Libby have finished eating dinner. Raleigh isn't with her. Francesca has nothing meaningful to report about what happened over there, the reason for all the commotion. The explosions, she says, were "just an experiment." As to why Raleigh is still on Ringrock, she says only, "He's busy," as she hangs the cabin-cruiser key on a pegboard by the back door. Sarah, the housekeeper-nanny-tutor-cook, offers to make a martini, and Francesca accepts. At the kitchen island, while the cocktail is prepared, meaningful looks pass between Sarah and Francesca. Young Libby is acutely aware that, with their eyes, the two women have agreed to talk later. Sarah is something more than housekeeper-nanny-tutor-cook, but Libby has never been able to find out what that something more is. Martini in one hand, her laptop in the other, declaring that she is exhausted, Francesca intends to retreat to the master suite to take a shower. Before she leaves the kitchen, her only interaction with Libby is to ask two questions about Aztec culture, currently in the curriculum, as a test to determine if the girl has been keeping up with her studies.

While Sarah clears the table of the dinner debris, Libby goes out to the yard to practice backflips, cartwheels, somersaults, and walking on her hands until the storm might eventually break and drive her inside. It's dark, but she could do gymnastics blindfolded.

Libby is fourteen, but she's not into boy bands and fashion and social media any more than she's into anorexia or cutting herself or suicidal thoughts. She can rock the piano, and she mainlines books as though they're heroin. Although she's home-schooled by Sarah, she is a raging autodidact capable of teaching herself almost anything, including hatchet throwing.

She read this article about the Logger Olympics, and the idea of throwing hatchets with incredible accuracy really got her juices flowing. Most parents would not buy their daughter six wick-edly sharp hatchets and a series of four-foot-diameter one-foot-thick Douglas-fir targets, but Libby is not saddled with a sensible mother and father.

Francesca and Raleigh, technically Mom and Dad, prefer that she call them by their names rather than their familial titles, for they believe that a family is more successful if organized strictly as a social compact rather than as a multigenerational blood-line. Libby has never received much in the way of affection from Francesca and Raleigh; however, she doesn't take their coldness personally. She long ago realized that each of her parents has a personality matrix with holes in it; lacking a capacity for affection, even for each other, they replace it with respect, which is at least something.

Libby *has* received from them a terrifically high IQ, and she's grateful for the effect of their combined DNA. They are scien-tists with multiple doctorates between them, and they are always learning more because learning is what they do instead of living. They have also given her a degree of freedom most kids don't have, anything she wants, to encourage her to develop emotional and intellectual independence, but also—she suspects—because in spite of their vast knowledge of so many subjects, they are basically clueless regarding the myriad ways that a child can hurtle off the rails when provided with no guidance.

Fortunately for herself and for them, Libby has never wanted to do drugs, guzzle booze, play with matches, or have a fourteen-foot python to call her own. Her interests are entirely wholesome and for the most part safe; even hatchet throwing is beneficial, because it develops upper-body strength, refines hand-eye coordination, and helps her work off the negative energy that is common in adolescence because of the body's struggle to figure out the correct production level of various hormones. And when a decade from now she marries a logger hunk named something like Paul Bunyan, they will share an expertise in an Olympic sport, besides wanting to jump each other's bones five times a day.

In addition to intelligence and freedom, Libby has been given the gift of Oak Haven. Francesca and Raleigh don't own the island, but it comes with their positions at Ringrock. Her father is the director of the project over there, and her mother is the übergenius who devised the institutional protocols, security systems, research procedures, and list of experiments that more than forty heavyweights in various sciences are carrying out. They have lived here seven years. It's cool having her own island, with no need to go to public school and be droned at. Sarah worries that Libby will grow up without being properly socialized, but Libby is confident that she will be immeasurably more socialized than Sarah.

Forty-six, attractive, smart, obviously well educated, funny, Sarah should be out there in the world, chasing men—or women, if that's the kind of chase that interests her. She ought to be running a business, taking cruises to exotic ports, getting ready to welcome her first grandkids into the world. Instead, for seven years, she has been on Oak Haven, taking just three one-week vacations each year, which she always spends with her mother in Indiana. Libby likes Sarah, but she doesn't understand her at all.

When Sarah is away, she is replaced by Marge, a mysterious woman who is in her fifties, not as smart as Sarah, and about as funny as toe fungus. There are reasons to suspect that Marge is an officer in the military, though it's probably the Russian military, in which you're allowed to smile only when you shoot someone or successfully invade another country.

Now, in the early dark, beyond Ringrock Island, the first lightning forks out of the clouds and stabs its bright tines into the great, dark plate of the lake. She counts three seconds before those fireworks are followed by a crash of thunder, and then counts three more until Sarah comes out of the house and calls her inside.

As Libby climbs the steps to the veranda, she says, "You know, I'm a thousand times more likely to accidentally chop my toes off with a hatchet than be struck by lightning."

"A thousand times? That supposes you're an extremely clumsy girl. To test your hypothesis, why don't you get your hatchets and practice here on the lawn? At the end of an hour, we'll see whether you're a pile of smoldering remains or just a five-toed girl."

"You're a lot snarkier than Mary Poppins."

"I can be more saccharine if you'd prefer."

"Gag me. Save your sugar," Libby says, as she opens the screen door. "I like you the way you are."

There's something odd in the air tonight, some quality of the oncoming storm, a *vibe* that encourages Libby to set aside discretion and press for answers she has never before been able to obtain, as if this is her last chance to get them. "I *do* wonder why you're here on Oak Haven instead of somewhere more exciting, being a captain of industry or a tech mogul or the mother of twelve."

"Twelve!" exclaims Sarah as she follows Libby inside. "So I should turn them out in litters?"

"You seem very fertile to me. Seriously. Why here?"

Sarah closes the door and engages the deadbolt. The house is locked tight every night, although no one else lives on Oak Haven and though the mainland is miles away. Raleigh has explained this routine by saying that even bad guys are smart enough to use boats.

"I like it here, Libby. I'm happy here. Anyway, I've nowhere else to be after . . ."

"After what?"

"After where I've been. Subject closed."

For at least the past two years, Libby has been mature enough to sense that under Sarah's apparent contentment lies a sadness that has long endured. She has done something that she regrets, and for whatever reason, that regret limits her options in life.

As they stand in the foyer, Sarah takes one of Libby's hands in both of hers and kisses it. She is given to such tender expressions of affection partly because that is her nature, but also no doubt because she is aware that Francesca and Raleigh are not capable of providing their daughter with such assurances of their love.

"You have your hypothesis about hatchets and lightning," says Sarah, "and I have a theory of my own, one that fills my days with purpose and makes me happy. A theory, you know, is better than a hypothesis. There's more evidence to support it."

"What theory?" Libby asks.

"I have gathered enough irrefutable facts to theorize with great confidence that one day you are going to be a woman of huge achievement, a person who *matters* in this crazy world, matters for all the right reasons, and it gives me deep satisfaction to be here for you, with you, during these years of your journey."

Maybe Sarah's intention is to so startle Libby, so overwhelm her, so humble the girl that she won't press the woman further on personal matters. If that's the case, it works. Tears flood Libby's eyes. She hugs and is hugged in return.

To her dismay, Libby doesn't know what to say after the hug. She bolts up the stairs like a discombobulated ten-year-old, for God's sake.

THE SOUND THAT IS NOT THUNDER

Meat and potatoes are enough to satisfy Katie. She is too agitated to take time to fold the filling into the crepes and flambé them. She washes the dishes by hand and puts them away.

A second glass of cabernet sauvignon can't protect her from anyone who might be roaming the night on Jacob's Ladder, but neither is it enough to dull her wits and worsen her situation.

After a long quiet, the low sound that she heard earlier comes again, a protracted rumble, hardly audible. If it's distant thunder, this is such a slow-building storm that it might never get around to letting loose the rain.

As she finishes filling her glass, the fox wakes, yawns, and cocks his head to study her. The ease with which he has adjusted to sharing this space with a human being makes Katie wonder if Tanner Walsh might once have domesticated the animal. Foxes can live twelve years, even longer; this one could have been on Jacob's Ladder when the writer lived here.

Michael J. gets to his feet and moves around the kitchen to the table, sniffing the floor.

"If I dropped something," Katie says, "it's yours."

He works his way under the table, between the chairs, and then toward the cabinets below the sink, his nose an inch from the oak flooring, on a sniffari and apparently oblivious of her.

She carries the wineglass into her study and stands before the unfinished painting.

Her supposition that the work can be successfully completed only by adding spectral figures in windows and puddled rainwater has become a conviction. Two men in medical masks and sunglasses. The vague suggestion of the Dodge. Each reflection must be distorted by the angle at which it's cast and by the usual quirks of light, so that the truth of it can be seen only with long study. Still better, Lupo and Parker won't be represented in a distortion of their actual appearance, as a comment on the condition of their souls, but will be portrayed in some symbolic fashion that as yet eludes her.

For the first time, she understands that she has long been aware of this solution to the problem of this painting and has not wanted to acknowledge it. She might not have the talent to pull it off, which will be a deeply dispiriting failure. And if she *does* pull it off, she'll be turning a corner from one phase of her life into another, putting a greater distance between herself and those she lost. Now, memories of her family warm her. With more distance, what cold might lie ahead?

She has obsessively painted this scene eighteen times. She destroyed seventeen. She's painted nothing else in two years.

Live, Katie. Live for me. Live for the girls. Live for us. As long as you live, we'll still live in you.

That is the Promise she made, to live for them. But she has been doing little more than surviving.

For her, especially now that she has no one, living means painting successfully, not merely this single fateful canvas, but also all the art that crowds her mind.

The fear visited upon her this strange day has shaken her into recognizing the other fear that has hampered her, the fear of moving on, which prevents her from fulfilling the Promise.

Michael J. enters the studio, still tracking whatever scent has mesmerized him.

The sound that before seemed like distant thunder now comes a third time. On this repeat, Katie realizes it's not a formidable roar reduced in effect by distance. It's a more intimate sound, subtle and close at hand, arising either immediately outside the house or from a source in these rooms.

GOODBYE TO ALL THAT

In her room, by the low light of a small lamp, Libby sits on her vanity bench, plucks Kleenex from a box, blots her eyes, and blows her nose. She stares at herself in the mirror, wondering if anything that Sarah said about her future might have any chance whatsoever of coming true. Maybe. No, no way. Well, okay, it's as likely as being struck by lightning, but not beyond possibility.

The geometry of the windows repeatedly prints on the room as the sky is fractured by lightning and a megatonnage of thunder. A wind like a blast wave hammers rain against the windows. Battalions are marching across the roof.

Libby is suddenly embarrassed to be studying her reflection for signs of future greatness. She feels like a self-absorbed doofus in one of those teen-themed TV movies that make her want to barf an ocean. She goes into the adjacent bathroom and splashes cold water on her face, careful to avoid the seductive mirror above the sink.

In her bedroom again, she turns on a second lamp and takes a paperback from her bookcase, a favorite novel that she has read twice. There's a character in it, a girl named Leilani Klonk, with whom Libby identifies. Leilani has a twisted leg that requires a brace and a deformed hand that surgery can't correct, but there are other things about her and her situation to which Libby can relate.

She sits up in bed, thumbing through the book, reading passages that she previously marked. The storm inside her is quieter than the tempest outside, but it's a storm nonetheless.

The weirdness of the recent tumult at Ringrock has knotted her nerves. She hopes reading about Leilani will untie them, but her attention is repeatedly drawn to the windows, to the night and the storm into which Ringrock has vanished as if it never existed.

Francesca and Raleigh think Libby doesn't know what work they have undertaken on Ringrock for the past seven years. It's as top secret as anything ever was. None of the computers at the research facility is linked to the internet, so they can't be hacked. The people working over there have security clearances for which God himself wouldn't qualify. When her parents bring work home, which they do all the time, it's always on laptops. At night, Francesca locks their laptops in the bottom drawer of a file cabinet in their study. The cabinet is bolted to the wall and features an alarm that will be triggered if an attempt is made to drill out the lock or pry open a drawer.

Libby is not by nature a snoop—or at least she doesn't think she is—but every girl of a certain age has some Nancy Drew in her; any girl that doesn't is pathetic. And when you've lived years on an island soaked in as much mystery as it is in sunshine and moonlight, with parents engaged in hugger-muggery and as uncommunicative as the stone heads on Easter Island, if you don't sooner or later attempt to satisfy your curiosity, your skull will explode.

Libby's skull has not exploded. Acquiring national security secrets required the successful completion of two tasks.

First, find the key to the file cabinet.

She had often seen her mother's and her father's key rings: the same two keys on each, one that worked the house locks, another for the thirty-foot cabin cruiser. She figured they hid the file-cabinet key somewhere in the study, for convenience. At every opportunity, when Francesca and Raleigh were on Ringrock and Sarah was busy preparing lunch or engaged in other work, Libby had searched the study. She'd found the key in an envelope taped inside one of fifty or sixty hardcover biographies that filled a bookcase. Francesca and Raleigh never read fiction for pleasure, only biographies. This one was the life story of Francis Scott Key.

Second, learn the passwords for both laptops.

Although her parents are for sure brilliant and strange—by some standards eccentric, by other standards grotesque—they are also human and therefore, with enough effort, readable. As a close observer of the dynamic duo, always sifting through their behavior and their more cryptic comments for clues, Libby has long known that the work they have undertaken scares them as much as it obsesses them. It's dangerous duty on Ringrock. Being anal, Francesca and Raleigh are certain to worry that if both of them perish in the same work-related event, the new leader of the Ringrock team might need quick access to the data and musings on their laptops. To prepare for that contingency but to ensure security in the meantime, they might have written down their passwords, sealed them in an envelope, and entrusted them to someone—most likely to the same reliable and enigmatic person to whom they entrusted the care of their daughter.

Sarah is something more than housekeeper-nanny-tutor-cook, but even after the exchange in the foyer minutes earlier, Libby can't begin to comprehend what that "something more" might be.

Sarah's full name is supposedly Sarah Stackhouse-Gaines. According to Google, no such person exists. Therefore, she must be a spook. Not the kind of spook who haunts a house. The kind who is an undercover agent for one government bureau or another.

Anyway, over a few weeks, feeling less like Nancy Drew this time and more like a sneaky little shit, Libby had surreptitiously searched her nanny-tutor's bedroom and bath—fifteen minutes here, twenty minutes there. She found a pistol, a spare magazine, and a box of cartridges, which didn't surprise her. If she searched her parents' bedroom, she would expect to find two guns. Everyone on Oak Haven had the air of people who are ready for something; what that might be was the question she hoped the laptops would answer. After the pistol, she turned up nothing else of interest until she found the envelope in a box of tampons in the bathroom, in the cabinet under the sink.

The envelope was of heavy cream-colored paper. An unbroken red-wax seal, impressed with her father's initials, confirmed that it had not been opened.

Raleigh was one of those men who wore bow ties and cardigan sweaters and corduroy trousers, who preferred wing-tip brogues with everything except pajamas, who smoked pipes, saw the world through wire-rimmed spectacles, and took comfort in such fussy details as wax seals and fountain pens that came with a variety of nibs.

Libby had taken the envelope to her room and hidden it between the mattress and box spring. A quick visit to the study confirmed that the supply closet contained a box of identical envelopes.

In her room again, she had violated the wax seal, torn open the envelope, and extracted the cover of an old paperback novel— *Alas, Babylon* by Pat Frank. The story appeared to be set in the 1960s and was definitely about the survivors of a nuclear war. Above the first word of the title, someone—not hard to guess who—had printed the letter *R* with a fountain pen and a flourish. Above the second word, he'd printed the letter *F*.

That night, when Libby had been sure everyone was asleep, she had gone to the study, put the paperback cover in a fresh envelope, licked the glue, sealed it, and used Raleigh's wax device to doubly secure the flap. The following day, when an opportunity arose, she had put the new envelope in the tampon box.

A little online research with her own computer revealed that Babylon was a city in the Bible that had been destroyed, reduced to rubble and dust.

The possibility that her parents were working on some new kind of nuclear weapon disturbed Libby so much that she needed a few days to build the courage to try the passwords.

Then one night when everyone was sound asleep, she had crept down to the study, taken the key from the book about Francis Scott Key, opened the file cabinet, removed Raleigh's laptop, and put it on the desk. *Alas* was an exclamation used to express sorrow, grief, pity, or the apprehension of evil. She hesitated before entering it, half afraid that, if it wasn't Raleigh's password, the security program would conclude she was a Chinese agent, and then the laptop would blow up in her face. It didn't.

As she opened files and pored through the contents, she had at first been bewildered by all the jargon, then merely perplexed—and then alarmed as understanding came upon her. By the time she backed out of the laptop and switched it off and returned it to the file cabinet, she was chilled to the bone. If all the brainiacs laboring on Ringrock were developing only a new kind of nuclear weapon, she might have gone back to bed and slept. No such luck.

That night of revelation had been eleven months ago, and Libby had for quite a while lived with anxiety that she needed to conceal, enduring nightmares worse than any she had known before.

It's funny, though not ha-ha funny, how you think you can't live with some newly discovered terror, how it crowds everything else out of your mind, but as time passes, it becomes just another horrific possibility—like cancer, blindness, an earwig laying eggs in your brain while you sleep, being beheaded by a maniac, a spinal cord injury resulting in quadriplegia, etcetera. You decide that, yeah, an asteroid as big as a mountain could slam into Earth and wipe out civilization, but it'll never happen in your lifetime. Sure, cancer is real, but you most likely have some genetic defense against all forms of the disease. Libby enjoys this capacity for denial no less than other human beings do. At first, it surprises her, and then not so much, and finally not at all. In fact, every time she starts to dwell on the purpose of those on Ringrock, she facilitates denial by focusing on something she enjoys, like a good book or gymnastics, or throwing hatchets, or imagining herself married to a logger and having kids of her own who will never have to wonder how much she loves them.

Right now, however, in the wake of recent events at Ringrock and considering the fleet of drones that had overflown Oak Haven the previous night, the fear inspired by the contents of Raleigh's laptop is sharper than it's been in months. Reading about Leilani Klonk doesn't provide enough distraction, and there's not sufficient open space in her bedroom to allow her to do cartwheels, and Sarah won't allow her to go outside to throw hatchets in a thunderstorm. It's times like these when it would be good to have reached an age when she'd have the option of boozing herself into a sound sleep.

She puts aside the book and gets out of bed and goes to the nearer window.

Dazzling light repeatedly washes down the night as though a door keeps swinging open between this life and Heaven. The shadows that leap and throb with each flare are mostly images of oaks cast off as if in a violent molting, but Libby has the impression that a spectral presence moves across the deep yard, independent of the lightning, some entity as dark as a shadow but not as insubstantial.

She usually enjoys storms, Nature at her rowdiest, but not this one. She is unable to shake the curious feeling that this isn't just bad weather; it's also cover, camouflage, and some beast moves out there that is more terrible than any monster ever conjured in all the nightmares ever dreamed.

The scream that shatters through the house has motive force, pivoting Libby away from the window, toward the closed door to her room and the upstairs hallway beyond. Shrill with rage and need, it's the ferocious cry of something that ravages whatever offends it and feeds on the remains. It sounds like nothing born on Earth—and yet Libby believes that she hears her mother's voice submerged in the louder shriek, not as if her mother is screaming in fear, but as though this is one beast with two throats, one throat within the other, crying out in harmony from a single mouth, human and unhuman hatred conjoined in a predator incapable of mercy. If this creature is what the information on Raleigh's laptop suggests it is, then when it finds Libby, it will bring her into communion with itself, but also with her mother, if Francesca is already one with it, as she must have been when she came home from Ringrock. Such a commune of flesh and mind, human and inhuman, in a rapture of blood lust and violence, will be an existence more horrific than anything that anyone has ever imagined Hell might provide.

It combines.

In the wake of the shriek, gunfire erupts. One, two, three shots. Something heavy crashes over and glass breaks and a door slams. Like a kraken risen out of the deeps, its voice never heard before in the world above the water, the intruder speaks again, a roar entwined with a squeal. This time Libby hears her name wrapped in the louder sound, attenuated and distorted—*"Liiiiibeeeee"*—not spoken in the yearning tone of a mother for her daughter, but as the dead and damned might call jealously to the living. Three more shots follow the first three.

Libby hurries to her desk and grabs the straight-backed chair. There's a privacy latch that's engaged by a button in the doorknob—no deadbolt. Although the door is solid, the latch is flimsy; it'll come apart if anything of size wants to get in here. She tilts the chair, jams the headrail under the knob. That ought to hold it for a while, but not all night, not until the Marines show up; anyhow, the Marines aren't going to show up.

Her breathing is fast and shallow. She's almost gasping, and her heart knocks loud enough for her to hear it. She can't calm her heart, but she hates the panicky sound of her breathing, and she takes slower, deeper breaths.

Her six hatchets are racked on the wall. She considers them to constitute a work of art. She has painted decorative designs on the handles—not on the grips, just the handles—and they're cool. She takes down two of them and stands across the room from the door. She puts one hatchet on the bed, within easy reach, and holds the other in her right hand, swinging it back and forth, letting the weight flex her muscles, stretch them out, get them ready.

Above the drumming rain on the roof and soughing wind at the windows, even above a hard roll of thunder, the sound of pounding footsteps thuds through the house. Someone is running up the front stairs. Now in the hallway.

"Libby!" Sarah shouts. "Libby, where are you?" She tries the door, finds it locked. "Libby, it's me, Sarah. Libby, open up."

She sounds like Sarah, and she probably is Sarah, but Libby remembers too well what was on her father's laptop. Sarah seems to be Sarah now, but what will she be two hours from now, an hour from now, in fifteen minutes? Francesca appeared to be herself when she came home, but evidently she was also something else; before too long, the something else was in ascendance.

It combines.

"Libby, we've got to get out of here, off the island. I can protect you, but we have to move fast."

Even as sharp as they are, two hatchets are a pathetic defense against Moloch. That's the code name that Ringrock's masters of science have given to the subject of their research. Moloch was a god of an ancient people who sacrificed their own children to him. He was insatiable, his hunger for human flesh so intense that he was not always able to wait for a child to be butchered on an altar for him. Then he descended from some nameless god country—certainly not Heaven—and fed on children *and* their parents, which ought to have taught them something about the inadequacy of their theology. There is no ancient god on Ringrock, only a project named for one, though Libby would rather be facing the original Moloch than some namesake of his that is perhaps now in the house.

Sarah raps hard on the door again and repeats her promise of protection, and Libby breaks the paralysis that has gripped her. She moves the tilted straight-backed chair, releases the privacy latch, but holds fast to the hatchet as she opens the door.

The woman in the hallway looks like Sarah, except she appears to be scared shitless, which isn't how Sarah has ever looked before. She says, "Come on, quick," turns away, and hurries along the hall toward the back of the house.

Libby has to trust her only friend, even though she doesn't know Sarah's true name. Francesca has never really been a mother to her, only a senior member of their "social compact," away at work on Ringrock more than she's at home, and now it's likely that Francesca isn't even human anymore. Libby has no one to trust except herself and Sarah. She can't survive alone. She steps into the hallway and rushes after the woman.

WHISPERING

A train of thunder passes across the lake and island, loud as it approaches out of the west, fading into the east. Moments later, another rumble arises within the house, soft and short-lived; the associated tremors are subtle, though strong enough to tremble the surface of the wine in the glass that stands on the drawing table.

As the fox sniffs his way out of the studio, across the hall, and into the living room, Katie follows him.

His behavior had at first seemed to be nothing more than that of an animal exploring a new environment. Now she associates it with the vibrations passing through the house, as though the scent that only he can smell and the sound she hears must be related.

This is not earthquake country. She's a couple thousand miles from California, in a stable part of the continent.

Remembering the depth charges released from the helicopters the previous day, she wonders if what she's hearing and feeling means that the people at Ringrock are dropping explosives again.

A different noise draws her into the hallway. The front door rattles against its frame. She might dismiss that as the action of the gusting wind, but not when she sees the knob turning back and forth.

Hampton Rice, in whatever demented condition, is still out there somewhere. So is Robert Zenon.

The ironbound oak is three inches thick, a lot sturdier than the boathouse door. Nevertheless, a few bursts from an AR-15 will blow out the lock.

When last she'd seen Rice, he seemed to have lost his weapon. If he found it, he might be too deranged to remember how to use it.

She recalls his eyes clearing briefly, reason returning to him, the sudden desperation in his voice. *For God's sake go, get away, save yourself. This is the epicenter.* If he had ever been her enemy, he wasn't her enemy in that moment. *Everyone living here will be dead soon. Everyone within a radius of miles. Miles and miles.*

If Zenon hasn't decided to replace the inboard-outboard engine and use her boat to flee, if he is still on Jacob's Ladder, then he is most likely in a condition similar to that of Rice.

Combine, integrate, aggregate. Who was isn't. Who will be won't be. So hard. So hard to make one and one be one other.

Watching the door, waiting to see the knob being turned again, Katie wonders what happened to Rice in the grotto. Is there a third person on the island? How is this mental degeneration transmitted—by toxin, virus, nerve gas?

I'm not combining well. It's only six hours . . . and already I feel I'm in a condition of rejection.

Whoever was at the door is evidently not there now. Maybe he's moved to a window.

Michael J. completes a circuit of the living room, returns to the hallway, and heads toward the kitchen, making a thin sound of anxiety.

The Glock is in the holster on Katie's hip, but the AR-15 and the shotgun suddenly seem dangerously far away, even in this small residence.

As she follows the fox into the kitchen, she hears whispering, which might be wind talking to itself in a flue, but which sounds so much like human voices that she draws the pistol. The only exterior door is intact and doubly deadbolted, and the windows are barred. No one can have gotten inside, but on this goblin night, she doesn't trust that what was impossible yesterday is impossible now.

She crosses the threshold low and fast, leading with the gun. There's no intruder in the kitchen, but the susurration is louder and more than ever like human voices, two or more, conversing in stage whispers, though she can't make out any words. She bends to the fireplace, but the sound doesn't come from there.

The windows are closed, and the shades are drawn shut. The candles pulse, burnishing the four urns with a quivering crimson glow.

Claws ticking on oak, the fox crosses the kitchen and lowers his head at the closed door to Katie's bedroom, the only chamber that he hasn't explored. He sniffs along the threshold and then looks at her.

She listens at the door, and though the whispering subsides somewhat, she's convinced that it's coming from the bedroom. Pistol in her right hand, she reaches for the doorknob with her left.

The longer she listens, the more ominous the sound becomes.

Both she and Michael J. reconsider and back away. She tucks the pistol in her holster and fetches the AR-15 from the table.

TO GO DOWN IN HISTORY

Breathing hard, Sarah pulls Libby into her bedroom at the back of the house, shuts the door, engages the privacy latch. Momentum deserts her. She freezes. "Be still," she whispers and then holds her breath, listening, as if it suddenly occurs to her that she might have closed them in a chamber where something is waiting for them. Contesting, jagged swords of lightning clash down the night. Bright flares at two windows provoke from the seamless dark the shapes of furniture throughout the large room, but nothing worse. Sarah moves again, and the wall switch brings a bloom of light to a bedside lamp.

She looks ghastly—as pale as bone, no color even in her lips, her eyes so wide they seem to be lidless. Terror has stolen her beauty.

She has a pistol in hand, the one that Libby found eleven months ago, when she searched this room for the passwords to her parents' laptops. This must have been the gun that fired the six shots downstairs. Sarah drops it on the bed along with the key to the thirty-foot cabin cruiser that Francesca drove home from Ringrock, the key that earlier hung on the pegboard in the kitchen.

Indicating the knob on the door to the hallway, Sarah says, "Jam a chair under that," and hurries into her closet.

The straight-backed chair isn't ideal for use as a blocking wedge. The back is padded. A chair with a wood headrail would be better. The silky fabric might slide out from under the doorknob when the thing, whoever-whatever it is, slams into the far side. Because it's all she has, Libby jams it under the knob anyway.

Sarah comes out of the closet with a pistol-grip shotgun, a box of shells, and a black nylon windbreaker with zippered pockets. She didn't have a shotgun eleven months earlier.

Tossing the windbreaker to Libby, she says, "Put this on."

Libby doesn't ask what the shooting was about, what creature issued that shriek of rage and need. She doesn't know what it looks like, but she knows what it is and who it once was. The windbreaker is too large for her, and it seems to resist her; she wrestles with it to get her arms in the sleeves.

Sarah says, "I'm going to tell you something crazy, but it's true."

"Moloch," Libby says.

Sarah looks astonished.

"I found the laptop passwords with your tampons. Sorry. But I had to know."

"When?"

"Almost a year ago."

"Jesus, Libby."

"I've been kind of scared ever since."

"Honey, you're something." Sarah throws aside the lid of the ammo box and spills the shells onto the mattress. "Fill your pockets with these." She loads the gun. "Watch how this is done. One in the breach, three in the tube. The gun is a semiautomatic. Gas-ejection spits out spent shells."

So many fears are contesting for Libby's attention that she doesn't have room for another, but it joins the mental circus anyway. "I've never fired a gun. That's big. I can't handle that."

"You're a strong girl. A gymnast, a hatchet thrower. This is an Italian gun with state-of-the-art recoil-reduction technology. Has a pistol grip. It'll shake you in your shoes, but it won't lift you out of them. I'll show you how to handle it in a minute. Now, just fill your pockets. And then zip them shut, keep the shells dry."

When Sarah returns from a second trip to the closet, she's wearing a quilted jacket, carrying a flashlight and a rifle.

"Not as scary as it looks. Just an AR-15. It'll do the job."

She quickly shows Libby how to hold the 12-gauge when on the move, how to stand while firing it. "Keep your finger on the trigger guard. Only slip it back to the trigger when you have to fire it."

"You were shooting at Francesca, weren't you?"

"She isn't your mother anymore."

"I understand." In all the ways that mattered most, Francesca never had been a mother to Libby, and yet there was a sharp pang of loss at the realization that the woman was taken, gone. "Where are we going?"

"To the mainland."

"Raleigh's never coming back, is he?"

Sarah meets Libby's eyes. "I'm so sorry. If not for me . . ." She doesn't finish the thought.

"Those gunshots," Libby says.

"Panic shooting. An early twofer is so damn quick. And you need a lot of hits to stop it."

"Twofer?"

"Technically it's called a fusion."

"Like it said on the laptop."

"But most of us call it a twofer. Graveyard humor."

"What I read—the fusion is a phase."

"We don't want to be here for what comes next."

"The spawning."

"Yeah. Stay close."

"Can they really be killed?"

"They're unstable. They self-destruct. All we can do is help them along, bring them down quicker."

"Are we going to die?"

"Not tonight."

As Sarah takes the chair out from under the doorknob, Libby says, "I don't even know your real name."

Sarah is surprised. "The laptop."

"I read what I could understand. But a lot was gobbledygook."

"I'm Shelly Framington. But call me Sarah. I don't like who Shelly was, what she did."

"What did she do?"

"Ruined everything. Out of pride. To go down in history. Now stand aside, behind the door, and pull it open when I tell you."

Libby stands aside, holding the shotgun as instructed. The weapon seems to be alive in her hands, the muzzle arcing up, down, up. She's got to control it before she can use it.

Sarah turns off the light and releases the privacy lock. She waits for something to erupt into the room. When nothing appears, she says, "Now."

Libby pulls the door inward, shielding behind it, as Sarah thrusts the AR-15 in front of herself.

There's dim light in the hallway. Nothing waits there.

The storm burns through the sky and speaks its power, while somewhere in the house, a woman whom Libby has tried to love is less than half who she used to be and perhaps incapable of human emotions other than hatred and fury.

Moloch's creations *are* unstable. They self-destruct. Maybe the Francesca thing has already spawned. Maybe all the spawns are dead.

Libby follows Sarah into the upstairs hallway.

BELOW

Except for the wordless yet malevolent whispering, Katie's bedroom is as it was—everything in its place, the bed neatly made, the windows covered by shades. She can't identify the source of the sound, which encircles her, as though spirits are striving to press through the gates of Hell and return to this world where they were once nurtured.

The fox hesitates on the threshold, but then follows her into the room.

Wolves are fierce and hunt in packs, but foxes are sly and mostly hunt alone, predators on a modest scale, omnivores that will eat all manner of other things when they can't get meat. Not known for challenging any creature their own size or larger, foxes live by the conviction that discretion is the better part of valor.

With his hackles raised and his flanks trembling, Michael J. is nonetheless boldly exploring the bedroom, his curiosity greater than his fear. One way to interpret his behavior—the only way that makes sense—is to suppose that he has caught the scent of something he has never smelled before, that he wants to understand, to know if it's the odor of something inanimate or alive, to be merely avoided or actively feared.

Turn by turn, he comes to the center closet of three. As he sniffs at the narrow gap along the threshold, the whispering abruptly ceases.

The fox backs away, his nostrils flared, his tail tucked, having evidently decided that whatever lies beyond is an active menace.

Katie moves past him, hesitates, and raps the barrel of the rifle hard against the door—one, two, three—to see if anything within responds to the provocation. Nothing happens. The whispering does not resume.

The only sounds are those of the storm and the panting of the fox, and Katie's heart thudding like a horse's hooves on turf.

She stands to the side of the door opposite the hinges. Uses one hand to turn the knob. Throws the door away from her, at once resuming a two-handed grip on the rifle. Nothing rushes into the room. She steps forward to inspect the closet. Nothing abides there.

The shelves concealing the entrance to the cellar are in place, secured with a hidden latch on this side.

She steps into the closet and listens. No sound issues from the realm below.

The latch is behind the drop edge of a shelf holding shoes. She feels for it with her left hand.

She looks back. The fox has retreated to the open door between the bedroom and the kitchen.

When her fingers find the latch release, she doesn't spring it. Instinct rises in her as strongly as it does in Michael J. Earlier, the susurrant noise, as of several voices whispering, had seemed to issue out of the air all around her because it was rising into every room from the cellar.

The cellar has no windows, no outside door, no vents. It can't have been invaded by anything substantial. Joe Smith engineered the foundation so well, installed such wide pea-gravel barriers and French drains all around, and slathered the concrete with so many thick coats of creosote that, even after decades, rainwater reliably flows away from the house during the rainiest years. The cellar has never presented her with a moisture problem. If water can't find a way in, nothing can.

Instinct insists. She eases her finger off the lock release.

The previous night, what creature had capered overhead, torqued the rain gutter when it dropped off the roof, and left a frost of some kind on the ground below the kitchen window? And what of the grass that had grown so much in but a few hours? What were the roots like, how thick and numerous, possessing what questing force? Could a subterranean forest of radicles have in such a short time probed through the long-resistant creosote and found tiny fractures in the underlying concrete and invaded the cellar? To what purpose? Merely to fill it with grass? No, not that, but something . . . something beyond comprehension.

She steps out of the closet, closes the door. There's no lock on it. The shelves concealing the entrance to the cellar are solidly constructed, but she doesn't know what insistent presence they might be required to hold back, if anything. She puts the AR-15 on the bed and drags a tall chest of drawers in front of the closet door. It doesn't provide a formidable additional barrier, but at least it will make a lot of noise if it is shoved aside or toppled.

THE HARD WAY OUT

From Sarah's room, the most direct route to the boathouse is down the service stairs to the kitchen and out the back door. They have a twelve-foot outboard runabout, but the much larger vessel Francesca drove from Ringrock to Oak Haven is better suited for a trip to the mainland on a stormy night.

The steady rush of wind and rattle of rain form a white noise which, in its constancy, barely registers with Libby, so that the residence seems to have fallen into a hush. In spite of her parents' emotional isolation, and even after Libby learned the nature of the work underway on Ringrock, this house has been a warm and welcoming haven by virtue of its proportions, elegance, and lovely detailing. At the moment, however, a change has come over it, the very geometry of the structure seeming to have been warped and shrunk by the power of the sinister presence that now creeps and shudders through it. The upstairs hall feels narrower than it once was, the ceiling lower; the room doors appear to swell with tension, as if set to spring open like jack-in-the-box lids. The perceived quiet is not a quiet at all, but instead an expectation of an imminent loud and mortal eruption of violence.

At the head of the back stairs, Sarah leads the way, although only for a descent of three steps, where she's halted by a noise in the kitchen below, a loud clatter. Something waits down there.

Sarah turns and ushers Libby ahead of her, retreating to the second floor. With the AR-15, she gestures toward the far end of the hallway. They'll have to go down the main stairs and out the front door. They move quietly over the carpet runner, raising no protests from the floorboards, though when Libby holds her arms too close to her sides, the sleeves of her windbreaker whistle softly against the body of the coat.

The main staircase is open, a single flight sweeping gracefully to the foyer. The chandelier cascades in a glitterless darkness of pear-shaped pendant crystals. The shadowy foyer immediately below is little illuminated by pale light issuing from one of a pair of doors to the living room. As they are about to start down, that open door eases halfway shut. This is a well-made house in which doors do not move under the influence of drafts.

Whatever lurks in the living room, behind the door, it is not likely to be the same thing that made the noise in the kitchen. The spawning has almost certainly begun, and perhaps it's complete. No way to know how many crawl the rooms down there, whether three or six, each wanting a successful fusion with something other than its own kind. They seek with urgency because their window of conjugation is very narrow; they are desperate entities of need and rage.

Sarah pulls Libby away from the head of the stairs, leads her to the first room on the east side of the hallway, the master suite. She closes the door behind them, engages the latch.

The clothes that Francesca was wearing when she came home are scattered over the bed and floor. It appears as though she literally tore off some of them. She had been aware that she was infected—or is it invaded, conquered?—not human any longer, harboring an entity that was fast remaking both her and itself into a hybrid creature. She hadn't stripped naked to shower, but instead to free herself of restraints that might inhibit the physical transformation impending, one that, by comparison, made all legends of werewolves and other shape changers seem ordinary.

"The window," Sarah whispers. "To the yard, the boathouse."

Three windows, all double hung, offer access to the veranda roof, two on the south wall, one on the east. The boathouse is to the east, so they try that one, but the lower sash is either warped or painted shut, and Sarah can't move it.

At the first of the south-facing windows, the thumb-turn lock is corroded, but it grudgingly moves in increments, with a rasping noise as the skin of rust cracks.

Perhaps overcome by a presentiment of impending death, Sarah confesses as she twists the lock and struggles to raise the stubborn lower sash. She reveals what she once was, why she's to blame, and how the government will try to contain Moloch once it reluctantly accepts that the threat is no longer confined to Ringrock Island—all in fewer than fifty words, rattled off in a state of terrified expectation.

Gripping the shotgun, Libby ducks under the raised sash, swings one leg over the sill and then the other, exiting to the roof of the veranda that embraces three sides of the house, into the whipping wet of the storm. She takes two steps and turns, sure that Sarah is already clambering out of the window—which is when the thing breaks down the bedroom door and catapults across the room and climbs the woman's back. Sarah reflexively fires four rounds with the AR-15, but she's taken so fast that she can't turn to face her attacker or lower the gun. Bullets pound the ceiling, dislodging gouts of shattered plaster.

Sarah drops her rifle or it is torn from her hands, and she is slammed forward, her face against the pane of the raised sash, her eyes shocked wide, her mouth open in an unvoiced scream. The thing that surmounts her is perhaps five feet in height, a hundred pounds of pale, muscular coils that appear to writhe in greasy knots, yet it has four pincered legs with which it fastens fiercely to her back. Her coat and other garments shred away like tissue paper. The assailant presses down as though thrusting in sexual congress, a creature so strange that no words can convey the horror of it. Like a demon in a dream, it seems to be ceaselessly changing, a million species encoded in its genes, so that it can summon itself into whatever form it wishes. The worst thing about it is the misshapen head; it's a human head in which the bones have become as soft as wax, and yet the face, for all its grievous detail, remains recognizable as that of Francesca. Her eyes are sour yellow, and her features twist into an expression of such fury that it far exceeds any emotion she might have felt when she'd been only her passionless self. This beast that has spawned—with others—from the fusion of Moloch and Francesca now appears not merely to ride Sarah, but also to conjoin with her, apparently remaking her flesh as easily as its own, and she screams against the window glass. The scream is human for a moment, but then it becomes two voices twined in an unholy shriek, simultaneously a cry of terror and one of glee, despair and triumph.

Fright pivots Libby away from the window, impels her across the roof of the veranda, around the corner of the house, from the south flank to the east, where the boathouse lies in the distance. Water streaming down the slope into the gutter, her feet slipping on the rain-slick slate, she almost falls, almost spills into space. She keeps her balance. Holding the shotgun in both hands and above her head, she halts and tenses her legs. She jumps and lands with feet as precisely spread as she might when dismounting from a set of parallel bars in a gymnastics competition.

The unearthly two-voice stridulation shrills through the night behind her. Prolonged lightning marries the sky to the earth; clouds seethe with white fire, while pale light billows across wet grass. Her spirit trembles as her body shudders her toward the boathouse.

HIS HANDS ARE INSTRUMENTS
OF JUSTICE

In the month following the shooting at the ice cream parlor, it becomes clear that some power unknown is obstructing the police inquiry. The exterior security cameras at the strip mall are said to have been malfunctioning and have recorded nothing of the events of that day. The seasoned detective assigned to the investigation is replaced by a callow young man with only one year of experience in the robbery-homicide division. A pizza parlor employee who had been preparing the business for its eleven o'clock opening the morning of the attack, a potential witness and initially cooperative, abruptly moves back to Mexico, leaving no forwarding address.

Avi is a former Marine and twelve years a Navy SEAL, who was awarded the Navy Cross. Since leaving the military, he has become a successful entrepreneur in the private-security industry. He has the knowledge, resources, and contacts to investigate the investigation. His grief is deep and black and unrelenting. When grief fails to mature into sorrow, he remains as anguished as he was in the hour that he learned his in-laws and his daughters had been gunned down. Convinced that the authorities are working to obscure rather than reveal the truth, he calls in every favor he is owed, presses every button, twists every arm that can be twisted until he learns there are three suspects who haven't been named. Off the record, the older detective who was removed from the case reveals the three names, making it clear that none of them will be charged, that if anyone ever is charged, he will be a fall guy. This is because the one named Parker is the son of a United States senator with presidential aspirations. Parker is now in a posh private hospital, a detox facility in scenic Big Sur, under the conservatorship of his parents; an attempt will be made to rehabilitate him. Failing that, he will most likely be deemed to have suffered brain damage due to an overdose and will be transferred to an equally posh long-term facility, where he will be medicated into a condition of permanent docile contentment. Lupo and Hamal, with the resources to begin new and prosperous lives, have been escorted out of the United States and will never return. This deal has been worked out in back rooms as handshake agreements, sans paperwork, and everyone involved finds the resolution satisfying.

Avi has always believed in the promise of his country; he still believes in it. He has also always known that there are good men and women who wish to serve and govern, as well as a worse kind who seek the power to rule. He has no illusions that wherever the latter are in charge, the law is not equally applied and justice is a dream rather than a reality. Having fought for the ideals of his country in numerous tours of duty in some of the world's most dangerous places, he feels confident that fighting for those ideals here in sunny California is no less his duty and more certain to result in a righteous victory. His experience of evil and its ways gives him an advantage, and his strong hands, scarred by combat, are instruments of justice.

Avi is not an angry man by nature. Excruciating grief can be a breeding ground for anger, however, especially for a man who feels responsible not just for those who deserve his protection but also for the triumph of evil in general. Perhaps his uncharacteristic rage renders him less prudent than he usually is, or perhaps this is a time when anyone searching the current darkness for an honest man is sure to wear out as many lanterns as he can afford. Although Avi knows that journalists are as likely as those in any profession to sell their souls for either ideology or mammon, he puts his trust in one who, by all indications and accounts, is a straight shooter. He arranges a meeting with the reporter in a park at sunrise, where they might be only two men who are runners on the same path. At the end of their run, he hands the reporter a thumb drive containing all the evidence he has gathered. Ten hours later, Avi is the hit-and-run victim of a man in a Porsche SUV traveling more than eighty miles per hour.

The vehicle is stolen. The driver abandons it two blocks past the point of impact and flees on foot.

Avi's injuries are so serious that he should die at the scene, but he holds on until, in the hospital, he can say goodbye to Katie and wrest from her a promise that she will not give in to despair, that she will live.

The driver of the Porsche is never found.

The journalist never writes a word about the meeting in the park.

FIVE

PURPOSE

KITCHEN

The house has been her fortress. Katie is reluctant to admit this has changed. But the house is not a fortress if something lives in the cellar and labors there to a hostile purpose. Her bedroom is no longer a place to rest, for it is there that whatever is in the lower realm might gain access to the main floor. In the studio waits the unfinished painting that she now knows how to complete but that she might never have a chance to finish; at the moment it not only represents not an opportunity to properly memorialize those whom she lost and thereafter live more fully but it also serves as a depressing caution that perhaps the resolution of loss is not possible in this fallen world. The living room has always been her least favorite room, because its very purpose is communal, a chamber in which to gather with others, and therefore minute by minute a reminder that she is—and might always be—alone, three of the four armchairs reserved for those who will never return to occupy them. Her safe space has been reduced to the kitchen, and even that seems less like a refuge than a cell, as she waits for an insistent knocking on the door or a beseeching, mad voice at one of the windows. *Mother, are you in there?*

Michael J. drinks from the bowl of water that she put out for him, and then he curls up on a sofa cushion that she brought from the living room. He watches her for a minute, as if he marvels at the alliance that these witchy circumstances have forced on them. Then he lowers his chin to his paws and closes his bright eyes and adopts the slow, rhythmic breathing of a sleeper deep in dreamless slumber.

Katie sits in candlelight at the table, rubbing one finger around and around the rim of the wineglass she retrieved from her studio. Although she slept less than five hours last night, she is certain that she won't sleep during the night ahead, for fear of waking to find a grinning apparition sitting across from her.

Watching the fox, Katie wonders at the stoic nature of all Earth's creatures other than humankind. Their lives are short and hard and ever shadowed by threat, and they endure periods of hunger when in their foraging they find nothing, and they persevere through sickness without understanding what it is they suffer, and they have seen others devoured by something bigger with sharper teeth. Yet in spite of all they have to fear, they sleep as if they are safe when unconscious, and they wake to each new day with enthusiasm. They mate and groom their offspring and play; foxes in particular gambol in fox games. Some say it is their ignorance of death and their instinct that ensures enthusiasm for life. After years of observing the animals on Jacob's Ladder, Katie has arrived at the conviction that, contrary to informed opinion, animals know what death means. It's not ignorance that ensures they are content with their lot. Instead, it seems they know something of great importance that humanity has forgotten; the knowledge comforts them.

After she sips the wine, the rim of the glass is wet. When she circles it with her fingertip, it produces a tone as silvery as a bell yet as eerie as if produced by a theremin, that instrument so often employed in very old movies of the Karloff and Lugosi era.

Suddenly, the whispering comes again. As before, it seems to be a chorus of voices, like the threats of a mob chanting promises of violence at a rally in some distant stadium.

She sets aside the wineglass and gets to her feet. This time, the sound doesn't issue from all sides but has a localized source.

Drawn to the sink, she stares at the drain basket, through the perforations of which the whispering rises.

The contents of the one toilet are flushed into a cesspool that wouldn't be permitted if the bungalow had been built later than the 1950s, after which a serviced septic tank would have been required. However, all the gray water from the kitchen and bath flow through pipes into a deep French drain, from there into the filtering layers of a cistern, in time through the ground and the bedrock, eventually into the lake, by then purged of soap and chemicals. If something has been able to penetrate the thick creosote and the concrete of the cellar walls, it could also have found its way into the French drain, into the pipes that carry gray water from the house.

As she listens, she begins to suspect that the whispering might not be produced by voices, but might instead be the consequence of agitation. The friction of something moving against the walls of a passageway or confining structure. Or numerous things moving against one another—brushing, whisking, writhing. She thinks of insects and snakes and rodents in great number, but none of those creatures seems to be a likely cause of this sound.

The drain basket is a two-piece unit that forms a watertight seal when the inner basket is twisted. She closes the drain.

From the pantry, she fetches a one-gallon can of fuel for the Coleman lanterns that she brought up from the cellar earlier in the day. She brings it to the sink and sets it on the counter. The noise is muffled now that the drain basket is sealed against water.

Michael J. continues sleeping.

The former owner, Tanner Walsh, had the old iron pipes, which were rusted and unreliable, replaced not with new iron or PVC, but with top-of-the-line steel. The pipes from here out to the French drain will withstand a flush of fire.

For whatever reason, Hampton Rice's voice plays in her memory: *Mother, are you there yet? Are you in there?*

She reaches for the drain basket.

Five thousand times five thousand years and then five thousand more. Who knows where, why, how long? Learn what it is, and you'll wish you hadn't.

She leaves the basket as it is and places the gallon can on top of it while she steps back from the sink to consider her options.

TO THE BOATHOUSE

The boathouse lies a hundred yards from the residence, the length of a football field. Libby has sprinted this ground countless times, on some occasions with her arms spread wide in imitation of a bird in flight. Now she falters and dodges repeatedly, like a broken-field runner with bad knees, progressing by fits and starts, because the darkness is not the darkness she has known all her life and is now as strange as an ink-black crater on the sunless side of the moon. The wind is colder than it should be at this time of year, the rain seeming to tick against her face as if it's sleet, or maybe the cold is not in the night but in her, rising out of her marrow. Blustering off the lake, the gale shakes the oaks, which rattle as if the skeletons of hanged men depend in mobiles of bones from their branches, and every burst of clattering is—or could be—warning of an attack, because in this world in its remaking, there might be monsters in the trees.

She has thrown back the hood of the windbreaker, alert for any sound that might indicate an imminent threat. However, the night is a cacophony of wind howl and all things shaken by the storm, and she is making more noise than she wants, unable to stop gasping both for air and in terror, feet pounding the ground and splashing through puddles. If there were to be a telltale noise—a growl, a hiss, a hateful cry—she is unlikely to be able to sift it from the tumult of the tempest in time to save herself.

Sarah is dead. *Sarah is dead.* Or if she is in any sense still alive and aware, then she's worse than dead, merged with a demonic entity, fused with it for purposes unimaginable. Dead or not,

Sarah is gone. That fact is intolerable, unbearable, undeniable. Francesca is gone. Raleigh is gone. After seven years on Oak Haven, there is no one for Libby to turn to except strangers on the mainland.

The storm isn't done with lightning, casting its arrows by the quiversful, figurations of oaks leaping with each fulmination, alien shapes capering across the ground as fast as cats, and faster yet— mostly shadows, yes, but perhaps not all shadows. Ricocheting through the grove, Libby expects to be seized, pierced, crudely mounted, and consumed, or to feel the earth open under her and to drop into a lair like that of a trapdoor spider. Although she holds the shotgun in both hands, in her panic she has forgotten most of what she was taught about how to use it. Even if in a mortal crisis she remembers what to do, she has no confidence that the weapon is sufficient to stop what might be coming for her.

A white rectangle, like a chapel without steeple or stained glass, looms in the night—the boathouse. When lightning flutters as it flares, the eight steps to the adjacent pier seem to topple into one another in a domino effect. At the top of the stairs, she turns and looks back through the grove, toward the house, amazed to find herself holding the pistol-grip shotgun as instructed, surprised but not reassured to see that no beast of inconstant biology is at her heels. The spawn of the Francesca fusion are out there, frantically seeking, for their time is short. The distant house glows not with the promise of shelter, but like a shrine to an ancient merciless god, and the woods are haunted.

Libby hurries along the planking, the boathouse to her left, the lake black and as vast as an ocean to her right. Only now does she realize that she is weeping, her eyes burning with the salt of tears. She is mortified to be crying not just for Sarah—and very little for her parents—but as much for herself as for her lost friend. She understands that even if she gets out of this place and this night alive, even if the thing on Ringrock can be destroyed, the promising future that once was hers is gone forever. This isn't a time for deep thinking—she needs to concentrate on surviving—but she can't help being who she is, and she's a girl who's *always* thinking. It's already obvious to her that, to a great extent, she will be defined by the fact that her mother and father were the scientists leading this project, among those whose hubris nearly destroyed the world, if in fact it isn't already too late to save it. Human nature is to look at a child and see the sins of the parents if the parents' actions resulted in horrific suffering and mass death.

They never lock the boathouse. Certain that the spawn born from the deterioration of the Francesca fusion are all behind her, Libby crosses the threshold, pulls the door shut, and fumbles for the wall switch. Circles of light fall out of cone-shaped fixtures that hang from the ceiling on chains. Only as the cabin cruiser materializes from the darkness does Libby realize she can't start the inboard engine. The key was in the pocket of Sarah's coat.

THE CALL

At the kitchen sink, Katie listens to the sotto voce chorus of some inhabitant—or horde—that must have originated deep in the pea gravel of the French drain but that seems to be drawing closer, now backflowing into the steel pipe.

Regardless of whatever extraordinary event has occurred on Ringrock, the siege of Jacob's Ladder will end sooner or later. There will be a resolution. Normalcy will be restored. Katie just has to ride this out, stay alive, and she will get her life back. She must learn from the fox, which still sleeps in a corner of the kitchen, learn from all the stoic animals, trust that in spite of what evil human beings may commit or facilitate, this world forged out of the void and fashioned in such imaginative detail is rightly ordered and will endure. She needs to remain calm, trust as the fox trusts—and kill the shit out of any person or thing that tries to take her out.

The unknown presence in the cellar is likely as hostile as it is strange. This isn't your grandfather's *Twilight Zone* episode, offering a pleasant chill for viewers of all ages. But the entity below can't get at her for now. Nor can Hampton Rice in his demented wandering through the night. Robert Zenon is missing in action. Depending on what is exploring the steel pipe from its terminus deep in the French drain, the sink might be a weak point in her defenses.

If she pours the lantern fuel into the drain and follows it with a lighted match, the fire won't be hot enough or last long enough to destroy or even compromise the steel pipe. However, the fumes gathered in that tight passage will almost certainly be thick enough to cause an explosion, which might destroy the integrity of the drain and result in a breach that is hard to patch or defend.

She returns the can of lantern fuel to the pantry and fetches two plastic jugs, one containing a rarely used drain cleaner and one full of Clorox. The former has two active ingredients that dissolve hair and grease, though slowly; she reads the label to be sure there is no ammonia, which when combined with the bleach would create a deadly gas. Good to go.

When she twists the inner basket, breaking the watertight seal, and removes the unit from the sink, the whispering grows slightly in volume but considerably more malevolent in its tone, suggesting that something is eager and encouraged in its advance. Issuing directly up the pipe, the voices are clearer and more nuanced than when they were rising through the floor from the cellar. She can almost make out a few words. For a moment, the open drain looks like the large-bore muzzle of a military weapon, but then it appears more benign, like the diaphragm in the cone of a stereo speaker, nothing more than a device to bring her clarified sound. She leans into the sink and turns her left ear to the drain, straining to decipher the words in that susurrant choir.

She realizes, after all, that there is nothing malicious in the whispering, that indeed there is a beseeching quality to it, a tender appeal for her consideration. More than that, she is valued, even cherished. She is *needed* as she has not been needed by anyone in three years. A sense of purpose overcomes her, an aspiration to go where she can be of value, where an important task awaits her.

Standing on its hind feet, forepaws against her leg, the fox nips her hand without breaking the skin. The bite is just sharp enough to startle but not frighten her. She looks down into his eyes as he makes a small fretful sound.

Without being aware of having stepped away from the sink, she has left the kitchen and gone into her bedroom. She is standing at the closet door that earlier she blockaded with the tall chest of drawers.

In an instant, bewilderment gives way to alarm. She remembers Tanner Walsh responding to the call of something on Ringrock. But he had been sleepwalking. She has succumbed while wide awake, perhaps because what called to her is not on that distant island, as it was when it reached out to Walsh, but is right here on Jacob's Ladder.

The fox drops onto all four. Bushy tail straight out behind him, he races out of the bedroom, into the kitchen.

CONTROL

The key to the boat.

The shock of Libby's situation is a hard blow that rocks her on her heels. For a moment she can't breathe, and when breath comes, the inhalation hurts. The pain in her breastbone quickly extends to a cramping in the gut.

She stands in the boathouse loft, at the head of the gangway, looking down at the thirty-foot cabin cruiser, an all-wood boat that is the most beautiful machine she's ever seen. On its transom, it carries the name *Fifth Day*, which is a mystery that only the first owner, long dead, could explain, and which has led to many theories. The residence and the boat are of the same era. A man named Lionel and his sons, Simon and Jack, visit from the mainland four times a year and anchor their vessel for a week to maintain the wood and engine and mechanical systems of the *Fifth Day*. The boat is fast and easy to handle, steady in rough weather—and useless without the key that starts the inboard engine.

Libby has taken turns at the helm, in open water, since she was nine. By now she is expert at docking and handling the cabin cruiser under any conditions. She pushes herself hard to excel in everything from homeschooling to gymnastics, from boating to scuba diving and distance swimming. Although she never expected Sarah to die, she's known the woman won't be part of her life forever. She's wanted to be as ready as she can be when the day comes that she's got no one but the parents who care less about her than they do about their professional accomplishments, ready to be able to rely on herself, to have *control* of her life to the greatest extent possible.

Now, as she looks down at the boat for which she possesses no key, she remembers something she read. *For want of a nail the shoe is lost, for want of a shoe the horse is lost, for want of a horse the rider is lost.* Which is true, but without hope *all* is lost, and she is not going to give up.

The man-size door between pier and boathouse can't be locked from inside. One of the remaining spawn might be tracking her, even now ascending the steps to the pier.

She presses the button that raises the large sectional door at the lakefront end of this boat garage.

In addition to the big, beautiful wood cruiser, the wide slip contains a twelve-foot boat with an outboard engine. She doesn't need a key for that, just the strength to pull the starter rope.

As the door to the lake rolls up, she hurries down the gangway to the floating slip.

She isn't the kind who gives up. Not ever. If she was going to give up, she would have done it during the first seven years of her life, before lovely Sarah, when her parents were even more distant than they have been here on Oak Haven. During those years, Libby was entrusted to Clarissa, who deemed the title "nanny" to be an insult. A twentysomething "childcare specialist," Clarissa earned a degree of some kind that impressed Francesca and Raleigh. She believed in the power of applied psychology, as she put it with a smile, "to shape the most stubborn little savage into a model citizen." Any dictator with a large population of political prisoners would have prized Clarissa for her skill at psychological torture, though she was not averse to resorting at times to pinches, slaps, and pokes. As young as Libby had been—preschool tyke,

then grade-schooler—she might have succumbed to her tor-
mentor if she hadn't been as smart as she was and if Clarissa
hadn't been stupid. Even so, if Clarissa had been willing to stay
with them when they moved to Oak Haven, and if Sarah hadn't
wanted the position as a form of penance, by now Libby might
have been batshit crazy. You can refuse to give up, but nonetheless
be broken in the process of not surrendering.

At the foot of the gangway, she hurries across the forward
arm of the slip and around to the smaller vessel. It's belayed to
cleats fore and aft. The door at the head of the gangway remains
closed; nothing has entered from the pier. She stows the shotgun
under the passenger thwart where it will be somewhat protected
from the rain, unties the lines, and swings aboard, onto the transom seat. She has to pull the starter rope three times, but the
engine fires. She throttles up and drives out of the slip, out of the
boathouse.

The sky is black, and the water is black, and the lightning provides no guidance. Exiting the boathouse, she is pointed due east.
In clear weather, the lights along the coast of the distant mainland
comprise a bright crack in the otherwise complete darkness, as
though the night is the shell of a fracturing egg. Through this
driving rain and the ragged tatters of windblown fog, she can see
no trace of the radiant shoreline. The cruiser has a compass; this
smaller boat has none. In the crossing, she will be all but blind.
With neither a compass nor visual references, disorientation is
inevitable. She might believe she's on course for the nearer coast,
when in fact she is bound south-southwest, past Ringrock and
into the full length of the great lake, where she could find herself
many miles from land, out of fuel, and adrift.

Back at the house, as Sarah had struggled to raise the window to escape the master bedroom, she had revealed, among other things, how the government would try to contain Moloch. Time to escape the cordon sanitaire was fast running out; the hammer was likely to come down long before dawn, perhaps no later than midnight, three hours from now.

Not sure that the outboard contains enough fuel to get her to the mainland even if she stays on course by sheer instinct, with a doomsday clock ticking in the back of her mind, Libby heads south. At the southeast corner of Oak Haven, she steers hard starboard, north-northwest, toward Jacob's Ladder.

Judging by all she's seen, Libby believes the woman on Jacob's Ladder lives alone. Whoever she might be, she apparently wants no company, for she has never reached out to her nearest neighbors on Oak Haven—not that she would have been warmly welcomed, especially if she had asked questions about Ringrock. However, she owns a cabin cruiser, a vessel smaller than the one Libby had hoped to use in her escape, but twice the size of this runabout; it surely will have a compass, if not also sophisticated navigation electronics.

The woman has sometimes cruised close to Oak Haven when Libby has been playing in the yard and has been friendly enough to wave. Likewise, when Libby has taken this outboard for a spin and has seen the woman on her pier, along her shore, or on the bluff where the small, stone house stands, they have waved at each other.

The crossing between the two islands is less daunting than the long journey to the mainland. Even in this foul weather, the lights of the Oak Haven house might not sluice away in the rain behind her before the lights on Jacob's Ladder swell into view. And if she is left without a guiding light either behind or ahead, the period of blind progress should be so short that she'll be able to avoid deviating radically from the correct course.

Lightning finds its way to water, the glazed lake seems to have no more depth than a mirror, the wind keens as though mourning the world, and Libby is alone as the night washes toward the Apocalypse or mere Armageddon.

DOWN THE DRAIN

Katie feels as if she has awakened not just from a state of dark enchantment, but also from the corrupt and mad world in which she has been living into one even darker and more insane. In the world fashioned by the nihilists who have ruled it for more than half a century, where children and their grandparents can be gunned down in an ice cream shop on a Sunday morning by men who pay no price for their actions, at least no hostile and mysterious entities had been in the cellar, no sirens speaking out of the plumbing to call her to the rocks of ruin.

Katie hurries from her bedroom into the kitchen, where the susurrant voices, capable of casting a hypnotic net over a listener, are spinning their audial filaments of attraction out of the drain. Somewhat to her surprise, to shield herself from the influence of that eerie chorus, she concentrates on the last four lines from "The Hollow Men" by T. S. Eliot, chanting them over and over as she uncaps the gallon of drain cleaner and pours it into the sink: "'This is the way the world ends / This is the way the world ends / This is the way the world ends / Not with a bang but a whimper.'"

Michael J. jumps onto a dining chair and watches intently, as though prepared to spring across the table and administer another bloodless nip if Katie slides away into a trance.

"'This is the way the world ends . . .'"

She doesn't think that whatever's whispering out of the drain is able to ascend through it, at least not in sufficient numbers to be a threat, because if that were the case, then they would already have erupted into the kitchen. She also doubts that the toxic substances she's pouring into the pipe will kill whatever is calling to her, but even a mild acid and bleach should be unpleasant enough to make the horde relent.

"'This is the way the world ends . . .'"

Finished with the drain cleaner, she quickly uncaps the gallon of Clorox. The whispering has subsided a little. She tips the mouth of the jug into the drain. Astringent bleach fumes steal her breath, and she turns her head to the right, seeking fresher air, rasping out the lines from Eliot's poem.

"'Not with a bang, but a whimper.'"

When the gallon is drained, she caps the jug and sets it aside and replaces the sink basket. She twists the inner unit, creating a watertight seal, which also blocks the fumes rising from the drain.

The whispering has stopped.

She turns away from the sink, taking deep breaths of clean air.

When her family had been ripped away from her, she'd had no one but herself, but at least she possessed the power to fantasize about vengeance and ultimately to decide to live for the Promise. If she had nothing else, she'd had the free will to shape her future, as grim and diminished as it might be.

This evening, however, for a few terrible minutes, even free will had been taken from her, that most basic and vital gift of human existence. She had been enslaved. If it can happen once, it can happen again.

From his perch on the chair, the fox watches her. He lifts his head, listening and sniffing. He drops down to the floor and returns to the sofa cushion that she has provided for his bed and curls up on it and rests his chin on one paw.

Katie can't stop shaking.

Her father had been afflicted with familial tremors, benign but annoying, that came and went. Red wine could often fade them.

She returns to the table and picks up her glass and drains what wine remains in it, medicating herself.

Still trembling, she stands looking at the ceiling, listening to the rain drumming on the slate tiles.

RALEIGH CONSIDERS MOLOCH

Six Years before the Crisis on Ringrock

From his personal archives as preserved in a high-security cloud account:

Let's dismiss with jargon and hundred-dollar words. Let's render it down to language that anyone can understand, even the most benighted of the Great Unwashed who don't recognize that science is the last bastion of honest individuals of every gender and race.

Five considerations will give you a basic grasp of the organism that I prefer to call "Proteus," but that has been named "Moloch" by several of my associates who are of a more flamboyant nature than I.

First: We know that all the matter in the universe was made from positive energy. At the moment of the Big Bang, there was no matter, only energy. (By "positive energy," I'm not making reference to the "power of positive thinking" and other self-improvement psychobabble with which credulous individuals stuff their heads.) Anyone who is interested in reading further about energy would do well to refer to F. J. Dyson's Order of Merit table of the nine forms of energy and the associated material to which this will lead you.

Second: As living beings—creatures made of matter—we sustain and grow and remain motive by ingesting other matter, our food.

Third: Now imagine, if you can, a life-form that feeds on matter, just as we do, but *also* can feed on energy—sunlight, heat, microwave radiation—and build matter from it as easily as it does from ingesting other matter.

Four: Further imagine that this life-form can produce new cells and organize them into tissues and complex organs thousands of times faster than we do.

Five: Such a life-form should be immortal. Assuming that the carbon dating of its dense shell has provided reliable data and that it is not the sole specimen of its kind, it should have become the dominant if not only life-form in the entire universe millions of years ago.

With those five considerations firmly in mind, there are three primary questions to consider.

One: Why isn't immortal Moloch the only life-form in the universe?

Two: Instead of merely consuming other life-forms, why does it instead attempt to combine with them and create a hybrid creature?

Three: Why, for all its splendid engineering power, does it fail, creating only freakish, violent entities that ultimately collapse?

Proper, intelligent exploration of these questions leads us to numerous theories that attempt to answer each. I have arrived at what I am confident are the correct answers, which I will render in simple terms in the next installment of this layman's guide, which is intended to assist politicians, bureaucrats, historians, and—frankly—certain other scientists to grasp the function of this amazing life-form, the historic nature of this discovery, and the implications for humanity.

When we understand the processes by which Moloch fashions living matter out of energy, we will have a technology that will transform human civilization forever and for the better.

THE CROSSING

Severe wind stirs the lake into turbulence, and the little boat knocks through the chop with such force that Libby clenches her jaws to avoid biting her tongue hard enough to draw blood. She has never been out in weather this rough or in a darkness this confounding. She works the throttle, seeking an ideal speed. When she slows too much, the boat pitches into the low swells, sometimes with such a downslide of the bow that there's a risk of taking on water. The one time she puts on too much speed, the vessel slaps across the waves, bouncing her on the transom seat; for a moment airborne, it comes down into a trough that causes it to roll so precipitously that black water laps over the port gunwale. As never before, her left arm begins to ache with the effort of holding the steering control on course.

When the glowing windows of the Oak Haven house are at her back, they confirm that she is headed north-northwest toward Jacob's Ladder, but they are being rinsed out of the rainy night faster than she expected. Soon they fade away completely, and still no lights appear ahead. The house on Jacob's Ladder is modest; its windows are few and small. As darkness envelops her, Libby leans forward, squinting, trying with an act of will to conjure even the faintest lamplight on the island that, she remains convinced, is directly ahead. Each bright but fleeting work of the storm reveals nothing useful before the sky folds its light away.

Encouraged by all the books she's read, her imagination has kept her sane these seven years on Oak Haven, but now it torments her. She remembers the golden afternoon of the previous day, when the helicopters dropped depth charges in the waters off Ringrock, when Francesca called to assure Sarah that nothing was amiss, that the unprecedented action was part of a scheduled experiment, and that she and Raleigh would be staying the night at the lab, as they did now and then. At the time, the "experiment" part seemed to be a half-truth; a day later, there can be no doubt it was a shameless lie. What was in the lake that had to be destroyed? What might have escaped the depth charges? In the best weather, this boat rides low in the water. Now it pitches when it doesn't roll. Water surges at the bow and then at the stern, to port and then to starboard. She half expects some infinitely strange and luminous swimmer to rise in the black water, to hook one fearsome hand over the gunwale and then another, to tip this small boat and spill her out of it—or slither aboard in all its hideous rampancy.

That neither Francesca nor Raleigh had warned Sarah to flee with their daughter to the mainland either confirms their narcissism and arrogance or reveals beyond debate that they were incapable of the affection that a parent should have for a child. Or both. They must have been so certain of their genius and their capacity to handle any crisis that they could not conceive of screwing up in a matter as crucial as preventing Moloch or any of its fusions with animals from escaping Ringrock. And once they had done exactly that, when they realized that doom was descending on them, were they drunk with a potent cocktail of self-esteem and despair, so lacking in sobriety that the fate of their only child was of no concern to them? What good is genius without humility? What value does it have if it isn't married undivorceable to kindness and empathy?

If she dies in this lake, she will be neither the first nor the last to have been lost in its depths. She has read much about death in novels as different from each other as *Little Women* is different from *Murder on the Orient Express*. Often she has considered her own death, the world in her absence, how those who had known her would be affected, if at all. There have been occasions—Sarah away on vacation; her substitute, Marge, off glowering by herself; Libby sitting on the veranda with her parents—when she has felt as if she'd died without realizing it and now occupied her porch chair as a ghost, unseen and unsuspected. Francesca and Raleigh always had much to say to each other—issues to discuss, theories to debate, career plans to develop, rivalries with others in their field to fume about—but they didn't know how to talk to children. Indeed, they seemed to think it wasn't necessary to descend to the simple and tedious interests of the young if the child in question was a good listener and could be socialized by attending quietly to the wise conversation of her elders. With her parents gone, by their deaths having earned her pity though not her grief, and with extreme peril awakening her to the full realization of who she has become, Libby knows that their indifference motivated her to be what they were not, to have what they would not give. Rather than fade away forever on the veranda, she's become more vivid, determined to immerse herself in the wonders of the world and delight in all that it has to offer. If she dies in this lake, she will be neither the first nor the last to be lost in its depths, *but she is not going to die here, not tonight, not tomorrow, not here or anywhere, at least not for a long, long time.* Although her arm aches, she holds fast to the steering control, the vibrations of the engine humming in her bones. Each time the boat slams into the chop rather than cleaving through it, she reacts to the impact not as if it might damage the vessel, but as if it is a thrill she'd happily pay for if this were a carnival ride. In the grace of this new understanding of herself, Libby yells into the wind and rain and dark. This isn't a scream of fear, but a shout of exhilaration, a defiant challenge to the storm and whatever leviathan might live in the lake, a refusal to succumb to any of the dire fates that the masters of Ringrock might intend to impose on her.

Through veils of rain, pale lights appear at an elevation above the lake—the windows of the house on Jacob's Ladder. At last the storm has something to illuminate. The boathouse is reconstructed out of the night. After its walls are painted by lightning and the sky goes dark once more, the structure has been revealed to the eye, and it remains visible as ghostly architecture.

At first, Libby intends to run the boat onto the beach, though that will likely damage the skeg, propeller, anti-cavitation plate, and driveshaft. Prudence counsels her that the pier offers another option. It is of unusual construction, one flank integrated into the masonry of the boathouse, which is built of stone, the outer length supported by a line of concrete pilings, which leaves a wider space underneath than there would be if two rows of pilings had been used.

She aims for the shelter under the pier, lets up on the throttle, and kills the engine, allowing momentum to carry her between the pilings and the stone wall. The vessel travels two-thirds of the length of the pier before wallowing to a stop and bumping against the pilings. The wave action in this shelter is minimal; the boat won't be damaged. She isn't likely to need it, but you never know. She uses the aft belaying rope to lash the craft to one of the concrete posts, and then she crouches forward to the bow to use a second line to secure it to another piling.

She settles on the passenger thwart, retrieves the shotgun from under it, and sits with the weapon across her thighs, taking deep breaths of air that smells of wet stone, wet wood, lingering boat exhaust, and dead fish. During the previous night, fish had washed up on Oak Haven, killed by the depth charges dropped off Ringrock yesterday afternoon. Evidently, similar marine carrion floated here, and the gulls failed to discover the portion of the smorgasbord that settled under the pier rather than on the beach.

Tipping her head back, blinking at the dark underside of the pier, breathing the air that streams in between the pilings and is marginally less offensive than that closer to the water, she collects her thoughts. She must convince the woman who lives here that a thing not of this world now rules Ringrock, that it has extended its dominion to Oak Haven, and that they must use her cabin cruiser to get safely to the mainland as quickly as possible. Considering the granular detail of the story she has to tell, that she has risked her life to come here in this weather, and that her audience will have witnessed the dropping of the depth charges, Libby hopes she will be believed. She needs to take a minute to figure out how to make the truth sound like the truth rather than like bullshit. Her story is, after all, fantastical. Her situation would be a lot better if she'd been able to bring Francesca's laptop. But all she has to sell her story are a direct stare, a sober demeanor, and whatever skills of narration she has absorbed from reading a few hundred novels.

Without further delay, she swings over the starboard gunwale with the shotgun held high in her right hand. Although she's close to the underside of the pier steps, which means she's close to the shore, she has no way of knowing how deep the water will be—maybe two feet, maybe six. It's up to her knees. Shotgun in both hands now, she wades forward, water sloshing noisily. Soft somethings bump against her, which she assumes are rotting fish. She steps to the left between the last two pilings, out from under the pier, onto a pebbled beach, into the clean-smelling wind.

Jacob's Ladder sits much higher in the water than Oak Haven, which slopes gently to its shore. The house is on a bluff, accessed by a set of stairs. Libby is on the second tread before she realizes someone is standing on the top stair, a human form nearly as dark as the night. Lightning cascades down mountains of black clouds, but it is in the northwest, far behind the figure on the stairs; therefore, it reveals no details, presents only a silhouette that might be that of either a man or a woman.

THE WHY OF IT

Carrying the AR-15, Katie patrols the house room by room, window by window, again and again. The residence has always been small. However, as she makes her rounds, the place seems to shrink, as if the structure is a pocket universe, with nothing but a void beyond its walls, as though this universe of hers is in a state of collapse, certain to close around her and become one room, that room then growing ever smaller, until eventually it is no longer a place for the living, but a home for the dead, precisely the dimensions of a coffin, in which she will cease to be able to breathe.

This claustrophobia is familiar, having afflicted her now and then following Avi's death, when her parents had been buried, when her husband and daughters existed only as memories and as ashes in urns. Alone in their house in California, she had at times felt as if the air were being sucked out of those rooms; she desperately needed to get outside, onto a patio, into the yard, to be able to fill her lungs. She suffered nightmares in which, though the house didn't shrink, the windows became as small as postage stamps, the doors no bigger than postcards, so that she could not escape.

Now, as she walks the residence on Jacob's Ladder, her distress has the same cause. It isn't grief or loneliness or fear that makes her feel as though she is being encased and crushed and smothered by the very place that should be a nurturing refuge. In fact, the sense of being weighed down and compressed to destruction has nothing to do with the house. Nor is it mostly related to the strangeness of recent events and the threat embodied in them. As always when this phobic reaction overtakes her, the cause is largely the same—her inability to understand *why*. *What* is happening matters to her less than *why*, because what happened is always known sooner or later, but the why of it, the true reason why, is often not revealed. And as long as the *why* remains a mystery, the *what* will surely happen again and again; there will never be any relief from it.

She is in her studio when the sound that is not thunder, the low rumbling, trembles through the house. This time, she is sure it comes from the cellar. She stares at the floor for a minute, until the sound fades, and then she continues her restless patrol.

Why? Why do the authorities allow the criminal gangs that terrorize neighborhoods and entire cities to thrive as they do? Politicians, attorneys general, district attorneys, and the FBI have the power to destroy the gangs and prevent most of the crimes they commit, the murdering and raping and human trafficking and the endless flood of drugs across the border, *the hateful murdering murdering murdering of faithful husbands and little girls in their Sunday dresses.* Yet the people with the power to stop men like Hamal and Lupo and Parker often facilitate their activities. Maybe the majority of politicians and their appointees are corrupt, but not all. Are those uncorrupted individuals so often ineffective because they are cowards or lazy or stupid? Does loyalty to party, class, club, or ideology matter to them more than doing what is right? Why? Why can't such people see that the crime and anarchy they permit to flourish in poor and middle-class neighborhoods will eventually metastasize into the enclaves of the elite where they live their privileged lives? Why do they have contempt for those not in their circle? Why can't they see that being *of* the people rather than ruling *over* them is the only way that they themselves will survive?

Katie is in the hallway when from the cellar come a crash and protracted clatter, as though something is shaking the supplies off the shelves down there. The commotion subsides into silence, and she continues to the kitchen. The house isn't really shrinking, but her options are, which exacerbates her claustrophobia. Until now, the choice has been hers to stay here or brave the night, but if what lives below decides to ascend and she can't defend against it, her only choice will be the night.

Whatever horror has been unleashed on Ringrock, it will prove to be the work of a "better class" of people, highly educated and sophisticated, but in one lethal respect alike to Hamal and Lupo and Parker, infected with the same grotesquely high self-esteem common to psychotic gangsters, with the same arrogance, with the same lack of humility and empathy, with the same dangerous incapacity for self-reflection. Although she doesn't yet know what has happened on Ringrock, she knows the kind of people who have done it. Even when she knows *what*, there will be no satisfying *why*. The thing that scares her the most, brings the walls in around her and lowers the ceiling, is that the people who pursued this reckless course and took inadequate precautions will have an explanation of their actions—the why—that will seem lunatic to all sane men and women. They won't examine their consciences to find their true motivations, for their self-image is only an image; no substance under it exists to be probed. They'll learn nothing from catastrophe.

The dread of facing some enemy unknown and unknowable, the strangeness and extreme nature of the threat, and the immediacy of it bring her to a point when she will either crack or experience a satori, a sudden enlightenment that might relieve her stress. She does not crack. Childless and widowed, to cope with her losses, she has sought—irrationally, she now realizes—to understand evil, even to concretize it in a visual metaphor within a painting that says to the mind and heart, *This is why.* Now she arrives at the realization that the *why* of evil is not to be found anywhere in the flaws of society or its institutions, nor can it be pinned down by even the most erudite and loquacious philosopher. The why of evil is in the human soul, which can't be examined with a CT scan or MRI to locate a dark mass, or dissected in an autopsy to learn in what artery the calcification proved mortal. Evil is a mystery for theologians, of which she is not one. Evil is irrational. There is no *why* formed so complete that it will satisfy her. Rather than spend her life in a fruitless effort to understand evil and those who commit it, she can do no more—and no less—than resist it. She'd taken it upon herself to view the Promise as having two parts—to live and to understand the why of what happened. Now she realizes that the second part is to resist.

When once again Katie enters the kitchen, the fox has moved from the sofa cushion to one of the dining chairs, where he sits alert, as he had been when she'd flooded the sink with bleach and drain cleaner. Perhaps the noise in the cellar convinces him that he is safer when he is at a distance from the floor.

At the sight of Michael J., Katie finds it easier to breathe. If the ceiling had lowered, now it rises to its former height, and the walls no longer seem to be closing in on her.

"When all this is behind us," she says, "I want to paint your portrait, Mr. Fox. Not from memory, either, but from life. Stay with me, trust me."

THE DEVIL OF THE STAIRS

When lightning steps down the clouds again, details of the figure at the head of the stairs remain unexposed, though judging by the silhouette, Libby is pretty sure it's a man. She's been under the impression that the woman she saw on Jacob's Ladder lives here alone. Maybe she's mistaken. The guy up there appears to be looking toward her. Although the night is deeply dark, he must see her directly below him, but he doesn't ask who she is or why she's here.

Libby takes the initiative, raising her voice to compete with the wind and rain. "I've come over from Oak Haven. My name's Libby."

He doesn't answer or move, just stands like a totem carved out of stone by a superstitious sculptor who placed him there to ward off the spirits of those who drowned in the lake.

"I need to get to the mainland," she shouts. "I can't make it there in my small runabout."

Still he says nothing, though he raises his arms and, once more backlighted by the storm, seems to mimic the pulling of ropes, as if to ring a carillon of cathedral bells like the hunchback in that old movie about Notre Dame that Sarah enjoyed so much.

Maybe he's drunk or of diminished mental capacity, which would explain why he's out in the storm. His silhouette suggests that he isn't wearing a rain slicker.

Libby can't stand here, shouting about Ringrock and monsters, and expect to be convincing. She climbs another step.

The man speaks but without sufficient force to be heard above the skirling wind.

"I can't hear you," she shouts.

He ceases pulling nonexistent ropes and raises his voice. "Mother? Mother, is that you?"

"No," she calls back. "I'm from the nearest other island. Your neighbor. I need help."

He repeats her last three words. "I need help. I need help. Show me the way, Mother. Are you there, Mother?"

"I'm not your mother," she shouts. "I'm just a girl."

"What's happened to Mother? Help me find Mother." Gesticulating agitatedly, as though thrashing at a cloud of annoying horseflies, he turns from the steps and moves away along the bluff.

In this tempest, the stairs are also a spillway, rivulets drizzling from tread to tread. Libby splashes to the top and glances toward the small, stone house.

When the stranger begins to call out anew to his mother, there's such desperation in his voice that Libby decides she has arrived in the middle of a crisis. The best thing she can do is assist in the search. The sooner they find the missing woman, the sooner this man might be persuaded to take her to the mainland.

Following him, she asks, "What's her name, your mother's name?"

He might indeed be drunk, for he lurches as if shoved this way and that by unseen tormentors. The wind is strong, but not powerful enough to stagger him. He halts and executes a stumbling turn, with the evident intent of returning the way he came. Instead, he grasps his head with both hands and, still the shadow of a man, drops to his knees, issuing an animal bleat of terrible pain and mental anguish, a sound beyond the capacity of a human voice.

As Libby halts ten or twelve feet from him, storm light breaks directly over them, a series of revelatory flashes. His hands are as white as fish bellies, the fingers darkening from first knuckle to nail; the nails are in fact talons that claw blood from the mottled skin of his hairless scalp. His face is more human than not, though the bone and flesh are being worked subtly and ceaselessly, as if by some cruel god who finishes designing his creatures only after first instilling life in them, so that they may understand they are born to everlasting agony and will not be permitted to entertain any illusions of grace and hope.

Because of the time that she spent with Raleigh's laptop, Libby knows what kneels before her. Some fusions are more successful than others, though all eventually fail in a day or two, resulting in the spawning that produces short-lived offspring. The vicious spawn either die within an hour or two, before having a chance to fuse with another life-form, or they find prey, whereupon this secondary fusion fails even more spectacularly than did the primary fusion. This hideosity before her is a primary fusion, part human and part Moloch, that has stalled in the process of combining. Countless lab animals—rats, dogs, chimps—perish one way or another after being exposed to Moloch cells, and one in five is condemned to this condition of incomplete combination, when the Moloch cells are for some reason inhibited from achieving complete integration with a host. This man, whoever he might have been, is a few hours—or perhaps a few minutes—from death.

A bolt bright enough to be the announcement of the world's end shears away the darkness and summons the fusion to its feet.

In the flare, Libby sees that one of its eyes is blue and human, the other black with an elliptical red iris like nothing on Earth. It lurches toward her, and she stumbles back, bringing up the shotgun, as the thing rapidly repeats an obscenity, demanding copulation, by which it means not sex but the melting together of their flesh, blood, and bone. She squeezes the trigger, and the recoil-reduction technology proves as effective as Sarah promised. Backing away, Libby fires again, and the fusion collapses, convulsing on the sodden ground. She is so close—easing closer to administer a third dose of buckshot—that she can see the skull swelling and shifting into inhuman shapes, the features being ceaselessly remade into what, in better light, would be a gallery of freak-show faces. She squeezes off a third shot, and the thing bucks with the impact. It thrashes off its back, onto all fours, crawling away from her, a thin keening issuing from it, and she dares to follow, firing the last round in the gun. The fusion collapses again, spasms violently, and then lies still, facedown in the wet grass and the mud.

Libby is sobbing with fright, with the recognition that this could be her last night in the world. There are no rounds left in the shotgun. She unzips a pocket of her windbreaker and fishes a shell from it. Her hands are shaking, and she cautions herself that the ammunition is precious.

If the damn thing is dead, it perished because of the anarchy inherent in its alien cells. If it is dead, Libby doesn't credit the shotgun, which at best might have hastened the creature's demise by a few minutes. *If it is dead.* According to Raleigh, Moloch itself, said to be securely contained on Ringrock, is immortal, a mass of dense but protean tissue, but for whatever reasons, the fusions cannot sustain. They die, they rot, and they do not rise again.

With her gaze fixed on the dark mass huddled on the darker ground, she slides a round into the breach. She transfers three more shells from jacket to magazine, then zippers shut the pocket.

Her ears ringing from the gunshots, she retreats a few steps before daring to look away from the fusion. Having stifled her sobs, she strives now to breathe less noisily, as she scans the night. If one carrier of Moloch has found its way to Jacob's Ladder, she can't rule out the presence of another.

The collapsed fusion doesn't move, doesn't move, rain beating on it as another minute passes. It lies silent and motionless, in whatever grotesque configuration it fashioned of itself during its last moments.

Libby looks at the house. The windows aglow with shade-filtered light had filled her with hope as she'd piloted the runabout toward the pier. Now she wonders what waits in there and what she risks by knocking on the door.

She considers going to the boathouse. Unlike the larger cabin cruiser at Oak Haven, the one here appears—at least at a distance— to have an inboard-outboard engine that, if she's lucky, will allow her to get it moving with a starter rope. It might even have simple electronic navigation gear, but if it doesn't, it'll have at least a compass mounted atop the control console. Even in this storm, she can find her way to the mainland with a compass.

Stealing the boat might be justified if she knew for certain that the woman in the house is no longer who she previously was, that she's become a fusion like Francesca, still passing for human but about to go into meltdown. However, if the woman is not one of *them*, then stealing her boat will be condemning her to death when the military moves against Moloch on Ringrock, as Sarah said they surely will before midnight, maybe sooner. Midnight is little more than two and a half hours from now, and sooner is—sooner.

If Libby takes the boat, she's saying it's all about her, just as her parents felt it was all about them, genius without empathy, without humility. And what did that get them other than dead?

Maybe the good die young, like they say, but who wants to die knowing she's treated other people like shit? Besides, no one lives forever, except perhaps Moloch, and who in her right mind wants to be that creepy bastard?

A KNOCK ON THE DOOR

A low, protracted rumbling rises from the cellar again. Katie feels it underfoot as well as hears it. Michael J. leans over the arm of his chair to stare at the floor. Vibrations clink glassware against glassware in a kitchen cabinet, and flatware rattles in a drawer.

No sooner has that phenomenon passed than Katie thinks she hears voices in the storm, one female and one male, shouting at each other, but she can't make out any words. Some nights, the wind talks in the fireplace flues, and it sounds like people in the distance, which is maybe the case now. She stoops at the kitchen firebox and reaches into it and briefly opens the damper, but she doesn't hear anything definitive. She listens at a kitchen window without putting up the pleated shade and opening the casement panes. From his perch in the dining chair, the fox watches her, but because his ears are by their nature always pricked, Katie isn't able to tell if he hears anything other than the storm raging.

The gunfire that follows the voices is unquestionably what it is, and confirms that the voices were not the wind's deception. Judging by the sound, she deems it a shotgun. In whose hands, she can't imagine. Zenon and Rice were armed with rifles and pistols.

Four rounds from the weapon suggest that if someone is dead, he wasn't easy to kill.

Katie waits for what might come next, and after a few minutes, a knock comes on the door, a hard rapid pounding, perhaps produced by the butt of a weapon.

Wary that someone might shoot out one or both of the deadbolts and fill the hallway with shrapnel, Katie sidles toward the door with her back against the wall, presenting as low a profile as possible. She reaches her studio and steps into the open doorway, out of the line of fire. After another series of loud knocks, when the visitor proves persistent, Katie calls out, "Who is it?"

The thick ironbound oak muffles the voice, but the words are clear enough to be understood. "My name's Libby. I came from Oak Haven. The island nearest yours."

She sounds young and afraid. She sounds sincere. She might be none of that.

"What do you want?" Katie shouts.

"Help. I need help."

"What help?"

"To get to the mainland. Before it's too late."

Trust is often answered with deceit. Such is the nature of the world in its long unbecoming.

"Please," the girl pleads in response to Katie's silence.

"What was that shooting?"

"I killed a man."

"What man?"

"He would've raped me. Killed me. Worse."

Rain is falling now; it had stopped falling that Sunday morning, outside the ice cream shop, where it puddled the pavement.

"How old are you?"

"Fourteen. You've seen me. We waved at each other."

The *tick-tick-tick* of claws on the wood floor. The fox has ventured forward from the kitchen. He looks up at Katie.

"You do cartwheels on the lawn," Katie says.

"You paint. I've seen you with an easel on your pier."

233

Considering the mysterious nature of this world, Katie wonders if it might be possible that this girl is the spiritual cognate of one of her daughters, brought here so that Katie can do for her what she couldn't do for her beloved Penny and Regina, and by so doing begin to better fulfill the Promise that she had made to Avi.

She returns to the hall, moves past the fox to the door. "I'm letting you in."

"Thank God. Thank you."

Disengaging the first deadbolt, Katie says, "I have a gun."

The girl says, "I won't put mine down."

"How stupid if we shot each other."

"I'll put it down when I know you're human."

Katie hesitates with her fingers on the thumb turn of the second deadbolt. *When I know you're human.* During the past thirty hours or so, her imagination has ventured into territory that she has never previously explored, and now it leads her onto a path darker than those before it. She unlocks the door and backs off a few steps. With the AR-15 held at the ready, she says, "All right. Come in, Libby."

The door opens, and the girl crosses the threshold, holding a pistol-grip shotgun in both hands. She's wearing a waterproof jacket but is otherwise soaked. Pale. Shivering. If a fever of fear sings in her mental wires, her expression is nevertheless one of resolve, her jaws clenched, lips compressed, eyes narrow with suspicion.

The girl doesn't use a hand to close the door, but shoves it shut with her body and stands with her back against it. "What's your name?"

"Kate. People call me Katie. Or they used to."

"That's a fox."

"Not just any fox. His name's Michael J."

"You have a fox for a pet?"

"He's not a pet."

"Then what is he? He seems tame."

"He wanted inside because he's afraid of what's out there. I suspect he knows more about it than I do, since I know little more than nothing."

"I know too much," the girl says.

"Then come to the kitchen and tell me." Katie lowers the AR-15, not because she is confident that the girl is incapable of deceit, but because she cannot kill a child. If Libby is not what she seems, then Katie will be riddled with buckshot and follow her family to the grave. To die rather than kill a child is not a failure to keep the Promise, but an honoring of it. Those who murder children have killed their own souls and exist rather than live, and neither live nor exist in any world to come.

Lowering the shotgun, Libby says, "We're running out of time. We can't stay here. I'll tell you everything I know on the way to the mainland or when we get there. My runabout has no compass, too little fuel. Your cabin cruiser is what we need."

"It's no use to us. It's disabled."

The girl looks stricken. "Disabled how?"

"Someone wanted to be sure I couldn't use it, took the engine. Maybe the man you shot, though there were two who put ashore here this morning, ISA agents."

The girl shakes her head. Her wet hair flings off raindrops. "But we've got to get out of here, to the mainland, or we'll die. I'm not sure if even that's far enough."

Katie goes to her and puts an arm around her and leads her, preceded by the fox, into the kitchen. "If we're out of time, we're out of it together, and at least not each alone. But one thing I know—just when you think it's over for you, it isn't."

RALEIGH ANSWERS RALEIGH

Six Years before the Crisis on Ringrock

From his personal archives as preserved in a high-security cloud account:

> Herewith, I will provide answers to the three primary questions that I previously posed. I will use the simplest possible language, in the interest of informing the general public (when security on the project is lifted)—as well as some among my colleagues who embrace unsupportable theories with the tenacity of ticks.

> Considering its talent for engineering complex hybrid living systems at a pace faster than God is purported to have taken to populate the Earth with its vast zoology, why isn't Moloch the only life-form in the universe?

> The answer has three parts.

> First, the universe must be even more fecund than we have imagined in our wildest dreams, with an infinite number of planets that support life. In an infinite-worlds scenario, an entity like Moloch could

spend eternity conquering a planet every year or two and never half finish the job.

Second, Moloch is a builder of biological civilizations, not necessarily technological ones. Consider how it travels across the light-years—not in a ship, but armored in its incredible shell, deep in a condition of stasis, apparently drifting as the solar winds and other forces either push or pull it, dreaming away the centuries. As such, it might encounter an inhabited planet only once every few thousand years.

Third, if Moloch is intelligent—an issue that may never be resolved—its intelligence is far, far different from ours. For one thing, as perhaps a unique organism, alone of its kind, it has no language and needs none. It is a different order of being from us. Humanity finds purpose mostly in conquering one thing or another—territory, other people, the many limitations of nature, ignorance. If intelligent, Moloch might have no interest in conquering worlds. Although it seems to be a predator and conqueror, the entity's purpose might be something else entirely, which I will address quite satisfactorily below.

Next question: Instead of merely consuming other life-forms, why does Moloch attempt to combine with them and create hybrid creatures?

The answer has two parts.

First, as previously noted, Moloch is able to feed on energy—light, heat, gravity—and create matter from it. Therefore, it never needs to consume other creatures. *And it does not consume them*, despite appearances to the contrary, per the following paragraph.

Second, Moloch is an incredibly condensed data-storage system of astonishing capacity, carrying in its flesh the DNA of perhaps millions of species from an unknowable number of planets. After almost seven years of study, I'm confident to declare that we should think of this entity in unconventional ways, and in addition to the two that follow, I invite other hypotheses by those of you who can exercise their imaginations on more than a superficial level.

Consider that Moloch (a name that needs reconsideration) might be a biological librarian, combining with other species only for the purpose of fully understanding the genome of each and storing it for posterity. Or perhaps it is a visual artist that takes as its sole purpose and satisfaction the creation of art, by which I mean the myriad hybrids it is capable of engineering. It is both artist and audience, which makes it among those most superlative of artists who create not to please critics or collectors, but for no other purpose than to make art.

The hybrids might be horrific to us, but wise men have long noted that beauty is in the eye of the beholder. In that case, Moloch (such an unfortunate name) is both the maker and the most sophisticated beholder of its art. Again, think outside the box.

Next question: Why, for all its engineering power, does it fail, creating only freakish, violent entities that ultimately collapse?

I can see three possible answers.

First, assuming it's a biological librarian, then perhaps it intends only to copy the genome of the specimen and telemetrically transmit the data to the mother mass in the shell. The hybrid then is nothing more than the mechanism by which this is accomplished. There is no intent for the hybrid to live past completion of its purpose. This requires us to assume that it has no moral compunction regarding the destruction of even intelligent specimens; but we need also to consider that by its standards, we do not seem intelligent.

Second, if it is creating art, then like many artists, Moloch may have a tendency to nihilism. Its intention might be to express, with irony, the meaninglessness of existence.

Third, if it's in fact tens of millions of years old, as the carbon dating of its shell and certain tests of its protean tissue tell us it is, who is to say that it has not gone senile? Or even insane. Unlike scientists, artists do go mad with some frequency—cutting off their ears, biting on shotgun barrels, murdering their mistresses, and so forth. I am attaching herewith a lengthy list of painters, sculptors, musicians, writers, filmmakers, and actors who have either been committed to psychiatric wards at various times, been sent for the remainder of their lives to sanitoriums and asylums, been sequestered by their embarrassed families, or have committed suicide while leaving incomprehensible notes that prove their minds were deeply unsound.

I invite the more imaginative members of the team to conceive of other purposes, no matter how exotic, that Moloch might have.

Although I have written much of insight in this journal, I am certain that I have only begun to record discoveries of immense importance involving Moloch. As we peel the onion of this entity's singular biology, we will eventually learn how to control our own biology, defeating cancer and all disease, and put an end to aging. Moloch (potentially Proteus) is our doorway to immortality.

AN EXCHANGE IN THE HALLWAY

The fox pads into the kitchen, but Libby halts and shrugs off Katie's gentling hand. Her face has lost what little color it had when she came in from the night, her skin is now alabaster and her eyes, by contrast, are midnight-blue.

"You don't understand. The mother mass is on Ringrock. That's what they have to hit. Take it out, take it out hard, and the theory is all the fusions die with it."

"Honey, this is Greek to me. Mother mass? Fusions?"

The girl urgently asserts additional concerns no less cryptic than the reference to a mother mass. "The fusions are linked to it by microwaves, like psychic or something. Maybe to kill them, you gotta overload the mother mass, fry the shit out of it."

Katie shakes her head. "I don't—"

"There's a nuke on Ringrock. It can be triggered remotely. They'll vaporize the place, everything on the island."

"How can you know—"

"My parents worked there!" Libby says impatiently. "They were scientists on the stupid project. They're dead, as good as dead, worse than dead."

The girl's earnestness and her near panic sell her warning. As incredible as it is, as shocking as it is, Katie doesn't doubt her.

"When?" she asks.

"I don't know. How would I know? At the latest—midnight. Maybe an hour from now, ten minutes, maybe *now*."

Jacob's Ladder is suddenly a more appropriate name for this island than it had been a minute ago. "We're two miles away."

"It's a big fucking nuke! Even the idiots who said they weren't afraid of the thing were scared crazy of it, so they planted the nuke. The mainland might be far enough to be safe, mostly safe, but not so much here, not Oak Haven. We're probably in the blast zone."

"I need to know everything you know."

"There isn't time, Katie. Your boat is everything."

"But it doesn't have an engine."

"Oh, God. Jesus, I don't want to die."

Katie props her AR-15 against the wall and grips Libby by both shoulders. "Panic will get us killed, honey. Panic quicker than the bomb." She pulls the girl into a hug. "You've got the right stuff. You're not the kind who panics. Stay with me, stay calm, and we'll get through this together. I don't give up, Libby. Are you someone who gives up? Are you a quitter?"

"No."

"Say, 'Hell no.'"

"Hell no."

"Say 'No, hell no, shit no, fuck no, I'll never back down.'"

Libby says it, and Katie lets go of her, and they look at each other, and a shudder of laughter escapes the girl, dark laughter but laughter nonetheless. "That was nuts."

"Totally," Katie says. "Come on. The kitchen. Let's do this."

SIX
BRINK

COFFEE

The night is replete with monstrosities slouching through the storm to what purpose none but they can know, and the little stone house, her refuge, is haunted by some basement dweller that, when it chooses to reveal itself, will be nothing as benign as a ghost. If the entire world is not on the brink of cataclysm, Katie and this young girl, this orphan, are balanced on the edge of an abyss, with no apparent way to bridge across it to safety. They need clarity of mind, focus, and luck; although coffee can't provide the third, it will help with the first two. They don't want a single-cup hazelnut or cinnamon-roll brew, no decaf, but a full pot of the real stuff, taken black, as Libby says she has taken it since she was seven, as Katie has drunk it since the days immediately after her family was ripped from her, when she strove to avoid sleep because of the nightmares that came with it.

When the coffee is ready and they are sitting at the table with full mugs, in the company of the inquisitive fox, which watches them with an inscrutable expression, Libby continues. "Anyway, Sarah's real name was Shelly Framington."

"An astronaut."

"Yeah. She was the commander of the International Space Station when the thing was found. She argued they should bring it back on the shuttle, got ground-control authority for that. They thought it was an alien artifact, which was a big deal. It wasn't something that could be studied in one of the space station modules. They isolated it on Ringrock, studied it for months before they knew a living thing was in it. I read about it on Raleigh's laptop, scared the bejesus out of me, but I didn't know Sarah was really Shelly Framington. She told me tonight, just before . . . before she died."

SIX YEARS BEFORE THE CRISIS ON RINGROCK

Raleigh Summarizes the Discovery of the Artifact

From his personal archives as preserved in a high-security cloud account:

> Although Air Force Lt. Colonel Shelly Framington, a former fighter pilot and subsequently an astronaut, underwent a three-day debriefing, I feel it is incumbent upon me to synthesize from her exhaustive testimony a simple abstract of the basic facts. This is unfortunately necessary because it has become clear that some who are involved in this project will seize upon insignificant details and inflate their importance in order to support hypotheses that are not in consensus with what most of us have determined after intense study of the alien artifact. As I and my wife were appointed by the president of the United States to plan and manage this most historic investigation, it is within my authority to ensure that the record is not muddied.
>
> As commander of the International Space Station, nearing the end of a six-month tour, Lt. Colonel Framington was, on the morning of the find,

informed that at some point during the night a siz-
able object of undetermined nature had lodged
between the large solar arrays nearest Node 3, the
module named *Tranquility.* This module contains
environmental control systems, life support systems, a toilet, and exercise equipment. The object
in question had somehow escaped radar detection
while incoming, and no alarm had sounded. There
appeared to be no damage to the solar arrays.

Attached to *Tranquility* is that module named
Cupola, which was installed in 2010. It provides seven windows from which the ISS can be
observed in its entirety. From *Cupola,* Commander
Framington saw an ellipsoidal object that would
eventually prove to be five feet six inches long and,
at its widest point, would have a diameter of three
feet four inches. Judging by all appearances, she
believed it was not natural in origin.

Commander Framington and a Russian astronaut,
Yuri Rogozin, conducted a spacewalk to examine
the object. On close inspection, they found it to
be pure white, as smooth as glass, of a material
not easily identifiable, with no signs of machining
or joinery, bearing no insignia or other indication
of national origin. Dust grains, traveling through
space at seventy miles per second, will over time
abrade any surface—but not this one. Framington
and Rogozin agreed that this was neither a natural

object nor space junk. There was every reason to believe it was an artificial construct produced by a highly advanced civilization. The object seemed less to be wedged in a gap between solar arrays than to be holding there by the exertion of some power such as magnetism, as though it might not have been adrift but might have homed on the space station. Nevertheless, Framington and Rogozin decided (rightly and bravely, in my estimation) to bring the object aboard via the airlock in Node 3.

After initial examination of the object in that laboratory module named *Destiny*, Commander Framington, to her great credit, lobbied most effectively that the artifact—at that time, informally referred to as "the melon" because of its shape—should be brought to Earth to be studied at a high-security facility. There were the usual negative voices, those skeptical of progress in general, who would have scientists restrain their curiosity and proceed at the sluggish pace of bureaucrats. They were not permitted to obstruct this great and valuable enterprise.

Days were spent as well in arguments over to which country the melon would be delivered and where it would be most safely studied. Ringrock Island was selected; a secret level-four biological lab engaged in researching defenses against bioweapons, it was rapidly retrofitted for this new purpose, and a team of scientists from nine countries was selected for the project. Commander Framington and the crew of the ISS were to keep the melon under constant observation for twenty days, when the next supply shuttle would arrive at the ISS from Earth and be able to transport the object. During those twenty days, the melon was as inert as stone.

With care, it was transferred to Ringrock and placed in an airtight containment lab, in a room within that room, an "isolation box" with bulletproof glass walls. Thereafter, it was handled only by wheeled robots with highly articulated hands, guided by scientists outside the isolation box.

The most intense scientific inquiry in all history proceeded initially under the justifiable theory that what we might have was essentially a large envelope, a message from the stars, containing samples of the music, art, and languages of another world, similar to what NASA sent into space as an introduction to civilization on Earth, with the hope it would in time be found by an intelligent species more advanced than humanity. Perhaps the melon would contain a star map, showing the galactic location of their planet, like the one NASA included in its good-will vessel.

We soon discovered that the melon absorbed heat and apparently used that energy to some purpose;

the only thing we could detect issuing from the object was a continually emitted stream of protons representing a mere fraction of the energy it took in. Now, after seven months of exciting discoveries, we have learned that beneath the six-inch-thick all-but-impervious "rind" of the melon is a hollow core containing matter of less density, as yet unidentified. We believe this is indeed a gift from an advanced civilization, even perhaps including all their scientific knowledge and technology. If we can discover how to reach this core and access the trove of data it likely contains, it could provide us with centuries of advances in but one year. I am convinced that those of us on this project will give birth to a new world of marvels and wonders.

MOLOCH

After fifteen intense minutes of mutual revelations, the girl can't sit still any longer. She gets up, moves around, the coffee mug held in both hands, as though she needs the warmth of it more than the caffeine.

Remaining in his chair, Michael J. turns his head to follow Libby wherever she goes.

"Only two scientists worked with the melon, the artifact, at any one time."

"Limiting risk," Katie guesses.

"Yeah. When they left the lab, they took four total-immersion baths in antimicrobe and antifungal solutions, submitted to long-wave radiation—whatever that is. They never went in the big glass-walled quarantine box, yet they wore face masks and breathed bottled air, so exogenous microbes wouldn't escape the lab."

"Exogenous?" Katie asks.

"Not native to the Earth. So eventually, when they figured out that the rind was six inches thick, they decided to breach it, get to the inside of the melon."

"With what?"

"Diamond drills, lasers. I don't know what all. Nothing had any effect. Then, after all those months, a hole just appeared in it."

"A hole. Appeared how?" Katie asks.

"It opened on its own, like from smaller than a pinhole to an inch in diameter, and a sort of worm came out."

"Sort of?"

"Wasn't really a worm. Later they called it 'amorphous tissue,' like living clay, about eighteen inches long, ready to be . . . well, whatever it wanted. It coiled like a snake does and waited."

"Waited for what?"

"For the big-brain experts to do something, I guess."

"What did they do?"

Libby stands looking down at the fox, and Michael J. meets her stare. She says quietly, "Everything's hanging by a thread."

"What did they do?" Katie presses.

Moving again, Libby says, "Through the transfer airlock, they put a rat into the quarantine box. The worm morphed into something that scared the piss out of everyone, something they never saw before and never wanted to see again. There wasn't any video on Raleigh's laptop like there must be in the main project files. They eventually called the thing 'Teratism One,' meaning *monster number one*. It went after the rat and combined with it."

"Combined?"

"So fast they could hardly believe it was happening, Teratism One flowed into the rat. For a minute or two, it was just a rat, but then the teratism and the rat became something that was a hybrid, a little like each of them, and even more hideous."

"They should have been ready to flood the damn quarantine box with cyanide gas or the strongest possible nitric acid, something."

"They weren't. The hybrid went into a frenzy, throwing itself at the bulletproof-glass walls, for like a few minutes, and then it scuttled back to the melon—which was really a shell—became like a worm again, slithered into the hole to rejoin the mother mass, and the hole closed up."

"They kept the project going six more years after that?"

"The shock wore off quick. The possibilities excited them."

"*Excited?* They ought to have been freaking terrified."

"A few were. After a year of more experiments, four researchers demanded the project be terminated and Moloch destroyed."

"Moloch?"

"That's a demon or god that ate children. They thought it was a cool name for the thing."

"Cool? Jesus, were these scientists thirteen years old?"

"Raleigh wanted to name it Proteus—"

"Classical myth. The sea god who could change shapes."

"On Ringrock they call it Moloch. If anyone there is still alive."

RALEIGH RECEIVES THE DEMAND

Five Years and Five Months before the Crisis

From his personal archives as preserved in a high-security cloud account:

> The same four resolute reactionaries who have been a thorn in our side from the beginning have now dropped what they believe is a bomb that will unseat me from authority and lead to the termination of the project. Choosing not to discuss the matter with me, these nervous Nellies circulated their foolish document to everyone on Ringrock and to those in government with security clearance and knowledge of our work, including the president and his wife.

We, the undersigned, herewith demand the immediate cessation of current research and the establishment of a committee to urgently determine the safest means by which to destroy or otherwise dispose of the extraterrestrial entity known to us as Moloch and currently held in an inadequately secure laboratory on Ringrock Island. Moloch is an entity of amorphous tissue with the potential to mimic any creature whose DNA it absorbs. If even the smallest amount of its substance were to escape confinement, and if that substance were able to grow, replicate, and invade multiple individuals and species, the fate of humanity and all life on Earth would be in the balance.

In nearly twenty months, for all our efforts, we have learned strikingly little about this organism, and yet what we have learned is entirely alarming. No single discovery regarding Moloch gives us any reason to suppose that we can learn anything about its cell structure, biological processes, or purpose that will in any way benefit humanity. The argument that in this creature lies biological information that will lead to the cure for cancer and all other diseases is nothing but happy talk based on illogic and self-deception. The nature of this entity is so beyond our comprehension— and will be a century from now—so resistant to all the standard tools of science, and such a constant threat to all who attempt to study it, that catastrophe is assured if the project continues.

The theories that Moloch is either a galactic "biological librarian" or an artist working in the medium of flesh are so ludicrous that we suggest those who entertain such ideas even in passing are, regardless of their credentials, insufficiently serious to be trusted to grasp the extreme danger posed by this entity and to keep safe the Earth and its creatures.

Reason leads us all but inevitably to the conclusion that Moloch is not of nature born, that its shell is not the product of evolution, but was engineered—along with its occupant—by some extraterrestrial species to serve as a weapon to which only its creators were immune. Perhaps such weapons were unleashed in great numbers on an enemy beyond our comprehension, at the far end of the Milky Way or even in another galaxy. We are capable of imagining that the ETs who created this thing might have been paranoid racists who feared there might be intelligent species on other planets and sent vast numbers of Molochs into space to ensure that they would never encounter a threat by a species of higher intelligence than their own.

We respectfully but adamantly demand that the entity known as Moloch be destroyed if a method of certain destruction can be agreed upon. In the event that it is determined that no lethal option can be guaranteed, we further demand that steps be taken—simultaneous with the committee's deliberations—to study by what means the entity could be safely encased and contained long enough to return it to space on a trajectory that will take it beyond this solar system.

Francesca and I thought we had surrounded ourselves with visionaries and individuals of courage.

Instead, four of them have proven to be intellectually blind and spineless cowards.

We have taken steps to prevent these misguided individuals from interfering with this vital research, which has unlimited positive potential for humanity. Eager to be part of this historic endeavor, they originally signed nondisclosure agreements with more teeth than a shark. They forfeited their right to adjudication of disputes in a civilian court of law. They further agreed to abide by the decision of a military tribunal. Should they reveal anything whatsoever about this project to anyone not already privy to it, they can be fined five million dollars for each violation and receive a sentence of ten years in prison without recourse to appeal. Now that they have made their threat, they are all under surveillance 24/7, their every action observed and every word they speak recorded. Should one of them make an attempt to contact a member of Congress, a journalist, or another problematic person, action of the greatest severity will be taken to stop them.

WHAT WALKS THE NIGHT

This island refuge that has sustained her now proves to be no refuge after all, for these days, the world is ruled by arrogant narcissists who have exchanged their souls for the promise of power, and in spite of all their talk about justice and the betterment of "the people," they care naught for any but themselves. In their high hubris, they are masters of destruction and press their many kinds of ruination into every crack and crevice, so that even the most remote sanctuary will in time receive the consequences of their insanity.

Katie has barely been able to manage her sense of urgency since hearing the word *nuke*, and because of the grim revelations that followed, her nerves have frayed further. She counsels herself to get a grip not just because of the Promise but also because of this girl who needs her. She gets up from the table, retrieves the empty satchel that hangs from a chair, and zippers it open. "You said these fusions break down into spawn that also fail."

Libby says, "They're disgusting, hideous."

"But Moloch can't be a thing that always fails. Failed life-forms just . . . go extinct."

"They believe it just needs practice, a lot of practice."

"That sounds like a joke."

"No. See, on Earth, we're carbon-based life-forms. Maybe life on other worlds has different bases. Living cells with different chemical structures. Unique proteins. Whatever."

Katie places the first funeral urn in the satchel—sweet Penny.

Then dear Regina. "So you're saying Moloch has to learn the rules of this world before it can successfully manipulate our cells, tissues, organs." The reality of cremated remains vies with the unreality of a voracious shape changer from another world for the best definition of *horror*. No contest. *Horror* is the ashes of those we love, even as we cherish the cremains as a symbol of all the beauty that once was ours.

"Yeah," Libby says. "To learn, Moloch has to try to fuse with a lot of local species, maybe hundreds or thousands of times, which it hasn't been able to do in the containment lab. All it's gotten are the rats, rabbits, dogs, and chimps they've given it."

As Katie carefully tucks Avi's urn into the satchel and, after it, the smaller bronze containing the ashes of Cassie, the dog, she says, "But once Moloch has been set loose, it can fuse with every living thing it encounters."

Setting her empty coffee mug on the table, Libby says, "Which has been happening since the escape yesterday."

"What escaped?" Katie wonders, slipping into her waterproof windbreaker and zipping it up.

Libby says, "Someone or something that evidently swam here to Jacob's Ladder. And today . . . Francesca. Maybe others."

"Something that could swim two miles?"

"A fusion could be part a marine animal from another world, something that once swam an alien ocean."

Hurrying to the pantry, opening the door, Katie says, "Go on."

"When it got here to Jacob's Ladder—I don't know—maybe it shifted into yet another form, a land animal. Something that climbs well. Maybe that's what you heard on your roof."

In the pantry, Katie sweeps from a shelf packages of pasta, crackling bags of corn chips, bags of dried beans, plastic jars full of dry-roasted peanuts. At the back of the bare shelf, a sliding panel reveals a foot-deep recess. A small backpack is crammed into that space. It contains twenty-five banded packets of hundred-dollar bills, a total of two hundred and fifty thousand.

As Katie comes out of the pantry, shrugging her arms through the shoulder straps of the backpack and then adjusting the hip belt, a protracted rumble rises from the cellar. Glasses against glasses, dishes against bowls, pans against pots—the contents of cabinets clink and clatter. The floorboards creak.

The fox leaps off his chair and sprints into the hall. He pauses there to look back at them, hackles raised, tail lowered, legs tensed.

When the disturbance passes and the only sound is the storm shattering its substance against the slate roof tiles, Libby says, "That's what you told me about over coffee."

Katie finishes securing the backpack. "I don't know what's down there."

"Maybe I sort of do."

"Yeah, well, I don't need to know." Katie yanks open a utility drawer in which she keeps a Tac Light, batteries, and other items.

Libby says, "When the failed spawn breaks down, it's kind of like, if I understood what I read, it's like this nasty mess of slip-slop, cellular soup."

Katie gives her a pair of scissors and a roll of duct tape. She positions the Tac Light against her right forearm. "Tape it in place while I hold it. The beam will be pointed wherever I point the gun."

As she winds the tape around and around the long handle of the flashlight, Libby says, "The cellular soup struggles to make itself into something, but it can't. It's lost the necessary complexity to receive instructions from the mother mass and shape itself."

"That's good. That's enough. Cut the tape."

"After a while, the spawn soup dies, it putrefies. It becomes nothing more than fertilizer, incredibly rich fertilizer."

Katie recalls the lush grass behind the house.

Putting down the scissors, Libby says, "But before it dies, if it can make contact with a living creature, no matter how simple, it can have a third life, diminished and not long, but still life. Fusion to spawn, then spawn to something less. That's what they suspected, based on observation of all the failed spawns in the isolation box."

The girl snatches the shotgun off the table.

Katie hands her the satchel of funeral urns. "It's heavy, but I'd rather you carry and I do the shooting."

"It's not heavy at all," the girl says.

"Okay. Then let's go."

"Go where?"

"The boathouse." Katie retrieves her AR-15. "I've got cans of fuel for your outboard, more than enough to get to the mainland."

"But in the dark and rain, near zero visibility—"

"I've been thinking. My cabin cruiser has a compass. It's mounted on top of the control board. We'll pop it loose, take it with us. We've got a chance."

The house quakes.

INTO THE OUTER DARK

Years earlier, people Katie has never met and never will meet, people who never think seriously about the lives of those who do not move in their circle, ordered the rapid renovation of the facility on Ringrock, threw the first tens of millions of dollars into the project, with too little planning, too little consideration of what might be at stake and how it might be lost. They were individuals of great learning and no prudence, their imagination enfeebled by the limitation of their dreaming to fantasies of power and utopian glory. They could have tethered the alien artifact to the exterior of the space station, where no member of the crew would subsequently have been at risk, could have ordered that it be carried around the Earth for a year, two years, a decade, for as long as might have been necessary to consider the many ways that disaster might ensue. It could have been kept off the planet until a better location than Ringrock Island could be chosen in isolate territory, a fail-safe facility constructed, and a crack research team rigorously trained in risk management. However, those who believe in revolutionary change and great leaps forward always thrill to the promise of the new to a degree beyond all reason. Whenever they rule a nation, they are the masters of its ruination—and in this case, they appear to be the engineers of the entire planet's demise. Whatever might be coming in the days ahead, they have here and now brought about the destruction of Katie's house and ensured that she will be driven from this unpretentious Eden into the outer dark.

The house shudders, and the floor rocks under her such that she nearly loses her balance, stumbles against the table, and knocks over one of the chairs.

Libby cries out as she is pitched to her knees. She scrambles to her feet and snatches up the shotgun that slipped from her hands.

The window shades flap like white flags, cabinet doors rattle, lights flicker, and the floor rocks. Underfoot, the tongue-in-groove boards buckle and crack; a swath of splinters prickles across the room as if the pine planks are raising hackles. Sure that something is about to erupt out of the cellar, Katie staggers after Libby, reaches the hallway, and looks back as, with a crash, the center of the kitchen floor instead collapses into the room below, taking with it the table and the chairs.

Although she left the cellar in darkness, a few lights continue to function down there. Shadows shudder through that subterranean realm, and whatever casts the shadows seethes through the rubble, the shattered flooring and the kitchen furniture and the overturned storage shelves. She wants to know, see, understand what lies below, and she can't stop trying to process what she's learned. *It feeds on light as well as matter. Each spawn soon dissolves into slip-slop, cellular soup, that binds with whatever humble forms of life it can find, still seeking to devour in its diminished form, struggling to become something more complex.* There is light in the cellar but also a supply of freeze-dried food, a rich trove of fuel on which this biologically chaotic creature might attempt to sustain itself even when it has devolved into a condition that leaves it unable to maintain contact with the mother mass on Ringrock. Katie's desire to *see* is as great as her fear, and as the whispering rises out of the cellar, as it did earlier, she realizes that once again she is being seduced into a state of curiosity and perverse attraction that holds her spellbound, as the fly is drawn by the dazzling patterns of the spider's web and by the promise of the liqueur offered by the Venus flytrap.

Libby realizes this, too, and tugs at Katie's sleeve. "Don't listen. Let's go, let's go, *get out!*"

Katie blocks the siren call by mentally reciting the lines from Eliot that saved her before.

The fox is at the far end of the hall, standing on his hind legs, forepaws on the front door, head turned and looking back, instinctively alarmed that his sanctuary has become a prison that might soon become a charnel house. He barks and then again, as he has not done before.

Katie knows how he feels. Once the whole world had been hers, past and present and future, but then she'd had only the island and the present, the past having become a wasteland and the future only a continuation of the present, offering hope but no prospects.

Although the hallway isn't long, it suddenly seems to telescope out ahead of her when she hears more of the kitchen collapse into the cellar and realizes that at any moment she might drop out of the main level into whatever hungers below. The overhead lights flash, flash, flash, and her shadow repeatedly flies forward toward Libby, like Death manifesting to scythe down a soul. Maybe the walls tweak, and maybe that's her imagination, but for sure she feels the floor cracking apart, sloping precipitously behind her, the floor joists and subflooring and pine planks falling away, a void opening at her heels. To her right, movement of the structure throws shut the door to her studio, but at once flings it open again, the bent hinges shrieking, as though the bungalow has come alive and is hostile to her; the lintel fractures and sags. And now there's no doubt that the bearing wall between the hallway and the studio is flexing, the studs cracking, nails squealing as they are tortured out of the wood that has so long and firmly gripped them. In the living room to her left, mortar crumbles and loose stones from the fireplace avalanche to the floor, knocking against furniture. The fox claws the door, and Libby struggles with the stubborn deadbolts, which are bound tight in the askew striker plates because the jamb has torqued with the movement of the building. The shiplap-pine ceiling clatters board against board with a sound like skeletons rattling bone on bone. One deadbolt relents and then the other, and Libby pulls open the door, and the night howls into the house as she and the fox flee.

On the threshold, Katie turns and looks back along the passage they have negotiated. The ceiling is cocked to the right. Walls lean aslant like those in a fun house. The hallway floor is mostly gone—a few fissured joists remaining, broken fragments of pine planking. On the main level and in the cellar, the lights flicker and pulse, sparks sputtering out of a fixture where a bulb exploded. In this pandemonium of coruscating light and capering shadows, a presence struggles to rise out of the lower realm, a mass too great to fit through the width of the hallway. If the spawn of a fusion dissolved into what Libby has called "slipslop," and if it drained through the soil and seeped through the foundation wall, it brought with it the genome of a worm; it is now the mother of all worms, as thick as a coaxial cable, wound in endless convolutions, writhing as if in ceaseless copulation with itself. She almost recoils from it and leaves it to bring down the house upon itself and deliquesce into death as all such end-stage creatures of Moloch supposedly do. However, one aspect of the thing so horrifies Katie that she is transfixed, as must have been the author of Revelation when he'd seen the beast come out of the earth and force every man and woman to take its mark and be bound forever to it. Here and there in the mass are human faces; some are entire heads and others are only countenances, and always the same face of a man in his fifties. Perhaps he was on the staff at Ringrock, a project scientist, seized by Moloch and shaped into a fusion that escaped and swam here and spawned at some point after its arrival. The entity that strives to surge into the hallway is grossly dysfunctional, sustained by light and freeze-dried food, re-creating the tormented face of its initial prey for no purpose, a face screaming without sound and rolling its eyes in terror though it is no longer that man, but is nothing more than a performance. Here is the fruit of arrogance, fallen from the tree of hubris, as rotten as the minds of those who believe they can learn all that exists to be known and can control anything they wish to control, who believe that it is their right, above the rights of all other men and women, to shape the destinies of their neighbors, cities, nations, and the Earth entire, according to their whims.

She backs off the threshold and pulls the door shut and turns to face the night, the girl, the fox. The intensity of the events in the house has to such a degree shocked and terrified her that for a moment she's been disconnected from the greater context of time and place; the wind and rain startle her. A thunderbolt speaks the fury of the storm and pulses its fierce searchlight across the island, and Katie cannot be sure that anything revealed is as it had been, that all of it hasn't changed and isn't changing further under the influence of an entity not born on this world.

With nuclear sterilization imminent, they need the compass, a can or two of fuel, and the runabout that Libby left tied under the pier. If they do not move fast enough and are vaporized, they will be erased from the history of humanity. They won't leave behind even ashes for an urn. There will be no one to mourn or remember them, no one to remember Penny and Regina and Avi, no one to live for them and keep the Promise.

"Stay close," she cautions Libby, and together, with the fox in attendance, they hurry toward the stairs that lead to the shore and the boathouse.

BEFORE JACOB'S LADDER:
THE CREMATORIUM

In this funeral home are many rooms, some in which the deceased are prepared, some in which the grieving can pay their respects at a viewing, others in which caskets are for sale and arrangements can be made for payment, a nondenominational Christian chapel, a chamber for those who prefer to meditate rather than pray, and additional rooms of mysterious purpose. There is, of course, a crematorium where mourners are discouraged from standing witness, and adjacent to it lies a waiting room with an adjoining half bath for those who feel the need to be present while flesh and bones become ashes.

This windowless room is small but, on consideration, most likely larger than it needs to be. Eight comfortable chairs are provided against the two longest walls. Between each pair of chairs is a small table on which are fanned a few magazines. At one end of the space, a wall-mounted television awaits any mourner in need of more insistent distraction than printed material offers. Against the fourth wall, the one nearest the door, stands a table on which a coffeemaker warms a pot; other beverages and a tray of cookies are available on request.

Katie has no interest in cookies, television, or magazines.

She needs only coffee and courage, the latter of which is in short supply at times during these sentinel hours.

The plush carpet is sapphire-blue, the wainscot dark walnut, the walls a paler shade of blue, the acoustic-tile ceiling white. The art has been chosen to induce serenity and convey a sense of eternity: a vast meadow leading to distant trees, all radiant in a golden twilight; a sequoia forest through which shafts of light reveal ferns bejeweled with recent rain.

The silence is deep, a hush, except for a faint rushing sound that, before long, Katie realizes is the noise made by flames fueled from pressurized gas jets.

When hours have passed, a grief counselor named Ariel brings Avi's urn to Katie. The contents have warmed the bronze. Ariel seems to know that, with this widow, no comforting platitudes are wanted and that the simplest of best wishes is the way to go.

A black Cadillac Escalade with tinted windows tails Katie out of the funeral home parking lot. Although the vehicle bears license plates, she doesn't bother to record the number because no one in authority will be interested. She is followed everywhere these days, and those conducting the surveillance want her to know that she is being watched. She goes directly home to put the urn with those that contain the ashes of her daughters.

Late that afternoon, she pays a visit to the cemetery where her parents are buried. A man stands on a knoll about fifty yards away, between two majestic phoenix palms, watching her through binoculars.

They will not arrange another hit-and-run or an accident of any kind, because even though these are people with extreme influence over the press, some journalists remain who would feel obliged to investigate yet another untimely death.

She believes that her phone calls are monitored. She suspects that anything she might say to anyone in the privacy of her home will be overheard.

She has no friends to bring light into these dark days. Some choose to keep their distance rather than bring themselves to the attention of dangerous people. Others seem to have been warned off and have taken the warnings seriously. In the interest of protecting those friends who have proved to be true, Katie withdraws from them, for they are too naive to understand the implacable evil of—and the risks to them posed by—those who protect the senator, his son, and his son's demented friends.

Although they dare not stage an accident, her enemies might attempt to murder her in such a way as to present her corpse in a convincing tableau of suicide. After all that she has lost, no one will argue that she is an unlikely candidate for self-destruction. For weeks, she hopes they will try it, will defeat her alarm and enter by stealth in the night, bearing whatever paraphernalia they require to sedate her without proof of a needle prick, to insert a tube down her throat after she passes out and feed her a lethal number of capsules of Nembutal or Seconal. She is heavily armed and alert, and the law cannot be twisted quite far enough to deem her a criminal for killing those who invade her home.

They don't come in either the night or the light of day, but neither do they cease monitoring her. She is eventually convinced that her only hope of peace, of escape from constant fear, is to retreat, thereby convincing them that she is at heart a rabbit, not a wolf. Jacob's Ladder awaits her.

WHO GOES THERE?

Katie knows her island by day and by night, knows it as well as if she were born here, having roamed it for hours every day, in fair weather and foul, in sun-shot summer days and bitter cold, because it is all she has of the world and all she ever expects to have, as if she has been shipwrecked here, no more likely to be rescued than if the place had been a South Pacific atoll and the year 1650. On this night, however, it is familiar only in the way that places one has never been are strangely familiar in a dream. With Libby at her side, hurrying away from the damaged house of which she has been dispossessed, she sweeps the yard with the Tac Light taped to her arm and, therefore, with the AR-15 that she holds at the ready. She has no fear of the spawn that metastasized in the cellar, because it will soon die of its internal chaos or, even sooner, when this terminus of the archipelago is suddenly, briefly as bright as the sun. She fears only what she can't anticipate, other manifestations of Moloch if perhaps the depth charges were in response to the escape of more than one fusion.

Thunder rolls in the distance, and the storm spends lightning in such a far place that the black clouds immediately above them are barely limned by the reflections that travel through their watery convolutions. Rain falls in undiminished torrents. The beam of the Tac Light reveals the concrete stairs that funnel down to a shore that is no longer common, the stones and pebbles of the shingle beach like cockleshells of some poisonous mollusk, the lake water seeming as dark and thick and foamless as a polluting sludge.

They trade the concrete steps for the wooden treads leading to the pier. The fox waits for them at the top, rain-soaked, looking not at all sly, but as bold and encouraging as a family dog that wishes to convey, by two quick barks, the urgency of the situation.

As they move along the boathouse wall, Katie smells fish rotting under the pier, a stench the wind can't entirely sweep away. A much fainter scent, at first merely chemical, quickly registers as gasoline. She halts, and Libby stops with her. Even the driving rain is slow to sluice away evidence of a recent fuel spill on the pier planks. Stubborn traces of cracked, refined petroleum float on the film of rainwater, iridescent blue and green and sulfur-yellow arabesques that shimmer in the beam.

When Katie switches off the flashlight, she sees a dim glow ahead, on the left, at the boathouse door. A fan of pale light grows wider only to grow narrower, wider, narrower. The fox pauses in the dim arc of light, raises his nose to whatever scents, and then hurries on to the end of the pier.

Katie hadn't left the light on earlier, when she had found the lock shot out and the outboard engine missing.

"Stay behind me," she says, and Libby does as instructed, and they move to the entrance.

The door sways under the influence of the wind, its hinges creaking. She puts her face to the gap, but she can't see anyone.

With the AR-15 gripped in both hands, she uses the barrel to press the door open. Quick across the threshold, tracking the rifle left to right, she encounters no threat.

A clank of metal on metal and a ratcheting sound draw her to the head of the gangway. Storm tides pressing under the big lakeside door enliven the water in the slip, which boils as slowly as the foul brew in a witch's cauldron. Distorted by the waves, reflections of the hanging lights seem to exist not on the surface but instead in the depths, like tentacular species of unearthly origin. The small cabin cruiser rides against the squeaking fenders that protect it from damaging contact with the slip. On the open deck, at the transom, a tall man bends to his work, reattaching the engine and its fuel tank. He drops a tool and stands erect, blotting his hands on his black uniform, the task completed, his back to Katie as she cautiously descends the gangway. The man turns, perhaps to release the belaying lines that are secured to the slip cleats.

When he sees her, he reacts not with surprise, but with that cool arrogance and barely disguised contempt that she first endured when she met him outside the grotto more than twelve hours earlier. "Ah, it's you," Robert Zenon says. "I was about to come to the house and warn you. We've got to leave. There's been an evacuation order."

"You took the engine and stranded me."

"Only so you wouldn't take off without me. I always intended to bring you with me when it was time to go. My partner, Hampton, he destroyed the boat we came in. He was . . . corrupted. I also didn't want him escaping in yours."

She says, "If your rifle's laying on the deck, don't stoop to pick it up. With an AR-15, I don't have to be a damn good shot, but I am, and I'll take your head apart."

"My rifle's in the cabin." He gestures toward the bow. "I'm not your enemy."

After treating him to a long silence, giving him time to look into the muzzle of the rifle, she says, "The pistol on your hip. Lift it out by the grip with your left hand, using just your thumb and forefinger, and drop it over the side."

"My ISA credentials are legit. We're on the same side here."

She fires one round, placing it so close to his head that he can no doubt hear the whistle of the round cutting air, even above the crack of the shot.

He flinches. "Damn! You're threatening an officer of the law."

"I'll trust any cop on a corner if he wears a uniform. But no law you pass can make me trust your type. You've got to earn the trust. Drop the pistol in the water, or I'll drop you."

Shifting his attention to Libby, who has descended the gangway, Zenon says, "Who's Shotgun Suzie?" He squints as he recognizes her. "You. You're their daughter. How the hell did you get here from Oak Haven?"

"Ignore him," Katie tells the girl. "He's nothing but trouble. Step away from me, honey. Away from him. Go around the slip to the front of the boat."

As Libby moves forward on the wet planking, Zenon pumps himself up with an air of authority and regards Katie with an imploring but stern expression. "Listen, you don't understand the situation. There's a crisis on Ringrock. This place isn't safe."

"Moloch," Katie replies. "Fusions, spawns, a nuke that could be triggered any moment. I understand some. Drop the pistol overboard."

Incredulous, he shifts his attention to Libby again. "They *told* you? They told a *child* all about it?"

Katie is sure that his astonishment is genuine, but she also knows he's stalling, hoping for a moment when she's distracted. "Hey, asshole, do what I told you. *Do it now!*"

"Okay, all right. I understand why you're so agitated. But I really am on your side." With his left hand, he reaches cross body and extracts the gun from the holster with his thumb and fore-finger. He drops it into the water.

"Now get off the boat," she demands.

"You can't leave me here. You're not that kind of person."

"I'm sure you've got a phone. Unlike mine, which you people somehow disabled, yours no doubt works."

He doesn't deny what she says. "No one's going to come for me now. Not with everything . . . the way it is, and the clock ticking."

"Get off the boat."

He lowers his head and stands in a pose of discouragement, but she suspects he's looking at his rifle where it lies on the deck, calculating, furiously scheming. In spite of what he'd said, he never had any intention of coming to the house and taking her with him when he left Jacob's Ladder.

She speaks softly, but her voice carries. "You're dead in five seconds. One . . . two . . . three . . ."

He swings over the gunwale and onto the slip. He looks fear-ful and defeated, but this is also a pose. He is alert for any advan-tage that might befall him. He will kill her if he can.

PITY

The stink of the fish rotting under the pier has not seeped through these walls, but in this extraordinary moment in time, the boat-house feels as much like a lodgment of Death as any mausoleum. The storm itself seems to have adjusted its rhythm and the roof to have become a drumhead, so that the rataplan sounds less like rain than like the cadence of a funeral cortege, a solemn and deeply unsettling announcement of inescapable fate.

Holding the AR-15 at the ready, Katie backs away from Robert Zenon, toward Libby, providing him with a clear path to the gangway. "Get up there, away from us and the boat."

"You can't do this to me."

"I'm doing it," she assures him.

"It's a death sentence."

"Your kind always find a way."

"Jesus, Katie."

"What about Him?" Katie asks.

"You're not without pity."

"Maybe I'm not, but I think *you* are. Get up the gangway."

He holds his hands out, palms up, a supplicant beseeching her to be a Good Samaritan. "How can I prove myself?"

She wants to shoot him dead. She will do it if he comes at her. However, she can't bring herself to cut him down in the absence of immediate peril. The Promise was to live for Avi and the girls, not to kill for them. "Why did you come to Jacob's Ladder?"

He answers without hesitation, "A scientist on the project became contaminated, a fusion, without anyone knowing. He was able to pass as himself for a short while, a few hours, until dysfunction set in. By then, he was in a position to escape."

"That's who you depth-charged."

"Yeah."

"It feeds on energy. A depth charge is a bomb—*energy*."

"You can't eat a hundred steaks at once. Moloch can't process unlimited amounts of energy. Any fusion can be overloaded, burnt out like a circuit. Which is what we were trying to do."

"That's just a theory—or proven?"

"Proven."

"So why did you and Rice come here this morning?"

"To be sure Shiff hadn't survived and made it this far."

"The scientist."

"Yeah."

"And what did you find?"

"Spawns. Two of them. In the grotto."

Remembering the face of the fiftysomething man that appeared in multiple iterations within the substance of the spawn, Katie says, "There's a third in the cellar of my house."

He appears surprised—perhaps that she is alive. "We destroyed the two in the grotto. Or I thought we did."

"They sent just you and Rice, not a platoon?"

"The more boots on the ground, the greater the risk of someone talking about what they saw, a breach of security."

"Do you people ever listen to yourselves?"

His expression remains that of a man humbled and afraid, but his stare sharpens with the arrogance that is the truth of him. "It was chaos in the grotto. Things got desperate. Rice and I—we were separated for just two or three minutes."

"And something fused with him."

"I didn't know it until Rice—the thing that was masquerading as Rice, that was still half Rice—attacked me. I fought it off, and then spent the day tracking him down."

"You didn't warn me."

"You don't have security clearance."

"No, you never do," she says.

Confused, he says, "Never do what?"

"You never listen to yourself. So where's Rice?"

"I killed him. He didn't spawn. Your island's clear now."

Her attention focused on Zenon, Katie calls out to Libby. "Honey, who shot Hampton Rice?"

"I did," the girl replies.

"How?"

"With this shotgun. He was stuck. He couldn't finish fusing."

For a moment, Zenon is silent and very still. Then he turns his head to look at the boat a few feet to his right.

Katie can read him as easily as the time on her watch. He is wondering if she would shoot him in the back if he scrambled onto the boat in an effort to get his rifle.

She fires a second round so close to his head that he startles and presses a hand to his left ear as if the passing bullet nicked it.

"Up the gangway. All the way to the top. Move your ass *now*."

His sneer of contempt is unsuited to a man his age, like that of a preppy, twentyish model in a men's fashion magazine whose sense of superiority rests on little more than his confidence regarding his taste in clothes. "You're as good as dead, cunt."

She nearly kills him then—and would have if he hadn't moved up the gangway with alacrity. Still covering Zenon with the AR-15, she calls Libby to her side. "Can you drive the boat?"

"I've driven ours at Oak Haven a lot, and it's bigger."

"Get aboard. Start her up. The remote for the door is on the control panel, in front of the throttles."

Libby leans over the gunwale to put her shotgun and the satchel of urns on the aft deck. She hurries along the slip and unties the belaying line from the forward cleat and returns to board the boat, leaving the second belaying line for Katie's attention.

Zenon watches from the top of the gangway, no doubt frantically racking his mind for a way to prevent them from leaving.

The big lakeside door begins to roll up, and wind charges inside, snorting like a frustrated bull released from a rodeo pen. The boat engine turns over with a roar.

Michael J. enters the boathouse, sprints past Zenon and down the gangway, his water-resistant coat defeated by the sheer volume of rain and pasted to him so that he looks as scrawny as a fugitive from some lab where the experiment requires that he be denied all sustenance. This debilitation is an illusion, for he quickens past Katie and springs effortlessly over the gunwale, onto the aft deck.

Keeping an eye on Zenon, Katie quickly releases the belaying line from the cleat and swings aboard the boat. On the deck, with the shotgun and the satchel of urns, is the agent's AR-15, just as she suspected.

She puts down her rifle, picks up his. She ejects the magazine; Zenon will have two or three others. There's a round in the chamber, which she fires into the ceiling. As the boat begins to move, she drops the rifle onto the slip, where he will be able to retrieve it. In spite of his claim that no one will answer his call for help, the ISA won't abandon him. Meanwhile, even he shouldn't be defenseless in a goblin night like this one.

Libby is a talented pilot, handling the vessel superbly and with necessary speed. They are out of the boathouse and into open water by the time Zenon reaches the foot of the gangway. The night will swallow them; without running lights they will vanish into the throat of the storm before the agent can jam a fresh magazine into his rifle.

SEVEN
PRACTICE

———

TO THE MAINLAND

At the wheel of the cabin cruiser, Libby knows that it isn't wise to think about her future. Envisioning the life she would have led if Moloch hadn't been brought to Earth, she risks despair, and by imagining the terrors that could still materialize in the hours ahead, she might be incapacitated by dread. However, she is cursed with a mind that cannot live only in the moment. The past is heavy on her, and if, by some stroke of great good luck, the future isn't a war for survival, it also won't be an idyllic life involving a logger husband with whom she competes in hatchet-throwing contests and whose bones she jumps five times a day. Maybe she was foolish, even childish, to imagine such a future, but it seemed desirable and achievable and fun—which are three qualities that do not inform any of the futures that she can currently foresee. What haunts her most of all is the specter of loneliness, of having no one who cares for her or about whom she deeply cares. The first seven years of her life were lived in isolation of the spirit, until Sarah came along—Shelly Framington, astronaut, will always be Sarah to her—and now that one friend is gone, never to return.

Michael J. lies curled up in a corner of the wheelhouse, wet and miserable but not whimpering. Libby has always thought animals live in the moment, their past dismissed as irrelevant, unaware that their lives are short and their futures fraught with danger. Again and again, however, the fox's behavior seems to belie that notion. Raleigh and Francesca had no patience for pets, considered them an even greater waste of time than, well, children. Maybe Libby's escape from loneliness will involve animals, which care more diligently for their offspring and might come to care for her.

"On course due east," says Katie, reading the compass. "You're doing great, honey."

The boat cleaves the chop with less drama than Libby's smaller runabout, and they are no longer in danger of being swamped. Holding true to course requires some strength because the wheel pulls to the currents and the wind broadsides the vessel, but she is not a weak girl who has spent the years lifting nothing heavier than bottles of makeup, tubes of skin cream, and lipstick.

They pass just south of Oak Haven Island, close enough that she is able to see the separate windows of the house that sheltered her for seven years, each pane softly radiant. Perhaps something that once was Francesca, that once was also Sarah, something that is now many worlds of life born in a single incarnation, is still searching those rooms for a girl to feed on. Whether such a creature remains alive or is dead, the Cape Cod structure with its fine veranda is no longer a haven, but rather threatens like a house in a story or poem by Poe, where the glow beyond the windows is the light of eternal horror, issuing from the lamps of Hell.

As Oak Haven recedes, hard rain washes the wheelhouse window, blurring the night beyond, which is itself a blur of rain and windblown mist. At this hour, in this weather, no pleasure craft are under way. The only traffic on the lake is commercial, large ships bearing numerous running lights. Even in this murk, she will be able to see one of those leviathans. If it's crossing her course, she can throttle back and, if necessary, wheel to port or starboard to pass astern of it. And if the president or whoever's in charge has made the decision to detonate the nuclear device under the facility on Ringrock, surely federal agents, using one deception or another, have already closed down or rerouted traffic from the blast zone.

During the quarter of an hour or so after Libby had knocked on Katie's door, they had shared, over coffee, their knowledge of the situation in which they found themselves, but she'd learned nothing about the woman's past—where she'd come from, how she'd wound up on Jacob's Ladder, why she was alone but for a fox. They can cruise the miles to the mainland in silent expectation of the explosion that might vaporize them or at least swamp their boat, which would make even this short journey endless, or they can distract themselves with conversation. In these circumstances, small talk is intolerably foolish, like chatting about recipes for apple pie while in line for the guillotine. Libby knows that the sealed bronze jars, different from one another, are surely funerary urns filled with ashes and must be as sensitive a subject as any she could raise. The universe might never have an end, time ticking on for eternity, but whatever happens this crazy night, her and Katie's time is limited, whether to ten minutes or fifty years, and with the silence of time's end looming over them, it seems that the only subjects worth talking about are those most sensitive. She dares to ask.

Katie takes no offense, nor does she hesitate. She condenses the ordeal into less than five minutes, her emotions repressed and her voice so haunted that she might be dead herself and speaking to Libby during a seance to which some spiritualist has summoned her back into this world. Her story is one of monsters, though all of them are human, and the grief she has suffered is beyond Libby's ability to fully comprehend. Detail by detail, the girl becomes aware that this is also an old story, presented in many books within a book and here distilled to its essence. It is the explanation of the world's condition that her parents refused to let her read and that she knows about only because of the books that Sarah smuggled to her, a story that reveals the origins of evil, that explains why the innocent suffer at the hands of those who have no use for the truth and why they have no use for it and how their contempt for the truth ensures a dark and ever-darkening world. For all the tragic loss and horror of Katie's story, she tells it some way that does not rob it of hope, a way of telling that Libby can't explain but that affects her nonetheless and leaves her dry-eyed and standing tall when she should be streaming tears, huddled, and shaking.

Katie finishes by saying, "We can't give in to evil, to those who do such things, because what they want is us to go still and quiet and never speak back to them. These past two years, I've been trying to figure out how to speak back and haven't been doing a good job of it. My Avi used to say, 'Always keep moving. The Fates are master sharpshooters, and the easy target is the one who's standing still.' By 'keep moving,' he also meant keep telling the truth, keep doing what's right, keep believing what you do matters, because when you give up on the truth, you become one of them."

The sky is black and the lake is black, but the compass has a light. Libby can read the lubber's line and the bearing line. She is true on course, and the night has not yet caught fire, and she means to stay on course no matter what.

FUTURE TENSE

After Katie's account of how she lost her family, Libby does not resort to platitudes but falls into a thoughtful silence.

The darkness is forbidding, the hour late, and the town toward which they're heading is small and short on nightlife, yet they are making such progress that Katie expects to see shore lights soon.

She wonders about the megatonnage. If it is a small device and four stories under Ringrock, it might turn much of the facility to dust and soot and puddles of molten steel, vaporize the mother mass of Moloch as intended, but do little damage beyond that island. In recent decades, however, many who govern have exhibited a tendency toward gargantuanism in all things; if a small solution is 90 percent effective, a program ten times larger is judged to be what is needed to solve the problem entirely. Would politicians, facing the threat of a malevolent ET annihilating the human race, choose to follow the measured recommendations of the experts or instead pack as much punch into the Ringrock self-destruct system as possible? If the nuke is not one that might be called tactical, if it is instead a metropolis buster that could level Los Angeles from downtown to Beverly Hills, then Oak Haven and Jacob's Ladder will sustain blast-wave damage and perhaps be set afire from end to end. Even then, damage on the mainland should be small or nil—except for the effects of radiation.

Always keep moving.

At last Libby says, "Wherever we go, if we live long enough to go anywhere, I want to go with you. Is that . . . is it possible?"

"Honey, you hardly know me."

"I know enough. You're . . . real. You take care of business."

"But your family will have their ideas."

"There was just Raleigh and Francesca. They weren't much of a family. I think they had me because being parents filled out their résumés better. That sounds mean and stupid, but I think it's true."

"You must have other relatives."

"Grandma Giselle. My mother's mother. She's eighty-four. She lives in Paris."

"She'll be concerned."

"The last time I saw her, I was six."

"Nevertheless—"

"She and Francesca were estranged. They haven't spoken in almost six years."

The girl had not seemed small before. She seems small now, and suddenly fragile.

"There's really no one else?" Katie asks.

"Raleigh had a younger brother and sister."

"One of them—"

"Undina died of a drug overdose when she was thirty-seven. Proctor is forty-eight. No way I'll go with him."

"Why?"

"He visited us on Oak Haven when I was nine. I thought he really liked me. What he liked was touching me."

"He molested you?"

"No. He grabbed my butt, kind of joking. Put a hand on my thigh and kept it there. Gave me neck massages I didn't want. He liked me to sit on Uncle Proctor's lap. But what he really wanted, you could see in his eyes."

"Dear God."

"I was only nine, but I didn't need long to figure it out. He's creepy." She stands on tiptoes to lean forward and read the compass. "I understand if you can't. I mean, all you're carrying, everything that's happened to you, it's already too much. I'm just afraid what they might do to me."

"What do you mean?"

"If they figure out I know about Ringrock, Moloch, all of it."

"The whole world's going to know about it soon."

Libby glances at Katie, her eyes shining faintly with compass light. "You think they'll admit the bomb was theirs? Why wouldn't they blame it on a terrorist? Invent a whole different story about what research was being done on Ringrock, make it something that one group of crazies or another would want to blow up."

"It's a nuke going off on American soil. In order to kill an existential threat. It's too big to cover up. There are too many people in the loop."

The girl looks ahead, on course. "They've kept Moloch secret for more than seven years. Does anyone take responsibility for what they screw up anymore? Maybe they say they do, but do they really? Don't they try to hide the truth or blame others?"

Since yesterday, Katie has been fixated on the strangeness and escalating eeriness of events. With the revelations of the past few hours, when the threat has proved otherworldly, her fear has been of the unknown; her plight is beyond human experience, the next turn of the screw unpredictable and therefore terrifying. However, she's now been reminded of what she never should have forgotten—that the true prince of this world isn't Moloch. The prince of this world is the father of lies, and his followers are legion. Those who control the narrative might in fact decouple

Ringrock from the explosion, might claim terrorists were fer-
rying the nuke from this lake to the next, with whatever city
as their target, when it detonated prematurely. Such a lie, sold
by the highest authorities, will not only cover up the reckless
project at Ringrock as if it never existed, but will also provide
them with an excuse to restrict freedoms and further consoli-
date power. The end of Moloch might be only the beginning of
something else as dark and menacing as that biological weapon
from the stars.

Libby is right to fear that she might be sought and silenced
one way or another. In a world where truth and virtue are more
often mocked than praised, the life of a fourteen-year-old girl
has little value. Every year in this war and that, even in our own
cities, countless children are killed, while those who spray the
bullets—or plant the roadside bomb, authorize the use of nerve
gas, send the drone with the Hellfire missile that strikes the wrong
target—shed not a tear, referring to those tender deceased as mere
"collateral damage," if they acknowledge them at all.

Nor is the life of a thirty-six-year-old widow worth anything
when she has accumulated the kind of knowledge Katie has
acquired during the past day. An island is not a sufficient refuge.
Neither is a remote mountaintop or an impenetrable jungle or
an arctic outpost. The only safety now requires her to become
someone other than herself. In the bedlam that will follow the
destruction of Ringrock, she and Libby might have a chance to
escape, flee far to the west, change their appearance, take on new
names, fabricate a different past as mother and daughter, and
hope for a future. Avi, bless him, has given her the information
she needs to rise phoenix-like from the ruins of her current life.

Libby says, "Shore lights!"

Six or eight thousand call this town home. It lies too far from the nearest city to be a suburb, although neither is it rural in its style or commerce. From late spring through mid-autumn, more than a thousand tourists at any one time—mostly families—come here for the pleasures of the place, for the beaches, boating, high-quality inns, and charming restaurants. That influx hasn't begun, but even in season, this isn't a Riviera of glittering nightclubs and noisy hook-up bars. The tallest buildings are four or five stories high, though most are two or three. As the town resolves out of the dark and rain, it appears to be an enchanted cove to which strange tides have carried precious stones to brighten and bejewel its shore.

STREETS OF REFLECTION

Waves slap the stone wall of the quay and slosh up the ramped cutouts from which boat owners can launch their vessels. Farther along, pale wisps of evaporating rain smoke from the warm metal shades of post-top lamps, and water littered with windblown debris churns among the pilings at the public docks, where the floating slips rise and fall with the restless motion of the lake.

Libby pilots the cabin cruiser into a berth. Katie debarks to belay it fore and aft, with the fox close at her heels.

The wind and rain are unrelenting, but the sky is no longer rumbling and firelit, as if a celestial stage manager has quieted the theater to ensure that the audience will be impressed by the nuclear opening of act three.

Katie with her backpack full of plastic-wrapped bundles of hundred-dollar bills and Libby with the satchel of urns ascend the gangway to the dock. With Michael J. in close attendance, they climb a set of stairs to a parking lot, splash across that windswept field of blacktop, and enter the first block of Main Street.

Katie has the AR-15, and Libby has the shotgun. They are loath to leave those weapons behind and rely only on a pistol for defense. In this small town, where crime and violence are largely limited to the occasional ill-considered actions of tourists who have had too much to drink, serious weapons openly carried will bring them to the attention of the police, who are certain to disarm and detain them. Each of them carries her gun at her right side, the muzzle pointed at the ground, using her body to shield it from the occupants of any vehicles that might pass in the street.

At this late hour, in this miserable weather, all the shops and even the restaurants are closed. A tavern or two might be open, but perhaps even the managers of those establishments have decided that one or two diehards nursing draft beer don't justify the expense of keeping the lights on, and have turned them out to stagger home. At the moment, Katie and Libby are the only pedestrians. As they hurry toward the first intersection, the sole vehicle in sight is a white SUV that crosses Main Street, motoring north to south.

They need to go only four blocks east, one block north, and then half a block along an alley to the rented garage where Katie's black Range Rover waits. As they cross the first intersection, she glances left, then right, whereupon she sees what seems to be a patrol car. It's two blocks away, has a roof-mounted lightbar that is currently dark, and is cruising slowly toward them.

"Cops," Libby declares.

Katie says, *"Don't run."*

At this distance, the fact that they're armed can't be obvious. Because they are the only people afoot, however, they will be of interest. Any police officer worth his badge will speed up and turn onto Main to have a closer look at them.

They cross to the next block, which puts the patrol car out of sight. Directly ahead is a bus-stop shelter enclosed on three sides and with a roof, where tourists can wait, in season only, for the jitney service that operates then. Katie rushes to it, ducks inside, slides her rifle under the bench, receives the shotgun from Libby, and tucks that away with the AR-15.

As they continue east on Main, heads ducked and shoulders hunched against the storm's barrage, she says, "No jitney service this early in the year. No one will find the guns. We'll come back in the Rover to get them in ten minutes."

"You're quick," Libby says.

Katie's smile feels as stiff as a rictus, but it's still a smile. "You too." A realization alarms her. "Oh, shit, Michael J. He's no dog, and we don't have a leash to pretend he is. The cop is gonna wonder what the hell."

Libby bends down and scoops up the fox, which neither bites her nor resists. She holds him against her chest, one hand atop his head to obscure that he's never going to audition for a remake of *Lassie*.

The patrol car turns the corner behind them. In its headlights, the rain shatters off the blacktop in crystalline bursts. The black-and-white pulls even with them and slows to match their pace. Katie turns her head and sees that the driver is the only one in the Dodge Charger. He is bent toward the center console, head lowered to study them through the passenger-door window. She smiles and gives him two thumbs up to convey that they're okay. He parallels them for a few seconds, but then speeds up and away.

"Michael J. is shivering," Libby says, "but I think he likes to be held."

She and Katie continue east on Main, as wind soughs through the trees and sings in the power lines.

Sinuous reflections of streetlamps slither on the water that sheets across the slick blacktop toward the gutters. The lamplight transforms display windows into cloudy mirrors, in which distorted versions of Katie and Libby stalk them from store to store, as if with sinister intent.

Near the end of the second block is a pizza parlor, and in the beginning of the third stands an ice cream store, and farther along lies a nail shop, the night rain ladling a dark luster over each enterprise. This minor coincidence has a larger impact on Katie than it should, as if a malevolent pattern is impressed on her life, the clatter of gunfire from the earlier tragic event to be a nuclear roar in this one.

In spite of this, she finds the town appealing, a place where she and Avi might have safely raised their girls with values that would have served them well in life. It's quaint, picturesque but real, well maintained rather than restored to some sentimental vision of a committee bent on the Disneyfication of everything.

As they hurry from Main Street to an intersecting avenue, she says, "Even if it's a tactical nuke, if here on the mainland there's no danger from the blast wave or a lot of radiation, I feel like we should do something, warn them to get the hell out, just in case."

"Me too. But who's gonna believe us?" Libby asks.

"Nobody. Not in time."

At the rented garage in the alleyway, she unlocks a man-size door, enters with Libby close behind, and turns on the light and sighs with relief when the Range Rover is where it ought to be.

The girl puts the fox down, and he shakes himself vigorously, casting off a lavish spray of rainwater. When Katie remotes the roll-up door between the garage and the alley and then raises the liftgate on the back of the Range Rover, Michael J. looks from the night to the vehicle to Katie—and then springs into the back of the Rover, where he cuddles in a corner.

As Katie closes the liftgate, Libby says, "You've got a self-domesticated fox."

With the girl in the passenger seat, Katie reverses out of the garage into the alleyway and heads back the way they came. "If things have gone haywire in Ringrock—and we know they have—why hasn't the bomb been triggered already? Why not hours ago?"

Libby slumps in her seat, as if thinking about this weighs her down. "Someone has to decide, take responsibility, like maybe the president."

Katie doesn't say as much, but she thinks that if a politician has to make the decision and risk the consequences, by the time he makes up his mind, Earth might have to be renamed Moloch.

She is headed west on Main, returning to the place where they secreted the guns, when she sees a lone man heading east on the sidewalk. He's tall, bent into the wind, moving with purpose, and carrying what appears to be an AR-15. Robert Zenon.

SCARECROW

Robert Zenon looks the worse for his rough journey from Jacob's Ladder. His black clothing clings to him in sodden swags, like grave windings that once mummified him but sag with the putrid softness of the deeply corrupt man who wears them. Bent into the wind, he holds the rifle with both hands, angled across his chest. His fierce aura of determination and demented rage suggest he has an all-important destination that he must reach at any cost, and as a consequence he seems oblivious of the town through which he slogs. As he heads east and Katie passes going west, he reveals no awareness of the Range Rover and never glances at it.

He'd evidently found Libby's runabout under the pier, took a can of Katie's fuel, and headed for the mainland at full throttle. If his phone still works and he has a compass app, that is how he has been able to stay on course and arrive only ten minutes behind them.

In the intersection, she hangs a U-turn, pulls forward to the curb at the bus stop, and says, "I'll keep him in sight," as Libby throws open her door and gets out to recover the guns they left under the bench.

On the move again, coasting eastward, headlights extinguished to avoid drawing Zenon's attention, Katie allows their quarry to remain a block ahead, his image shimmering through the lens of rain, briefly clarifying with each sweep of the windshield wipers. Perhaps he is intent on putting as much distance as possible between himself and the lake before Ringrock blows. The ISA has a budget in the tens of billions, more agents than the country has dentists, and vast fleets of vehicles. Zenon could have called to have transportation standing by—or to have Katie and Libby apprehended when they tied up at the public docks. Evidently he has lost faith in the agency's ability to contain this crisis and is now concerned only about self-preservation.

A police car, perhaps driven by the same officer who had taken an interest in Katie and Libby earlier, turns the corner onto Main Street, less than half a block in front of Zenon.

Katie pulls to the curb and stops, but she leaves the car in gear, her foot on the brake.

The lightbar brightens on the Dodge Charger, casting off flares of blue and red, making gay confetti of the rain, and the motorized spotlight puts Zenon center stage. This understandable reaction to the sight of a man with a rifle is predicated on the expectation that, in this heretofore peaceable town, the figure of interest most likely has a legitimate reason to be openly carrying a firearm and that he has at least a modicum of respect for the law. Indeed, it's possible that the cop knows Zenon is with the ISA and is engaged in activities coordinated with local authorities. Whatever the reason for the officer's confidence, he pays the ultimate price for it, as the federal agent brings the AR-15 to bear. Bullets pock, pock, pock the windshield; it dissolves. Zenon keeps firing as he approaches, and steam like a spirit being exiled from this world billows from the grille as the radiator proves to be no match for a high-velocity round with a full-metal jacket. The agent yanks open the door and drags the driver out of the vehicle. The corpse tumbles to the pavement. Zenon gets into the Dodge and spends a minute or two evidently trying to get the car moving, as if he can't comprehend that he has killed both man and machine. He throws open the door, clambers out, and stands by the car as he slaps a fresh magazine into the AR-15. The officer is surely dead, but Zenon puts two more rounds into him before continuing on his way.

Even from a block away, the murder is ghastly. Katie regrets that Libby has seen it. The girl has witnessed worse on this night, but each new offense against her innocence further scars her soul.

"He's moving like a scarecrow," Libby says. In their whisking, the wipers impart a stroboscopic stutter to Zenon's progress, but it's true that he also lacks the grace he possessed on Jacob's Ladder. "It's like he isn't used to walking."

Indeed, as Katie watches the ISA agent make his way to the far intersection and turn into the cross street, he lurches as though he's just unhooked himself from a cornfield cross and hasn't quite yet gotten a handle on this mobility thing. The machinelike stride he exhibited prior to encountering the patrolman has deserted him.

Libby gives voice to a thought that Katie is only now forming. "You remember what I said about Moloch and practice, about learning the intricacies of our chemical structure, our unique proteins, hormones . . ."

Zenon hadn't been like this in the boathouse on Jacob's Ladder. If he'd been a fusion then, he'd been successful, convincing. And if he is soon to spawn, maybe his spawn will be still more successful when they in turn fuse with people. Maybe they will be *entirely* successful, able to pass for human until suddenly they morph and attack.

Whether or not the ISA agent is an existential threat to the entire world, he is an imminent danger to the citizens of this town, to whomever he seeks, if he seeks anyone in particular, and to any luckless soul whom fate leads across his path. The gunfire has not gone unrecognized in the storm, not even in this commercial district where few people live, but any response to it is sure to be confused and too late to save the next person on whom Zenon sets his sights.

As the man disappears into the side street, Katie swings the Range Rover away from the curb and, with headlights still off, races past the patrol car and the dead officer, past the cross street into which the scarecrow slouched toward whatever unholy rebirth might be his destiny. In the middle of the next block, she brakes and hangs a hard right turn into a parking lot between businesses. She angles the SUV to the left, puts it in park, sets the emergency brake, and switches off the engine.

Her AR-15 is propped between Libby's seat and the dashboard, and as Katie retrieves it, Libby says, "You gonna kill him?"

"That's the general idea. Look after Michael J."

She is compelled to act not just because Zenon is a cop killer and might be the biological revolution that, for seven years, Moloch has schemed to dispatch into the world beyond Ringrock. These recent events have summoned her from a dream of permanent escape to the reality that in a well-lived life, there is never any escape from commitment, from responsibility not merely for family but also for others whom the violent would sweep away. She has been awakened as well to the realization that though perhaps half of humanity has no such sense of responsibility, their indifference is no justification for her to retreat into a life of self-interest. If someone had ever stepped up to force Lupo, Hamal, and Parker to face justice for one of their many crimes before that Sunday morning at the ice cream shop, Katie's parents and her daughters and her husband would be alive, and what she must do now is be that someone, that avatar of justice, for those not yet dead at Zenon's hand.

Libby grabs her shotgun. "The fox is safe. I'm coming."

Katie says, "Honey, no."

The girl opens her door. "Your husband said 'keep doing what's right . . . or you become one of them.'"

"You're only fourteen."

"No, my folks never gave me a chance to be that young."

Katie needs to be an example to this girl, but she understands that Libby's desire to prove herself to herself is also a necessity. Such are the exigencies of human nature that allow for heroism even as they court tragedy.

The parking lot, with a row of marked spaces to the left and another to the right, connects Main Street to an alleyway. As Katie and Libby hurry toward the service lane behind the stores, wind squalls over rooftops and blusters between buildings and whistles through streets, and heavy rain raises the many voices of water from high gutters to downspouts to drains, though still no sirens signify that a motorcade of justice is attending to the murdered officer whose blood the storm dilutes.

They turn right into the dark alley. The north-south street into which Zenon fled is half a block to the west.

FIVE DAYS EARLIER: GRANDMA'S KITCHEN

Grandma Giana Gasparelli was once a svelte dark-eyed beauty with silky black hair; at eighty-nine, however, she is a tub with a bosom that time has grown into an impressive shelf that can serve as a rest for her crossed arms. Her eyes are black olives in the well-worked dough of her face, and her hair is not pure white, as you might expect, but in part pale yellow and peppered with gray, as if she washes it in urine and finishes it with a small spray of soot. Of all the things about her that you can't find in the photographs taken sixty years earlier, the most striking are her arms; back then, they were slender and feminine, but now they are—and for decades have been—as formidable as those of a long-shoreman, as if she has for most of her life exercised with barbells in the privacy of her bedroom. These days, most grandmothers wear pink jumpsuits or the equivalent, but Grandma Giana insists on housedresses, as if it's still 1955, though where she finds satisfactory garments in the patterns of that lost age and in her size is as mysterious as the origins of Stonehenge.

She is Robert Zenon's maternal grandmother, and he owes her everything. Forty-one years earlier, when he was just a boy of five, his mother, Palomita, died of a heroin overdose. Because Palomita claimed the father's name was Aristotle Zenon, she hung that surname on her son. No one has ever been able to find an Aristotle who would admit—or deny—that Bobby is his progeny. Grandma Gasparelli took him in without complaint. She was at that time forty-eight, a widow for five years.

Bobby Zenon never knew his maternal grandfather, Nino. Although fourteen years older than his wife, Nino nevertheless died young, at fifty-seven, in a dispute with a business rival whom Grandma Giana never named but to whom she sometimes referred as "that damn Jew," sometimes as "that damn Spic," and sometimes as "that damn Polack." Whatever the ethnicity of Nino's competition, things were changing in those days; a minor mafioso was no longer able to count on the enforcers who served the families in the big cities. After thirty years as the capo of organized crime activities in six or seven lakeside communities, however, he'd been able to leave his bride with enough money to ensure that she would never want for anything.

Grandma Giana has lived all her life in this town and in this handsome water-view home ever since her marriage. A staff of three young women clean the house, do the shopping, and drive Giana everywhere she wishes to go. "They adore me, Bobby, they really do, though the little bitches are still stealing me blind. What's an old woman gonna do? Better little thieves you know than bigger thieves you don't. There's no honor among the young these days."

On this evening, Bobby and his grandmother are alone in the house, dining together in the kitchen. She is a marvelous cook, and there is excellent red wine. They start with *acquacotta*, a Tuscan peasant soup with cabbage and beans. There's also focaccia with onions, Genoese-style.

News of family comes with the soup.

"Your uncle Vittorio—he's seventy-six—just took his fifth wife. She's thirty-four. I love my brother more than life itself, but you and I both know, he coulda done something bigger with his life if he didn't make every decision with his dick.

"Your cousin Camilla, she's so dumb you'd think she must be some French baby was put in an Italian crib by mistake. She's all excited her youngest boy is gonna be a priest. Now, we all need priests to marry us and pray us quick through Purgatory, but what kind of crazy bitch wants one in the family?

"Your cousin Paulie, he has prostate cancer. Who knew he's man enough to have a prostate?"

After the soup, she serves baked polenta with Bolognese sauce, about which Bobby sincerely raves before he says, "Nonna, everything you did back in the day to get me into Harvard is about to pay off in a big way."

"You got yourself in Harvard with your grades, *dolce bambino*. All I did was stuff money in the pants of them blueblood admissions bastards to persuade them your family come here with the fucking Pilgrims."

"Well, being a Harvard grad greased my way into the FBI."

"Your nonno woulda died if he'd lived to see you go over to the law."

"And I was right to make the jump to the CIA after six years."

"At least that got you out of law enforcement, God bless your nonno's soul. When you took the job with the ISA, *then* he woulda been as proud of you as he was of his own father for being friends with Mussolini."

Around the time Bobby signed with the ISA, his grandmother had informed him of her conclusion that the government was engaged in a strange project on Ringrock Island, which she could see from various rooms of her lake-view home. She is suspicious by nature and almost supernaturally gifted with the ability to recognize when others are going to lengths to conceal their true intentions. Bobby took her seriously. Over a few years, he exploited contacts in the CIA and used his position with the ISA to compile rumors regarding Ringrock and develop rumors into facts. After much maneuvering, he became head of security for the Ringrock project the previous year.

"I've got it all, Nonna, the biggest story of the century, of *any* century, and I can make it pay off big."

"Tell me."

"An alien, not from some third-world shithole, but from another planet." He lays it all out for her, how he has all the records of the project on thumb drives, and she is rapt.

"*Dolce bambino*, I gotta hear how you'll use this information to get the biggest bang. But first, I'll put the lamb on the table."

The lamb is pan roasted with juniper berries, finished with cracked pepper, and served with asparagus.

As they attend to the delicacy plated before them, Bobby says, "The experiments they're conducting on Ringrock are dangerous beyond comprehension, insane, the work of insufferable people who think they can't make mistakes. And here's the best part—year after year, the president has personally seen to it that black budget funds are directed toward the project in ever greater sums—billions!"

Nonna Giana frowns. "What president?"

"Of the United States. He's—"

"A simpleton."

"Yes."

"But our simpleton."

"You don't even vote."

"They can steal it without me."

"Here's the thing, Nonna. After all the government has screwed up in recent years, the public will be terrified to learn about the crazy risks they're taking with this Moloch. Flat-out terrified. I've got video. It'll make the pandemic hysteria a few years ago seem like nothing. This will blow up the current administration. If I wait till the other party nominates a candidate and then I bring this to him or her—who do you think is going to be the director of the ISA after the election this coming November?"

Nonna Giana's grin is so wide with surprise and delight that a morsel of lamb falls out of her mouth. She claps her plump hands and declares, "You! You're gonna be director of the secret police."

"Semisecret. People know we exist but not what we do."

"Bobby, when you sit in that seat, that *throne*, you can learn all their secrets, everything about all them bastards, even the president, and then you will *own* them."

"All because of you," Bobby says, "all you did for me, all you taught me."

"I am *sopraffatta*," she says, blotting her eyes with her napkin as if she is capable of tears.

Later, after salad, over a dessert of black grape pudding and ricotta fritters, she says, "Promise me, *dolce bambino*."

"Promise you what, Nonna?"

"Once you know everyone's secrets, rule with an iron fist."

"I will. Don't worry about that."

"With an iron fist, not like a sissy-ass Harvard boy."

"Harvard boys are as vicious as they come, Nonna. Heartless backstabbers. The women, too."

"But under it all, they're weak," she says. "Don't be weak."

"I promise I won't be weak."

"Break the fuckers, sweetheart, break them to your will."

He pours shots of grappa, and they toast each other, and she blots her dry eyes again to make sure that he knows her heart is full.

THE LIVES OF OTHERS

If for a moment it seems to Katie that the rain washes them through the night and town, it is not the rain, and if it seems they are blown by the wind, it is not the wind, nor is it any instrument of Nature that propels them, but a compulsion born within them that both excites and terrifies her. The motive is not courage, though courage is required, or at least they need the boldness that arises from a fear of being cowardly and is called courage. In the height of action, it is best not to put a word to the reason for their resolute commitment to such dangerous intentions, because no word will be adequate, and in fact any word will cheapen what they feel, diminishing their excitement and increasing their terror.

The alleyway leads them half a block from the parking lot to the avenue into which Zenon vanished after murdering the policeman. Assuming that he didn't turn back toward the heart of town, but continued south in his shambling scarecrow gait, they forgo the sidewalk for the center of the street, the better to see all before them.

In this block, storefronts gradually give way to residences. After a hard winter, the deciduous trees, striped maples, have begun to leaf out in a tentative fashion. Where streetlamps rise above the lower branches, shadows like grotesque arachnids with too many legs bent in weird configurations scrabble without progress across the pavement. Zenon is nowhere to be seen.

Beyond the next intersection, the businesses relent entirely to houses, and the trees are a variety of spreading conifer, evergreen baffles that limit the spill of lamplight, allowing darkness greater dominion. Out of that gloom comes a rhythmic sound like the knelling of a buoy marking some channel in the night, its bell note flat and varying in tone from strike to strike. The storm wind is too erratic to produce such a measured clink, and at this hour in these blusterous streets, it's unlikely that anyone other than Robert Zenon is afoot.

Side by side, guns at the ready, Katie and Libby step quickly through the brighter light that pools across the intersection, into the fragrance and shadows of the soughing pines, where they proceed with less haste, alert to all that moves in this shuddering night. Dead needles, shed from the trees, weave a shifting and potentially slippery carpet, and airborne others, like brittle insects, flick Katie's face. The metronomic clinks and clanks continue as if the malformed gears of a large machine are meshing teeth in the grudging performance of some ponderous task.

Along both curbs, residents have left vehicles that exceed the number of spaces in their garages. Lamplight silvers windshields, and swaying pine boughs pattern those mirrors with illusions of sinister occupants in the front seats beyond the glass. On all sides, the night is full of false presences, spectral distractions that provide Zenon with cover.

In many houses, the windows are dark, and in most of those from which light shines forth, the residents are on the second floor. A day earlier, Katie would have passed these homes with no thought of the people living there, other than with a simmering distrust of strangers. Now she feels a kinship with them, a kind of communal sympathy and poignant sense of their grave vulnerability. Something vital in her that was moribund is revived, and she sees her own life in the lives of others.

"There!" Libby whispers, and points with the barrel of the shotgun.

At the far end of the block, on the right, with hardly more apparent substance than a shadow, a tall man strides past vehicles that are humped like elephants paused in a circus parade. He proves they're merely machines by swinging something—no doubt his rifle—at each back wheel and then each front, rapping the muzzle against metal, as if the sound emphasizes some mental count he is keeping as he reviews the tasks he must perform to fulfill whatever mission has brought him here.

As Zenon proceeds into the brightness of the next intersection, a siren shrills elsewhere in town. No more than four minutes have elapsed since the shooting of the officer on Main Street, a common interval between a call to 911 and a response, though it seems much longer than that. The ISA agent quickens through the crossing, into another block of wan lamplight muffled by the dense boughs of the ordered pines.

Unable to discern whether the siren might be approaching Main Street from a direction that will bring the patrol car past them, Katie and Libby slip between two SUVs, trading the traffic lanes for the sidewalk. With the cover of the vehicles to their left and the deeper darkness that the overhanging trees provide, they hurry after Zenon, hoping to close on him, surprise him, and discover if he is only what he seems to be or is a harbinger of the transformation of the world.

By the time they reach the intersection and transit the cross street, they lose sight of him. The siren is louder but behind them, not coming this way. They move faster and with less caution into another tunnel of conifers. Katie worries that they should turn back and take no further risk. Whatever Zenon is, he's no good, whether an arrogant and lawless ISA agent or a fusion. The midnight hour is coming; second by second they are farther away from the Range Rover, which is their only means of escape, if escape is even possible.

Fear is useful when it's on a leash, but it's always a bad dog when you let it run free in your mind.

Perhaps a hundred feet in front of them, Zenon steps out from between two vehicles and crosses the sidewalk and passes through an open gate, taking no notice of them.

The property encompasses the two lots at the end of the block and is encircled by a wrought-iron fence topped with spear-point pickets and decorated with scrollwork. Two ornate gates, one at each end of the circular driveway, are at the moment open. The house is more or less Georgian, brick with limestone or cast-stone window surrounds, fronted by an impressive columned portico through which the cobblestone driveway passes. It must be the most important house on this street, perhaps in all of the town, and it surely has a lake view.

A second siren swells, weaving its shriek of alarm with the first, as Katie and Libby crouch at the base of a pine tree and study the house through the fence pickets. Robert Zenon follows the driveway to the portico, no longer lurching as dramatically as he did before, though there is still an oddness to his movements that reminds Katie of Karloff in his signature film role. Perhaps Zenon was injured in his flight from Jacob's Ladder. He climbs a few steps to the door and enters the house so briskly that he can't have used a key or rung a bell.

Libby says, "If he spawns—"

"We don't know if he's a fusion," Katie reminds her.

"He is. He must be. You can see something's wrong with him."

"Something's always been wrong with him."

"If he spawns," Libby persists, "everyone in that house is screwed."

"It might be his house. He walked right in. There might be nobody else in there."

One siren dies, and then the other, and Libby protests, "We didn't come after him to wimp out."

"A strange house can be a trap. I'm not going to let you die in there."

After a silence, the girl says, "Penny and Regina weren't your fault. You've got nothing to atone for. And me—I throw hatchets, you know. I can use a shotgun. I'm not a little kid. I grew up long ago, and the last thing I want is to be like Francesca and Raleigh, looking out for myself so much that I'm blind to everyone else."

"That's not it."

"That's it," Libby insists. "That's exactly it. If this is the last night of the world, I don't want to do the wrong thing. Turning away from this, letting Zenon do what he wants, is the wrong thing. If there's judgment at the end, how do I explain why I did nothing?"

"It isn't the last night of the world," Katie says.

Libby speaks quietly, not argumentatively, with a reverberant conviction that echoes back through Katie and animates in her a sense that they are not trapped in a horror show, but are instead swept up in a series of mystical events that will either confirm the sacred nature of the human soul or condemn humanity to the status of prey and chattel. Libby is just a girl, but it was a girl of her age who raised the siege of Orléans in 1428 and broke

317

the English army, and no one can say what a girl might have the capacity to endure or achieve. "Maybe this is the last night the world still has a chance of hope and freedom," she insists. "If practice makes perfect, if Zenon is a stable fusion, the first in seven years, if the brainiacs are wrong when they say vaporizing the mother mass will destroy the fusions linked to it, then he's loose—it's loose—and the world is gone. *And they've been wrong about almost everything.*"

Swollen with water that their hard cuticles and waxed needles do not easily absorb, the boughs overhead gather rain into rivulets and channel it to branch tips and anoint Katie and Libby with dark streams that bear the incense of the pine, which is alike to the fragrance of the yew tree. A few blocks away, men of the law attend to the murdered body of one of their own that lies on the pavement, as if it is the useless flotsam of a shipwrecked society, as if it never was inhabited by a mind of infinite possibilities. So did Avi lie on a busy city street, in shadowless sunshine, his spine cracked and his vitals punctured, holding fast to life only to be able to say goodbye and to secure from her the Promise.

Katie says, "Whether Zenon is only the man he's always been or he's something else, there can be no mercy, and that will be on us."

"I know," the girl assures her.

"Then let's do it."

EIGHT
NEST

———

GRIMM

As she and Libby follow the arc of the cobbled driveway, Katie remembers reading somewhere that the road to Hell is paved with the bones of faithless priests and that the way is lighted by lampposts that are bishops who, in life, violated their vows without remorse and now burn eternally. She doesn't know why such a macabre image should occur to her in this fraught moment, unless she's being given a warning, a presentiment that this house will prove to be a preview of Hell writ momentary and in miniature.

Under the roof of the portico, they throw back the hoods of their jackets, climb four steps, and peer through the beveled panes of the sidelights that flank the door. Beyond lies a spacious foyer brightened by an immense chandelier with at least a hundred long crystals like obelisks hung upside down, their pyramidal points as sharp as ice picks, as if they could be released by a switch and bring a rain of death down on an intruder. To the right, a graceful limestone staircase with a Persian carpet runner curves to the second floor without pausing for a landing, and directly ahead a hallway leads to a closed door at the back of the residence.

Even in this time of rising crime and epidemic drug use, this is a town where people have left doors unlocked for generations and still do. No hamlet in America remains so safe that Beaver Cleaver can ride his bike into the evening without at least some risk of being abducted, raped, beheaded, and discarded in a dump. However, this community isn't accustomed to regular outrages that, elsewhere, have left many of their countrymen numb to violence so cruel as to seem almost satanic. Katie is prepared to find another way into the house—perhaps through an unlocked window—but when she tries the front door, it opens without the slightest sound of protest.

They enter the foyer and close the door behind them and stand dripping under the crystal dirks that imprint symmetrical patterns of gray lines on the pale limestone floor. The house is so well built that the voice of the storm hardly penetrates its walls, and no sound of internal origin gives any indication where Zenon has gone or how many others reside here.

To the right, before the stairs, a door stands open to a dark room. If she can judge by the handsome desk that is in part revealed by the influx of foyer light, it is a study.

The rubber soles of their shoes squeak thinly on the limestone as they step with caution out of the foyer, maintaining two-handed grips on their weapons. To their left, an archway trimmed out with layered moldings leads to a generously proportioned living room that is nevertheless crowded with large sofas and armchairs and antique Italian sideboards. The walls are adorned with paintings of famous Roman buildings in rococo gold-leafed frames, and all is warmly lighted by stained-glass lamps of rich provenance.

A Persian runner absorbs the rain they shed and quiets their sodden shoes as they pass a dining room currently illuminated only by a pair of Lalique sconces. Step by step, as the storm seems to go mum beyond the thick walls, as not a ripple of house sound disturbs the pooled stillness, Katie feels more threatened by the hush, for it seems to be the silence of surveillance, as if the wallpaper design is cunningly flowered to conceal tiny cameras that transmit their progress to a video screen where a smiling observer waits for the right moment to trigger some device that will snare them in heavy nets or open a trapdoor to drop them into a great depth of darkness where they will find themselves among the bones of those who took the plunge before them.

They arrive at a swinging door with a push plate of brushed stainless steel. No doubt the kitchen lies on the other side. A brighter light than that in the hallway leaks from beyond, defining the thin space between the door and jamb. That crisp light brings with it no sound. Katie looks at Libby, and the girl nods, and Katie keeps both hands on the rifle as she shoulders the door open and passes into a room that smells pleasantly of garlic and basil and fresh-baked bread.

A kitchen of this size, with its many appliances and dining table covered in red-and-white-checkered oilcloth, is the heart of the home. On the large island stands a platter of fresh artichokes awaiting use and a bowl of large black plums ripening.

The old woman—about five feet two, maybe two hundred twenty pounds—wears a short-sleeved ankle-length dress of a silky fabric, patterned with small blue-and-yellow birds bearing pink ribbons in their beaks. Her hair is gathered into a bun and pinned and further constrained by an elastic net, as though she is soon headed for bed. The seams of her fleece-lined slippers are partially sprung and her feet appear to be swelling out of them. She stands at the island, in front of a cutting board, carving and eating paper-thin slices of pepperoni. Beside the board, a squat glass contains red wine and a bottle of Chianti offers more.

She looks up when Katie and Libby enter the kitchen, chews, swallows, and says, "You got some complaint about Nino, you're forty-six years late. That damn Polack killed him and widowed me before you was born."

The woman's equanimity is not only too strange and calculated to be convincing, but it is also belied by how she changes her grip on the knife, clutching it in her tight fist, as if she hopes for a chance to use it like a dagger.

In addition to the swinging door, the kitchen presents Katie with four others, too many to remain properly alert to all of them. One is an exterior door with four panes of glass in the upper half. One is probably to a pantry, another to the basement, the fourth to a half bath or maybe a set of back stairs.

"Do I know you girls? Well, I must."

"Where is he?" Katie says.

"This is my house sometimes." The old woman looks around, as if confused. "Then sometimes it don't seem my house."

"Where's Zenon?"

She frowns. "What's a Zenon?"

"Robert Zenon."

"Some man?"

"We saw him come in here."

"A *vecchia donna* like me don't need a man."

"He's dangerous."

"Men, they all are."

"He killed a policeman."

The old woman doesn't respond to that revelation. She puts down the knife. Her sudden, sweet smile is almost convincing—except that her stare is as sharp as that of a viper. "You girls, are you my girls? You work for me? Why're you working at night?"

"I'm not buying the senile act, grandma."

"If you're not my girls come to work, you must be company. I don't get company so much like I used to."

"Cut the shit. Where is he?"

The old woman clicks her tongue in disapproval. "Such a potty mouth. Jesus is listening, young lady." She turns away from them and shuffles around the far end of the island, muttering in Italian.

"What're you doing?" Katie asks.

"Gotta treat company right, like my own mama taught me."

"Stop where you are."

She stops and sweetens her smile. "Homemade *sbriciolona* with a glass of *vin santo* or maybe port. Won't that be nice?" She is on the move again. "You get out the nice dessert plates with the pierced rims, dear, and don't forget the fancy napkins. No paper napkins for company. Everyone should be treated like the *capo di capi*."

As Libby stands with her back to a wall of cabinets, trying to watch four doors at once, Katie heads around the nearer end of the island to confront the old woman.

"I maybe got a fresh *ciambella*, too. I flavor it with anise, not lemon. It's good dunked in sweet wine."

Katie blocks her as she reaches for a yellow-enameled dropdoor box on the counter between the two Sub-Zero refrigerators. "Lady, I don't want to hurt you."

Looking bewildered, the old woman says, "It's my bread box. You don't like *ciambella*? I also got some *crema fritta*—or is it black grape pudding?—in the fridge. I made it yesterday, if I made it, or maybe I ate it."

Holding the AR-15 in her right hand, finger on the trigger, muzzle at the woman's throat, Katie uses her left hand to open the drop door. The bread box does indeed contain what appear to be delicious homemade baked goods—but also a 9 mm pistol.

"Seriously? You were going to try to shoot us, go against a rifle and a shotgun?"

The old woman pretends bewilderment. "Shoot someone with a *ciambella*? I never shot no one with a pastry ring."

Katie takes the pistol from the bread box. She steps back from her would-be murderer, out of reach. She ejects the magazine from the pistol and pockets it, shakes the round out of the breach and pockets that. The island contains a trash compactor that opens with a foot pedal. She drops the unloaded pistol in the waste bin and pushes the compactor shut.

"Robert Zenon," she says. "Is he upstairs? In the basement? Where exactly? Don't make us go room to room."

The old woman's face is a large lump of potato dough that hasn't been worked into a proper gnocchi, or that has been worked too long and now is heavy and coarse and incapable of being shaped into an appealing dumpling. Her black eyes are foul matter fallen into the mix from whatever rodent. When she speaks now with clear mind and undisguised intention, spittle sprays in a toxic mist and bubbles on her lips, as if it might well be venom. "Get out of my house, you syphilitic whore. Took me a year to have that Polack Spic bastard put through a meat grinder for whacking Nino, but I got him, and even after all this time, I still got a piece of the action and friends in the right places."

Katie can no longer imagine any of the ways she expected things to unfold after they pursued Zenon into the house. This grotesque old woman is unpredictable, and the chaos she adds to an already pandemonic situation puts them in greater peril second by second.

"Listen, calm down. We don't have a beef with you. This guy killed a cop. He really did. Just minutes ago. Why hide a murderer? What is he to you?"

"My grandson. My only *nipote*. I don't care he popped a hundred fucking cops. I hope he kills you, too, whatever you are."

Still with her back to the cabinets, nervously watching the five doors, Libby says, "It's not just that he killed a policeman. He's not who you think he is. Not anymore. He's a monster now."

Infuriated by her impotency, the old woman snatches a large plum from the bowl on the island and throws it at Libby and misses. "You ignorant little twat. *You're* a monster. This bitch with you is a monster. *I'm* a monster. This is a world of monsters, and anyone thinks she's not a monster—she'll be the first eaten alive."

Libby says, "Katie, for God's sake, tell her about Moloch, make her understand."

Tense, expecting another bread-box trick from the woman, Katie is watching her when Libby mentions Moloch, and she sees the twitch, the flare of nostrils, the widening of the eyes. "*You know.* You know about Ringrock."

"Who are *you* to know?" the old woman demands. "You don't look like somebody. You gotta be *somebody* to know about this."

"He's corrupted, infected. Your grandson. He isn't who he seems to be. It happened sometime in the past day, on my island, Jacob's Ladder. He's the most successful fusion so far."

Grimacing with anger and perhaps now with genuine confusion, the woman puts one hand to her forehead as if feeling for a fever. She tries to run a hand through her hair, having forgotten that she'd pinned it up, and the hair net startles her, tangles in her fingers. She plucks it off with a thin cry, as though for an instant she believes it's alive, a clinging insectile invader from another world. She throws it to the floor and stamps on it twice. "Piss and shit! Look what you got me doing. You got me in a state, busting in here like you done." She glares through ropes of hair that overhang her face like a Gorgon's snakes. "How would you know about him, my smart boy, what he is or isn't? You don't know nothing. My Bobby's too smart to get infected. You're a dumb slut is all you are." She turns away from Katie. "Now you fired up my sciatica, damn you." She limps toward the table with the red-and-white oilcloth. "You fired up my sciatica. Sweet Jesus, I got to sit down. Why don't you just shoot an old lady in the head and be done with her?"

What Katie learned from Avi over the years, coupled with her intuition, has kept her alive thus far; now her internal alarm bells are clanging as loud as they did when the crone was shuffling with arthritic pretense toward the bread box. Her severe limp appears too extreme even for Captain Ahab on deck during a wild chase after his white whale, and in spite of it, the woman moves with alacrity, face contorted by what she means to be an expression of pain but what looks like blackest hatred. Katie gets between her and the table, barring her way, enduring her curses. "Libby, check under the table and chairs. Start at that end, where she was headed."

"Check for what?" the girl asks.

"Ciambella," Katie replies, *"sbriciolona,* maybe some black grape pudding."

Libby crosses the room and puts the shotgun on the table and gets on her hands and knees and crawls under the draping oilcloth.

Face-to-face with Katie, the old woman says, "If I was your age, you'd be dead. I'd be cutting out your tongue for how you disrespected me."

Five doors. One behind her. Another far to her right, not quite in her peripheral vision. Katie doesn't want to look away from the old woman, who's within arm's reach. This geriatric psychopath has her hands in the pockets of her housedress, and you don't have to be paranoid to suspect she has a simple weapon in one or both of them—a nail file, a penknife, a razor blade—that she'd like to use to slice into a carotid artery or take out an eye.

"He told you about Moloch," Katie says, "but you don't get it."

"I get more than you'll ever get if you live to be a thousand. Bobby never shot no cop. He's in control of Ringrock. He brought me big news, good news, gonna tell me after he takes a shower. He's top dog on Ringrock, but a liar is all you are."

Libby crawls out from under the table and gets to her feet and holds up a pistol. "It was fixed to the underside with a spring clamp."

This is the kitchen of a witch. Katie and Libby are two Gretels without a Hansel, and they could still end up baked in an oven.

"Check that chair," Katie says.

The girl sits on the chair toward which the old woman had been headed. She feels under the seat with both hands. "It's clean."

As Libby rises to her feet, Katie tells the old woman to sit down, but the witch refuses. "I don't need to no more. My sciatica suddenly let up. I gotta go potty, unless you're a pervert likes to see an old lady piss herself."

On the second floor, something falls over with a hard crash that reverberates through the ceiling and rings glass against glass inside the cabinets, like the high-pitched laughter of evil elfin presences living secretly in the kitchen's many cloistered spaces.

A DISAGREEMENT

Libby doesn't know how many times her heart can beat per minute before it ruptures, but she figures she's two-thirds of the way to the lethal speed even just thinking about going upstairs to see what Robert Zenon has become.

In the kitchen, one of the five doors opens to the back stairs, which comprises two flights and a landing, so that if they're on the lower flight, they won't be able to see what might be waiting on the upper one until they turn at the landing. At that point, face-to-face with whoever or whatever, they would have to stand their ground or be attacked from behind as they turned and fled. These stairs are also as enclosed and narrow as a slaughterhouse chute. No way.

By contrast, the front stairs are open, curving up without a landing, and they can see all the way to the upper hall. When they get up there, all bets are off, but at least during the ascent, they aren't blind to what threats await them.

Whatever's upstairs can elude them by coming down the back way. However, the offspring of Moloch have so far not been reluctant to engage in confrontation.

Libby would like to lock Grandma Dracula in a closet or tie her in a chair, but there's no time. Besides, the witch is probably able to speak her way out of chains and through locks with one spell or another, and the last thing they need is her surprising them with one of the maybe hundred other guns she has hidden around the house. Katie wants the old woman to lead the way, keep a gun on her back, and force her to be the first to encounter her beloved grandson in whatever form he might currently have taken.

After the crone has turned out the pockets of her dress and submitted to a pat down, she decides to give them grief again by refusing to go upstairs. Katie tells her that if she takes the lead, she'll have a chance to talk to Bobby and somehow get him to prove he's not a fusion, but if she refuses to do that, then Katie will shoot him on sight.

When the battle-ax responds with an obscene suggestion and spits in her face, Katie surprises them—and maybe herself—by in an instant reversing her grip on the rifle and slamming the butt into the crone's mouth, splitting her lips and staggering her backward against the refrigerator. In the thin wash of blood, a broken tooth slides down the old woman's chin, not quite as yellow as a kernel of corn, and drops among the birds carrying pink ribbons across the shelf of her bosom.

"No second chance," Katie warns. Her face is so changed by wrath that she looks like a different person. "Everything isn't about you or about the arrogant grandson you fucked up. There are other people in the world, you selfish bitch, and they matter. You take the lead now, or I shoot you in the gut, let you lie on the floor and scream yourself to death."

This has a remarkable effect on the old woman, as if it never occurred to her in more than eight decades of life that anyone would raise a hand against her. Except for the bright blood dripping from her mouth, she is as white as a hard-boiled egg, and a greasy sweat slicks her face. Her eyes are wide with shock, maybe with something more than shock, with a cold fear that is as new to her as humility would be if that virtue could be instilled with as little as a hard blow to the mouth. She doesn't quake or cry.

She continues to curse Katie, but her swearing and blaspheming are no longer in a voice of challenge and contempt, but muttered as if for no purpose except to reassure herself that she is no less a dragon lady than she's always been. Holding a hand over her mouth, she leads the way to the front stairs without further contention.

Katie looks at Libby and then urges the old woman through the swinging door. In that brief glance, Libby reads not just anger and fear, but also a certain sadness and regret. She knows she isn't reading more than is there to be read. As a girl who has journeyed through a few hundred books, she has become an insightful reader. People are books of a kind, each one a story. Sometimes, with no more than a glance or a gesture or a poignant word, they turn a page for you and reveal a deeper truth about themselves than you've seen before. In these extreme circumstances, Katie has done only what was necessary when she struck the old woman. Nevertheless, being Katie, she will pay a self-imposed price for what has happened, because she understands that necessity doesn't fully excuse meanness.

Following the two women into the hall, Libby knows that if they live through this night, she has found in Katie the mother who for fourteen years has been denied her, the rock of love and selfless giving who will encourage and sustain her at all times and without fail. She says now what she has never said to anyone, not even to Sarah, "I love you," but she barely whispers it for fear that she will jinx this last, best hope if she speaks those words too loud.

ELECTRICITY

The upstairs hall is not just a place but also a representation of Katie's dread, a pulsative-throated passage clotted with darkness that will swallow anyone who steps into it. One of the switches at the bottom of the stairs brings light above, but banishing darkness doesn't discharge the aura of menace up there.

The old woman leads reluctantly. With her right hand over her mouth, muttering into her plump fingers, left hand on the handrail, from step to ascending step, she carries the burden of her flesh and also her humiliation, which is by far the heavier weight. She has been shocked by her vulnerability, although not to any extent that will result in useful self-assessment. Katie can almost hear the woman scheming to settle the score. The crone knows about Ringrock and understands that a mistake there can imperil the world, and she may even suspect that something is wrong with her grandson, but the fate of humanity probably matters not at all to her because she's too much of a narcissist to believe she will die along with everyone else. Evidently, she has led a life cosseted in a criminal culture of inherited position; she also seems to possess an impressive talent for sustaining power relationships over a long period of time. Most octogenarians at least occasionally contemplate their mortality; however, when this one considers her eighty-nine years, maybe she sees her longevity as evidence that another eighty-nine isn't unlikely. Those for whom self-love is the only love are very skilled at creating fantasies in which they live contentedly until reality threatens to pop their bubble, whereupon they can be capable of any atrocity in defense of their delusions. Ideally, this woman wouldn't be leading the way, but she can't be trusted at their back. Killing her must be a last resort in respect of Katie's conscience and out of consideration for how such a scene would forever fester in Libby's memory.

Last in their procession, the girl sidles up the stairs, her back to the railing, so that she will know at once if something creeps into view behind them. She holds the shotgun low, ready to fire from the hip, aware that what creeps might also be capable of springing upon her in an instant. Even with its recoil-reduction technology, the 12-gauge will challenge her balance if she has to fire it with her feet on different treads.

Whatever the cause of the crash that initially alerted them to activity on the second floor, no sound follows it—until they reach the top step. Then a sibilation as thin as the summer-night song of insects seems to rise all around them. As they pause, turning their heads to seek a source, the hiss swells and clarifies until it is an electronic keening like the tinnitus that, in response to stress, troubles insomniacs. With their ascent complete, they are above the grand chandelier that perpetually cascades to their left, beyond the railing and above the foyer. The pendant crystal dirks reflect the sound until, among them, it is not a single voice but an ominous chorus reminiscent of hornets swarming.

Stepping into the upstairs hall, the old woman lowers her gore-gloved hand from her mouth and wipes it on her dress. As if she has forgotten her pain and, for the moment, put aside all thought of retribution for the loss of a tooth, she takes three steps into the hallway, turning her head left and right, looking up at the ceiling, seeking. The sound is unnatural and too shrill to be of no serious consequence; it is the sound of pressure rising toward a blowout or a meltdown, with damage inevitable.

Hanging arm's-length at her sides, her hands curl into fists as she considers this new offense. She calls out—"Who's there?"—as though it could be someone other than her grandson, some malefactor who ventured in here to pillage and vandalize, unaware this is the freehold of Nino's widow, where no crimes are tolerated except those committed by the owner. Katie wants to avoid drawing attention and thereby lose the element of surprise, if in fact they have any left, but she's sure there's no way to silence this bullheaded octogenarian brat short of shooting her. As the eerie keening grows louder, the woman raises her voice. "Hey, asshole, this is *my* house! You know *who I am*? Where are you, what the fuck you doing?"

Her features clenched in rage, the old woman heads toward a door on the right, bloody foam dripping from her chin, as if she is infected with rabies. Anger is her staff of life, nourishing in her a fierce confidence that has reliably cowed those who would resist her. She clearly expects that it will serve her well again.

Frightened by the crone's recklessness, Libby says, "Katie, do something."

Katie motions for the girl to climb the last two steps and join her in the hall.

The old woman throws open the door and crosses the threshold and clicks on a light. She's out of sight less than half a minute, but when she returns, she is angrier than ever, her face empurpled with rage. Somewhere in these chambers, a violent creature born of Moloch waits, and judging by the shrill keening, which now grows louder, it's engaged in an activity they haven't seen before, but this woman exhibits no fear of the unknown. Her self-love seems to have doubled and redoubled over the years, metastasizing until she believes that she knows or correctly intuits everything, that the unknown—especially the category of the Unknown requiring the word to be capitalized—exists only for other people, the benighted and the foolish. The blow she took from Katie can be forced down a memory hole now that this new offender gives her an opportunity to assert herself. As she crosses the hall to another closed door, her eyes appear lidless and swollen in their sockets by the pressure of her fury. She doesn't so much as glance at Katie, but shouts at the imagined vandal. "Quiet! Stop whatever you're doing, stop it this minute!" She opens the door and storms into the room and abandons a curse midsentence, her abrupt silence almost as unsettling as a scream.

"Stay sharp," Katie tells Libby, and she moves cautiously to the threshold.

The old woman stands agape, staring at something at the far end of the bedroom, a sight blocked from Katie. She uses the rifle to ease the door open wider, all the way back against the wall, and steps inside.

If Moloch is a weapon, as Libby reports that some who studied it contend, it is designed not solely to slaughter, not just also to terrorize, but equally to dispirit. Whatever civilization conceived it and produced it and set it loose—perhaps in legions, millennia ago—must have been evil personified, apostles of nihilism who meant to prove the meaninglessness of the universe by waging eternal war on every intelligent species, on planets known and unknown to them, even after the extinction of their own kind. They must have been at war with hope and the idea of transcendence, because the biological chaos on display here mocks the concept of benign creation and the value of the soul, inspiring despair and surrender to oblivion.

Robert Zenon's clothes and weapons lie discarded on the floor, and he sprawls on the bed, a gross obscenity. It's not his nakedness that is obscene, but what he has become and is becoming. If he was a hundred and seventy pounds before, he's more than three hundred in this incarnation, the folds of his flesh compiled in layers not as any human body arranges tissues, but reminiscent of the hard fungus, *polyporus igniarius*, that drapes the lower trunks of some trees on Jacob's Ladder, like a slide of pancakes slightly offset one from the other. The vast corpus glistens with a substance that appears oilier than sweat. Broad feet, toes hooked and carapaced with a hornlike material. Enlarged hands, fingers long and spatulate. His neck is as thick as his head, his head half again as large as it ought to be. Even with his distorted features, he is recognizably Zenon, the ISA agent. The question of whether there remains anything of the *person* he once was, any quality of mind and degree of self-awareness, is too awful to contemplate. He makes no eye contact, but stares at a fixed point above their heads. Neither does he cry out in misery or entreaty, for from his open mouth issues the sound that began as a sibilation and has escalated to an electronic shriek.

How he, a fusion, could increase so dramatically in size in the short time since he murdered a policeman and took refuge here is no mystery. Libby has said that Moloch and the hybrids it creates can feed on pure energy to build matter at an astonishing rate. From the spine of this freak issues a cord about an inch in diameter, like a coaxial cable with vertebrae, which trails off the bed and to an electrical outlet in the wall; the cover plate has been torn away, and the snaky extension of the Zenon hybrid has inducted itself into the receptacle, sucking power with which to grow. Now Katie realizes that the mountain of flesh subtly throbs, that even the skull pulses as though the bone continuously restructures and expands. If this feverish rate of growth isn't just chaos, the purpose eludes Katie—until it becomes manifest.

The old woman is transfixed by what has become of her grandson, although she doesn't recoil from the sight of him. Neither does she tremble nor stand with her hands fisted in a characteristic posture of anger. Indeed, a hard to define aspect of her expression, an odd set to her mouth, something in her black eyes that isn't light but seems like light—these things suggest, inexplicably, that what's happening to Zenon evokes in her not horror, not fear, but a sense of wonder that she has never felt previously. His transformation is a display of power beyond anything she could previously conceive, and she is a woman to whom power is the only thing to be devoutly worshipped. As if in a trance—as if called by that siren voice that Tanner Walsh followed into the lake the night he drowned, the same voice that spoke to Katie from the kitchen drain—the grandmother approaches the repulsive thing on the bed.

"Bobby?" she says.

"No," Katie warns.

With greater speed and fluidity than an amoeba reproducing by fission, the beast on the bed forms a deep division groove and, with a sound like lava oozing-chuckling-crackling from a volcanic vent, it separates into two entities in no more than twenty seconds. At first, each individual has the mass of one Robert Zenon distributed through a body with a single leg and single arm, as if this is the victim of a bad judgment by an unwise King Solomon. In each case, a lone eye glares from a malformed skull that is convex on one side, flat on the other. The substance of this bifurcated being is as plastic as amoeboid cytoplasm; the flesh flows into the fullness of two Zenons, like air filling out half-collapsed balloons.

Heart knocking furiously, Katie backs three steps toward the hall door as the newly formed Zenon, the one not attached to a wall plug by an umbilical cable, rises from the bed. He is as apparently real and well formed as any man whom she's ever seen—except that he lacks testicles and a penis, as though in recognition of the fact that he's a product of asexual reproduction. Considering the hyperrealism with which the rest of him has been crafted, the absence of those organs seems to be a statement of contempt for procreation via coitus, and perhaps for all that issues from it, such as family and the bonds that tie generation to generation.

Practice makes perfect. Moloch has attained full knowledge and mastery of the human genome, the proteins and chemistries required for faultless mimicry. Patience is the devil's only virtue, though seven years is but a week—a day, an hour—for this creature that has traveled across a thousand times a thousand galaxies.

"Bobby?" When the old woman speaks his name, he turns his gaze on her and says, "Nonna."

Whether drawn to him by a siren voice or by her twisted psyche, perhaps by both, she marvels at this risen double and touches his face with one hand. "Bobby?"

"Nonna Giana," he says, his voice flat and cold.

On the bed, the other Zenon seems insensate, lying against the stack of pillows, still gazing toward the ceiling, his mouth open. Only then does Katie realize that the one-note squeal is to a degree diminished and is no longer issuing from the reclining figure. It comes instead from the adjoining bathroom, where the door stands ajar and darkness pools beyond.

There were always two electronic voices shrieking, precisely coordinated. Abruptly, the volume increases to its previous level. Once more, two sources emit the piercing sound, as the Zenon on the bed begins to pulse. New flesh forms out of him in offset layers like depending fungic masses of *polyporus igniarius*.

The naked man who stands before Nonna Giana is evidently not the first that the reclining Zenon manufactured out of the flow of electricity. Another must be in the bathroom, umbilicated to a power outlet, reproducing a replica of its own.

Breathing hard and fast, unaware of having moved, Katie finds that she has retreated to the threshold of the room.

The Zenon who has risen from the bed embraces the old woman, pulls her tight against him. As though she's not a creature of flesh and blood, merely energy in the form of matter, he absorbs her, his entire body a sponge. No spray of blood, no crack of splintering bone, no cascade of viscera. Only a sound like the much amplified suction of a thick milkshake being imbibed through a straw. Faster than human science can explain, she is gone as if she was never more than vapor, her clothes fluttering to the floor, jewelry no longer of value to her, fleece-lined slippers standing untenanted. The grandmother's bulk inflates the Zenon. As he was formed by fission, so now he becomes a fusion. Bloated, slick with some oily excretion, this massive consolidation slumps to the floor beside the bed and begins to split in two, in the manner that the Zenon on the bed had previously divided.

The spectacle is horrific but equally mesmerizing, seeming to involute Katie's soul like a fully bloomed flower curling its petals into a tight and colorless bud, so that she has no courage to move.

The fission occurring before her spews off a third entity, much smaller than the two Zenons who are becoming, for there is more mass than needed for the twins. Smaller than a two-year-old child, this thing squirms across the carpet, like a cocoon made mobile by the wriggling of what it contains, shaping itself as it moves, tucking itself in a corner as it becomes a minikin of the grandmother, her aged face in the body of an infant. She glares across the room at Katie, her black eyes twice as large as they ought to be, her stare intense, her hatred palpable, working her toothless mouth until teeth begin to sprout, not Nonna Giana, only a mockery of her, but also a thing of pure evil that has drifted countless light-years through a void to the precious ground of Earth.

Although she hears no siren voice stealing her free will, Katie feels spellbound, perhaps by cold terror distilled to a potency that paralyzes the mind. She hears herself resort to different lines from Eliot—"All shall be well and / all manner of thing shall be well. All shall be well and / all manner of thing shall be well"—as if by this incantation she can break the dark enchantment that grips her.

In the corner, the minikin of the crone hisses like a serpent, and from beyond the bedroom Libby calls out—"Katie!"—and the bathroom door swings open on darkness, a tall shape looming.

Katie pivots to the hallway, pulling the door shut behind her. She grabs the girl by one arm, compelling her toward the front stairs. *"Run!"*

DIABOLIC

This house is a madhouse and a realm of witchery in which evil can be conjured merely by the expectation of it. The front stairs are no more than fifteen feet from the door that Katie pulls shut between her and the room where replicas are shaped into the world like demons summoned from a cauldron. Nevertheless, as she and Libby reach the top step, yet another Zenon moves out of the ground-floor hallway, into the foyer, under the obeliscal crystals of the buzzing chandelier, to the foot of the stairs.

The science of this advanced alien civilization, having been refined through tens of thousands of years, seems like magic, though not of the Disney variety. When science has no goal but power, it mantles itself in wickedness. Those who wield such power, convinced of their immortality, worship no god other than Death, and Death is obedient in their service.

Katie and Libby halt at the sight of the replica below. It must have been the first individual formed by the plugged-in Zenon, must have gone down to the kitchen by the back stairs, in search of them. Because it is born to terrorize as well as kill, *because it can*, it calls forth from its omnibus of alien genomes an alternate design to human bipedalism, morphing into an armless man with six muscular but vaguely insectile legs, the better to dart up the stairs low and quick.

"Back door!" Libby says as she hurries away along the upstairs hall.

Katie agrees that the back stairs and the kitchen door are their best way out, but she hesitates long enough to squeeze off four rounds from the AR-15. At this ideal range and angle, the creature takes four hits, at least two in the head, and tumbles backward, though Katie has no expectation that it is dead or can be killed. She hopes only to delay the thing for a crucial half minute, while it heals its protean substance and regains its form. As she turns away to follow the girl, she is aware that no blood burst from the bullet wounds. She also believes she sees—but doesn't tarry to confirm—chunks of curved skull and a broken slab of the face with an eyeless socket that, by some ghastly method of locomotion, are crawling toward the twitching replica, to marry themselves to it, while wads of matter on the stairwell wall unite with a similar intention.

She sprints along the hallway, quick after Libby, gasping for breath not because she's physically exhausted, which she is not, but because she feels an incipient dizziness that she must stave off by flooding the brain with oxygen, fears spinning like a carousel of shadows through her mind. Moloch's displays of biological mastery are an invitation to madness for any who witness them. Back in the day, the loss of her family and the failure of the system to punish those who committed murder had tested her sanity to the brink of destruction. From that ordeal, she seems to have acquired immunity to madness, if not also to despair, and she keeps moving as the dizziness relents.

Waiting at the end of the hall, Libby cries out, "Behind you!"

Katie angles to the wall, rolls against it to face the way she came, and opens fire on a pair of Robert Zenons, each on two legs, as she backs toward the girl. Six rounds remain in the magazine, and she expends them, doing enough damage to knock down both pursuers, though they are incapable of being long discouraged.

Marine wife, Marine widow—always faithful, as the Corps' motto pledges—with the Promise to be kept, she ejects the spent magazine and slaps in a fresh one. She races after Libby, down the back stairs, leaving the stairhead door open behind them because it has no lock. As much a chute as a stairwell. Worn rubber treads peeling off the wood. The lower run of steps ahead lies out of sight beyond the landing. Anything might be waiting, ascending. She should have gone first, even though the girl has the shotgun, should have gone first, damn it, although if one of them is going to die in this hateful shaft, then both are going to die here.

Nothing waits on the lower stairs. Libby and then Katie plunge into the kitchen, into the aroma of garlic and freshly baked bread. The infernal electronic shriek is louder than ever. Katie slams the door to the stairs. It lacks a lock. With one hand, Libby hooks a chair from the dining table and shoves it across the floor. Katie snares it and tilts it on its back legs and jams the headrail under the doorknob.

Nothing in the kitchen. The swinging door is closed. The Zenon with four legs too many might be scurrying to the second floor—or coming this way. Go out the back. The only option.

Opening the door to the porch, Katie is pummeled by an influx of wind bearing the scent of rain and of ozone lingering from the lightning earlier. As she steps out of the house, she hears what for an instant sounds like thunder, but she realizes that it's a child of Moloch running across the roof overhead. Having come out of the window at the end of the second-floor hallway, one of the Zenons leaps to the lawn beyond the porch, morphing as it drops and rolls. It rises transformed, strange beyond all understanding, a thing that the conditions of this world would never have brought forth. It is a construct suited to scuttle across the floor of an unearthly sea, in heavy waters black and poisonous, as spinose as a thorny cactus, armored, with several eyes as red as blood. She empties the magazine into it, but it comes on like a Lovecraftian menace.

She backs into the kitchen and slams the door and locks it, but a pane of glass explodes, then another. At the same moment, a great weight crashes hard into the braced door at the foot of the stairs. She joins Libby, putting the island between them and the barriers that are under attack, fumbling her last magazine into the AR-15. The swinging door is to their left and might offer an escape—or a confrontation no better than the two that are impending.

The staircase door is battered, battered, the chair stuttering under the knob, and two more panes shatter in the back door. A chair leg cracks. The chair sags. The leg splinters. The chair collapses. Simultaneously, the back door is torn from its hinges and flung away onto the porch. Into the kitchen surge entities no less abhorrent than those in the hideous throng that poured *out* of Poe's Haunted Palace.

Many miles out on the great lake, the aborning light swells and for an instant shrinks as if it will collapse in upon itself, into a black hole of immense gravity created by its own fruition. Then it flares in such brightness that shadows of porch posts and window muntins imprint upon the kitchen, like hieroglyphs of urgent but indecipherable meaning. In that wild light, an abomination that might be the king of Hell himself hulks just inside the back door, and lesser devils loom out of the stairs, and time seems to have stopped. Then the shock wave comes, and the roar. The bones of the house rattle in the walls, and window glass hums, and all manner of things clink and clatter. Nothing breaks, nothing topples, nothing burns, and the house lights merely flicker, because the blast is at a significant distance, produced by a large tactical weapon four stories underground rather than by a city-leveler detonated at altitude.

Linked by microwave to the mother mass on Ringrock, the vicious progeny of Moloch stand sentinel, motionless and alert, perhaps in expectation that their maker is going to draw the massive release of energy into her loom and weave it into her substance until she grows to many times her current size. Katie and Libby stand eye to eye in the desperate hope that the creature has instead been overwhelmed and vaporized. The turbulence quickly subsides. The tide of hard white light simmers to orange and recedes, leaving the house to its lamps. Those entities whose origin traces back countless millennia and innumerable light-years to a nameless world and a nameless race suddenly shed their structure more rapidly than late-made snowmen on a sudden summery day, masses of substance sloughing to the floor and puddling not like snowmelt but obscenely, like the ancient flesh of vampires, sustained by the blood of others, might swiftly decompose when exposed to the cruciform made famous on Golgotha. That alien tissue, once so talented at mimicry, lies inert and gray and growing grayer, neither straining toward any shape nor churning chaotically. From it arises a putrid stench in part like rotting meat and sewage, but as well like burning rubber and melting copper, a stink that surely confirms that Moloch will have no resurrection.

The only sounds in the house are the susurration of the rain and the wheeze and whistle of the wind, issuing from the doorless doorway to the back porch—until a siren arises and then another.

Katie and Libby look at each other, but neither speaks, for there are no words adequate to the moment.

If it seems that they are spared and safe, they both know that safety is an illusion. If those responsible for bringing Moloch to the surface of the Earth choose to conceal the facts, they will craft a narrative involving terrorists or other villains. They are excellent at suppressing the truth and dazzling with fictions of convincing complexity. They'll give no quarter to anyone who knows the truth and might expose them to the wrath of the citizens they purport to serve. They will be certain that Libby knows too much. What they'll find on Jacob's Ladder is sure to convince them that Katie, still bitter about the injustice she endured in the past, is a threat to the ruling class, which in their minds is the same as being an existential threat to the state.

She and the girl are not in imminent peril. They have a few days to scheme their way out of their true past and into a future where they will be other than who they really are. However, they need to get on the move, away from the lake and the town and this state before roadblocks might be erected to support the deception that terrorists are being sought.

To be sure the girl understands, Katie says, "We leave it all behind."

Libby nods. "Everything we want is nothing here."

"Then let's go do it."

NINE
AFTERMATH

THE FOX AND THE ARTIST

In the aftermath of the explosion, with fear rampant and the authorities suspicious of everyone old enough to walk, anyone who openly carries a gun will likely be forced to surrender it or use it. Coats from Nonna Giana's foyer closet are swaddling clothes in which to conceal the rifle and the shotgun, so that the weapons can be carried like babies wrapped against the rain.

In the years ahead, the world becoming will have its monsters, although they will be exclusively of this world, born of man and woman, innocent and harmless until they are transformed by envy and hatred and ideology. Against the children of Moloch, firearms were of minimal effectiveness; however, in crises to come, they will be essential to the defense of the just and innocent.

The sky is an inverted ocean, its substance falling in waves of dense spray, and in this bleak moment, Katie feels as if the works of humanity are at risk of being naught but shipwrecks on the shoals and beaches of pitiless time. As she and Libby hurry along the curve of the cobbled driveway, through the open gate, under the conifers, the wind batters and mocks them. The trees toss their crowns, shake their limbs, flail their branches, and pitch down cones that bounce like live grenades along the pavement. Street drains are clogged, gutters overwhelmed, intersections flooded. The blast on distant Ringrock has awakened townspeople; light fills the glass of windows previously dark, where faces with shadowed features peer through the streaming panes. At many houses, people have come onto their front porches, sometimes entire families. As usually happens when normal life is unexpectedly rattled on its foundations, even on those occasions when a momentous event seems dire but is not yet fully understood, a not unpleasant excitement thrills through those gathered and seeking news, as though coded in the human genome is a profound awareness that history is laboring toward an apocalypse of which this might be but the beginning, when the horror of the human condition will be at last explained and the world made right at a price but a price worth paying. From their porches they call out to Katie and Libby: *"What's happening, what was that sound, what was that light, where are you going, what have you seen?"* They have seen everything, but nothing that will satisfy the unconscious longing of those who call out to them, and they respond to no one.

Sirens sweep through the night in numbers that seem peculiar for a town of six or eight thousand, as though every patrol car, ambulance, and fire engine has been summoned. There are no apparent fires, though a new odor of burning and ashes has come ashore from Ringrock even on this wettest of wind. The shock wave wasn't fierce enough to cause damage on the mainland. Few hearts are weak enough to suffer a cardiac event because of an explosion miles away. Katie can't help but wonder if, in the minutes immediately before the detonation, a federal agency gave a heads-up to local authorities for the purpose of engaging them in the response with as little delay as possible. If that's the case, the need to get out of town is more urgent than ever, before it's closed down.

In the mid-block parking lot, between the alleyway and Main Street, the Range Rover stands where they left it. At a rear window, Michael J. watches them without evident anxiety, as if he never doubted they would return.

Katie is surprised by the emotion that swells in her at the sight of the fox. He means more to her than seems reasonable. He is what he has appeared to be, in a time when not much has been what it seems. His beauty is the truth of the world, an answer to all the ugliness that has been imposed on it by those whose reason has deserted them. If she is to paint again as she hopes—not to seek the *why* of her subjects but to present entirely the *what* of them, the uniqueness that, if properly appreciated, answers the hardest of questions about the meaning of life—then she must start with this humble fox and do justice to his glory.

First, she and the girl need to stay alive. And free.

They put their weapons on the floor of the back seat, covered in the coats. Katie takes off the small backpack full of money and the Tac Light taped to her arm, and puts them with her rifle.

She gets behind the wheel, and Libby settles in the passenger seat. They're soaked and cold to the bone, but when the Rover starts with a push of the ignition button, they smile at each other, as if the rumble of the engine is predictive of the destiny they seek.

They negotiate the town by its alleyways and secondary lanes, eluding all the sources of the sirens. As they enter one backstreet, about a dozen teenage boys on foot, none dressed for the weather, come racing at them, though not with bad intention. They're excited, calling out to one another as they run toward the lake, on some midnight adventure in the wake of the explosion, perhaps having heard that the forests of Ringrock are ablaze with such intensity that the rain can't extinguish them. If authorities are concerned about radiation, they apparently haven't begun to alert the locals to evacuate or at least stay inside to minimize exposure. Maybe the consensus is that the volume and velocity of rain will purge the air of fallout, washing radioactive particles into the diluting volume of the lake before they can reach the mainland. Or the device was less dirty than a standard tactical weapon. Or maybe the people who should care about the consequences to public health don't care about anything other than concealing the truth and shifting the blame to nonexistent villains. Some of the boys slap the flanks of the Rover as they stream by on both sides, and some make comical faces, bright presences in the headlights, fading as they pass. In the rearview mirror, they're reduced to shadowy shapes reflecting the red of taillights, like embers blowing toward extinguishment.

THE EAGLE, THE LION, AND THE CROCODILES

Katie is a widow only three days when a friend who is Avi's part-ner in their security company, a former Marine named Sudi, pays her a visit. He brings a package he was entrusted to deliver in the event of Avi's death.

Sudi is as formidable as a supernatural visitation, tall and strong and the black of polished ebony, father of four, husband of Shanda, warrior and mensch. He has wanted to take up the fight that led to Avi's murder by hit-and-run, but Katie has forbidden that. She is the godmother of their oldest child and honorary aunt to all four, and she will not see those children's father taken from them. On the battlefields of war, where the lives and free-doms of millions are at imminent risk, evil must be resisted by all means available and with overwhelming force. However, on the battlefields of daily life, different rules apply; collateral damage is less justified, and resistance to the wicked must be at a time and place—and of a kind—that is not their choice but instead the choice of those whom they have wronged.

The package that Sudi delivers is just a nine-by-twelve manila envelope containing eight pages of information. The self-sealing flap is further secured with a sticker depicting the eagle, globe, and anchor that is the enduring symbol of the United States Marines.

They sit at her kitchen table with coffee while Sudi explains the envelope. Avi had asked him only to deliver it, and the words are Sudi's own. All Marines aspire to the vigilance, courage, and nobility that the eagle represents, and nearly all conduct their careers in full honor of the Corps and its traditions. "But some," he says, "are greater eagles than others, and we both know Avi was one of those. Not many have earned the Navy Cross. For all of that, he was humble. He'd never call himself an eagle, but he believed you were a lion. After your parents and the girls . . . when he took it on himself to find the truth and get justice, he worried what you would do if anything happened to him. He was concerned you'd be all fight, no fright. He wanted you to live—and know a lioness isn't a coward when she backs away from a fight with a family of crocodiles. He wanted you to have the knowledge you'd need to give you options if he was taken out and you were alone."

Gazing into her coffee as if she is a master of elaeomancy and can read the future in the characteristics of a liquid surface, she says, "He made me promise to live for him, for them, and I've never broken a promise to him. I never would. I've just got to figure out *how* to live."

"One way might have to be that you become someone else." He taps the envelope on the table. "This gives you what you need to know if events force you to make that choice."

After Sudi leaves, she opens the envelope. She does not expect a love letter, and there isn't one. She and Avi didn't need to write down their love in words, for they lived it in their every action, every day of their lives. Avi has given her a detailed explanation of what she needs to do to disappear, to fade as Katie and become someone else so effectively that no trail remains to follow. In the course of the investigations he'd done for corporations, charitable foundations, universities, and others, he'd tracked down individuals who had remade themselves with new identities—but there were others he failed to find. From the failures, he learned as much as from his successes, including the names and addresses of a few providers of ID and related services who are the best at what they do and always loyal to those whom they shepherd into a new identity. In the last paragraph, he urges her to memorize every word of his advice, including those contacts, before destroying the document.

She needs four days of intense study, twelve hours a day, to engrave every word in her memory. Her eyes burn, and headaches come and go, but the task gives her something to do other than grieve, and it keeps her sane.

Instead of at once putting this knowledge to use, she chooses instead to serve as executor of her parents' estate, sell their house and her own, dispose of her interest in the security business, collect on life insurance policies, and retreat to Jacob's Ladder. If the senator and those who would smooth his way to further power decide that she is unfinished business, they will know where to find her—and she will be ready for them.

OUT OF THE DARKNESS

An occasional display of lightning reveals the thunderheads like mountains reshaping in slow motion, but these are the late-storm soft pulses that travel the hills and valleys of the sky without drama. The rain remains heavy, but the wind is diminishing, and better weather lies ahead.

Westbound on the interstate, they seek news on the radio. For an hour, they can find no mention of an explosion that must have registered at least four on the Richter scale in territory where earthquakes of even a modest power are rare. Music for every taste, infomercials, men who want everyone to know Jesus as well as they do, post-midnight talk radio about out-of-body experiences and shadow people from other dimensions are plentiful, but when news can be found, it's regarding current political skirmishes, celebrity divorces, and public officials denying rape charges. The absence of a story about the destruction of Ringrock might be a consequence of journalistic laziness, but Katie and Libby are in a mood to suspect that the story is being suppressed until authorities can figure out how best to manage it.

In the eastbound lanes, a van appears, crowned with an array of strobing red and white lights that brighten the dark rain into blood and tears, though it emits no siren. It's the herald of a convoy of what appear to be military eighteen-wheelers, although they lack insignia or identification of any kind. Eight, ten, twelve of the big trucks flash past, as ominous as the cars of a Hellbound train, the urgency of their mission implied by the flashing lights that precede them but also by the fact that they are greatly exceeding the speed limit and have launched at an hour when the rest of the world assumes a slower pace.

"When will we be safe?" Libby asks.

Katie glances at the dwindling convoy in the rearview mirror. "Not tonight."

THE MOON AND THE MAN

As Katie races west, the rain moves east. Twenty miles after she has no further need of windshield wipers, the clouds wither and the once drowned moon is resurrected.

During a night of fight and flight, they have been made quicker and stronger and more alert by adrenaline, and they're still powered by it. However, she wants to put a few hundred more miles between them and Ringrock as fast as she can, and the time is coming when exhaustion and the need for sleep can be staved off only with caffeine. The Rover, too, is going to need fuel soon, and Katie is relieved when a sign announces a truck stop eleven miles ahead.

"After we've got a full tank, you can sleep," she tells the girl. "I'll be okay with black coffee."

"No way. I want to be totally caffeinated. I don't want to sleep till I'm so freakin' tired I don't wake every hour from a nightmare."

"Too much caffeine might make the dreams worse."

"I'll risk it. When we're missing, will they think we're dead, victims of Moloch?"

"Maybe. If we can make this Rover disappear. But we'll need to change the way we look."

"Change how?"

"New hair styles for both of us. A new hair color for me. Small things will be enough if they really think we're dead."

"We don't have ID to be other people."

"I know how to get it."

"How?"

"You'll see."

"Who will we be?"

"Mother and daughter. That okay with you?"

After a silence, the girl says, "I'd like that. I mean, if you think that would be good."

"I think it would be."

"I don't have any money."

"No need for any."

"I'll have to pay you back someday."

Katie is pleased to find that she can smile. "Damn right you will. I can't abide freeloaders."

"Me neither. We'll need a story."

"We're pretty creative. I bet everything I own, we'll come up with something."

The truck stop is a town in itself, employing hundreds, serving countless thousands, offering more than gasoline and diesel fuel, comprised of a motel, restaurant, pharmacy, gift shop, barber shop, chapel, repair garage, and more. Four fueling islands are provided for trucks, two for cars; in the latter, Katie finds that two of the six pumps are not limited to credit cards and will still honor cash.

After fueling the Range Rover, they park in an area reserved for vehicles other than big rigs, under lamps casting a necrotizing light that bleeds all the color from everything, makes white gloves of their hands, and chalks their faces. Katie pockets three hundred dollars from the small backpack and then straps it on. Leaving Michael J. to guard the weapons concealed behind the front seats, she and Libby head for the main entrance to the complex.

The gift shop caters primarily to truckers. Katie purchases a tin of caffeine tablets, as well as two large thermos bottles that have modern insulation but that re-create the ribbed-aluminum design of thermoses from the 1950s, with screw-on tops that also serve as cups. In the adjacent restaurant, at the take-out counter, they present the thermoses to be filled with coffee. They order three cheeseburgers, one without onions, and two cinnamon-pecan rolls. While they wait for their order, they stand listening to a Garth Brooks classic followed by an Alan Jackson gem, as if the world hasn't recently almost ended.

When they return to the Range Rover, a man looms beside it, shadowless in the hard, plumb light, peering in the starboard window of the cargo area. He's fortysomething, wearing boots and jeans and an untucked plaid-flannel shirt, his hair tied back in a ponytail.

"Can I help you?" Katie asks as she and Libby approach him.

He turns to consider them with disapproval. The funereal lamplight emphasizes the moonish quality of his round, pitted face. Eyebrows that haven't been trimmed since New Year's Eve and a shaggy mustache appear to have been applied for some stage production. His earring is a silver circle pierced by an arrow, which Katie assumes is a meaningful symbol, though of what she doesn't know. He says, "You have a fox in there."

Michael J. is at the window, regarding the man with a puzzled expression.

"You shouldn't have a fox," the stranger says. "A fox isn't a pet. It needs to be free. It was born free. It isn't property."

Adopting a tone of friendly good cheer that sounds real even to her own ear, Katie says, "Isn't he sweet? But he's not a fox. He's an Australian cattle dog mix."

The man stands taller and lifts his chin as if posing as Mr. April for a calendar of righteous citizens. "That's a fox. His tail alone proves it."

Hugging a plastic bag containing the thermos bottles, Libby pushes between the man and the Range Rover, perhaps to put distance between him and Michael J., and she gets into the front passenger seat as Katie says, "Oh, Australian cattle dogs have very furry tails. And pricked ears like a fox. Anyway, Mel Gibson—we mostly call him Gibby—is some kind of mix, like I said. We rescued him from a shelter."

The man's face puckers in an expression of contempt. "What's he a mix of—fox with fox? If you domesticate him, you'll ruin him. He won't be able to survive in the wild any longer."

"Well, you have a nice day," Katie says. Carrying the bag of food, she gets in the driver's seat and pulls the door shut and puts the bag in Libby's lap and starts the engine.

The stranger has gone to the back of the vehicle.

"He's trying the liftgate," Libby says.

"It's locked," Katie assures her, releasing the emergency brake and putting the Rover in drive.

"Or maybe he's memorizing the license plate."

"Who's he going to report us to at this hour? The highway patrol doesn't have time to chase down illegally adopted foxes."

Nevertheless, three miles from the truck stop, they leave the interstate for a town about the size of the one they escaped less than two hours earlier. The streets are quiet, the houses dark. In an alleyway, in a commercial district, while Libby feeds Michael J. the burger without onions, Katie uses a screwdriver from the Rover's tool kit to remove the license plates, which she tucks under the driver's seat. In a residential neighborhood, while Libby keeps a lookout, Katie removes the plates from a car parked at the curb. At the dead end of a dirt road that leads to a cornfield, Libby lets Michael J. out of the SUV to toilet, and Katie transfers the stolen plates to the Rover. They are both concerned that Michael J. might scamper off into the night. However, good rescue dog that he is, he springs back through the liftgate. Less than fifteen minutes after leaving the interstate, they're back on it, rolling westward. The burgers are cold, but they're still delicious. Cinnamon-pecan rolls washed down with hot, black coffee seem to prove that the world has meaning and, therefore, a future.

NEWS

Thursday, dawn rises in rare red flamboyance, and the sea of night ebbs low across the land, revealing a vast plain spreading before them, with hillocks in a few places and farmed nearly to the horizon. Katie's hands ache from gripping the steering wheel. Her mouth tastes sour, and her eyes burn, and the daunting distance between them and safety inspires a headache centered above the bridge of her nose.

Libby switches on the radio, scans the frequencies for news, and is at last rewarded. An explosion of terrible magnitude has destroyed an Environmental Protection Agency facility on Ringrock and set a few square miles of forest ablaze with such intensity that even the rain—now ended—couldn't quench the fire. None of the sixty-six who live and work at this unique research facility has survived. The source of the blast seems to be a natural-gas pipeline passing through a system-monitoring tunnel under the island.

"There's no pipeline under Ringrock, is there?" Libby asks.

"Maybe. Probably not. But hating natural gas is popular these days, so the explanation resonates."

"If there's no pipeline, some reporter might report that."

"If anyone will listen. They say everyone is entitled to his own facts. So then, what is truth?"

"But the radiation."

"Why would there be radiation from a natural-gas explosion? No need to check for it."

"What if there's a lot more cancer, birth defects, and stuff?"

"It'll be years before it shows up in the statistics. They'll have a lot of villains to blame, and Ringrock won't be one of them."

"You could just google—"

"Yeah, years from now, if people google Ringrock Island, maybe they won't find any history of an explosion. Some will decide it never was a big deal. Others will wonder if they dreamed it."

"Some will be smarter than that," Libby says.

"But most of the smart ones will be chilled to find that the incident has been scrubbed from the records. They'll wonder how easily they, too, can be scrubbed away in every sense. All but a few will decide that silence and forgetfulness is the best response to such power."

"All we need is a few to expose it all."

"Maybe. The internet is the greatest repository of knowledge in history. But when history is kept in electronic files, the internet is also an efficient memory hole, and truths can be erased as easily as untruths can be fact-checked and sold as the new history."

Katie presses the Range Rover to chase its morning shadow, and the sun remains in steady pursuit until the only shade the vehicle casts is entirely under it.

THE JAWS OF THE VISE INVISIBLE

The day is humid, unseasonably warm, birthing swarms of flies as if by the discredited science of abiogenesis.

Aboard the Range Rover, with windows up and air-conditioning pumping cool air through the vents, in a corner of a supermarket parking lot, they eat thick deli sandwiches wrapped in wax paper and drink Pepsi. In the cargo area, Michael J. feasts on sliced turkey and drinks bottled water out of a disposable aluminum baking pan Katie had bought in the market while waiting for the sandwiches.

She and Libby talk about where they might most like to make a fresh start in life, about the advice that Avi prepared to help her disappear into a new identity if she made that choice, about the source of forged but credible documents in Las Vegas. In spite of their weariness, they discuss all this with enthusiasm, though Katie can hear in both their voices a tentativeness that reveals doubt as to whether they have a real chance of living long enough to be other than who they are.

Nevada is far away. For now, they might be thought deceased, subsumed by Moloch and dead twice when the mother mass was nuked. However, eventually the authorities will realize that a Range Rover is registered to Katie with the DMV, and the hunt will be on. In the material that Sudi delivered to her, Avi had explained that a GPS emits a unique signal by which any vehicle can be quickly located, and he explained how to find and disable it, which she had done when she'd moved to Jacob's Ladder, at the height of her paranoia. Her Range Rover can't be tracked by satellite. Cell phones also can be located by the microwave signature they emit, but neither she nor Libby has a registered phone any longer. There's a disposable phone in the glove compartment, which can't be traced to her; she replaces it every eight or ten months. In the chaos of recent events, the ISA might need a few days to realize that Katie is alive. Or they might already have found the empty garage and have issued an APB through the National Crime Information Center, of which Avi has warned her; in that case, every police agency in the nation already has a description of the Range Rover and photographs of Katie, and they have been told, without specificity, that she is a threat to national security. If the town from which she fled has security cameras in public spaces, like the docks where they left her cabin cruiser, or traffic cams—and no town these days is too small to be free of such surveillance—they will know she had a girl with her and will deduce who that girl must be. The switched license plates won't be disguise enough if they are stopped for any infraction of the traffic laws. Nevada is very far away.

When they finish eating, Katie drives to a big-box store that is two blocks from the market. She has a list of sizes that Libby has given her. Their clothes dried out hours ago, but the garments are wrinkled, dirty, and don't promote the anonymity needed. She is loath to leave the girl in the SUV, but by retreating to the back seat and keeping the fox with her, Libby should be able to conceal him from any animal-welfare do-gooders who wander by the vehicle.

As she walks through the phalanxes of parked cars, hovering flies hang in the moist air as if stuck on gluey paper. Heat snakes shimmer off the blacktop. Sunshine splinters off the vehicles and pricks her eyes. She squints into the glare and bats at the flies with one hand. These annoyances, layered on top of her exhaustion, give rise to a sense of unreality, as if she is in a waking dream.

At the entrance to the store, a double dozen protestors are gathered for a purpose other than a strike. Some carry signs that espouse their complaints in such ideological jargon that Katie is not able to interpret them. Whatever else they seek, they want to prevent people from shopping here. For many of her fellow citizens, this isn't an age when disagreements can be addressed through debate and persuasion, but only by vocal and physical intimidation. Her way is repeatedly blocked, so that she must weave through the crowd as if they're athletes in a slow-motion soccer game played without a ball. Each of them seems to be half again as large as she is, their angry, contorted faces looming in grotesque mummery, assembled here for a Halloween masquerade more than six months prior to Allhallows Eve. She endures the torment but is shocked and dismayed when they begin taking her photo and filming her with their smartphones. They can have no purpose other than to upload her image to the internet and post her on whatever wall of shame they have erected in their fervor for bullying. Too late to cover her face, Katie bows her head, pushes through the back line of their offense, and steps through the pneumatic door into the comparative quiet of the store.

She will have to run that gauntlet when she leaves, pushing a shopping cart. The fact that she's been photographed gives her more reason to hasten through the task at hand. Two suitcases. Two pairs of jeans for her, two for Libby. No need to try anything on. An approximate fit will be good enough. Two T-shirts each, one sweater each, socks, belts, underwear. Two baseball caps, one pink and the other black. Toothbrushes. Essential toiletries.

No employees make reference to the demonstrators outside. A few security personnel wander the maze of aisles, observant but for the most part smiling as though it's just another day on Sesame Street. To acknowledge the mob, even in a sincere attempt to placate them, will only incite them further. The police could be summoned, but that would be bad publicity—and they might fail to answer the call, being as sensitive to bad publicity as is the store manager.

With a large, laden cart of goods, Katie dreads departing the premises, but as she reaches the exit, a bit of good luck befalls her. Four or five new arrivals to the scene, a group of young men in their early twenties, do not abide the harassment; they respond to the bullying with laughter and ridicule. Resistance in the form of mockery particularly enflames the mob, which rises in a great fluttering and cawing, like an angry assembly of crows interrupted by other birds while feeding on carrion. The shrieking throng is so distracted that Katie is able to pilot the shopping cart past them, through the rows of vehicles, to the Range Rover unnoticed.

Hurrying away from the uproar, she is struck by the absurd but eerie thought that the thing on Ringrock Island wasn't the first invader from another world, that some other species has come down from the stars to possess once rational people and convert them into creatures of perpetual discontent and restless vexation, with Earth in the process of being conquered.

The purchases fit on the floor behind the front seats, leaving the cargo area for the fox. As Katie drives away from the store, Libby says, "What is all that about, what are they so angry about?"

"Life," Katie says.

She needs ten minutes to find a once-thriving industrial park where the buildings now stand derelict. Weatherworn, rust-cankered, roofs swaybacked and windows cataracted with filth, the structures stand testament to the economic advantages of slave labor in faraway lands. She drives behind an abandoned warehouse, out of sight of passing traffic.

While Michael J. is loose to explore and attend to business, Katie and Libby unpack the purchases and repack the items in the two suitcases, discarding the empty boxes, bags, and wrappings. Soon, the three of them are on the road again.

Katie had hoped to stop in this place overnight, but she is now eager to put distance between them and the store where she'd been photographed. She feels as if they are in a vise invisible. Someone unknown is turning the handle clockwise, the slide block is closing the front jaw toward the back jaw, and Nevada is very far away.

BY A ROUTE OBSCURE AND LONELY

Libby is intrigued and perplexed to find that, in addition to the disposable cell phone, the glove compartment is packed full of maps, some devoted to two states, others to as many as four. When Katie removed the GPS, the Rover also ceased to have a functioning navigation system.

"You're the navigator now," she says.

The girl sorts through the maps, finds the one appropriate to their current location, partly unfolds it on her lap, and studies the dazzling AAA cartography with a sense of wonder. "This isn't *anything* like a Google map."

"Google Maps," Katie exaggerates, though maybe not excessively, "are for the timid who need to see the world simplified in order to understand it. *These* maps are for those big, bold, pioneering souls who love complexity—explorers, adventurers, lovers of byways and alternate routes!"

Traveling the state with her index finger, Libby says, "So many towns, hundreds and hundreds of towns."

"And people who love every one of them. Although no one will ever write a hit song about most of them, there's beauty and magic in every place if you know how to look."

They crest a low rise. All rises are low in this territory. Before them a patchwork of kept fields lies in broken light. A police car stands along the right shoulder of the road, radar cone aimed their way. Katie is driving two miles per hour under the limit, but she knows about radar traps where the patrolman's facts, different from hers and incorrect, will nevertheless decide the issue.

She does not reduce her speed, but proceeds past the black-and-white, hoping Michael J. is not peering out a window. She spends as much time watching the rearview mirror as the road ahead, until the cruiser dwindles to the mere suggestion of a car.

At 4:20 in the afternoon, numbed incommunicative by profound weariness, they come into a farm town from which prosperity hasn't yet fled. The streets are graced with trees. The houses are well maintained. The community has a quaint and humble aura.

Of three motels, Katie chooses a mom-and-pop operation that might rate two stars. She tells a brief but convincing story about the theft of her credit cards, and they are happy to accept cash in advance for one night in a room with two double beds. The only ID they require is the license-plate number of the car.

Katie carries the luggage and then the wrapped guns into their room, which is clean and comfortable. Self-domesticated, the fox submits to Libby's embrace, and she smuggles him inside.

Libby showers first and returns pajamaed from the bathroom. Moving as if zombified, she checks the deadbolt on the door, which she has checked twice previously, after Katie engaged it and the security chain. She falls into her bed and says, "Leave a light on, some little light."

"All right," Katie says.

"I don't want to wake in the dark."

"I'll leave a light on, honey."

"Just a little light." The girl closes her eyes, says, "I love you," and at once is fast asleep.

On her way to the shower when those words are spoken, Katie turns to stare at the girl. Libby is not Penny or Regina; she never can be. She is her own precious self, with a quick mind and a heart for caring, long unvalued but not broken. A gift. Dizziness sways Katie, and she holds her arms out, palms down, as if to still the world that is rushing too fast away with her.

Michael J. has curled up on an armchair. Resting his chin on his crossed paws, he yawns and closes his eyes.

In the bathroom, as she disrobes, Katie discovers that her face is wet even though she has not yet turned on the shower.

At 5:40 p.m., when daylight is still bright at the edges of the draperies, she rests her head on her pillow and closes her eyes and dares what visions sleep may bring.

The troubled mind creates a troubled world, whether waking or in dreams. Puddled blood and rainwater quiver in the light breeze, as the echoes of gunfire go on forever. Lupo and Hamal and Parker have been shot. Inside the ice cream parlor, Avi stands at the window with his daughters, gazing out in solemn witness. Emma and Harry—Mother and Father—kneel among the dead men, in whose eyes reflections of tattered clouds in miniature move across still-moist corneas. Although in life they had no belief in faith healing, Emma and Harry are here engaging in the laying on of hands, praying that God will close the wounds of these men and release them from death. Increasingly frantic, Katie strives to make her mother and father understand that these three were evil, that if they are called back into this world, they will be returning from a kingdom far below Heaven. But her parents are blessed and cursed with innocence that blinds them to the nature of such beasts; they pray more ardently. The dead men's eyelids flutter and, as one, they turn their heads, whereupon Katie's image is miniaturized in all their glistening corneas. In terror, she backs away from them, searching the pavement for her AR-15, but no guns furnish the scene. She turns toward the ice cream parlor, eager to hurry her husband and daughters through the store, out the back door, and away. Libby. No. Libby stands at the window with Avi, Penny, and Regina, in a tableau graced with the quality of light and shadow seen in the paintings of Correggio, that sixteenth-century master of chiaroscuro, who rendered holy figures with such tenderness and mystery. They know their fate and are prepared to go to it without resistance. Lupo, Hamal, and Parker rise, lantern-eyed and of inconstant form, not gangbangers, but children of Moloch; they open wide their greedy mouths, from which issue the screams of ten thousand murdered species woven in a cry of despair.

Flung awake, Katie throws off the covers and sits on the edge of the bed, gasping for breath as if the struggle to extract herself from the nightmare was equivalent to running a marathon. The bedside clock glows 3:36 a.m. She has been asleep almost ten hours.

Per Libby's request, a narrow wedge of light from the bathroom frosts the far end of the room and also illumines the realm within the mirror on the sliding doors of the closet, an alternate-world motel unit that seems not merely reversed but possessed of a depth and some sinister purpose beyond nightly rental.

As she mends her ragged breathing, Katie hears stifled sobbing. She imagines the girl is crying in her sleep, but when she whispers, "Libby," the child replies, "I'm sorry."

Katie moves from her bed to the other, sits on the edge of the mattress, and puts a hand on Libby's shoulder. "Sorry for what?"

Lying on her side, face turned away from Katie, the girl seems smaller than fourteen. "I'm too old to cry."

"No one's ever too old to cry."

"What's the point, anyway? Crying doesn't change anything."

"It reminds us that we care. And must never stop caring."

"It's crazy though."

"What is?"

"Caring for people who never cared for you."

"Maybe they did, in their own way."

"No. I won't lie to myself. I always hoped it would happen, but it never did."

Katie gets into bed and gently pulls the girl into her arms. "One-way caring is the virtue of virtues, honey. It's why we're on this world."

A silence passes between them.

Katie says, "You know what?"

"What?"

"It *has* happened. Here and now."

The girl needs time to speak without her voice breaking. "I guess maybe it has."

"No maybe about it."

"I want to listen to your heart," the girl says, and lays her head on Katie's breast.

The fox is an undefined shape on the armchair, known by the shining eyes with which he watches them.

"Whenever the night willies get hold of you," Katie says, "never try to deal with them alone. Wake me."

The girl's silence signifies that she doesn't trust herself to speak. Soon her breathing reveals that she has fallen asleep, each inhalation and exhalation matching a beat of Katie's heart.

Katie and Michael J. regard each other in the gloom, and it seems that he, no less than she, wonders at the bond between them and the mystery of their existence.

When the fox falls asleep again, the lamps of his eyes shaded, Katie remains awake for a while, alone with her thoughts. If ever she were to tell the story of these past two days, it wouldn't be primarily about a threat from another world or about prideful and imprudent scientists. It wouldn't be about reckless power-crazed government officials and corrupt authorities. All that would be background to a story about grievous loss and the improbable hope that can grow from it in a heart that remains open to grace.

However, she can't help but wonder how much loss a heart can endure before it beats only with foreboding.

Nevada is very far away.

BAD NEWS

Stars still diamond the predawn darkness this Friday morning. As Katie and Libby load the SUV, lights come on at the restaurant across the highway from the motel. It's a white clapboard structure with two dormers and a front porch, rather like many houses in this town. The sign says GLADIE'S PLACE. Minutes later, when they're ready to hit the road, three pickups and a larger truck with slatted side walls on its cargo bed have already parked over there, evidence that those who work hard for a living find the food satisfying and fairly priced.

Katie's strategy has been to eat deli and chain-restaurant takeout in the seeming sanctity of the Range Rover. Now that they are almost seven hundred miles and four states away from Ringrock, following their marathon drive, a true country breakfast seems worth the risk of taking a table in Gladie's Place. She parks at the end of the restaurant lot farthest from the building, where Michael J. is least likely to draw attention, and Libby promises to bring him something tasty. Katie carries the small backpack full of cash as if it's a purse.

Oak floors, tables instead of booths, padded captain's chairs, pale-yellow walls, bright chintz curtains, and copper chandeliers with soft lights aglow in the inverted bowls give the establishment a homey quality, as if this is just one large eat-in kitchen where family gathers. Their twentysomething waitress, Esther, is cute and freckled and as wholesome as if she stepped out of a 1950s sitcom. Omelets, hash browns, corn fritters, cinnamon-raisin toast with whipped butter—all of it is delicious.

By the time that Katie and Libby are finishing breakfast with a last cup of coffee, Gladie herself stops by their table to make sure they're satisfied, which they assure her they are. She's fiftyish, good-looking, with raven hair swept up in a bun, wearing a blue Mother Hubbard with a white apron. "You ladies new in town or just passing through?" She has been chatting up all the regulars and clearly enjoys the interplay.

Nevertheless, intuition tells Katie not to be passing through, to claim instead local ties of some kind. "Actually, we're moving to the area."

"To Saddledale," Libby says brightly, putting her recent map studies to good use.

"Why," says Gladie, "that's just a hop, skip, and a jump from here. I hope we'll see you time to time. Where you moving from?"

"Boston," Katie says. "My husband and I work from home. We're sick of cities. He grew up in this part of the country. We love it."

"I can have a horse!" Libby declares. "That would *never* happen in the city."

"Darlin'," Gladie says, "God made horses and dogs so we poor misguided human beings will have constant examples by which to better ourselves."

"We have a dog named Michael. He's in the car," Libby says. "We ordered a hamburger for him."

"Tell you what," Gladie says. "I'll upgrade that burger, make it two thick slices of pork roast, no charge."

"Oh, that's not necessary," Katie says.

"Maybe not to you, dear. But I suspect if we asked Michael, he would say it's *essential*. When you've settled in Saddledale, come see us now and then."

"We will," Katie said. "Thank you. You're very kind."

As Gladie moves on, Katie feels as though she has drifted into normalcy for the first time in years, and she wishes that the story she and Libby concocted had some truth in it.

Esther arrives with the check as well as slices of pork roast in a little takeout container. "You pay the cashier. And when you get that horse, bring us a picture of it with your good selves, so we can post it on the 'Friends of Gladie' board out in the foyer."

As Katie weighs down a generous tip with her empty coffee cup, she says to Libby, "You tell me about hatchet throwing, but you don't say a word about earning a drama degree?"

"I thought I sounded stupid."

"You sounded real. Because you are."

In the foyer, a few dozen photos are thumbtacked to the Friends of Gladie corkboard. To the eye of an artist, the display is as moving and profound as the contents of any art museum.

The cashier is a Norman Rockwell granny with curly gray hair, wearing a cardigan over a turtleneck, sitting on a stool at the cash register. She asks if everything was to their liking, and Katie says it was all superb as she tenders payment.

To entertain herself between customers, the cashier has a small TV in her cramped work space; it's tuned to a network morning show, the volume set low. As Katie waits for her change, she sees her face appear on the screen. The photo is old, taken before her life fell apart, used in a brochure for a one-woman show of her art in the gallery that once represented her work. Her hair is stylishly short in the photo, but it's now long and pulled back in a ponytail. In the black baseball cap and without makeup, she is far less glamorous than she is in the studio portrait on the TV. Although the volume is not loud, she can hear herself described as a suspect—not a mere person of interest—in the murder of two ISA agents. What agents? Zenon and Rice? How can there be a murder investigation when there are no bodies? What confection of lies have they spun to entrap her? As the cashier counts the change, the photo on the TV is followed by smartphone video of Katie outside the big-box store the previous day, where the mob harassed her. "Wait," the cashier says as Katie reaches for the bills and coins on the counter, "I think I almost cheated you out of thirty cents," and she recounts the change as the morning show drives home the final nail by presenting a picture of a black Range Rover. "Yes, indeed, I almost shortchanged you," Granny says, and adds a quarter and a nickel to the change. She turns to see what's riveted Katie's attention on the TV, but they've gone to a clip from a forthcoming Henry Golding movie. Granny says, "Last thing I'd ever want to be is twenty again, but if I was, I'd drive out to Hollywood and find that beautiful man and make him honest."

When Katie thanks the cashier and turns to Libby, the girl is rigid with alarm. She has seen.

DAMNATION ALLEY

This bright early-morning sunshine feels tentative, as though, at the command of some malefic power, a total eclipse is imminent, during which the rest of the day will unravel in an ashen quarter light that allows evil men to do their work in perpetual shadows.

Crossing the parking lot to the Rover, Libby says, "Everyone in the country was looking for that guy who killed his fiancée. There was all that video he took of her where she was so pretty and seemed so sweet, but he strangled her or beat her to death. Everyone knew what the creep looked like, and everyone wanted to find him so bad, but nobody could for weeks and weeks, *for months*. Why won't we be just as hard to find?"

"We can hope," Katie says.

"Well, hey, we've *got* to hope. Keep moving like your husband said. The Fates are sharpshooters. They want you to stand still. We don't stand still. We aren't quitters, are we?"

"No."

At the Rover, Libby says, "Come on. Say it. 'No, hell no, shit no, fuck no, I'll never back down.'" Katie smiles and says it. The girl makes fists of both her hands and punches the air and declares, "We've got this. We can do this. Let's go do this."

"I'll give Michael J. his pork roast. You get aboard and take the maps out of the glove box. We've got some planning to do, and we'll do it on the move."

Behind the wheel, on the road, Katie calls forth from memory an address in Kentucky, one of the contacts in the document that Sudi delivered when she was just three days a widow, from the eight pages she memorized. This is not the address of anyone who can produce a new identity that can withstand meticulous investigation. This is instead a place where people will welcome her and Libby, shelter them, and scheme with them to plot a safe path through this passage at arms in which the ISA and others intend to find and finish her.

She can't endure the thought of surviving Moloch only to be served up to Leviathan, to the tooth-lined throat of the techno state with its billion eyes and billion ears, chased down by its millions of minions. They want her only in part because she knows about Moloch, and otherwise because, in the senator's eyes, she is more than ever a dangerous piece of unfinished business. Libby's photo hadn't been included in that morning-show report, most likely because her surname would lead some to connect her to her parents, who were famous in some scientific circles. Considering their specialties, if Francesca and Raleigh get drawn into this, it will be harder to sell the lie that Ringrock was an EPA facility and that a natural-gas explosion destroyed it. Even if Libby had known less about Moloch than she does, it would be necessary for those responsible for that fiasco to make sure the girl ends up as fertilizer in a remote field.

Katie says, "Forget the interstates. They're more heavily patrolled than other highways. Even if we push ourselves to the breaking point on secondary routes, we'll need two days or longer to get to Vegas. Too far. We won't get halfway there with cops looking for a black Range Rover. There's a place in Kentucky, a few miles from a small town called Casperton, where there's someone who'll help us. You find the best route. The maps have drive-time tables. It'll be good to know not just how far but how long it'll take to get there."

Sorting through the maps, Libby says, "Maybe we should ditch the Rover."

"I wish. But . . . have you stolen a car lately? Jacked one? Yeah, neither have I. It's not in my skill set. Anyhow, there's nothing gained by switching from one hot car to another."

"Casperton? C-a-s-p-e-r-t-o-n?"

"That's right."

"Who's there?"

"Spencer and Marion. My Avi served in the war with their son, Jack. Jack died over there. Back in the day, Avi accompanied the body home, the way they do in the Marines, always in uniform with the casket across half the world, so the deceased is never alone."

"They won't know we're coming. Maybe we're too much, you know, too most-wanted for them."

"That's not the kind of people they are, honey. I'll use the burner phone to call them when we're getting near. They'll take us in, help us get a different car and figure out Vegas. When you're blooded in the Corps like we are with them, you're family forever."

With her lap for a table, the girl unfolds a map, unfolds another atop it, and sets to work. "Here's Casperton. It's just a tiny circle on the map, like it's very small. I'll work backward from it."

"The faster the better," Katie urges.

In the cargo area, Michael J. grumbles as he circles that space, his tail held unusually high, before he finally settles.

After only two or three minutes, Libby says, "Okay, like six miles ahead, maybe seven, you'll come to a state route that'll take us south. Doesn't look like getting there is gonna be a straight run. We'll be doglegging it a little. This'll take some figuring."

Katie owes Libby rational optimism, a virtue that isn't easy to sustain in the current circumstances, but she is not about to go full-blast Pollyanna, cruising south while singing "Happy Days Are Here Again." However, this strong-willed and courageous girl has borne so much with such grit and grace that she deserves a calm companion who will inspirit rather the dispirit her. Besides, Katie has the strangest conviction that their situation is not as dire as it seems, senses that she has an advantage not yet apparent to her, some power that, in a crunch, will get them to Kentucky. Maybe this is reliable intuition, or maybe it's the resolve of one who has suffered so many offenses that she will die rather than endure one more outrage, which is a state of mind that can sometimes inspire a boldness and an almost supernatural strength that can carry the day. Whatever might be the cause of this glimmer of hope, she's convinced it isn't merely wishful thinking.

They transfer to the state highway and are motoring south when Libby finishes her calculations. "The way we have to zigzag to stay off interstates and go around the big cities, it looks like five hundred and forty-two miles and maybe a little more than ten hours. Because we gassed up yesterday before we checked into the motel, we won't need to stop to refuel more than once. We're most vulnerable when we stop, right? People get a closer look at you and have longer to register you're in a black Range Rover."

"Five hundred forty-two miles," Katie says. "That's doable with luck." She conceals her dismay. She doesn't have a proper sense of distances in this part of the country, thinks of these states as compressed when compared to the vastness of California and the West where she lived until Jacob's Ladder. She expected Libby to say at most three hundred miles, six hours; even three hundred would be a daunting distance when they are so intently sought by the ISA and all the federal and state authorities that sinister agency is able to impress into its service. On the other hand, it's a big country, and the ISA can have no idea where she's headed, though they might think that, for whatever reason, she is being drawn into her past, to California. Because the ISA must keep Libby's involvement secret lest they blow up their big lie, the girl provides Katie with cover; the public—and most likely state and local police—aren't looking for a mother and daughter, but for only a harried and desperate woman alone. "It's doable," she repeats. "On straightaways, wherever I can see it's safe, I'll push the speed up, otherwise just five miles an hour over the limit, try to trim an hour or ninety minutes off those ten hours. Meanwhile, look over the maps again and see if there might be a shortcut somewhere."

"I'm on it."

Katie suspects that these five hundred and forty-two miles will not be a highway to any kind of heaven, but Damnation Alley. She is alert for a variety of demonic manifestations.

OTHERNESS

They travel ninety miles in excellent time, but Katie enjoys no sense that luck is with them. The morning light seems too thin, as it might if the sun were dimming toward some apocalypse, and in the windless day, the trees stand as if they are carpentered by other than Nature. The buildings they pass seem to be stage flats with no architecture behind them and no lives unfolding beyond their faux windows and doors. This is a mere impression, of course, inspired by the extraordinary events of the past few days, but it feels eerily, disturbingly true in a figurative sense.

After all, this world isn't the one in which she grew up; it's changed radically. There's a disquieting otherness about it. These days, virtue is constantly and loudly signaled but seldom practiced. Freedom is called oppression, mindless violence is called justice, and science bends to the demands of culture. The world has changed so fast, shaped by the powerful with reckless indifference to the lessons of history, and the momentum of change promises that in twenty years, the new world that follows this one will be crueler. She hopes she's wrong, but experience suggests her foreboding is justified.

They have gone a hundred miles when a patrol car appears in the northbound lanes, approaching them, lightbar flashing but no siren sounding.

Katie lets her speed fall precisely to the posted limit. Her hands tighten on the wheel, and her body tenses, but whatever might happen, she's no stunt driver and isn't going to try the Hollywood response. When she had a family and lived in California, TV news helicopters would cover chases that lasted two or three hours, with a dozen police units in patient pursuit along freeways and surface streets, as one dimwit or another tried to outrun them until he crashed into an innocent motorist or rolled his vehicle or ran out of gas. The days of Bonnie and Clyde are a century in the past, and there's no escape when the boys in blue have eyes in the sky.

With a short burst of its siren to clear traffic, the patrol car passes and doesn't cross the median to pursue them.

Libby says, "All right," but softly.

"Yeah," Katie says.

They fear that a bolder expression of relief will invite the Fates to commit mischief. During the next hundred miles, they engage less in conversation, until they sit in a silence of superstition, as tense as if they are in fact being pursued.

After switching highways a few times, they have traveled two hundred fifty miles when they round a curve and discover half a dozen vehicles backed up, the pavement littered with shattered safety glass. Two cars are on the shoulder of the roadway, damaged in a collision; a county sheriff's cruiser is parked in front of them and another behind. There appear to be no serious injuries. One deputy talks to the rattled motorists while the other waves traffic around the scene.

Libby grins and waves back at him, and he smiles. They are on their way unmolested, neither of them daring to comment.

Thirty miles farther, deep in farm country, passing a freshly furrowed field where a large green machine is issuing seeds and covering them with raw earth, they are suddenly aware of a drone that executes an elevator maneuver, dropping out of nowhere to parallel them for half a mile. It has a camera, of course, possibly more than one, and Katie is reminded of the much larger drones that scanned Jacob's Ladder on Tuesday night. She isn't sure what to make of this, but it spooks her. Unconsciously, she accelerates, and the drone makes a ninety-degree turn, speeding away across the field.

Libby exhales a pent-up breath. "It's just monitoring the planting."

At half past noon, the fuel gauge indicates they have less than an eighth of a tank when the answer to their needs appears ahead.

The combination service station and convenience store isn't a sleek and plastic unit of a national chain, but a local operation in a clapboard building painted pale yellow with dark-blue trim. The fueling island offers four vintage pumps and an air hose for tires. Katie sends Libby inside with enough cash to pay for what gasoline they need. "Tell whoever to unlock pump two, and get the key to the restroom. After you've used it, bring it here to me. The less time I have to spend inside, the less chance I'll be recognized."

Task accomplished, coming out of the store on her way to the restroom, Libby gives Katie two thumbs up.

By the time Katie has filled the tank, Libby returns with the key. "It's cool. No stink, no cockroaches either dead or alive, and liquid soap that smells like oranges. The store clerk is a nice old guy. I think he's the owner."

Katie says, "We need cold sodas, candy bars, and whatever else to get us through to Casperton. Plus something tasty for Michael J."

"I'll go see what looks good."

The pumps more or less screen the Rover from the highway, so Katie leaves it there while she uses the lavatory. As she washes her hands, she studies herself in the mirror. Without makeup and with the baseball cap, she doesn't look much like the photo that was on TV, although a little too much like the woman captured on video at the big-box store.

She's reminded of something Avi once said to the effect that the hardest fugitives to find are those who never appear furtive, who act cheerful and friendly, as if they have nothing to hide. All right—house lights down, stage lights up, open the curtain.

Chimes announce her when she opens the door. The store is weighted heavily toward beverages and snacks. The man sitting on a stool behind the counter looks as though he sings with a barbershop quartet, if such things exist anymore. With white hair, muttonchop sideburns, a walrus mustache, and a candy-stripe shirt, he has the air of a guy who doesn't think the word *merriment* is old-fashioned.

Alert for Katie's entrance, Libby calls out, "Hey, Mom, what about these for the dog?" She's got packages of beef and chicken jerky.

"Seems like just the thing." Katie takes them from her and indicates a cooler stocked with sodas. "One of those sixteen-ounce Pepsis and whatever you want."

They are the only customers in the store. Perfect.

To the left of the cash register stands a display of packaged nuts—cashews, peanuts, almonds. As she drops two bags of peanuts and two of cashews on the counter, along with the jerky, she favors the cashier with a wide smile and asks, "How're you today?"

"Never been better, ma'am. Leastways, iffen I ever *was* better, I done forgot, so I don't have no reason to feel sorry for myself. One of the benefits of dementia."

"You have a nice place here."

"It's a place, anyway," he says. "I'll sell you beer, wine, all the fatty snacks you want to shut down your arteries, but I won't never sell no dirty magazines or cigarettes."

"I like a man with principles," Katie says as she pulls a thin fold of tens and twenties from a jacket pocket.

He begins to ring up the items. "I don't know about principles. I think I heard of 'em. What I do got is a healthy fear of Hell."

Libby puts two cold bottles of Pepsi and a few candy bars on the counter.

The cashier says, "My daddy smoked himself to death, back in the day when the advertisin' touted the many health benefits of tobacco." To Libby, he says, "Don't never start that nasty habit, young lady."

She says, "I think people smoke 'cause they're bored. I'm never bored. Always reading books, doing gymnastics, throwing hatchets."

Before the cashier can react to the hatchet comment, the chimes announce another customer. Two. One is white, about five feet ten, with thick blond hair, and the second is black, maybe six feet two, with a shaved head, but in the only way that matters, they are the same, alike to Zenon and Rice. They stand just inside the door, staring at Katie and Libby, as expressionless as ancient entities created prior to human beings for the task of harvesting souls, as if they have seen everything, done everything, and still perform their work as assigned, with a passionless but refined appreciation for the nuances of sanctioned murder. The otherness of the day and the world that has dawned with it is likewise embodied in these men.

Katie considers her options, which are few and dismal. She puts money on the counter to pay for the purchases, proceeding as though no one of special interest has entered, only two new customers, as if insistence on this will make it so.

No doubt with some experience of those who covet the meager contents of his cash register drawer, the old man behind the counter stops ringing up the snacks. In a voice less folksy than that with which he has been speaking, with a cool authority that might have inspired second thoughts in men of ill intentions who weren't sure of the wisdom of their plans, he says, "Iffen you gentlemen are from that company insists on sellin' me a better video-security system, I'm pleased as puddin' with what I got, how it uploads in real time to the cloud." He smiles at Katie. "Sorry iffen it offends, ma'am, but you been recorded for posterity since you come through the door. Costs me nineteen dollars a month but worth every penny."

She will forever remember the sadness in his eyes even as he favors her with a courteous smile.

The younger of the newcomers says, "That's amazing, real time to the cloud. I never heard of such a service."

The older one says, "I heard of it, but I never imagined a backwater shitcan like this would be so state of the art."

"And only nineteen dollars a month," says the younger one.

His partner says, "But then what profit does he have left after a month of labor and worry? I suspect that same nineteen dollars would have been it."

The younger one evidently intuits that a gun is shelved behind the counter and that the old man is nearing the end of calculations regarding the need for it, because he reaches under his sport coat and draws a pistol and fires twice. The second shot is wide of the target and unnecessary; the first round is a particularly fortuitous head shot, entering through the left eye. The old man falls off the stool, following the back of his skull and a mess of brains, onto the floor, as if he never was real, but was only the idea of a man, which is all he had been to these creatures who mocked him and cut him down.

HANDBASKET

As the old man pitches backward off his stool, Katie looks at Libby, and the girl stands rigid with her eyes closed, having been aware of what was coming and determined not to see it. There is no cowardice in that, especially for a girl of fourteen; it is nothing more than psychological self-defense, essential in the world of this time, when those who mean to kill you prefer to assure themselves of the fullness of their power by first breaking you emotionally and mentally before they take your life. As the echoes of the second shot fade along aisles of food and beverages, Libby opens her eyes and meets Katie's stare. Neither of them has cried out in fear or horror, and that means something, speaks of a wild faith in which there is strength when needed. As incongruous as hope is in these circumstances, Katie feels on the brink of a sudden enlightenment.

The older of the two agents turns the deadbolt on the front door and works a dangling cord and drops a shade across the glass. The fabric is translucent, and the early-afternoon light reveals on it the word CLOSED, which from this perspective is reversed, as in a mirror. It is only the backward shadow of a word, but the reflexed letters seem to have the incantatory power of an inscription on a tomb, warning away the living.

The younger man comes to the counter, and Katie backs off from him to stand beside Libby. With one thumb and forefinger, he flicks at the nuts, jerky, and candy bars. "On a diet like this, you girls will be as fat as pigs."

Neither Katie nor Libby responds.

393

As the other agent walks to the back of the store to check out a closed door, the killer says, "These aren't the kind of supplies you'd be loading up for a long drive, like all the way to Mexico."

His expression isn't quite a smile, although he shows a high count of white, perfectly matched teeth that suggest his job comes with excellent dental benefits.

"So where were you running to?"

Katie shrugs.

"I can't translate that. I need words. Where did you think you could ever be safe?"

"We hadn't figured that out yet."

"When did you plan to figure it out?"

"Maybe never."

"You're running just to be running?"

"We're in a fix. No choice but to run till we find somewhere to go to ground."

"A fix? Is that what you call it?"

Katie is silent, but Libby says, "You didn't have to kill him."

"*You* killed him, kid, by just coming in here. We can't have him gassing off about your girlfriend and you being taken into custody. We need you girls just to disappear."

"You could have waited for us outside somewhere," Libby says.

"Too public. This is perfect. Take the money from the register, it was just a stickup. If there's video in the cloud, we erase it."

The other agent returns from the back of the store. "Nothing there but Santa Claus's office."

The killer says, "You think the dumb shit looked like Santa?"

"More than you do," his partner says, and he plucks one of the candy bars from the counter.

"While you were at the North Pole, this bitch told me she thinks they're in a fix."

Peeling the wrapper off the candy bar, the agent says, "Honey, you're far beyond a fix. You're in a handbasket on the way to Hell."

Giving Katie that not-quite smile again, the killer says, "Who do you know that's ready to take you in?"

"No one."

"So you were just going to drive till you found a cliff, go off it like Thelma and Louise. Is that what I'm supposed to believe?"

"I didn't say that."

"You didn't say that."

"No."

The killer glances at his partner. "Didn't she say that?"

"In so many words," the older man agrees.

They aren't handling this any way Katie would have expected. They're too casual, too sure of themselves.

"Some of our people are waiting to question you, both of you," the killer tells her. "They have a lot of questions."

"Hours of questions, *days* of questions," his partner says around a mouthful of candy.

The killer says, "But your friends wherever you were headed— we need to know who the fuck they are."

The older man says, "We've got questions for them, too, like what you told them about Ringrock."

"Maybe you can imagine," the killer says, "we think it's urgent we talk to them. Me and my friend here, we're ambitious. We want all the glory in this. We want to hand up the whole package, not let some big-ass chair pilot in DC take the credit."

"There isn't anyone who'll take us in," Katie insists, a lie that she follows with a truth. "We haven't told anyone anything."

The killer has been holding his pistol down at his side. At times he almost seems about to holster it. "So maybe we strip this little girl naked and make her get down on her knees and teach her something new to do with her mouth. How much of that can you watch before you tell us what we want to know?"

Katie remembers how, after breakfast and hurrying away from Gladie's Place, in spite of seeing her face on TV, she had been overcome by the strange conviction that she possessed an advantage not yet apparent to her, some power that, in a crunch, would get them to Kentucky. Here is the crunch, and she begins to understand what information these men lack that has resulted in their reckless yet self-assured behavior.

"She's just a child," Katie says. "What's wrong with you?"

The killer regards his partner with sham embarrassment. "What's *wrong* with us?"

"Does she want a complete list?" the older man asks.

The killer frowns at Katie. "Do you want a complete list?"

"Never mind," the older man says. "We don't have time for that. It'll take hours."

The weapons in her armory on Jacob's Ladder had all been bought from black-market sources, as Avi had advised. No one had known that she possessed them until Zenon and Rice intruded in her life. Zenon and Rice are dead, and at no point during the events of Wednesday were either of them likely to have had reason to inform anyone that she was armed. If there is street-cam video of them carrying guns when they docked on the mainland after boating from Jacob's Ladder, maybe no one has yet found it, or perhaps the quality—taken at night in a heavy rain and mist—is so poor as to be worthless.

"Besides," the older man says, "fourteen isn't any child. Who thinks fourteen is a child these days?"

"In my book," the killer says, "a twelve-year-old isn't a child these days. Maybe a ten-year-old."

"Some ten-year-olds," his partner says, "but not all."

The agents are having their sick fun because they didn't take time to search the Range Rover standing at the pumps, in which the AR-15 and the shotgun are hidden. Because they know her history, they see her as a timid woman who, after her family was murdered, reacted with cowardice and hid herself away on a remote island. They don't know the full story of what happened at Nonna Giana's house or that she and Libby were even there. To them, she is just someone who knows too much about what happened on Ringrock and is running away both from the horror of it and from the fatal consequences of being witness to what must be covered up at all costs; they believe she can be easily intimidated. And in their arrogance, they haven't the capacity to imagine that a milquetoast like her might have a pistol in a belt holster under her jacket.

"Leave the girl alone," she pleads with what she hopes is the right note of distress. "I'll tell you where we're headed, who we expect to take us in, hide us. I'll tell you everything. Just don't touch the girl. Please don't touch her."

The killer forms a real smile this time and favors his partner with it. "Why, Tom, the lady is an upstanding citizen after all, just wants to do the right thing. Makes you proud to be an American, doesn't she?"

Katie's pounding heart feels as if it is swelling beyond the capacity of her chest to contain it, and a bitter mass rises in her throat, giving her voice an authentic note of anxiety and choking dread. "They were friends of my husband. They don't know anything about Ringrock. There's no reason to come down hard on them. You talk to them, and you'll see."

This is not like shooting Zenon, who was a child of Moloch when she turned a gun on him. These are human beings, two of the worst kind, but human nonetheless. Crossing this bridge is also crossing an abyss, and there is no way back.

"I've got the address right here," she says. She reaches in an exterior jacket pocket, then in another, feigning confusion. "Where did it go?" She reaches cross body with her left hand, as if to an inner jacket pocket—sees sudden suspicion in the killer's eyes—and draws the pistol and takes it in a two-handed grip and places two hollow-point rounds in him, point-blank chest shots that take him down so quick that his gun falls out of his hand before he can even reflexively fire a round. The older man, Tom, has just stuffed the last chunk of the candy bar into his mouth and has no gun in hand, but he goes for his holstered weapon, his face twisted in hatred so intense that it almost seems that his humanity is as much a pretense as that of Moloch's replicants, goes for it instead of raising his hands and trying to con her into an act of mercy. She executes him, which is how she needs to think about it—he the unrepentant enemy of freedom and life, she the embodiment of justice.

With the air redolent of gunfire and blood, her ears ringing, Katie turns to Libby.

Unspent tears shine in the girl's eyes. "I'm so sorry you had to . . ."

"So am I, sweetheart. But I'm not sorry I did." She holsters her pistol. She plucks the bottles of soda and packages of jerky from the counter and hands them to Libby, leaving the candy behind. "If the old man had a car, it must be parked in back."

They hurry through the store and into the office. A pegboard is fixed to the wall beside the back door. Among the keys hanging on it are a set for a vintage vehicle that rolled out of Detroit decades before anyone conceived of electronic keys.

Behind the store waits a white-and-tan Ford LTD Country Squire. The station wagon has been so lovingly maintained that it appears as though an automotive museum has curated it since the day it first appeared on a showroom floor in the 1970s.

Giving the keys to Libby, Katie says, "Open the tailgate. I'll bring the Rover."

Michael J. is at a cargo-space window of the Range Rover when Katie rounds the corner of the building. Fifty yards north of the store, a dark sedan sits as if abandoned on the shoulder of the road, surely the agents' vehicle.

She drives the SUV behind the building and parks beside the station wagon, out of sight of the highway. She and the girl quickly transfer the long guns, the concealing garments, the suitcases, and the satchel full of funerary urns from the back seat of the Rover to the back seat of the Ford.

By now an accomplished traveler, Michael J. bounds down from one vehicle and springs up into the back of the other. His territory in the station wagon is more spacious than that in the SUV, and he explores it, sniffing, fascinated by the decades of subtle odors that have accumulated here largely undetected by any human nose.

As they drive out to the highway, Katie sees that the gas-gauge needle pegs out at full. Even in this big beauty of profligate fuel consumption, they should be able to cover the remaining two hundred and sixty miles without stopping.

Together, she and Libby consider all the ways their plan could go wrong, not because negativity has gripped them after the events at the convenience store, but because being alert to the risks might give them an advantage at a crucial moment. Avi always said that speaking the devil's name doesn't summon him, but pretending there is no devil will ensure that proudest of demons will put in an appearance to mock you.

The sign on the door at the convenience store had announced farm-country business hours of 4:00 a.m. to 6:00 p.m. The old man won't be the captain and entire crew of his humble enterprise for fourteen hours. At least one employee will cover part of the day. It's reasonable to assume that a man of the owner's age would choose the shorter noon-to-six shift, leaving the eight-hour morning to an employee. They had arrived at half past noon, which might mean that the owner would be alone there until closing time. Unless another employee came to work after lunch to stock shelves and clean the premises. Unless the owner has a wife—now a widow—who visits him sometimes at work. Unless, unless, unless. Until the bodies are found, the station wagon isn't a hot vehicle, though if they are stopped for a traffic-law violation or are involved in an accident, they are screwed.

The dead agents who, by whatever cleverness or stroke of luck, found the Rover had evidently not called for backup or even reported their find. Katie remembers what the killer said: *Me and my friend here, we're ambitious. We want all the glory in this. We want to hand up the whole package, not let some big-ass chair pilot in DC take the credit.* Most likely, neither the ISA nor other authorities are aware that the fugitives are no longer in the

Range Rover. Until the agents fail to call in on schedule, if they're required to call in. Until a sheriff's deputy becomes curious about the abandoned sedan with government plates, fifty yards north of the convenience store. Until an employee goes to work there or the widow can't reach her husband by phone. Until, until, until.

Hour by hour, worry by worry, they make their way at last into Kentucky, off the Pennyroyal Plateau, into the Bluegrass region with its rolling hills and lush meadows and enormous oak trees. Seven miles from her destination, she pulls to the side of the road and uses the burner phone to call Spencer and Marion. He answers, but before the call is completed, Katie has spoken to Marion, as well. After the murders at the ice cream parlor and before his death, Avi consulted them regarding the possibility that Katie might one day need shelter—and at a danger to anyone who provides it to her. She wants them to understand that she is in a car that will have to be disposed of in some manner untraceable, that she has with her a fourteen-year-old girl being sought by the corrupt ISA, which wants to silence her forever, and that she herself is sought not only because of what she knows about the senator's son, but also because the story of Ringrock Island is the biggest lie of the century, to which she could speak the truth if she dared. To all that, Spencer says, "You come on over here straight-away. Minute we saw your face on TV this mornin', we made up a guest bed, and Marion baked her famous piña colada cake. We knew we're first on Avi's list of safe havens, and we've just been prayin' you could get here in one piece. You tell the girl we'll go now and make up a bed for her, and set another place for dinner. If maybe she doesn't much favor piña colada, we have chocolate cake, too, and pecan pie."

Katie switches off the disposable phone and puts the car in gear and pulls back onto the two-lane blacktop.

Libby says, "We forgot to tell them about Michael J."

"They'll be cool with him. I suspect they might be cool with him even if he were a tiger."

This territory is home to hundreds of horse farms, properties defined by miles of plank fences painted either white or black, or by native-limestone walls. The spring-green bluegrass pastures roll away in a copper-gold haze of late-afternoon light, once grazed by bison in centuries past and now home to magnificent thorough-breds. Some horses from here will win the Derby, the Preakness Stakes, the Pimlico Special. Rarer specimens will dazzle by winning the Triple Crown and become legends in the racing world, for this is a place where achievement is valued more than power, where Nature and her own have not been evicted from their high place in the order of creation. Early-leafing oaks canopy the lane and shadows deepen as Katie slows dramatically and points to the right, where a stallion and two mares stand at a white fence under a thinning of oak limbs that allows coppery light to fall over them. Their eyes wise and soulful, the horses watch the lane as if they are paying homage to a presence only they can see, three solemn guardians of a revelation yet unrevealed in a world where truth has waned and waits to have its flame renewed.

HOUSE

On these hundred sixty acres stand a barn, three stables, and four houses. The graceful Kentucky manor house is white with black shutters and trim, encircled by a deep and columned veranda, shaded by enormous willows. The two managers' houses are removed from the main house and are smaller, complementary versions of the manor. The bungalow is farther removed, built of limestone, overlooking a lake; it once served as the residence of Marion's mother, Jeanette, who is now deceased. Spencer and Marion occupy the main house. Their son Travis and his wife, Laura, live in one of the manager's houses with their four children. Their son James, a former Marine, lives in the second manager's house, and in spite of a prosthetic left leg that replaced the one amputated above the knee, he is as good with the horses and as much a demon for work as is Travis. On a knoll beyond the stables, under an oak, in a grave meticulously tended, not far from a flag that flies dawn to dusk, lies Jack, whom Avi escorted here from half a world away, forever home from war.

Katie, whose name is now Nora, and Libby, who has become Rebecca, live in the bungalow overlooking the lake. Nora's hair, always before a chestnut-brown and previously long, is now ash-blond and cut in a pleasing shag. Rebecca's hair, previously short and blond is now longer and still blond. Their story is that Nora was once Jack's lover when he was stationed in San Diego and that Rebecca is Jack's child, whom he never lived to know he'd fathered. For a long while, Nora hadn't been aware that Jack had died, had been misinformed and thought that he simply chose not to return to her. When years later she learned the truth, she contacted his parents. With much joy all around, she has been brought into the family. It is quite a story, fashioned over several dinners and glasses of Kentucky bourbon.

The documentation of these new identities can withstand any degree of investigation. After Katie and Libby underwent a modest makeover, Spencer flew to Vegas with their photos and fingerprints. In a week, for fifty thousand dollars of Katie's money, the master forger created a history that exists now not only in paper birth certificates and other documents, but as well in the computers of public archives, as integrated in the data files as any legitimate entries.

Brigandine Farm frequently rings with the shouts and laughter of children, and there are always horses in the day, many glorious horses to be raised and ridden and loved. There are races to attend, mounts and riders to cheer on, wins to celebrate, losses to learn from. There are holidays and excuses for holidays, all requiring elaborate decorations, church and long family suppers on Sundays. There are dogs, those that are most attached to their people and those that are more attached to their horses; many thoroughbreds find canine companions calming.

And for Nora, there is her painting. Hyperrealism remains her style, though even the most perceptive art dealer or critic will not connect her work to that produced by a once rising star named Katie something, who has faded from the scene. She doesn't any longer paint to find the what and why of the subject, but only to portray the what of it to a depth she'd never before been able to attain. She once painted only the works of humanity—buildings, bridges, towers, still lifes of arrayed objects—whereas now she paints only animals—dogs, cats, horses, rabbits, many of a certain fox. These portraits have such power that people stare at them for long minutes in silence, and some are moved to tears but can't say why. Although she is unable to adequately explain what she means by this, she seeks to paint the full beauty of a thing, the beauty lying within as well as what any eye can see, for it is in the beauty of nature that the why of all things is coded for us to decipher if we can.

A year passes, during which her affection for the family grows steadily, and it is on the first day of a new spring when James asks her on a date. As graciously as she can, so that this sweet man will not think it's his prosthetic that inclines her toward rejection, she begs off by referring to herself as a faithful widow whose heart has been in part reduced to ashes and interred in three bronze urns. Rebecca, no less determined than the girl who once learned to throw hatchets like a logger, argues Nora to a reconsideration; she says that the profound beauty in all animals is also to be found in those people who have not chosen darkness, and that it is in James. On the first day of the following spring, Brigandine Farms holds a wedding to which the family rides on a procession of garlanded horses. Nora and Rebecca and Michael J. move from the limestone bungalow to the second manager's house, and the girl who, at fourteen, had parents who were parents in name only, now has a mother and father.

Some nights, when the sky is clear and the stars shine like channel buoys in an infinite sea, Nora walks the farm with no one but Michael J. and talks softly to him about things that seem too pretentious to discuss with anyone else—about good and evil, about why the latter exists, about loss, about love that even death cannot diminish. He remains a mystery to her, an intent listener who never more than briefly grumbles or barks once in commentary. She thinks of him as an intermediary between her and whatever presence might exist in the hidden foundation of this world, from which emanates the beauty she seeks to paint. She will not be surprised if one night, on a walk together, the fox speaks to her at length, as in a fairy tale or fable, revealing the secret of secrets. After all, she has experienced stranger things.

On *this* night, among much else she says, Nora tells him that she had thought of the house on Jacob's Ladder as the house at the end of the world, at the end of *her* world, where she would one day die alone. "Now here I am in a new house, happier than I could have imagined back then. There is no end of the world, Michael, because in every end, there's a new beginning. That house has become this house, and so it goes, life into life. But you know that already, don't you? I wish I knew what it means, if it means anything at all."

The fox walks in knowing silence at her side, and the oak trees are hushed in the windless moonlit night, and the crickets scissor forth no sound, and the lesson she takes from all this stillness is that the knowledge she desires will not come to her as words, but by her continued study of beauty and her seeking of its deepest source.

ABOUT THE AUTHOR

International bestselling author Dean Koontz was only a senior in college when he won an *Atlantic Monthly* fiction competition. He has never stopped writing since. Koontz is the author of *The Big Dark Sky, Quicksilver, The Other Emily, Elsewhere, Devoted,* and seventy-nine *New York Times* bestsellers, fourteen of which were #1, including *One Door Away from Heaven, From the Corner of His Eye, Midnight, Cold Fire, The Bad Place, Hideaway, Dragon Tears, Intensity, Sole Survivor, The Husband, Odd Hours, Relentless, What the Night Knows,* and *77 Shadow Street.* He's been hailed by *Rolling Stone* as "America's most popular suspense novelist," and his books have been published in thirty-eight languages and have sold over five hundred million copies worldwide. Born and raised in Pennsylvania, he now lives in Southern California with his wife, Gerda, their golden retriever, Elsa, and the enduring spirits of their goldens Trixie and Anna. For more information, visit his website at www.deankoontz.com.